PLUMB

by the same author

THE BIG SEASON
(*Hutchinson*)

A SPECIAL FLOWER
(*Hutchinson*)

IN MY FATHER'S DEN
(*Faber*)

A GLORIOUS MORNING, COMRADE
(*Auckland University Press/Oxford University Press*)

GAMES OF CHOICE
(*Faber*)

UNDER THE MOUNTAIN
(*Oxford University Press*)

PLUMB

Maurice Gee

OXFORD UNIVERSITY PRESS

Wellington

in association with Faber and Faber

First published in 1978
by Faber and Faber Limited
3 Queen Square London WC1

This edition published in 1979
for sale in Australia and New Zealand
by Oxford University Press
222-236 Willis Street, Wellington
Reprinted 1980

Printed in Hong Kong by
Brighter Printing Press Limited

© Maurice Gee 1978

ISBN 0 19 558054 0

In memory of James and Florence Chapple

On the morning of my departure I stood by the open window with my trumpet to my ear, hoping to hear the thrush in Edie's plum tree. That bird and its forebears have sung to me for thirty years. I remind myself that other families than mine have made their home in Peacehaven. On that morning though the bird was silent, so I put my trumpet aside and went along to breakfast. Although on festive or family occasions I carry the instrument with me, more to satisfy expectations than out of a wish to hear, in normal times I'm allowed my aural blackness. Indeed, I enjoy it. It sharpens my other senses, especially my sense of otherness.

I had no sooner sat myself down than Meg was at my elbow, shouting something in my ear, of which I heard only the word 'see'. From her gestures I understood she wanted me to follow her to the kitchen, where I would find something I must admire. Her face was pink and her eyes held the expression of shy delight she takes from Edie. That expression, and her workworn hands, Edie's hands, are thorns of remembrance. They start in me a pleasurable pain. It prompts me to my journey, my gathering in of my children; prompts me to a searching of my past.

I had the wish to please her and so followed the poor girl to the kitchen. Her pleasure, I saw, rose from the brand-new object in the corner: an electric stove. Contraptions, engines, have no interest for me, but they have the habitual effect of bringing Emerson to mind—my son not the great transcendentalist for whom, laughably, he is named. The effect is so strong in fact that I looked about the room for him. Of all my children he is the strangest to me; although I recognize and hail in him enthusiasm, faith. He dropped me a letter one morning from his Gypsy Moth, flying not a hundred feet above my lawn. The blossoms fell from the plum tree in a fright.

'Oven,' Meg shouted, opening the door of the stove and showing me its polished insides. 'Elements,' and she raised

9

three fingers to show their number—on one of which a pot of porridge boiled glueily. The thing, I saw, was called Atlas. There was even a picture of the god kneeling under his burden. These are promiscuous days. Atlas, Vulcan, Milo, Thor. I expect before I die to see some contraption named Jehovah: a wireless perhaps.

'Scrimp and save,' Meg pronounced, recounting the history of her purchase, and I nodded approvingly, for I was glad to see her brought to life. The things she had wanted had once been very different. She stirred the porridge and shifted the pot to the back of the stove. Then she turned a knob, cutting off the flow of electricity. I saw a further sign of approval was needed and as a tribute to the magical qualities of the machine I laid my hand on the element, expecting to find it cold. The pain was like being bitten by some fierce animal. I cried out and Meg shrieked and for five minutes the house was upside down. Raymond and Rebecca (come running at the noise) ferried me to the bathroom and sat me on the edge of the bath, into which, half fainting, I almost tumbled. They coated my burn with vaseline and wound a bandage round it. Outside the door Fergus gave poor Meg a dressing down. He's careful of my person. Knowing that Peacehaven comes to him and his wife when I die, he makes it a matter of principle to keep me alive.

We had cold porridge for breakfast. Meg lacked the confidence to re-heat it. I explained my belief that electric stoves cooked with electricity not with heat, and Bobby shouted down my trumpet (fetched by Rebecca, for this was a special occasion) that really I didn't belong in the nineteen-forties. I agreed. I agreed that one of the new hearing aids would serve me better than my antique trumpet. But they could not get me to agree to try one. My trumpet I see as companion to Edie's coal range, still in its place by Atlas in the kitchen. Neither will ever bite me.

After breakfast they were all away: Bobby to the teachers' training college, Rebecca to her job selling buttons, Raymond to school, and Fergus in his shining new van, with blowtorch, bag of tools, quantities of lead pipe and lavatory basins, off to
10

some brand-new housing estate. *Fergus Sole, Plumber.* A good and useful man, enjoying his first taste of success, and dying a little to his wife and children daily. Meg, the most vulnerable of my girls, the most open in soul, married for love.

I have known much disappointment in my children, seeing so many of them disappoint themselves. Although they have moved on the margins of my life, each has known his path to the centre, and all have come, all have taken comfort in their need. They have brought little comfort to me, but that is no proper complaint. I have never wished for comfort, but for thorns, for battle in the soul's arena. I have had what I wished for. And the thorns that prick me now are the thorns of remembrance. Children, followers. Along that other way, where I found so few to accompany me, and for distances so short, I reached my goal. The striving is done. I turn at my end to other cares. Life on the margins has a pain the sharper for my knowledge that here those I love are in a state of exile.

2 After breakfast I walked in the orchard: Edie's orchard. She was always the planter, the one who wished to put down roots. For me movement and stillness are in the spirit, going forth and coming home for the soul. The most I can say of Peacehaven (the name Edie chose) is that it was pleasant to have my body lodged in this spot during thirty years of my journeying. If I love the place now it is because I loved Edie.

I crossed the little brick bridge beyond the plum tree, pausing to look at the eel-haunted creek where my younger children and my children's children swam. Meg had slipped some crusts into my pocket for the eels but with my burned hand I could not take them out. I do not know why I enjoy calling these creatures up from their deeps. Slimy and snake-like, they drive themselves through the water like thoughts better not admitted. Do I still have evil passions? No! I have conquered. My ideal was Wordsworth's, plain living and high thinking, and all I have ever known

11

of lust or rage or envy or greed I have plucked from my heart and put from me and the very places where they had their life I have burned in the cleansing flame. It is not pride that speaks.

The eels that come for my crusts are God's creatures like the thrush in the plum tree. How foul this new symbology of the mind that sees a creature of darkness in every thought. Even the poets, the half-poets of this poor crippled time, creep about on all fours:

> I think we are in rats' alley
> Where the dead men lost their bones.

No! And again, no! Men must be fed with Angel's food. Only then will they arrive at God.

Enough. This is not to my purpose. I walked in Edie's orchard, among the ripening fruit. It has been my habit to walk there daily. Sheep graze among the trees in place of the house-cow Robert milked. Robert (for whom today's rough Bobby is named). The bravest of my sons, but the simplest too, not understanding his way but taking it from instinct. I walked by the apple tree from which he had fallen and broken his collar bone. A fearless climber after fruit, but always the ripest was for me or his sisters or Edie. He took the one part of my way his understanding made open to him and spent the war behind spiked wire as I spent part of that other war in Lyttelton jail. He rests now, on his community farm, among the 'God-fearing' folk who have taken him in. He tends the sheep, milks the cows, prunes the fruit trees, gathers the honey. Quiet is all he desires. Robert, my son, bruised beyond his endurance. The rest of his life is a convalescence.

I walked along by the creek or stream—Edie in the Englishness imposed on her by her mother would have it stream, would have the paddock field, would even have the ti-tree picnic hut Robert built on the lawn a summer-house. She never adjusted to colonial ways, least of all the ways of her rough sons. Rough sons? Oliver, dry Oliver, rough? But Emerson, Willis, Robert, their edges caused her pain. My Edith was a lady—gentleness,

12

fineness, were the air she breathed. Every act of hers was a spiritual act, an act of praise. In her weariness, in her pain, she praised; scouring pans, mopping floors. Giving birth, she praised. But a sense of their bodies was natural to my sons. How in this rough land could it be other? Their loudness struck Edie in the face, their language, their ugly vowel sounds, drove her out of the room. But she fought for them. I brought my sons to her by their ears; and then got out of the way into my study, or into my deafness. She set their hands on the ivory keys. Their fingers thumbed out tuneless sound. And Edie wept inside herself for their stillborn sensibilities. Oliver, though, tried hard. A mannerly lad. No pine-gum on his fingers. He is a good square pianist to this day. Edie, I do not criticize you. I would not have had one hair of your head different. I understand the approval you felt for him; as I understand your love for that other, the one I do not name. Who died to me on that morning long ago.

Let it stand.

I walked by the hollow where the stump of the quince tree rots. I neither looked nor turned my face away. Wife, I know to whom you were going on those mornings you pulled on your gloves, settled your hat, gave me your sad apologetic smile that set me at naught. I do not judge you. I understand your love for the person, your son. Alfred. My hand does the work. I pray that one day I may speak his name.

In the hollow past the quince stump bracken grows, young pine trees raise their heads. This is a lesson to me. Along these paths I may travel to the Light that shines in my life in every place but this.

3 My hand was causing me pain. I lifted the edge of the bandage. Great blisters had come up under the vaseline. A good thing, I thought, it isn't my writing hand; for being deprived of that activity would be as damaging to me as being deprived of food.

In fine weather I write in the summer-house. From the top of the orchard I saw its skeleton roof, and saw too Meg pegging out washing on the line. In this world, I thought, there are so few voices and so many echoes. Goethe; and I smiled at my quickness in turning him up. But I wanted my notebook under my hand and my pencil busy. I walked down the line of the stone wall, scattering the silly sheep, and along the path by the Butters's rose garden. Merle was kneeling on a cushion, snipping with her secateurs, and Graydon forking compost by the greenhouse. I stepped off the gravel and went along quietly. These two have been kind neighbours; and great robbers of my time. I hoped to get off on my trip without their goodbyes.

But once in the summer-house I found my thoughts no longer worth recording. I sat there remembering Edie. Her presence in this place is like the scent of a flower or rustle of a leaf. I see her beautiful hands on the worn yellow keys, see the wave of her hair, her gentle eyes; and see her lips parted breathlessly over the beauty of a Chopin nocturne—but not fully willing, as at some struggle in her puritan soul.

4 Mrs Hamer, a widow, was a teacher of pianoforte, and Edie, her younger daughter, assisted her. Florence, the older girl, was devoted to good works, and indeed a more selfless and patient creature I have never known. She was a doer of good and kindness, an angel of mercy. This is Edie's terminology, and I adopt it without hesitation. I am aware of modern 'discoveries' that would see in Florence's long life of service—the sitting up with the sick and dying, the sewing of garments for the poor, etc.—a form of self-punishment, a species of religious hysteria. Cleverness passes for knowledge in these times. Florence was good and kind. What more needs to be said? She put self to one side and discovered her real self in loving others and in loving God.

As for her disappointment, it took place before I met the

family. The story Edie knew was only part of it. Mrs Hamer, that sharp and clever woman, knew the rest. Florence was nineteen and engaged to a young Church of England curate; a promising young man from all accounts, and handsome, easy in his ways, attentive to his elders, jolly with the young. He was very popular, and she very much in love. One day this young man vanished, simply vanished. He took nothing from his rooms, no clothing, no books. Only his bicycle was gone. The police began enquiries. But at the end of two or three days his bishop received a letter. The young man explained that he had undergone a crisis of soul, had come to understand he had no calling for the church. He had thought it better in the circumstances simply to take himself off. He had left Christchurch and was leaving the country.

Florence's letter—it arrived in the same post—told another story. He had met a young lady, the curate said, and fallen in love with her, and he wished all arrangements for the coming wedding cancelled. He was leaving, he said, for Australia, where his wife-to-be would join him presently. A tale that need not have been so cruel. I doubt he was as gifted as people believed. The truth, never known to Florence or Edie, but told me in confidence by Mrs Hamer, who had not wished me to believe another young lady preferred to one of her girls, was this: the curate was bicycling in the country when he found it necessary to answer a call of nature. He retired behind some bushes, looked about to be sure of his privacy, made water, and turned, buttoning up, to find himself observed by a party of ladies out picking wild raspberries—wives and daughters of members of his church. In that time, the eighteen-eighties, in the place of his curacy, a suburb of well-to-do tradespeople and professional folk aping the genteel ways of Home, he took his only course. He mounted his bone-shaker, rode off down that country road, and through the town of Christchurch, and on again, and stopped somewhere to write two letters, and for all I know is riding still. And Florence, jilted, kept to her room, refused to go to church; but emerged at last to find a life that suited her very well.

Edie was deeply affected by her sister's disappointment. For several years she believed she would never marry. By the time I met her she was not so sure, but no young man had yet found the way to her heart. It was, in truth, a way that was strait, a daunting way to the frivolous and shallow. She was at that time troubled by the rituals of her church. Something in them too much of the world had begun to repel her. At the very moment when I was finding myself attracted by the austerities of Presbyterian worship, she felt its simplicity making a deep call to her. So that when we came to speak—but I go too fast. There was first a different meeting: that first tremulous delighted touching across the gulfs of loneliness. Popular literature has debased the term 'love at first sight'. ('He's so handsome.' 'She's so glamorous.') I use it to describe a spiritual meeting. When I first saw Edie I knew I was looking at my Wife; and she at her Husband. The moment was sacramental. (Of course, we were too young and too immersed in the orthodoxies of the time to phrase it so then.)

I saw her first on a hot Saturday afternoon in Linwood, Christchurch. February 4, 1893. I was fielding on the long leg boundary in a cricket match. Let me say now, I have always been impatient of those who sneer at sport. Nothing better promotes deep and free breathing, which is the basis of health. And indeed a physical skill has its own beauty; and benefits the mind, which it exercises. Walking, cycling, fishing, cricket, bring a rare conjoining of our mental and physical being—but I preach; another of my sports. Let me just say, I loved my cricket. I was no batsman but a tireless bowler of what today is known as the in-swinger. My team-mates called me the steady little trundler. And there I was on the boundary, resting between overs, when Edie and Florence and Mrs Hamer walked by.

I saw a young woman fashionably dressed, in the full-sleeved and be-ribboned style of that day, but—I could not see how she managed it—quietly dressed. She carried a parasol that kept her face in shade. From that well of coolness there looked into me the finest hazel-brown eyes I had ever seen, eyes full of

16

calmness and purity and determination and womanly modesty. How can I describe their quality? Beneath a brow both delicate and noble, the eyes of saint, nurse, mother, helpmeet. Wife. Companion of my soul.

And what did those eyes see? A young man in cricket flannels and cap, a rather sweaty young man (to you his sweat was perspiration, Edie); short in stature, red of hair, small in hand and foot. Grass stains on his whites, I believe, and an untidy belt holding his trousers up. An undistinguished young man (to whom Mrs Hamer gave no second glance). But in *his* eye the knowledge of a meeting.

5   I bowled another over, took a wicket. On the boundary, under the trees, one of the ladies softly clapped her hands. Her companions drew her on and out of the park.

I wasted no time in finding who she was, discovered in fact before the day's play was over by the simple means of questioning a legal acquaintance of mine, an international batsman, who had raised his cap to the ladies as they strolled by.

And so on Monday evening I presented myself at Mrs Hamer's house as a student of pianoforte. That clever lady was not long deceived. Before half the lesson was done I made the suggestion that a person of my poor abilities had best be left to an assistant. She understood, gave me such a sharp appraising look that it was all I could do not to describe my prospects on the spot; and rose with dignity, saying, 'Very well, Mr Plumb. My daughter has a good way with beginners.' She left me trembling by the piano in that little front parlour, and returned in a moment with Edie, whom she introduced and left with me. There was a good deal of nonsense about Mrs Hamer, but none in matters of real importance.

Edie trembled too. She sat down at the piano and asked me to sit beside her.

'Do you know the keyboard, Mr Plumb?'

My mother had taught me that much, so for the next few moments I answered her shy questions sensibly. But she stopped them soon. Her nature was too serious for pretence. Looking at me straight, she said, 'I don't think you've come here to learn the piano, Mr Plumb.'

'No, Miss Hamer. I've come to see you.'

'Yes, that's what I thought.'

'Do you want me to come again?'

'I think I would like that. But I shall have to tell mother.'

'She knows already, Miss Hamer.'

Edie smiled. 'My mother is very clever.' But she was not untroubled. 'You are very good in your cricket, Mr Plumb. Do you care for it a great deal?'

'There are things I care for more.' She thought games frivolous. 'It's a diversion from my studies.'

'What are you studying?'

'The law.'

She was neutral about that. I think she wanted to ask me my church; but instead she said, 'And do you like music? Or was that just a pretence?'

'I like it.' And because, in spite of our knowledge of being joined, we laboured a little, I asked her to play something for me.

She chose a Chopin nocturne. I saw her lips open as I have described: the music enraptured her and yet she was disturbed that beauty should exist for itself. She was, I came to know, a person eminently practical, of that religious nature that finds its way to God through man and concerns itself with works ahead of faith. In this she was not a natural Presbyterian. She seemed so, as I did, for we were attempting to come before God less by strenuous labour, less by subjective faith, than through a form of worship. It took us many years to discover our error.

But our similarities we discovered at once, in that little front parlour, on the double stool. (Her mother was not in too much of a hurry and made us play the game out.) The nocturne done, we talked about our parents. She found my story sad. My mother

18

reminded her of Mrs Hamer. Both had been widowed in middle life but had not let it get them down. Both were very much concerned with appearances.

6 Mr Hamer died when Edie was thirteen. He remained when I met her ten years later the man against whom all other men were tried. His chief quality, she said, was kindness; though its greatest measure, I suspect, was saved for his younger daughter. Because of his kindness she overlooked his failings (her mother did not), the worst of which, in any case, was simply bewilderment in the face of the world. He left his wife in what we called 'straitened circumstances', although the house was secured to her. The garden, large and beautifully tended, supplied many of the family's needs and would have brought in money if the widow had not been too proud to sell its produce. Edie and I spent many happy hours in it in the summer and autumn of 1893. Our favourite place was a wooden seat under the quince tree in what Mr Hamer had called his fruit garden, a term Edie used too in preference to orchard. From there we looked down through the trees, cherry and white heart and pear, greengage plum and prune and almond, and over the patch of gooseberries and black and red currants, to the vegetable garden, the woodshed and potting shed, and the house, overgrown with scarlet japonica and jessamine and rambling roses.

'My father gave way to mother in everything,' Edie said. 'But he never would come in out of the garden, even when she grew angry. We sometimes had visitors and father would stay out here with his trees. He used to come round to the front gate as they were leaving with baskets of plums. One old lady thought he was the gardener. Poor mother.'

Mrs Hamer possessed the most delicate of mechanisms for what I can only call the measurement of her due. But though no one would ever have judged her less than a lady there was a streak of coarseness running through her. It distressed Edie; for

19

it was moral coarseness, and pride its manifestation. When some unfortunate soul came to the door and asked to buy fruit it was pride not generosity that made Mrs Hamer say, 'We don't sell fruit but I will give you some.' And pride it was, not concern for them, that made her keep her daughters out of service in the days of her worst need before Mr Hamer's affairs were put in order. 'No woman,' she said, 'shall be able to say that one of my daughters ever worked for *her*.' The teaching of music was acceptable for a lady. I paid for the lessons I never took before Edie and I graduated from parlour to garden; but paid unknown to her, in a moment carefully engineered by her mother; paid with embarrassment, in a most thick-fingered way, into a performance quite beautiful of refusal by murmur along with acceptance by hand. Well, she had the need, just as she had need of her sense of her station; and, too, of her belief that in marrying Walter Hamer she had married beneath her.

This was the thing that hurt Edie most. Her father, her gentle loving father who had carried her through the garden teaching her flower names, who had built her a swing in a pear tree and bought her dolls to play with when her mother turned neighbour children away at the gate. Poor Edie, poor lonely girl, with her sister away at a 'school for young ladies', she would sweep under her swing, put a clean sack on the ground, and with her dolls on her lap sit and swing for hours, until that ailing kindly man, already unable to face the world, came from among his vegetables and walked in the flower garden with her, saying, 'Japonica, Edie. And this is jasmine, my mother's favourite flower. It has a beautiful scent, especially at night.' He died, and she remembered him and loved him all her life.

She loved her mother too but was troubled by a suspicion that she did so out of duty. The nearest she came to rebellion was after her father's death when Mrs Hamer refused to let her work in his garden. That was no occupation for a lady. She might pick fruit from time to time, no more. But Edie wanted to do what he had done. She wanted to dig, she wanted to plant and weed and prune and spread manure. Gardening, she knew, was more than a matter of collecting ripe fruit in a basket. It was a moral act, a giving as much as a taking. It was a discipline and a duty and its rewards were not in harvesting alone. More than once in later years I heard her tell one of her sons that he could cure his boredom or discontent by getting out into the garden and doing some digging. But in her mother's house she obeyed her mother's rules. So for several years the gardens became a wilderness. When money was a little more plentiful Mrs Hamer hired a man but his best efforts never managed to restore them to the perfection they had known under Walter Hamer.

Edie inherited many of her mother's tastes and attitudes. She loathed common-ness, poor speech, expressions that were inexact or coarse. She disliked showiness in dress. Colours that were too bright or varied she called a peacock display. Her rings and brooches were always modest. She hated cheap lace, or jewellery that was not the real thing. She used to say, in her mother's voice, 'Better none than imitation.' I do not think she would have cared for my mother.

7 For that dear lady was a lover of bright things—she collected them like a magpie. Perfume, of which Edie was sparing, she spilled about her person in a most extravagant way. My mother's arrival was always heralded by an olfactory wave of the boldest, the most unsubtle and sugary kind. Her dresses were gay and her hats—I can do no better than Edie's term, a peacock display. And yet I believe it was love of life, a hunger for the beautiful, that drove her to these excesses. My father found no fault with her. To him she was everything that was feminine, she existed in a magical enclosure, a glittering and perfumed garden, from which the loud sounds and rude activities of the world of men (a world in which he was very much at home) were excluded. My father mentally took off his boots in mother's presence. He was always a little breathless, a little

apologetic—and yet there showed through a fierceness, a pride in possession.

I never managed to explain my parents to Edie. Her pity for me was always too quick: to lose a father at seventeen in such a dreadful way (he choked on his food after taking too much to drink at what has come to be called a stag party) and then have my mother abandon me and fly back to her family in Kent! It was useless for me to explain that I was happy, that my mother was happy. I had been home the year before and found her most affectionate and generous. An American gentleman called Weedon, a follower of Mary Baker Eddy, was paying court to her. Little in this picture appealed to Edie. She had a grievance against my mother and held it till the day she died. There had been a failure in both duty and love; there had even been, I believe she suspected, cruelty, and this was the unforgivable sin. It was not so of course, but my Edie was, in some things, an obstinate woman.

8 'George,' she said to me one day as we sat beneath the quince tree, 'do you think a person should put off doing something he believes is right because he knows it will hurt somebody else?'

I was a little alarmed. But I knew her well enough to answer a serious question in a straight way, so I said, 'I think as a general rule one must do what is right. And who is going to be hurt, my love?'

'Mother.'

'How?'

'I think we should be married at St Andrews.'

'I see.'

'That is where we belong now. And so I feel we should be married there.'

I agreed. I knew there could be no argument. For this was a serious matter, one that touched us in our profoundest feelings.

We felt that to carry on as Anglicans, to take in that church the most precious of sacraments, simply to avoid hurting Mrs Hamer in feelings that after all were no more than social, would be to call into question the special, the religious quality of our union. Mrs Hamer, seeing us sit on that wooden seat with fingers intertwined through the long hot summer, had supposed us talking sweet nothings. But we were exploring our beliefs, we were mapping out our lives under God. Already we had attended Presbyterian services. We did not keep this from Mrs Hamer, she simply did not ask. (Florence had begun to move in that way too and so did not give us away.)

What did I believe in those days? The doctrinal part is remote from me and when I try to bring it back seems so trivial I find it hard to believe two earnest and intelligent people exercised their minds on it ardently, as on a matter of life and death. But it was so. I had told Edie I was happy—but I had been unhappy, sick with a malady of the spirit that caused me to see man as banished eternally from God. This was worse than the Manichean state, for I had no sense of the divine. *I know that my Redeemer liveth.* 'I know it not,' my answer would have been. My sense was of evil. I saw it in the lusts of the flesh, in the ambitions of the mind (both known to me, for I was my father's son). It fed in a way both hoggish and refined upon the spirit and substance of my life. The point of light on which somehow I managed to keep my eye was simply that, a point of light, without warmth, without content, and further off than I believed I could travel in a dozen lives. But I kept my eye on it: and slowly worked my way out of the darkness towards it by the practice of bodily and mental austerities that now make me shudder to think on. But this, this foretaste of a dark night of the soul, this devastation of spirit, marks the point of my beginning. And I do not find it in me to sneer at the step I put my foot on because it will no longer bear my weight. It was a rock. I said, 'I enter in at the strait gate. I shall have to stoop, i.e. subdue my nature and my ambitions. There will be hard struggle and little company. There is no other way to God.'

23

For a time I kept up a form of worship in the church of my fathers, but I no longer took communion for I had embarked on a harsher way and trod now the path between Bozez and Seneh. The time came when I found myself among a sterner sort of folk (the first thing I noticed was that this worshipping body smelled of soap and shoe leather, not confections and emollients and sachets). And soon Edie and I were both there. I had not found myself long without company.

Sitting under the quince tree, we prayed for guidance; prayed that the light of understanding would shine on Mrs Hamer.

We went inside to break the news to her.

9   A man called Matthew Willis, an importer of cotton goods, had come to take afternoon tea, and with him his schoolboy son. Mrs Hamer was at that time busily introducing me to influential men. Willis was self-made. He had come to New Zealand from Australia and worked on the West Coast diggings. After a few years, seeing no fortune was to be made, he had set up as a storekeeper, and done well enough at that to sell out and buy a half share of the Christchurch importing business he now controlled. He was a difficult man to talk with. His structure was geological: a stratum of self-importance, formed in the years of his success, with below that the shrewdness and tightness of a shopkeeper, and lower down again the miner's open-ness and practicality. The trick was to chip down deep, for there one found a man worth talking to. On that day he was all pomposity.

'So this is the young man,' he said, in imitation of some lordly figment, and he studied me benignly, though with an air of not yet being fully satisfied. 'And they give me to understand that you have carried off our fairest rose.'

I could not take too much of this (nor could the boy, who blushed) and the shrewd shopkeeper part of Willis saw it. He

24

turned the conversation to my prospects. I named the seni
in the firm I was articled to, and he recounted an anecdote
each to show his familiarity with them. Mrs Hamer wa
with a mixture of edginess and approval. I sensed her longing
to correct, to shape, Mr Matthew Willis, and a colour that came
to her cheeks now and then set me wondering. It was not until
Willis mentioned he was a widower that I understood. I looked
at Edie for her response. But Edie was withdrawn, her mind still
on our religious concerns.

'My son, John,' Willis said, 'has made up his mind to study
for the law.'

We looked at the boy, and he said in a tone of forced manli-
ness that he hoped his studies wouldn't interfere too much with
his cricket. He began to talk with me about the game. I understood before very long that he was a clever boy, and one troubled
in some obscure way. Perhaps, I thought, the loss of his mother
has put him off his balance. He spoke with too much emphasis,
as though he believed force would disguise his unhappiness; and
there was in his way of saying 'my mother', which he did several
times in the few minutes we talked, the suggestion of some inner
compulsion, and a delicacy, a defensiveness, and indeed a flush
of emotion, that hinted at a love still having part of its course
to run. This, I thought, is close to a sick condition. And I saw
that the boy did not want Mrs Hamer for stepmother, or any
woman for that matter. I saw too, and drily stated, that he was
not interested in cricket. He went pale and retired to a corner;
and I was sorry.

Florence brought in tea and Mrs Hamer poured it. Edie too
was brought into this play and Willis paid her one or two heavily
roguish compliments. He grinned at me and winked—the miner
now. Had we not both found the colour? I felt myself warming
to him at the moment when Mrs Hamer went cold. It was her
he must please: he pulled himself together. 'And when are the
banns to be proclaimed?'

I frowned at Edie, warning her that now was the wrong time
to speak, but she had put her cup down.

'We hope to be married in the Spring. At St Andrews church, mother.'

'But that,' Willis said; and stopped.

'Yes, Mr Willis,' Edie said, very pale, 'it's the Presbyterian church. George and I are becoming Presbyterians.'

'George,' Mrs Hamer cried, so loudly Florence placed her hand on her arm, 'this is your doing. I hold you responsible for this.'

'No, mother,' Edie said, 'we've come to it together. We've talked about it and it's something we must do.'

'I shall get Mr Willis'—forgetting for the moment he was there—'I shall get the vicar. He will put this straight.'

'Please don't, mother. Don't distress yourself.' And Florence added her voice.

'Mrs Hamer,' I said, 'there are some things that can't be altered. Edie and I haven't decided this lightly. It's a matter of how we can properly use our lives.' And being young, I began to preach, saying that in these times men were too wise and that the early Christians had been babes and that we must return to that simplicity and freshness and cleanse ourselves in the Holy Spirit for our minds were corrupted from simplicity in Christ. 'Be ye filled with the Spirit,' I said, and, 'Out of your inmost soul shall flow living waters.' But Mrs Hamer broke in upon me, crying that spirit was all very well for those who go to China but we had to live in Linwood. And she cried, 'I blame you, George Plumb. My Edie didn't have a religious thought in her head until she met you.' It was her honest opinion. Proper observance was for ladies, intensity of faith was not. We could not calm her. That was the work of Matthew Willis.

'Mrs Hamer,' he said (the shopkeeper speaking), 'make the best of it. They mean what they say. And after all, it's no great tragedy. It's a perfectly respectable church. It could have been the Wesleyans. Or something in the Other Direction.' And while she sat biting her lips, he said, 'I've attended many churches in my time. And I've almost come to think the one round the nearest corner is the best.' He shocked us all. Perhaps he meant to.

26

'Matthew,' Mrs Hamer cried, 'keep such opinions to yourself'—a cry that showed us plainly how things stood between them.

Willis smiled. He asked Florence politely for more tea. He was pleased with himself, for with two minutes work he had had himself admitted into the family.

The talk went round and round, as it will on such occasions. We were called selfish, wilful, ridiculous, enthusiastic (a very hard word), and even thoughtless—but there was a good deal of forcing in the performance. For Mrs Hamer's life had changed its course.

Willis knew it. I caught him once grinning like a Cheshire cat.

10 We were married in the Spring in St Andrews church; Mrs Hamer in the Autumn at St Bedes. My mother sent us fifty pounds along with the news that she too intended to marry, to Mr Weedon. Her home would be in Philadelphia. And so we all changed course. But the time for decision-making was not yet done.

The season changed. We sat by our winter fire in our cold little house. Edie knitted. Our child was growing within her. Booties, bonnets, tumbled from her needles. She was utterly familiar to me, utterly strange. I never knew from moment to moment whether our love was to be holy dread or pikelets and sweetened tea. On the night I speak of I said, 'How shall we use our lives?' It was ground we had covered before. We had even seen what our decision would be. But it remained unspoken, waiting its sign. I said, 'I can go into the firm when I graduate. Mr Barclay called me in today. And I didn't know what to say, my love.'

Edie put down her knitting. She handed me our bible. I read aloud from St Paul's first Epistle to the Corinthians, whose key word is wisdom. I came to that chapter in which the apostle praises charity, 'Though I speak with the tongues of men and

27

of angels and have not charity, I am become as sounding brass, or a tinkling cymbal.' Part way through I felt her touch on my arm, and fell silent a moment, and read again the verse at which she had stopped me: 'When I was a child, I spake as a child, I understood as a child; but when I became a man, I put away childish things.'

My career in the law (and I wanted it very much still) was a childish thing. We saw it plainly. And because our spirits were ready, our minds prepared, the call that came to us was neither obscure nor arbitrary.

I said, 'They're liable to send us anywhere, you know. Even the Coast,' mentioning it as though it were Brazil. For a door had clanged shut behind us, there was no turning back, and I wanted her to know where it was we stood. 'Rough people and no comforts, and probably the house will be tumbling down.'

'Then,' she said gaily, 'we'll build it up again.'

'It will mean more study. And loneliness for you.'

'You forget.' She laid her hand on the child to be born.

'Yes. But Edie, think how upset your mother will be.'

'Bother my mother,' said Edie.

And so we talked and laughed and were very excited and gay, and frightened too, for these were our lives, and this our love for each other, we dedicated to the service of God. It was a great and terrible thing we were doing and Edie's calm fled away and she wept on my shoulder. But nothing in this life could have made us change our minds.

'I'll get you some cocoa, my love.'

'No, I'll get it,' for she never would let me do a thing in the kitchen and in any case I would have been helpless there. When she was out of the room I prayed, placing my hand on her cushion for I wished to include her, and the child too: 'Lord, accept our lives. Make us useful, Lord.' It was best, I believed, to pray short and pray hot, and pray in confident expectation. I had not the least doubt I would be useful; and believed it sinful in any case to offer more than one could give.

28

I sat in the summer-house with climbing roses drooping about my head and thought of Edie's loving eyes and her cheeks wet with tears of happiness and fright. But I was troubled, as though by the buzzing of a mosquito or fly. In a moment I became aware of Meg shouting at me on my left, which for some reason she believes my better side. She was trying to draw my attention to visitors.

I was not pleased to see Merle and Graydon Butters, smiling ingratiatingly and bobbing their heads in unison, but behind them, cutting her self off by a sideways stance and a half indignant look, was Wendy Philson. And Wendy I am always pleased to see.

I motioned them in and accepted my trumpet from Meg; placed it to my ear, and the world began to squeak.

'—do hope you're going to enjoy your trip,' shouted Graydon.

'—enjoy your trip,' echoed Merle.

'But what have you done to your hand?'

'—poor hand?'

'It looks so painful.'

'—painful.'

'Doesn't it, Merle?'

'Yes.'

'Yes.'

'It must have hurt so much.'

I left it to Meg to explain, left them my hand to exclaim over and delicately prod, and beckoned Wendy to sit beside me. She too was concerned about my burn. I cut her off and asked what she had been doing.

'Nothing,' she said.

'Nothing?'

'I've been learning German. Reading Jung.'

But I did not want to hear about her reading, and she would

29

not have talked about it with Merle and Graydon by. We could not, in fact, talk at all, so I sat and enjoyed her company, which has meant so much to me since Edie died, while Meg kept the Butterses entertained.

But soon they came back at me, like two puppets worked by the same set of strings. Edie and I met them in 1919 when we bought Peacehaven. The Butterses lived next door, and they were enchanted to meet the well-known jail-bird. Merle and Graydon are cultists; a pair of butterflies flitting from movement to movement, not in any frantic or driven way, but charmingly, intelligently, and always in perfect accord the one with the other. I am fascinated and repelled by the perfection of their dance: he turns, she turns—impossible to tell which was first; he executes a tricky step, oh so lightly, and there she is completing as he completes. Their flashes of understanding are in common, their turns of phrase the same, even their dreams identical. If he had been Theosophist and she Steinerite, or she with the Oxford Group and he a Rosicrucian, I might be able to take them seriously; but no, they have gone hand in hand, in perfect step, through every movement of the last thirty years, safe and charming behind the glass wall of their money. Lately they profess themselves socialists, and pacifists to boot, and believers in the Higher Consciousness, and some extraordinary *mélange* of these, some politico/mystical porridge, they have the impertinence to call Plumbism. For they are followers of mine.

Graydon shouted that he and Merle had written an account of their most recent experience of illumination. It had taken place in the rose garden and in intensity it almost matched that experience of Wordsworth's at Tintern Abbey. Almost, not quite, they had known the Brahmic Bliss. Would I read it? Graydon asked.

I said no. I had not the time. But if he liked to read it I would listen; and I pointed my trumpet towards him and smiled benignly. (Meg went off to make tea.) Graydon read, a little flushed in the face, for loud speaking is a strain to him. Merle nodded emphasis. I heard a word here and there: '—that serene
30

and all-pervading light . . . we stood in a state of perfect still-ness, perfect harmony, etc.' I was overcome with weariness. Half my life has been spent listening to nonsense. Why, I thought, can't these people look into their hearts? Why must they inflate what they feel? And I wrote in my notebook for Wendy to read: *How long does this go on?*

She took my pencil: *Are you tired?*

Knowing her capable of asking the Butterses to leave, I shook my head. She wrote: *They're fools.*

Merle was watching. I began to be alarmed. And having my trumpet by chance at the right angle and hearing the words, 'We shall arrive,' I said, 'Bravo!'

The Butterses went pink with pleasure. Graydon read on. Merle reached out and held his hand. I was touched. I felt ashamed. For they love each other, these two. And have known sorrow in the death of their son.

When Graydon finished I said I felt they were close. I agreed they were still in the twilight but if they held themselves open one day perhaps the true light would shine. For this cowardice I do not blame myself. The truth is I needed my cup of tea; and I asked Merle to see what was keeping Meg. She went off, Gray-don followed, and I was left alone with Wendy. At once she took my hand. Her touch was comforting. She put my notebook on her knee: *Are you well?*

'Yes,' I said.

Truly?

'Yes.' I raised my burned hand. 'This is nothing.'

Why are you going?

'To see my children.'

Felicity?

'Yes. And Oliver and Robert.'

But why at this time?

'It's summer. I don't want to catch cold.'

She wrote nothing more for a while, then suddenly scrawled: *Why have you been avoiding me?*

'Me?'

You haven't written.

I sighed.

I'm sorry. I don't want to trouble you.

'You don't trouble me, my dear. You've never troubled me.'

'Do you mean that?'

'You've been a great comfort to me.'

And that was no more than the truth.

12 My daughters disapprove of my friendship with her. It is not that they dislike her. Meg and she have much in common. It is simply that they believe themselves looking after Edie's interests in chaperoning us. They do not understand. Edie was my wife, my life's companion. There is a coarseness in the girls, in Esther especially, that prevents them from understanding. One might say *Wife* and *Life's Companion* and still they would not see it. They measure things by the marriages they made. Edie is in no danger.

I do not forget though that Wendy made an effort to be my wife. And when I explained to her why it could not be, offered to bear my child. The time is long gone, the possibility faded, and something in Wendy faded too. She is not now even my pupil—just a woman I can sit with comfortably and tell my thoughts to. She is the only one I invite to a 'paper chat'—Edie's term. It makes my poor Meg jealous.

13 Wendy heard voices approaching and let go my hand. She wrote: *Can I come and see you when you get back?*

'Of course. I'd like that.'

How long will you be?

I did not know. I had not planned. 'A month possibly. It depends on Felicity.'

Meg came in with a tray of cups, Merle behind with sugar

32

and milk, and Graydon with biscuits on a plate. Meg frowned when she saw Wendy writing in my notebook.

I read: *Look after yourself. Goodbye.*

'Stay for a cup of tea.'

She shook her head and I watched her make her goodbyes to the Butterses and Meg. She kissed me quickly on the forehead. Then she walked across the lawn and down the path: a short squarish woman with swollen legs and a large bottom and a self-conscious set to her head. One would never look twice at her, except . . . Much of Edie's beauty had been in her eyes. All of Wendy's is there.

I drank my tea, and kept my trumpet at my feet. Merle and Graydon fretted. But when I leaned forward and tapped the manuscript in Graydon's pocket and smiled encouragingly they cheered up; and after fluttering about me for a while and wishing me *bon voyage* they took themselves off.

'Do you want anything else?' Meg asked.

I said no.

'How does your hand feel?'

'It hurts.'

'—doctor?'

'No. I'll go in Wellington if it's still sore.'

She gathered up the tea things and went to the house, walking a little dejectedly. She feels always there is something more she should be doing for me and so all our exchanges have an unsatisfactory ending.

14 The Revd Mr Geddes interviewed me in the vestry of St Andrews. He seemed not in the least surprised at my request, but showed no approval. He began to catechize me at once in a contemptuous manner. I thought it official and did not object, but decided later it rose from a disapproving nature.

'You came to us from another communion?'

'The Anglican.' There was in this a whiff of Rome, even to my nostrils. I was not surprised to see a sour expression on his face.

'Your wife too?'

'Yes.'

'It's unusual. An unusual direction.'

'For a time,' I said, 'I attended no church.'

'For how long?'

'A year or two.'

'Exactly, please.'

'Fifteen months.'

'You made no religious observances? None at all?'

'I went to one or two Salvation Army meetings.'

This did not impress him. 'What was the nature of your doubt?'

I told him as clearly as I could, which was not very clearly. And he said, 'You understand we must examine this fully. There's a self-indulgence in this—this terminology, that frankly I find distasteful.' And he began to put to me those questions I had already answered on entering the church. He made no deviation from the form. I was offended, with the feeling of one who offers himself for matriculation and finds himself placed in an elementary class. But as we continued I began to experience a cleansing of spirit. My resentment, my pride, fell away from me, and I thought, I offer myself to a life of service and I must behave with humility. And I answered in a simple and childlike way, yes, that I acknowledged myself depraved and corrupt in nature; that I knew my salvation lay in Christ, etc. And I promised to contribute according to my ability (Mr Geddes put extra weight on this phrase) for the support and extension of the Gospel, and by a holy and active life of Christian usefulness to adorn the doctrine of God our Saviour.

Mr Geddes looked upon me with not a jot more favour when this was done. 'You must understand, Mr Plumb, our first consideration must be not your willingness to this work but whether you have seen the Glory of God in the Person of Jesus Christ.'

'Yes,' I said.

'No other gifts you may possess can compensate for a deficiency in Christian conviction.'

'I understand that.'

'It is essential that you do. I'm disturbed by your lapse from worship, even in that communion. You have found your way to us by your own efforts—perhaps too much so. Independence can lead one into unsound doctrine.'

'I hope I've avoided that.'

'Or grievous heresy.' And he examined me in the Statements of Faith. I saw that my perfect responses troubled him. But he had to give up, for how can a true test be made? If one is a parrot one is through. I was feeling clever again by the time he stopped. He saw it, and left me to pray. He was a man who knew his business. Again I had to face myself, and face my pride. I prayed in humbleness; prayed for the purging of my soul; offered nothing, asked for nothing except to be shown my place and to be made useful. After I had finished I remained on my knees, and in this attitude Mr Geddes found me when he returned. He was refreshed (had been, I believe, for a cup of tea). He sat down and motioned me into the chair before him.

'I can hardly think you a proper candidate, Mr Plumb. But then, I may be wrong. It is not for me to judge. I shall forward your application. I should like to say something about your educational suitability?'

I told him. He was, I think, impressed; and showed it by looking sour. 'If the Presbytery accepts you it will want you to complete your degree.'

'Yes, I want to complete.'

'The law has much to offer an ambitious man.'

'I have no ambitions. Except to be useful in Christ.'

Mr Geddes was silent. 'Who shall judge usefulness?' he muttered. We both knew the answer to that, but neither spoke, and presently Geddes dismissed me.

I walked home through the cold and windy night. I was disheartened. Yet I had learned much from this interview. I must not look for approval in others and must beware of approval

35

in myself. I had not lost my belief in my calling; but it had been shown me (what before I had simply heard) that the gate was narrow and the way lonely. In my ministry I must learn to stand with Christ and with no other. I thought of Jeremiah, whose life was a prolonged martyrdom. He served forty years of ministry, this man so full of shrinkings, and prophesied with invincible perseverance. What cannot the weak do? I thought (who knew myself strong); and I said over several times, 'For thou shalt go to all that I shall send thee, and whatsoever I command thee thou shalt speak.'

15 The ordeal by Geddes was the worst. (His name became useful to us. 'Now George, don't play Mr Geddes,' Edie would say, when my severities threatened to run away with me.) Mr Timmins and Mr Stephenson, appointed by the Presbytery to examine me, were a pair of cheerful gentlemen, pleased to welcome a candidate so obviously suitable, and the Presbytery itself was full of encouragement. Early in the following year I was asked to proceed to the town of Kumara on the West Coast to take up the duties of a Home Missionary.

Willis and his son John helped us pack. Florence took the child Oliver off Edie's hands, and Mrs Hamer (I never could call her Willis) looked in once and sorted Edie's half-dozen pieces of jewellery. She was upset at our going. She refused to accept that I was called, regarding this as a delusion. Willis himself was disappointed. He had hoped, he said, to take me into his firm. But he became the miner soon enough and entertained us with stories of the Coast. He had once owned part of a sluicing claim in Kumara and still had an interest in a sawmill there. He had known Richard Seddon well, in his days as mayor of the town and publican of the Queen's Hotel. He had been a supporter of Seddon in the election of 1879 but changed sides in 1884 over some mining issue. His conversation became technical at this point, full of sluice-heads and sludge-channels. Willis had been a 'back number man' and Seddon a 'prior rights man'. I never came to understand this. But I remember Willis's feeling as he declared it had been a black day for New Zealand when Seddon gave up serving beer and learned to spout.

Later in the day he told me of Sullivan, the Nelson murderer. And this tale had a profound and terrible effect on me. Sullivan and his henchmen were ticket-of-leave convicts from Australia. They preyed on miners bringing in their winnings to the towns. It will never be known how many men they killed before those five in 1866 on the Maungatapu mountain. Willis had been a young man then and had left the Coast for the Marlborough diggings. The news came back to Deep Creek of how Sullivan, Burgess, Kelly and Levy had waited on the track from Canvastown and ambushed first an old flax-cutter, Jimmy Battle, and later a party of three shopkeepers and a miner. They had robbed them and killed them all, by strangling or shooting. Several days later the murderers were arrested in Nelson. Sullivan turned Queen's evidence and saved his life. His companions were hanged.

Willis had seen Sullivan; come, he said, in spitting range of him. He was on the steamer that took the man to Hokitika after the trial, where he was wanted for questioning about the murder of Dobson, a surveyor. It was Willis who shouted out to the mob on the wharf that the police had taken Sullivan away by dinghy to another landing place. Sullivan was nearly lynched that night. But the police saved him; he gave his evidence; was imprisoned in Dunedin for a time; and pardoned. And vanished then from the knowledge of the Coast. Such was Willis's story.

It brought down on me a feeling of dread, a sense of things abominable. I experienced again that devastation of spirit, that dreadful knowledge of being lost in the darkest of nights, that I had known in my days of alienation from Christ. I smelled the stink of evil, felt its slimy touch. I believe I almost fainted for I felt Willis's grip on my shoulder and heard his voice crying to his son to bring me a chair. But I put their hands off. I wanted no touch upon me. I said I was all right, I had these turns now and then when I worked too hard. I let them bring me water. And I begged them not to worry, and above all not to tell Edie. And then Edie herself came into the room, carrying Oliver, whom Florence had just returned, cradling him in her arms and making to him those small cooing bird-like sounds women alone have the secret of, and everything was right with me again.

But when I was alone I prayed, and I gave thanks to God for the light that shone upon me, for I saw clearly that I was a soul lost and damned the moment my foot strayed an inch from His path. I thanked Him for the sight He had given me of the abyss, and the soul of the murderer Sullivan writhing therein. The slope was long and slippery and my foot not an inch from its edge. I was not saved beyond damnation. And I saw that I stood where I did by an act of will as much as by the grace of God. I said, 'I must work. Or else I die.'

So as I embarked on my career I fell into what our friend Geddes would have called a grievous heresy. In it I have remained until this day.

16 We came up from the junction in a horse-drawn van, a journey of some four miles. The town had the appearance of a thriving little community—shops of every kind, a newspaper office, a school, a police camp, a hospital, four churches, and, we saw with alarm, twenty hotels at least. It was though, as we discovered, a town in decline. While we were there five of the hotels closed and two or three of the shops. But even in our first drive through the main street I felt the rough vitality of the place and I told myself that here was a stony field and one that a young and active man could test himself in the tilling of. Home missionaries were sent to these hard and difficult places to see what they were made of and to find if they were really in earnest. I did not know then that my sternest battles were to be not for the souls of men but against wet bush, swollen streams, rough and muddy tracks.

38

We drew up at the Manse and began to unload, and soon I saw my joke about tumble-down houses had been a bad one. No door or window opened without a battle. The floor, covered with oil-cloth worn to its fibre, undulated like a sea and had several holes rotted in it, into which the dust and refuse of many years had been swept. We discovered that night that the roof leaked. 'We'll never be short of water,' Edie said.

While we were unloading, several ladies arrived to give us tea. They brought new-baked cakes and loaves of bread. Their pleasure in Edie's clothes was childlike. She told me later theirs were a good ten years behind the fashion. This did not put them out. They were pleased the wife of their minister should outshine those of the Wesleyan and Anglican. I did not pass muster so easily. One lady was troubled by my tan shoes. 'You're no going to preach in those things, are you?'

'Why,' I said, 'what's wrong?'

'They look like circus boots. If you've no black ones my boy will lend you his.' She was our strictest sabbatarian, but a kindly soul. She sent her boy, who turned out to be her husband, to mend the holes in our floor. He also made several of the windows work. But I preached in my tan shoes of course, beginning as I meant to go on.

The Kumara station had been empty for several months when I arrived, the congregation attending Wesleyan services, or none at all. The charge was a large one including the towns of Dillmans, Humphrey's Gully, Greenstone and Stafford and a number of scattered preaching stations. I began pastoral visiting at once, and services on our first Sunday in the town, but before really coming to grips with the district and, too, embarking on my studies, I knew I must put the house in order. So I worked with paint and hammer and saw for several weeks and the little house began to look brighter. Edie scrubbed the walls and floors, made new curtains, put out our few pictures and ornaments. ('The likes o' these are not seen in Kumara,' our sabbatarian said.) Just as she had promised, we built the house up again. Watching her work about the place with her hair pinned up and an apron of sacking tied about her waist; listening to her sing or in her firm and friendly voice direct the girl Kate we had taken on to help with the household work; seeing her with our son Oliver, washing him in the tin bath, towelling him, dressing him, singing him to sleep; and feeling when I was worn out with my work, her loving hand upon my shoulder, on my brow, I knew that I had been blessed. We lay in our iron bed listening to the Coast rain thunder on the roof. With my body I thee worship. It was so. And in our spiritual journey we were side by side. I knew that with this woman I would never be lonely. She was my home, my rest.

Of physical rest I had little. I had chosen a faith whose traditions were evangelical. There was no time even for thought. People flooded into my life and filled it to overflowing. The Wesleyan and Anglican ministers came to my door, axes on their shoulders, and took me off into the bush to chop a winter supply of firewood. The friendliness between the churches was something I came across in no other place. We had our socials and picnics together and even the Catholics joined in. Father O'Halloran would have come along on our wood-chopping trip if he had not had a burial to attend to. From a hillside over the town we watched the procession pass through the main street and climb up to the cemetery.

'A good chap, O'Halloran,' said Montague, the Church of England man. 'Takes a drop too much, of course. If you see him fall off his bicycle you must tell any children standing about he's had a heart attack. He has frequent heart attacks.'

Brice, the Wesleyan, was not amused. But he was a great hand with an axe. Our pile of rata logs mounted up. Late in the afternoon we carried them down to the roadside, where a dray was waiting to take them to the Manse. The drayman had boiled a billy of tea. He was a Catholic and called us Father indiscriminately. He wanted to know if I played cricket and tried to enlist me in a team playing against Dillmans the following Saturday. It was a temptation, but I said no, I must study every Saturday.

I saw he judged me a poor specimen. Father O'Halloran was a great cricketer and wrestler and player of billiards.

This drayman mended the bicycle I found in a shed behind the Manse and on that rickety machine I made my rounds. Sometimes my way was on roads, sometimes on tracks or paths in the bush, sometimes along the old horse tramway. But whichever the way it was muddy. I came to love the West Coast storms, they exhilarated me and I stood in them many a time laughing and shouting, and was taken for mad. But the electric rain, falling in sheets with an elemental roar, and the brilliant sunshine after: all other weather is tame after this. With my shoes in my pockets and my bicycle on my back I waded across rivers and streams to visit old miners, relics of 'the golden days', living in their shacks in the bush. Or I cycled down the road to Dillmans for the Sunday afternoon service, into a landscape that seemed of another world: great craters and cliffs sluiced in the fields, water races on their spindly legs, and blind iron sheds. Or I took a rutted and pot-holed track out to a mill, and over the scream of the steam winch and breaking-down saw bellowed my way through Christian counsel to some stump-armed or three-fingered sinner. Then home to long evenings of Latin and Greek and Theology.

Edie protected me. 'The minister is busy in his study.' (Obstinately she called me minister.) And then, knowing her loneliness, I dug grimly into my books; into that dreadful work of Hodge, *Systematic Theology*, from which I took nothing but headaches and dust in my eyes. 'The minister is busy in his study.' But one night I heard her call 'George' in an urgent way, and hurrying out saw that another time for joy had come. And leaving her with Kate, I cycled down the road to fetch Mrs Cornish, who advertised herself as Midwife and Lady's Nurse. We walked back, I pushing my bicycle with Mrs Cornish's bag strapped on the back, and failing to hurry her; she had a voice like Napoleon, this woman, and meant to be obeyed. Sensible Kate had Edie in bed; Oliver, who had woken, pacified; and everything ready. But Mrs Cornish put me to work, as a matter

41

of principle I believe, and I could not, as I had meant to, get to my books. I was left holding Oliver, while Kate helped Mrs Cornish in the bedroom.

It was an easy birth. Edie cried out several times, but apologized later. At one o'clock in the morning I was allowed in to see my second child, a daughter. Edie was pale but happy and the child red. I placed my hand on her head, cupping her tiny damp brain-case in my palm, and as I had done for Oliver and was to do for each of my ten other children, prayed for her and pledged her soul to God. Mrs Cornish watched with approval. Edie cried and laughed. Kate made tea. And Oliver, again disturbed, set up a squawling.

We named the newcomer Felicity.

17 By the start of our second year I had visited everyone whose name was in the Blue Book except one couple, Edward and Mrs Gardner. They had not appeared in church and all I could discover was that he was a retired miner who lived in a bush clearing with his wife along a track off the Goldsborough road. Edie came with me on many of my visits and so one summer afternoon as I prepared to set off in search of the Gardners I heard her say that she would like to come with me. I warned her of the distance, but secretly I was pleased, for it gave me great satisfaction to have her with me when I spoke to plain honest folk (I was proud of her, she was so sensible and simple and beautiful), and too it gave me delight to walk the roads with her as though we were courting. So we set off. But this is her story, which I take from a notebook she filled many years later in idle or pensive moments. As I copy it down I hear her voice:

G.O.P. said that perhaps this time I ought to stay home as it was a *long way*, but the day was lovely and I wanted to go. Kate could mind the babies quite well, I said. After a little argument I had my way. So we set out. But neither of us had known quite how far it was. Up hill and down dale we went, until our shoes were yellow with mud and the hem of my dress was heavy as lead. I became *very tired* indeed and so did my husband. But we felt it would be silly to turn back—and I enjoyed it so much when he carried me over streams, and so did he. We kept on *walking, walking, walking*. At long last, through trees and along a one track path, we came on a little tumble-down house, almost overgrown with weeds. An old woman answered our knock and looked astonished and almost frightened to see us. We told her we were the new Church minister and his wife and of course she asked us in. She called her husband from the back-room, a poor infirm old worn-out looking man, and my husband talked to him and I talked to the old woman. It was nearly tea time and they asked us to stay for tea. The place was anything but *clean*, and as it was beginning to rain we thought perhaps we had better go. But it *poured* with rain, and the West Coast (or wet coast) is proverbial for heavy rain. So we had tea. Mrs Gardner put her hand in the teapot and pulled out the leaves and threw them out the front door. The bread looked dark in places, almost like marble cake. There was jam which she had made, and condensed milk mixed with hot water. It was not a very comfortable meal, but they were so pleased with the visit. Then as the rain had not stopped, there was the problem of our return, which seemed *impossible*, as we would be *drenched*, and it was getting *dark*. Mrs Gardner said we must *stay* the night. She had no proper accommodation, but there was another shed room and a sack bed, and of course we had *no choice*, and had to make the *best* of it. She took us into the room where we were to sleep, it had a bed made of sacks, filled with straw. She said a man who had worked there slept on it one time. The sacks looked clean, but we had to have a little ladder to get into it, it was raised up from the floor. There were pieces of bacon hanging up, and strings of onions hanging from the roof. One string was over our faces. We took things *humorously* and G.O.P. laughed as he pulled me up the ladder.

Mrs Gardner brought in a new pink flannelette nightdress, which she said she had *never worn*. I thanked her. Then she brought in a big white chamber, trying to hide it from my husband. She apologized for not being able to give him *night* clothes. My husband read the Bible to them before we went to bed. I kept on thinking, *whatever would they do* if *one* or the *other* was *suddenly* taken ill.

Next morning it was *breakfast* I *wished over*. My husband went outside. In front of the house was a plum tree with *ripe fruit* on it. When Mrs Gardner called him he said, 'I've eaten so many plums that I *really* could not eat porridge.' I had to manage to eat a little.

The sun was shining and we started our long walk to Kumara. When we got home everything was *all right*. The baby had been *good*, and Oliver. My husband said, 'Oh Kate, make us a good cup of tea, *as fast as* you can.'

In the winter Mrs Gardner fell and broke her hip and her husband trying to walk the track into town to fetch help for her lay down at the side of a stream and did not get up. So they died. I was away in Christchurch and became weatherbound getting back. I telegrammed Edie that she must ask Brice the Wesleyan to take the service, or read it herself. She chose to read it herself.

These were our days on the Coast and this was my wife.

18 I put my suitcase in the hall; a small case, for these days I need very little. Meg had borrowed Graydon Butters's car and was driving me to Esther's for lunch. While she turned it round in the yard I walked about the house. I was an old man and it was quite on the cards I would not see it again.

But I could not work up much feeling. Rather I found myself recalling small annoyances and triumphs. The bed for example, 'the monster' as Meg's children call it; a huge four-poster, ugly I admit, but stately too, and speaking of birth, generation, death: this Meg has been at me to sell. The making of it breaks her back she says, and she tries to persuade me I would be more comfortable in a single bed. But Edie and I shared this and I mean to keep it. I have had my way so far. A triumph.

And in my study I found Browning's *Poems* on my desk. I had been reading it the night before, looking at *Paracelsus.— progress is the law of life—man's self is not yet Man!* As I picked it up it fell open at the fly leaf, and there were the smiling orange sun and purple birds and blue trees Raymond had drawn with his crayons twelve years before. My study was forbidden, but he had crept in and defaced half a dozen of my books. I would have whipped him but Meg took him behind her. I cannot instil into these two generations a proper feeling for books. And I stood there and felt the blood beat in my temples.

Meg blew the horn; but then, remembering my hand, ran up the path and took my bag herself. We drove down to the gate.

'Stop at Bluey's, Meg. I want to see him.'

'Do we have to?'—or something like that. She has Edie's dislike of Bluey Considine.

'He doesn't know I'm going.' I had deliberately not told him. He would have been upset and pestered me with visits. (I had known the risk I took in renting him the cottage but he had been very good and not come to see me more than two or three times a week.) He was sunning himself in a wicker chair as we drew up, and his friend Sutton pottering in the garden.

'Reverend,' he cried, heaving himself to his feet like a steer. He made me take his chair. Meg went off to wait in the garden and this drove Sutton, the woman-hater, out. He came to the front yard, but could not stay there, being a parson-hater too, so he went inside.

'Well Bluey, I'm off for a week or two.'

'Eh?' he shouted. Our conversations are like this. He too is deaf but refuses to do anything about it. Once or twice, exasperated, I have tried to ram my trumpet in his ear but he pushes it away in a kind of terror. He thinks himself unworthy.

'I'm going away, Bluey.'

'What's that?'

'To Wellington. To see my son and daughter.'

Sutton, who must have been listening, came out with a grin, and set off for the creek, carrying a fishing line baited with a lump of rotten meat.

'Eels,' Bluey shouted. 'He's after the eels.'

'Don't you let him catch those. They're my pets.'

'Eh?'

'Don't try that with me.'

He cupped a hand behind his ear, grinning.

'You can hear.'

'No I can't, Reverend.' And at this joke he wobbled with laughter. A clever one, Bluey. He had got past the eels all right.

'You can pay the rent to Meg while I'm gone.'

'You're not going away, Reverend?'

I explained again. Shouting tires me and I found myself little moved by his distress.

'Reverend . . .'

'All right, Bluey.'

'There's a little thing that's been troubling me.'

So I ran through for him the anthropological view of the hell myth. For Bluey is bog-Irish and though he threw his religion off as soon as he was able to think for himself, it comes back now to claim him. He came to me as a political follower, but in these days, both of us over eighty, it's my rationalist hat he wants me to wear. As I talked—or shouted rather (and a cyclist on the road turned his head in amazement)—I saw from workings in his eye that this was a battle I would lose. The dread of hell is in his bones; was fed him with his potatoes; and I knew that on his deathbed he would call for a priest. I grew disheartened. I like Bluey Considine. I watch with a humble respect his kindness to the little cripple Sutton, whom he has taken care of for fifteen years. He washes the man's club foot and oils his hump. I have seen him chase jeering schoolboys with his stick. It saddened me on that morning to see fear brighten his eye.

'Bluey, there is no hell. God is kind.' I shouted it to him as though he were a child.

'I know, Reverend. I know.' He did not know.

Meg came from the garden and tapped her watch. I said, 'I've got to go now, Bluey.'

'You'll come and see me when you get back, Reverend?'

'Yes. Don't you let Mr Sutton catch my eels.'

'Eh?'

'You're a rogue, Bluey.'

He came to the gate with me, heavy as an old elephant. Even through my deafness I heard his wheezing.

'You look after yourself, Bluey.'

'You too, Reverend. You give them politicos down there a bit of your old stuff.'

As we drove away I saw Sutton limping up from the creek, a red carnivorous grin on his face, dragging an eel twice as long as himself.

19 'Impossible,' Meg cried, and I told her to be precise. But she could not. My children are short of language.

'Bluey Considine is a good man.'

She shrugged and her lips moved again, making some word I did not bother to hear.

'He was kind to you when you were a girl.'

'—dirty and smelly. Mother——'

I suspect the rest was 'hated him.' But that was not true. Edie hated no one. She hated cruelty and selfishness. But while she could not hate Bluey Considine, she disliked almost everything about him; his coarse language and coarse manners, his greed, his way of calling her 'Mum', his betting on race horses, his fatness and smell and smoking; and, especially, his way of taking me off to my study after dinner and closing the door. He had made off, she calculated, with years of my time. (A different matter if he had been worthy.) She stamped her foot when she saw him on the drive. But I reminded her Bluey was a good man, an intelligent man. Brought up on prayers and 'spuds', Bluey Considine. Brought up under Rome. And look, he had won free. And he was kind to the children. He brought them chocolate fish.

I reminded Meg of it. But she cried, 'Oh, I couldn't eat those dirty things. They had bits of tobacco stuck on them. Robert and I used to throw them in the creek.'

I was shocked—although I did not believe what she said about Robert. I could not see a hungry boy throwing good chocolate fish in the creek. But I could see a girl brought up by Edie, with her notions of cleanliness. And I thought, gentility is the enemy of life, it gets in the way of natural response, it's like trying to eat your food with gloves on or drink tea from a thimble. Gentility had been Edie's vice. Not puritanism. Nothing wrong with that, it's maligned by the ignorant and self-indulgent. I have been a puritan all of my life. Meg on the other hand is not. She has not sufficient intelligence for that, she has too much hunger. She's a modern woman and is not going to deny herself. Genteel is what she is. She gets her share of cake, but eats it in the manner Edie taught her.

She saw she had upset me and she took one hand from the steering wheel and patted my face. This is a female trick I hate. They take on this nursery manner, try to overcome us with their specialism. I don't deny there's some good feeling in it, with Meg at least. But there's more of looking down. They can't manage us as men so they make us babies.

I said rashly, 'I'm going to let Bluey have the cottage rent-free.' And having gone that far, told her something else: 'I'm leaving it to him in my will.' I almost believed it. But not quite. The cottage will go to Robert, of course.

20 When we arrived at Esther's the two girls retired to a bedroom to discuss my latest delinquency. I prowled about the house. I can never rest there. It has the air of camp, not home. It has taken nothing from the people who live in it. Fred and Esther come back here to eat, sleep, drink wine, and listen to the races. Their real lives are lived in some other place. And the house shows it. It has a depressed and temporary air for all its expensive furniture and glossy ornaments.

Fred Meggett is more to blame. Fred is busy accumulating wealth (which Esther, to be fair, finds to her taste). He left his father's butcher shop to become a land agent, and bookmaker on the side. And money began to find its way to him like tacks to a magnet. He missed the war (for which I do not blame him); he dealt in some obscure way in American army surplus; he quit bookmaking; and now he's in land again, in a big way as the saying goes. He saw before anyone else that our town must change its centre and he bought up the land where he thought it must go. And it goes there, of course. The shops are starting to spring up now, all owned by Meggett or on sections bought from him. Esther jokingly calls the place Meggettsville. It doesn't seem to be a joke to Fred. I admire him, in the way one can admire a weasel or stoat. I enjoy reminding him I'm a socialist.

'Dad,' Esther yelled, coming up on me with a glass of some purple drink in her fist, 'what's this about the cottage?'

I did not want to argue. My hand was hurting and I wanted my lunch. 'That was just a joke.'

'It'd better be. Old Bluey'd sell the place and blow it all on the races.' But she's a good-hearted girl in her clownish way, and she put down her glass and unwrapped the bandage on my hand almost without my feeling it. 'As soon as you've had lunch you're seeing a doctor.'

'No——'

'Yes. Don't argue.' The smell on her breath was wine. 'And don't turn up your nose. Mum liked her little drop.'

'She did not. That was invalid port.'

'You stick to that story. Come on, let's eat. I've made a bacon and egg pie.'

After lunch she took me to see a young man with oiled hair who bandaged my hand again and tried to talk me out of going to Wellington. He turned my trumpet over in his hands like some Hippocratian relic. I was short with him. And when we were back at the house I told the girls I was going to take a nap. Esther led me into David's room, took off my shoes, laid my burned hand on my chest. She tiptoed out. And there on my grandson's bed, I dozed the afternoon away, surrounded by photographs of football teams and film stars.

21 The time for my ordination arrived. Edie and the children returned to Christchurch, taking Kate with them (she was part of our family now). I went down to the junction to see them off. I was to stay on a week to welcome the new Home Missionary.

Many people from my flock travelled down. Edie was much loved. There were tears; and a passing of goodies and cakes—the largest from our sabbatarian (kind and spiteful lady), who assured Edie it was full of butter and not 'reekin' wi' grease' like all the rest. And so my dear ones left and I went back to Kumara and prayed in my church for guidance on my way, which I knew would be hard. I was going to a world less simple than this, and to folk whose needs were less plain to them. I did not expect to be liked as I had been liked. But I had the clearest knowledge of my duty.

I preached one more time in the church, reading the lesson from Isaiah 61: 'The Spirit of the Lord God is upon me; because the Lord hath anointed me to preach good tidings unto the meek: he hath sent me to bind up the broken-hearted.'

And I read on through words I would hear again at my ordination but would not recognize even then as prophetic, as laying on me an injunction, 'to proclaim liberty to the captives, and an opening of the prison to them that are bound.' It was the first part of the verse that spoke to me and I would have declared then, if asked, that my special care was for those it named, the meek and broken-hearted. The rest I took for underlining. I spoke that day on Christian kindliness and the counsel one man may bring to another; on the sense in which all may be the Lord's anointed. Geddes would have seen error in this but to the simple folk listening that day it was no more than common sense.

On Monday morning I set out to make some visits. There were many old miners living in shacks round the town; old-timers who had come to the Kumara rush in the eighteen-seventies and stayed to work on sluicing claims or in the mills, and built their little huts to see out their days in. I took special pleasure in visiting these independent old men. They asked for nothing, many rejected counsel, but they enjoyed a yarn and I had fallen into the habit of calling on them for the pleasure of hearing them talk. Johnny Potter was my special friend. He had been a forty-niner, and worked on every Victorian and Otago and West Coast field. Gold was his life, the 'colour' his *ignis fatuus*. When the fields died, when all that was left was sluicing or dredging, Johnny took his shovel and pan and headed for the mountains. He was bent like a bow, his fingers were set in a hook, before he came down to Kumara and built his shack.

With Johnny I did talk religion. He was a free-thinker (beautiful word, much to be preferred to Huxley's agnostic). He could not read or write but from somewhere, perhaps from half a century of camp-fire talk, he had picked up many of the rationalist arguments. To him they were simply natural sense and I found myself more than once stopped in my flow of scriptural exposition by some simple, some practical contradiction, some 'fact' as plain to Johnny as that wet kindling won't take fire. He came down especially hard on the First Cause argument,

51

enjoying tremendously his picture of endless Creators, each bigger and better than the last, stretching on into infinity. Darwinism he had not fully grasped; and one of my tasks was to explain it to him. So I, a Christian missionary, sat in his little tin shack on many a wet afternoon, with my bible on my lap (for he let me read now and then), taking him through the arguments he would use to attack my faith. I refuted them of course as I went along, but this gave Johnny special delight and he would cackle in his high cracked voice, 'Wriggle, Reverend, wriggle. This is one hook you won't get off.' He made me tea, a painful business. Wet camps and icy rivers had locked his joints. But he made no complaint. He had enjoyed his life and had no quarrel with the way it was ending.

But on that Monday I had no talk with Johnny. As soon as I came to his door he told me his 'mate' Tom Clarke was 'cashing in' and wanted a preacher. I had no Tom Clarke on my book, and told him so. Perhaps, I said, he wanted Mr Brice or Mr Montague.

One preacher's as good as another,' Johnny said, 'so save your gab.' He took me along the road and up the tramway, a walk that took us an hour or more, and would not talk as we went along. I could not help improving on the occasion, saying that in the face of death the way to Christ became broad and open. Johnny had a simple answer: he spat.

We turned into a track in the bush and found at the end of it a small wooden shack. Johnny sat down on the step. 'Tell him I'll be in when you've finished your gab.' I went inside and saw an old old man, whiskery and filthy and jutting with bones, lying on a sack bed in a corner. The room was full of unclean smells all magnified horribly. I had to push my way through them like a fog. There was no chair or stool so I knelt on the floor. The man scratched at his bedding with hands dry and horny as a turkey's claws. He had true *facies Hippocratica*: pinched nose, sunken eyes, pendent lips, etc; but had a kind of residual redness in him, a flicker of life. He hung on to complete something.

I leaned forward. 'Tom Clarke.' I held my bible up so he might understand a 'preacher' had come. 'Tom Clarke, I've come to pray with you.'

His eyes reached the Book, and came on to my own. He made a sound with his mouth—a magpie gabble. I thought for a moment it was the rattle of death; but he had not spoken for many days and his tongue had the stiffness of wood. I caught the word 'confess'. It caused me to think he was a Catholic and I wondered if there were time to fetch O'Halloran. I had a strong desire to be out of the shack, and away from this mad filthy sinner on the bed; for it had come to me suddenly, through no sense I can name, that here was an antechamber to the Ultimate Darkness, and here, in this man, a being who had Commerce with the Devil. I held my bible tighter and said, 'Are you a Catholic?' and when he made no reply, ashamed of myself, said, 'I'm going to pray for you. Can you hear my voice?'

He nodded, and said more strongly, 'Confess.'

'What is it you want to confess?'

He replied with a word I thought was 'Nothing'; but when I repeated my question, spoke again; and I understood it was, 'Murder.'

'Yes?' I said, beginning to shake, for there were rustlings and shiftings in the place and I could not keep my eyes from straying to the corners. I lifted my bible. 'Are you saying you have killed somebody?'

He made a choking sound: 'Murder,' again.

'Who?'

And then he spoke with clarity, like someone calling a list he had by heart, or checking off goods. The names came out. I did not record or count them, but there were a dozen or more, and several amongst them I knew: Battle, Kempthorne, Pontius, Mathieu, Dudley. I was looking at the Maungatapu murderer, Joseph Sullivan.

I went to the door. 'Johnny, wasn't it a priest this man asked to see?'

'Preacher, priest, they're all one to me,' Johnny said.

'Go and get Father O'Halloran.'

'It's a long walk, Reverend.'

'Then I'll go.'

'I reckon old Tom'll be dead by the time you get back.'

'That can't be helped.'

Johnny said, 'What's the matter, Reverend? Doesn't your bible tell you what to do?'

I went back to the bed. 'Are you Joseph Sullivan?'

'Joe Sullivan.'

'Tell me about the men you killed.'

I kept the Book between us. And I listened while the middle of the day passed, and the afternoon, and night began to come on. Once, late, I looked for Johnny but he had gone. I lit a lamp against the darkness of the place.

He had been a prize-fighter, a baker, a thief; a transported convict, a ticket-of-leave man; then a storekeeper and publican, and proprietor of a sparring-ring. He was a man with great strength in his hands. When he killed he preferred to stab or strangle. He killed George Dobson by strangling, or 'burking' as he called it. He looked on as Burgess choked the old flax-cutter Battle with his hands, and the next day showed him a better way, strangling Dudley with a sash taken from the victim's waist. He shot Pontius, stabbed or 'chivved' Mathieu. And the others . . . Why go on?

His remorse was greatest for his killing of Dobson. He had mistaken the young man for a banker, but once he had stopped him could not let him go. He wept. 'He was joking with me.' And then, and many times, scratching with his hands and clutching my coat with a sinewy strength, 'I am deeply dyed with the blood of my fellow creatures.'

He had lived many years without remorse. Greed had drawn him back to New Zealand. As Tom Clarke, ten years older than Sullivan, he had gone to Nelson, meaning to dig up the gold buried after the murders. But there superstition caught him. He crept up on the place, he circled it, but the closer he came the more dreadful it seemed. He heard voices, heard the sounds of dying men. Several times he had come within yards of the spot, and once got his shovel into the ground, but had known if he lifted the sod the ghosts of the murdered men would spring on him and devour him. So he crept away, and crept away, and each time he tried to go back found himself stopped shorter. For a while he haunted Nelson, but there on a hill was the jail where Burgess, Kelly, Levy had been hanged. Kelly, whom he called Noon, preyed on him specially. Kelly, it seems, wept as the judge passed sentence and cried, 'I don't want to be hanged,' and Sullivan counted him as one of the men he had murdered. At length he came to rest in Kumara, and there he lived fifteen years in greed and fear—and in the end remorse.

I asked him the proper questions and heard his replies, and prayed for him, and so guided him into the Church Universal. I was not happy about it. It seemed too easy. I told myself the judgement was not mine. I let him hold my bible on his chest.

Johnny came back with some bread and a billy. He lit a fire in the yard and boiled up tea. I asked him why he did not use the shack. He replied that he had never been able to touch any of Tom's things.

'So you know who he is?'

'He's Tom Clarke.'

'Did he ever ask you to get his gold?'

'It don't be gold.' He looked angry, as though I had tried to mark a stain on his life. We drank the tea and ate the bread. Johnny told me he had known Sullivan as soon as he'd set eyes on him. He had fought him once in Ballarat for two pounds.

When we looked at the man next he was dead. I closed his eyes. I was glad Johnny was with me for I could not be sure evil was out of the place. I had no sense of having won this man's soul to Christ. I had felt evil but not its defeat, I had known as though by putting my hand on it and feeling its texture the corruption that can feed and flourish in a human heart, but I had not felt the redeeming Blood of Christ. Why? I asked myself in a kind of torture. Had I not carried the offer to him?

Had we not, between us, put the abomination out, and had he not freely and gladly come into the arms of the Redeemer?

Why did I not know it?

The question was troubling me still on the morning we buried Tom Clarke or Joseph Sullivan. Scroggie, my replacement, had arrived. We followed the undertaker's cart with a dozen old miners, Johnny amongst them. The old men dropped out at the bottom of the hill and left their *crêpe* hatbands hanging in a tree for the undertaker to pick up as he came down. They went back into town to a hotel. Scroggie and I walked to the cemetery. He took the grave-side service; and I saw my congregation was in good hands. The remains of Joseph Sullivan sank into the ground. '. . . earth to earth, ashes to ashes, dust to dust; in sure and certain hope of the resurrection to eternal life, through our Lord Jesus Christ . . .'

And indeed I began to have some knowledge of it.

We went back to the Manse and I packed my bag. After that for many months I had no time for thought.

22 Fred Meggett hums like an electric motor. It's a fearful energy that possesses him, driving him on to what he calls success and I damnation. (He means of course power and possessions and I the lost possibility of becoming a Man.)

When he came home late in the afternoon the smell of the world of gaining and getting was on him; the reek of money. He tried to relax with a glass of beer and a racing guide, but as he sat in his over-stuffed chair he was shaken by small mental explosions that made him clench his face up like a walnut. He tried to talk to me. (He's one person who doesn't need to shout.)

'Well George, they tell me you're off.'

'Yes, tonight.'

'That's a hell of a trip, that *Limited*. You'd do better to fly.'

'If God,' I said, 'had meant us———'

'Sure, we'd have wings. And wheels if He'd meant us to ride.'

A point to him. In spite of my disapproval of Fred, and hatred of what he stands for, I find myself liking him at times. He's a boy.

'How many widows and orphans have you put on the streets today, Fred?'

He enjoys this game. 'None. But I fired a girl.'

'What did she do?'

'It's what she didn't. She forgot to write an appointment in my book.'

'Was that serious?'

'Not much. I wanted to get rid of her, that's all. She was too dumb.'

'Will she be able to get another job?'

'Sure. Plenty of jobs. She can go and work in the jam factory. That's about what she's good for.'

'Fred, when the revolution comes you'll be first up against the brick wall.'

'Not likely,' he said. 'I'll probably have the contract building them.'

We exchanged a grin, pleased with ourselves and each other. I had, in fact, switched off a part of myself, otherwise I would have been angry. Fred Meggett is dangerous—Fred and his kind. Other people are not real to him. He's surprised to see them move and speak, and outraged if they show feelings. They must be pushed here, pushed there, and fitted into the places made for them even if arms and legs get knocked off in the process. Fred is a dictator, a brother under the skin to Hitler and Stalin. I've told him this frequently, demonstrated it, but it drives him into a pious rage; so I did not try that afternoon. I had a sore hand and a long journey ahead of me.

Meg looked in to say goodbye. Fred pounced on her. 'You tell Fergie I want him down at those shops first thing tomorrow. Sure—' he waved her quiet—'I know he's got other jobs, but I got that contract for him and now I want some action. O.K.?' He grinned. 'You're looking well, Meg. Esther been feeding you wine, has she? Esther love, when's tea?' You could almost hear the switches clicking on and off under his skin.

Meg kissed me and left. I joined the Meggetts at table. These small families seem unnatural to me. Esther has David, seventeen, and Adrian the late child, five. Where are the others that should have come between? What chemicals, what techniques, prevented them? My life and Edie's together was a tree that bore fruit in its season. In every sense what came from it was natural and blessed. I look at David, I look at Adrian, greedily gobbling his food, and I think, Why not those others, the poisoned ones? I find it hard at these moments to put food in my mouth.

'Is your hand sore, dad?'

'No.'

'I don't think you should go.'

'I'm all right.'

'Can't you put it off a week?'

'Felicity's expecting me.'

'We can send a telegram.'

'They cost too much.'

'Oh, dad.'

They think I'm mean. I turn them aside from all sorts of other ground by pretending it.

23   Edie never complained at the shortage of money. Not only our early days were hard, but all our days. There were many mouths to feed and bodies to clothe. We managed. I have never had much satisfaction from it. But minds—that's another matter. There were young minds to feed and clothe.

Oliver was born in Christchurch. Felicity and Edith in Kumara. Willis, Florence and Agnes in the town of Emslie, where I was called on my ordination. Emerson, Esther, Rebecca (who died at thirteen), Alfred (who died to me one day at Peacehaven), Margaret and Robert, in Thorpe. After 1910 there were no more babies. Edie was not strong enough.

Some of my children have told me I cut myself off from them. But those years, 1895–1910, were years of hard work for me, and bitter struggle. They were years of growth and self-education. I left day-to-day matters to my wife, and never heard her complain. And if at the end of her child-bearing she was bone-tired and aged beyond her years, if her face was lined and her eyes weary, and her hands, her beautiful hands, were those of washerwoman rather than pianist, she would have said it was no more than proper; her eyes and hands and hard-used body were those of wife and mother, no more; she had done her duty in the eyes of God, in the service of her loved ones. There's a modern piece of cant about happiness being our due; and those who utter it do so with a greedy look on their faces. Happiness equals self-gratification! There's a truer sort that can only be found in service.

She came to me one day with a piece of paper on which a child had written: *Our father which art in his study writing a sermon.* She was shocked, and amused a little. I was neither (though pleased at what I took to be the beginnings of literary skill).

'Is this Felicity?'

'Yes.'

'She's got a good hand.'

'I don't think she meant any harm.'

'Send her in to see me.'

The child came in pale and quaking. They were used to coming to my study for punishment. (I beat the girls, but only with my hand.)

'Did you write this, Felicity?'

'Yes, father.'

'What did you mean by it?'

'Nothing.'

'Come now, child. You can't write a sentence and mean nothing.'

'I only meant you were in your study writing a sermon.'

' "Our father which art in his study." Some people would say that was blasphemous.'

She began to cry. She was only eight.

'It's all right, my dear. I'm not going to beat you.'

'You only come here to read,' she sniffed.

'Only!' I was shocked. 'You mustn't speak to your father like that Felicity. Otherwise I *will* have to punish you.'

'I'm sorry.'

''Come here, child.' I took her on my knee. 'I come to my study to read, and to write, and to think. I can't think with children running round me, can I?'

'No,' she said.

'That's why your mother brings my meals in here. Now, look. Can you read that?'

She read, hesitatingly, from my notes, 'The wider bible of literature.'

'This is an essay I'm writing for the paper. I'll be paid for it, just a little bit, and that will buy us food. But that's not important. The Wider Bible of Literature. Do you know what that means?'

'No.'

'It means we can learn about God from other places than the bible. From books men have written. When I became a minister Felicity I had not read much. Mostly the bible and books about the bible. But now I'm reading other things. And I'm learning more about God. That's my job. Do you see? So I can help other people learn about Him.'

She said she saw. I read her a little poem of Ella Wheeler Wilcox:

> Let there be many windows to your soul,
> That all the glory of the universe
> May beautify it. Not the narrow pane
> Of one poor creed can catch the radiant rays
> That shine from countless sources. Tear away
> The blinds of supersitition; let the light
> Pour through fair windows broad as Truth itself
> And high as God.

60

'Now, you take this book away and learn that poem and come back and recite it to me tomorrow night.'

After that I made it my practice to have one of the children in for half an hour each evening after tea. It should have been longer. I should have given them more. They crept in so pale, with such a hunger in them. Yet I did much. I have seen Oliver sitting quietly in the corner reading *Sartor Resartus*; heard Felicity read me her first poems; seen the shine in Willis's eyes as I read him Emerson's great words, 'God will not make himself manifest to cowards'; and in Emerson's as I read him *Locksley Hall*. Oliver had the sharpest mind, but alas, a narrow pricking thing; Felicity the bravest; and Willis or Theo the strongest sympathies. (I had discovered Browning shortly before the child's birth, and through Browning Theophrastus Bombastus von Hohenheim, or Paracelsus. So Willis got his useful second name.) Emerson was a practical lad, not easily taught, but easily moved. A good boy. Edith, Florence, Agnes: intelligent children, eager for knowledge, eager for the blossoming of spirit that, had I known it then, creates from man *Man*. I gave them much but should have given them more. I was a child myself and did not know.

The later ones—well, there were other books and other evenings. Only let me say that of all of them, all of my children, it was Margaret or Meg who pleased me most. Her soul sparkled like water; and when she lifted her tender eyes to me, Edie's eyes, my heart grew full of joy in my love for her. Margaret, who grew up to marry a plumber and smoke cigarettes and worry about the colour of her lipstick.

Edie looked after their bodies; their food, clothing, schoolgoing, household duties. The girls as well as the boys worked in her garden. From her they had their lesson that idleness is a sin. And their reverence for growing and living things. Their everyday morality (the higher from me). And of course their manners and habits. Meg showed me a letter given her by Edie on her wedding day:

61

Teach your children to be *good*, *clean*, *honest* and *truthful*. A child is an *unwritten* page, a 'bundle of possibilities'. Teach them to have clean habits, clean teeth, clean finger-nails, and never to spit before people, or blow their noses *violently* as that is a habit that assaults the nerves of the eyes, ears and throat. Teach them to value their *eyes* and their *teeth* because one set of permanent teeth and one pair of eyes are to last them *all* their lives and they are *precious* possessions. Teach them to have nice manners. They should not pick their *teeth* or their *noses*, or *scratch* their heads. These things if they *must* be done should be done when they are *alone*. Teach them not to sneeze loudly in company. I once lived near a woman who used to come to her back door and sneeze so that all the neighbours could hear her. That is a *vulgar* thing to do. Make them respectful to elderly people. I hate to hear a young boy address an elderly man as Tom or Jack. It makes life more pleasant to be with *good-man-nered* people. Watch their speech, don't let them fall into the habit of *bad grammar*, like [oh my dear good Edie!] children often do. It does not take more than a minute to correct them. Also teach them good manners at the table. I have seen many a meal *spoiled* by a naughty child. *Punish* them for *swearing*. Make them *abhor* it. *Good strong* men *don't* need this filthiness to make their words *tell*.

Remember your father's prayer for his children, 'Let them be *original*.'

Never call your children 'kids'.

24 My time in Emslie was a time for gaining strength. The little town of tradespeople and farmers was a stonier field than Kumara. I met with kindness there, and with many good people, but I met too complacency and selfishness and greed—what I came to call, and plainly, from my pulpit, a fatness of the soul.

It did not take me long to discover that I was in a town of haves and have-nots, and that the distinction was carried into my church. And I would not have it. I made it known in Session that I would allow no renting of pews, and at once a storm broke about my head. One would have thought I proposed some new theological doctrine. They were elderly and in the main prosperous men, and I was young and poor. But I stood my ground. I reminded them I was their pastor; that not a month before they had attended my induction and promised me (and I spoke the words) 'due honour and support in the Lord'. They wagged their ignorant heads. It was not that sort of argument, they said. This was a financial matter, a matter of organization, and my duty lay elsewhere, in the care of souls. And Cheeseman, who had seen ministers 'come and go', reminded me that a part of *my* promise had been to promote unity and peace within the Church. I grew angry. I would not be told my job by these satisfied men. Unity and peace, I said, were not promoted by the sale of favours. I told them I was disappointed to see such an appetite for precedence in my congregation, such a concern for worldly things. 'Beware of the scribes,' I said, 'which desire to walk in long robes, and love greetings in the markets, and the highest seats in the synagogues.' And I said renting would stop at once. If recompense must be made then we would run a sale of some sort to raise the money. Or, I said, it could come out of my stipend. One or two looked ashamed. But not Cheeseman. He gave in, of course. He was politician enough to know battles are not won or lost round a table.

When I told the congregation on the next Sunday that renting was finished, they murmured a little—at least those in the front—but I saw no rebellion. The matter was left quiet. But on the next Sunday the same people were in the front pews. And the next. I was stumped. I could not scourge them out.

Cheeseman said to me in Session, 'It's all very well laying down the law, but people are used to their seats and the ones up the back won't come down the front simply because you say so. They like it where they are. Some of them have been sitting there for twenty years. You wouldn't shift Mrs Carter with a block and tackle.'

'Very well,' I said, knowing I had lost. 'They may sit where they please. But from now on we won't take rent.'

'Then how will you pay for a roof?'

'We'll manage.'

The roof began to leak. And soon I was having to use my handkerchief to wipe water drops from my bible. (It kept the little boys amused.) I had to set about organizing galas and jumble sales and cake stalls to raise money for repairs; and all this was a great strain on Edie, whose job it was to see them properly run.

25 Cheeseman: dangerous as a jersey bull. I can still hear him bellow, still see him paw the ground.

One day I took as my text Matthew 26:40: *Inasmuch as ye have done it unto one of the least of these my brethren, ye have done it unto me.* I said a teacher in the town had told me her children were falling asleep at their books. One small boy had toppled out of his desk and curled up on the floor and not stirred for an hour. Others had been found in the playground, sleeping under the trees. Their health and their work were suffering, I said. And why was this? A good half of the children in the school came from farms. And most of them were called from their beds at 4 a.m. to work in the milking sheds. When they arrived at school they had already been labouring four or five hours. (Some even came unfed.) Whatever their parents might call it, I said, this to me was sweating; and sweating was evil.

I told them of child labour in factories and mines, and how in all civilized countries it had been stopped by enlightened legislation. I told them of the work of Rutherford Waddell— a Presbyterian, I emphasized, a minister of their church—who, almost single-handedly, had wiped out the practice of sweating in New Zealand. But some classes were less fortunate than the girls who had sewed moleskin trousers for fourteen hours a day at twopence halfpenny a pair. And these were children, whose parents could do with them practically as they chose. Drag them from their beds, I said, these eight- and ten-year-old mites. Send them out into the mud and sleet, work them till their fingers froze and their bodies trembled with fatigue and hunger. Then send them off to school unfed, or with only a gulped plate of porridge; and complain as you did so at the loss of wage-free labour. And when they came home work them again. Then come to church on the Lord's Day, into the presence of Christ, into His very house, and ask, nay demand, His blessing? Never, I said. Never while I was pastor of this flock. I would have, I said, no sweaters in my church. And I led them in prayer: Almighty God, most merciful Father, forgive us thy servants who have fallen into evil ways, purge us of our greed and hardness of heart—and so on.

During my sermon several people left the church. There was much stirring and grumbling. But I saw that some were moved and as I led them in the singing of the hymn—I had a fine clear tenor that put a few choir noses out of joint—I had a feeling I had not yet known in the pulpit: a sense of good work done, of a burden shouldered with joy and ease, and of the long hard way I must carry it. And I told myself that at last I had begun my ministry.

Cheeseman was of the opinion I had ended it. He was a farmer, his son was a farmer. It was his grandson who had fallen out of his desk; a fact I had known. Cheeseman read me a lesson in the economics of farming. He complained that my sermon had been no sermon at all but a piece of socialist rabble-rousing. Where, he asked, was the doctrinal content? The Presbyterians of Emslie went to their church for religious reasons, not to be told how to conduct their lives.

I could not believe what I had heard. 'Would you say that again, Mr Cheeseman.'

He had the good sense not to. But he cried: 'I challenge you, show me the Christian doctrine in that sermon.'

'As ye do it unto the least of these,' I said. 'That should be doctrine enough for anyone.'

'The way you twisted it,' he cried, 'it was socialism.'

'Socialism not to want children exploited? To want them to get their education?'

'Book-learning. Where does that get anyone? Work is what children need. Hard work—that's the way to the Lord. Not fancy ideas. I worked. We all work in Emslie. And we won't have any city preacher coming out here and telling us how to live. You think these children are hard-used. They'd be into mischief if they weren't kept busy. I know. My father made me work and I thank him for it. I was out in the sheds from the time I could walk. I was milking a dozen cows a morning, and afternoon too, by the time I was ten. And look at me now.'

I looked at him, at his meaty face and swollen eye, and I thought, This is the enemy. I was shaken. 'Mr Cheeseman,' I said, 'it's my business to look after the spiritual welfare of the Presbyterians of Emslie. I'm surprised I have to remind you conduct is a spiritual matter. Unless you do good——'

'Faith in the Lord is all we need. No more. *I* remind *you* that we are among the elect. The grace of God is upon us.'

'Unless you do good how can you come into the Lord's house——'

'Works,' he roared from his bull's throat. 'You ask us to seek salvation through our works.' And from some Calvinist hole in his mind dug out the tag:

> 'Doing is deadly thing.
> Doing ends in death.'

The enemy, I thought. But doctrinally he was on safe ground. It was mine that was shaky. I contented myself with saying, 'Good works are good works, Mr Cheeseman. They're no road to salvation, as we know. I would hope we do them not to be saved but because we are saved.'

He did not let the matter lie, but raised it in Session. He wanted authority to report my sermon to Presbytery. He had some support in this, most noisily from a storekeeper called Hay who thought too much schooling bad for children and hard work and beatings a way to the Lord. I learned, without surprise, that he had been raised in that way. 'I was beaten every morning,' he said, 'for the good of my soul. And taken away from school at ten. I've no complaint. I learnt enough reading and writing to do my accounts—and read my bible.' This, of course, was back-blocks Presbyterianism. I reminded them of the church's work in education, that its ministers were university graduates. A mistake—it enraged Hay and Cheeseman. I was claiming superiority now, they would not put with it. But one or two of the others were uncertain. And I took the opportunity to produce my strongest argument. They beat me about the ears with Presbytery; I beat them in turn with the Southern Synod (soon to be joined with our own Assembly). Simply, I took from my pocket and read: 'The Synod deplores the existence of the sweating system in the Colony, and instructs the ministers and the office-bearers to discourage it by every means in their power, and enjoins all to bear each others' burdens and so fulfil the law of Christ.'

It silenced them quicker than a biblical text. They came on to the attack again—Cheeseman and Hay, at least—but cautiously. Was not this an historical document? Twenty years old at least? Ten, I replied; the principle as sound now as then, and the instruction as clear. But sweating, they said, was an industrial matter, and we were talking of children in milking sheds.

So the argument went round, and Cheeseman and Hay warmed to their task again. My concern, they declared, must be for the spiritual welfare of my parishioners. I must keep my socialist rabble-rousing out of the pulpit, etc. We fought a war of texts. I began moderately, 'But whoso hath this world's good, and seeth his brother in need . . .' They bombarded me with fundamentalist nonsense—hellfire and damnation and worms that dieth not. I lost my temper and cried, 'I have seen the wicked in great power and spreading himself like a green bay tree'; which I suspect they had meant to use themselves. We were like schoolboys throwing stones at each other. I saw it and was ashamed, and going to my wider bible, said, 'In Religion What damned error but some sober brow Will bless and approve it with a text?' They took it personally. Useless to explain I had aimed it at myself. So I apologized. They did not. They complained to Presbytery.

But they were complaining to educated men; narrow perhaps and limited in their religious understanding (as I was then), but men who knew the importance of book-learning. When they discovered that children were falling asleep at their desks they came down firmly on my side; advised me though to fight my battle discreetly. Which I did; and won some ground.

Cheeseman and Hay were a thorn in my side for the whole of my stay in Emslie. Edie called them 'the Bullock' and 'the Crab'.

26 I see myself cycling home from a pastoral visit, a small red-headed man, hair a little thin, hearing a little dulled; hot in my suit of grey and turn-around collar. People smile at me and call, 'Lovely weather, Mr Plumb.' I come to my gate, unsnap my trouser clips, put my bicycle in the shed. Children run to meet me from the garden, their fingers stained with weeding. They hang about my knees, and one, Emerson, climbs me like a tree and perches on my shoulders. Through an open window I hear my wife playing the piano. She allows herself a quarter of an hour each day. It is *The Rustle of Spring*. She welcomes me home with a gay tune. Kate clatters dishes in the kitchen. (Dear Kate, plump and bossy, more mistress to Edie than servant.) I go into the parlour, kiss my wife, and drink a cup of tea. I tell her about my day. Kate looks in, demands her in

the kitchen, and she goes off with a smile of apology. I walk in the garden, examine the children's weeding, put the boys to stacking firewood. I eat a plum, think about my sermon for the next Sunday. And some neat turn of phrase drives me to my study, where I begin to write.

An hour later Edie comes in with my dinner on a tray. I tell her the children have been very quiet and she grows pink at my compliment. I have got a lot done, I say, and I read her some of it. She approves; and goes out to eat her own meal. Later a child creeps in. They are always excited and nervous. This is Aladdin's cave. I hear her recite:

> All wondering and eager-eyed, within her portico
> I made my plea to Hostess Life, one morning long ago.

I praise her and sit her down on a stool to read; and feel her kiss on my cheek when after half an hour she creeps out. I do not look up. I have found a new argument.

Later I hear the sounds of children going to bed. There are tears, and I watch the door to see who will come in for punishment. It is Willis. He tells me he has been bad. He has drawn a moustache on Edith's doll. It is a small offence and I strike him only once with the cane. He says he is sorry and goes out smiling bravely. The house is quiet.

I write a letter to the paper. Some bigot in a religious column has said the Sabbath-breaker is as bad as the murderer. A sensible word is needed on this. I go out to the sitting-room and read Edie what I have written. She is darning socks, but she listens and approves. I see how tired she is and tell her to get an early night.

Then I read for two hours: Emerson on the Over-Soul, or Behmen or Swedenborg; or the new London Ethical Society pamphlet with its account of the debate between Joseph McCabe and the Revd Waldron. No doubt about the winner.

At eleven Edie brings me a cup of tea. She sits and talks to me. She tells me we must pay Kate more; that she has seen some cheap material that will do for dresses for Felicity and Edith. Oliver needs a new shirt and winter shoes. Willis's teacher says he is getting on well. I am pleased at that. She kisses me and goes to bed. After reading in my 'bible' I follow her.

This is my life until 1910, in Emslie and Thorpe. I fish in the rivers, and walk in the hills, and play cricket. (I bowl leg breaks now but they still call me the steady little trundler.) People look sideways to see Edie expecting again. We smile and say, 'The more the merrier.' On Wednesday nights I lecture at the Literary Institute: Wordsworth's *Prelude*, the novels of George Eliot, the bible in literature, Dickens and the poor, Thoreau, Richard Jefferies' *The Story of my Heart*, Hardy and Meredith, Browning and Tennyson, Plotinus, Emerson as poet, Emily Brontë, the *Satires* of Juvenal, Socialist thought in the English poets. I am learning to speak, to spout. It shows in my sermons. I am told I declaim too much. Others say I am too insistent. Nobody yet has accused me of doctrinal error. They accuse me of socialism. In this they are right.

27 I joined the Socialist Party in 1902, shortly after I moved or, to use the ecclesiastical term, was translated to St Andrews, Thorpe. The move was a happy occasion. It brought us closer to Christchurch, which we thought of as home; closer to Edie's mother and sister; into a familiar landscape. I expected it to bring me in touch with like-minded men.

I was straining to break my bonds. Years of ministering to simple folk had made me familiar with much that is noble and generous in human nature, but it had also brought me close to the dark. There are holes and corners in the mind, lidded tight. I had prised loose some of the lids and seen spring out genie-like, and swell to giant size, things whose names are ordinary enough, greed, envy, cruelty, race hatred, class hatred, lust, sloth, hatred of man, of God, and of the self; but whose shapes can shrivel the mind. An example: I was called to a house where the police had found a four-year-old child tied to the leg of a table. It had not been freed since it had learned to crawl. It was filthy, emaciated, clothed in rags, and it made its wants known in grunts and whimpers, like an animal. We had it taken away to an institution but it never recovered human shape or mind. Another: a young boy, given for the first time his body's evidence that generation requires a physical act, hanged himself from a rafter in his father's barn. Another: the behaviour of 'the Bullock' and 'the Crab', whose belief was a tightly closed door; who saw with naked glee those outside consumed by eternal fires.

In Thorpe, and even in my church, I expected to meet men and women whose minds were open to the light.

I joined the Socialist Party, the Eugenics Education Society, and became a subscribing member of the Rationalist Press Association of London. For several years I had been reading widely in socialist literature. I was master of the doctrines of communal Utopians and Marxians alike; and if as a Christian I found myself settling at first somewhere near the former, as the years went by I travelled leftwards and became a root-and-branch man. My key text in those days was the one I had used against Cheeseman and Hay: But whoso hath this world's good, and seeth his brother have need, and shutteth up his bowels of compassion from him, how dwelleth the love of God in him? A good question, and not to be answered by donations to charity.

I could not say from my pulpit that socialism was the answer. But I said it on week nights, in halls about the town. I spoke on the need for a eugenic programme. For it seemed to me socialism and eugenics travelled hand in hand. The socialist state must be the eugenic state, where men and women could be healthy in mind and body and morals.

These were days of intense mental labour for me, of wide reading and wider enquiry, and the beating out of ideas to a fine gold leaf; and it gave me joy to walk in the country with friends, to talk and joke and dispute with them and try upon

71

their intellect and spirit the ideas working within me and drawing me with an inexorable force, elated mostly, uplifted, but sometimes, I admit, shrinking and nervous, into my life of rebellion. They came about me, a band of brave and open-hearted men: Edward Cryer, John Jepson, Andrew Collie, John Findlater. And there was too the young John Willis, a lawyer now, who came down frequently from Christchurch. These were men on whom I leaned, who gave me comfort and support in the cold times that slowly crept upon me. Later there was Bluey Considine. But at first it was Edward Cryer and John Jepson who were important.

Edward was a member of my church; at least his name was in the Blue Book, but I seldom saw him at a service. I saw him at my Literary Institute talks and my Trades Hall talks (and later at the Unitarian Hall). He was shy. He was ugly and inarticulate, and full of pain at unregenerate man. He approached me after a talk I gave on William Morris, working his way up like a yacht tacking against a breeze. He asked me if I knew the writings of Robert Blatchford. 'Of course,' I replied haughtily; offended that anyone should suppose I did not know of *Merrie England*, know of the *Clarion*. Edward drew back as though I had struck him. It was an instinctive animal-shrinking from danger. He mumbled something and turned to make his escape. But I took him by the shoulder. I apologized. We walked home together and drank a cup of tea and talked (at least I talked); and we became friends. I drew him slowly into a closer intimacy than I was ever to know with another man; into comradeship. And in that state he lost his halting manner of speech and talked as well as I, and often to greater point. His mind was more sensitive than mine, and he had a greater purity of ambition. Self played no part in it.

Edie grew fond of him and my children called him Uncle. He never came to see us without flowers for my wife (he was a florist), sweets for the younger ones, and a book for Felicity and Oliver. I whipped Willis severely one day for aping Edward: pushing out his ears like flags, beetling his brows, and thrusting

72

out his jaw prognathously. And stopped Felicity's puddings for a month when I learned she called him 'Old Hairy Ears'. Edward brought her bags of cakes to make up for it.

John Jepson was different. A bluff and hearty man. No nonsense about solid John. He was well-to-do, the owner of an aerated-water factory. His library was the best I have ever seen privately owned. He too came to me after one of my talks. He offered me the use of his library. I went along expecting the usual half-dozen shelves of books, expecting perhaps no more than one or two titles unfamiliar to me; and came, like my children, into Aladdin's cave. Infinite riches in a little room. It took my breath away, I almost fainted. It took the ordinary—a glass paper-weight, a chair, John himself, a glow of honest pride on his face, moving to stack green pine-cones on the fire—to bring me to myself.

'You may borrow what you like, Mr Plumb. Except my prize birds here.' And he showed me a glass case of eighteenth-century first editions—a set of *The Rambler* I remember, *The Deserted Village*, the *Poems* of Ossian. I made polite noises; but was drawn, even as I spoke, to the other shelves. For here, without doubt, was the wisdom of the ages. And here, especially, was modern thought, modern heresy. Here was the future if I could only hammer it out from these shelves.

We must have talked, although in my memory I simply sat down and started reading. His wife came in with tea; a disapproving Presbyterian lady—yes, one of mine. She sniffed at the book-leather smell, the pipe-tobacco smell, the smell of male clothes (I was wet with rain), as though she detected something going off; but John dismissed her with a wave of his hand.

'Women and books don't mix. Now, have you seen these?' He placed on the arm of my chair a dozen brand-new titles, just out of their wrappings. We fell to dipping, and talk, and quoting, and the reading of passages aloud; and our tea went cold on the table. (Mrs Jepson removed it without a word.)

So John Jepson became one of the group about me. He made

73

me careful. He made me think before I spoke. He would not be carried away. I can hear his voice: 'Yes George, but these are just fine phrases. What exactly do you mean when you say "higher ethical altitudes"?' (Or, 'sublime democracy', 'world-wide communal soul', 'eugenic knowledge', 'one-man humanity'.) I came to value him for more than his library.

I remember those afternoons when we strolled along the by-ways and over the hills. John and Edward became friends, though not as close to each other as each was to me. They had a competition to see who could provide me with the funniest joke for my next week's talk. Edward's were innocent, boyish, and often, I thought, without point. John's leaned towards earthiness. I made it a condition of telling that each man should demonstrate the usefulness of his joke to my argument. Those were vigorous and manly afternoons. We walked hard—John at fifty and Edward at forty-five perhaps a little less hard than I: they sometimes sat down to rest while I went ahead or off to one side to get some quicker or wider view. John had the habit of whacking stones with his stick, using it like a golf club. Edward gave us the name of each flower and bird. I hear his voice (a little less free than if he and I had been alone): 'George, I came across a beautiful phrase the other day. The understanding silence of a long married life.'

'Is that your joke?' cried John. 'It's easy to see you've not had a wife.'

'I think it describes my marriage very well,' I said. 'At least the part of it I've had so far.'

'Then you're a fortunate man. But tell me how you can work it into your talk.' (For my subject was marriage.)

'Well,' I said, 'I'd have to give it some thought. Perhaps Edward can tell us.'

'That,' he said, 'is how I imagine marriage. And one of you has told me I'm not wrong.'

'I'll tell you you're wrong,' John cried. 'Haven't you heard the Chinese proverb: A woman with a tongue six inches long can kill a man six feet high?'

74

Edward and I both found this improper. He was married, and we knew his wife.

We were, I remember, a full company that day. Andrew Collie, John Findlater, John Willis, had joined the band; and we made an unusual sight—six men of varying ages and varying dress (John Findlater was casual, and John Willis coloured, and I of course in my dog-collar), inclined very much to laughter and declamation, and the scribbling of notes in pocket books, and the spouting of poetry. John Willis said, 'There's another proverb, John. God could not be everywhere and so he made mothers.'

'And what of the dying man?' Edward asked. 'He caught sight of the Other Side and said, "That is my mother's land." '

'That could mean the opposite of what you think,' John Jepson said; and we roared with laughter. 'In any case, we were talking of wives. And George, I offer you this. Women are good for making butter and trouble.'

Andrew chimed in in his uncompromising Scots. He could recite the poems of Burns from front page to back; and now he gave us:

> John Anderson my jo, John,
>   We clamb the hill thegither,
> And monie a cantie day, John,
>   We've had wi' ane anither;
> Now we maun totter down, John,
>   And hand in hand we'll go,
> And sleep thegither at the foot,
>   John Anderson my jo!

'There's your answer, John,' Willis said.

'*An* answer,' John replied. Like Edward and me he was impressed by Andrew's courage in reciting the poem. We three knew his story. He had been engaged to a young woman in Aberdeen and had come to New Zealand to establish himself in business. He would send for his girl as soon as he was able. The story is common enough. He met another, and fell in love

75

with her; and wrote the painful letter home; and prepared himself for marriage. And then came the horror—I choose the word with care. His *fiancée* would not release him. She wrote that he was pledged to her. She loved him and would keep him to his contract, which he must honour as an honest and God-fearing man. She would be on the next ship out. Well, Andrew was God-fearing no longer, but he remained 'honest'. So he gave up his dream of happiness, and lived in the nightmare. He cut himself off from the girl he loved—her agony was something he could not bring himself to speak of—and married the one he did not. They had been together now for fifteen years, in bitterness and hostility. There were never any children. The marriage—if I can call it such—was, he told me, never consummated.

We walked along, talking of women and morals. John Findlater, a cricketing acquaintance, flicked a ball from hand to hand, or practised his strokes. He was a lover of poetry, and would-be poet himself. His verses, which he read without shyness on these walks, were full of lark-song and breaking bud, pretty enough, but for men of our belief almost without content. He was, too, politically ignorant. He believed the government of the day—Seddon had just died and Ward was running things—a benevolent institution. We had undertaken to educate him. Indeed, he was often in a state of shock by the time we finished our walks. But he came along nicely and was one of my great supports in my times of trouble.

'I would have all marriages as happy as my own,' I said. 'And,' I said, 'I would have all marriages cease to exist that are less happy than mine. For happiness is the end of marriage—that is the divine purpose of it. Happiness and children are the fruit. And a barren tree should be chopped out at the root. The law and religion drag behind this truth. I would have divorce made easy, and the immorality of marriage without love put an end to. It cannot be called marriage, in the sight of God or man. It is prostitution.' I did not spare my friends in the pursuit of an idea.

'Now George, now George,' John Jepson said, 'what do you mean by divine purpose?'

'And what,' Andrew asked (an atheist), 'what do you mean by God?'

'Look here,' John Findlater cried, 'that's going too far.'

Young Willis was on another line. 'Just think of the women in bondage to cruel men. Think of them—delicate creatures, forced to yield to the embraces of drunken tyrants.'

None of us cared much for his tone, or his choice of words. He was still harbouring, it seemed to me, a too personal view of things; though I could not see how drunken embraces fitted in. His father had long been a total abstainer (from strong drink, I mean). But John was a generous and cheerful boy, and sharp-minded enough when his filial emotions were not in play. So I welcomed him to the group when he came down and hoped long walks and country air and the company of my friends would freshen that part of his mind where he kept his obsession.

'What we must aim for John is to prevent unhappiness in marriage. There are many sorts of unhappiness besides the one you mention. I don't advocate, John'—and I turned to Findlater here—'free unions and free divorces. What I do say is that the higher ethic is to ease the way for the separating of unhappy couples.'

'What do you mean by higher ethic?' John Jepson asked.

'What God does not hold together by love, let not the Church paste together by texts and laws,' I quoted.

'Very fine,' Edward said.

'And all very well, but how do we go about changing the church's mind?'

'There's too much talk of the church here. And God,' Andrew cried. 'You don't change their minds, you sweep them away. They're part of the rubble of the past. Sweep away God and the church, I say.'

'But good heavens,' John Findlater said, 'what would become of morality? Why, there would be nothing to restrain us.'

'Morality is not the property of the church. Morality has its

77

home in the free mind. All else is superstition. The free mind needs no restraint. The free mind,' I said, 'is God.'

'Hear, hear,' Edward said.

And we marched along.

28 But how was I to reconcile all this with my position as minister of St Andrews? A murmur had begun and it grew with the passing years and at last even my children began to hear. For people shrewdly guessed that my political and social beliefs must have as their companion an unorthodoxy in religious doctrine. If challenged I would not have been able to deny it. But it did not enter my church. I married people, and baptized and buried them; I gave the Lord's Supper. Sunday had become an annexe to my real life; one I found it harder and harder to enter. Only when I had pulled the door shut behind me, closed the shades, so that no light from the wider place should enter; only then could I remind my flock that they were corrupt and depraved, call them to repentance, speak of the passion of Christ, and declare that faith in Him was the single pathway to salvation. I was in a curious state; for in that little room I was a believer. My years of intellectual acceptance and emotional need had placed a part of me in thrall, and this my rebellious self, the new man, failed to win over. It was a Dark Tower, the old need and superstition, and I came to it like Childe Rolande many times, and set my slug-horn to my lips and blew; but the beast did not emerge and the tower stood. And while it stood I remained in my ministry.

This is high-flown language. Yet I believe it accurate. Those were painful and emotional days as well as being full of intellectual striving; as well, that is to say, as being joyous. I preached and prayed, and remained doctrinally sound in these activities —though less heavy than most of my flock must have wished. I administered the sacraments according to form. In my visiting I gave comfort and counsel. And socially I was very good, very good indeed. Mr Plumb at a picnic was a wonder to behold. He sang and joked and blessed the food (and did not forget to praise the cooking). He jollied old ladies and little children; he sat on the greasy pole, drove nails in the nail-driving contest; shied the cricket ball; he judged the children's races, strolled in the shade with the ladies, talked plumbing with plumbers and law with lawyers and the Good Book with a pious elder. He climbed a tree to rescue a trapped child. Spanked his naughty son. Gave his arm to a faint young bride. All beautifully done and much approved. At the end of the day he stood by his pretty wife and called his healthy children close about him. An ideal Christian family. He saw them into their trap—a squeeze. He made a joke. His parishioners laughed. Just for this occasion they were pleased with Mr Plumb.

And Mr Plumb waved, dignified now, and drove off to his home; where he unwrapped the mail he had turned his mind on all through the afternoon—the latest copy of the *Hibbert Journal* and the latest reprint from the R.P.A.

I have forgiven this man his duplicity. But I will never make him my close friend.

29 I was sorry we had no workman in our group (sorry too we had no woman, but found only Edward agreed with me in that). We went on a good deal, I said, about our faith in the working class to sweep away capitalism and imperialism and establish a world of peace and plenty, but which of us had as friend a man who worked with his hands? It was a challenge. And one that Edward answered with Bluey Considine.

He was not sure about Bluey. The young man (an aging young man) had come into his shop to buy roses for his girl. But, they discovered, he had left his money at home. 'Now how did I manage that?' He turned his pockets out like a stage comedian. Then they talked about progressive literature. Bluey had read books Edward had never heard of (he invented some of them).

Edward was impressed; and let him walk out in the end with a dozen of his best dark reds, sprinkled with water and done up in coloured paper. The following week Bluey was back, and did it again, this time with a grin; paying in talk. But on his third visit wanted no roses, except perhaps one for remembrance: his girl had found a young man she liked better. Edward brought 'Mr Considine' to meet us; and whispered that he would not vouch for him.

I discovered fairly soon this talkative County Corkite was more vagabond than workman. But at first I was delighted with him. He was not only a wharf labourer and union man but a fugitive from Rome as well. Early in our acquaintance he turned up at my home unasked just as we were sitting down to dinner. It was Sunday. We were back from morning service. I was not pleased to see him; but soon recollected my claims for myself —I was a Christian and a Socialist. And here was a brother in Christ, and one of the exploited. So I asked him inside and introduced him to Edie and sat him down at table with my family.

And Bluey began to gobble—there is no other word for it. He carried great loads of food to his mouth and chewed them noisily. We saw half potatoes, lumps of meat, travelling down his throat like fish down a seagull's. He stretched his arm half the length of the table to snatch bread or butter or salt from under Edie's nose. 'Push that gravy along, Reverend.' He forked a piece of fat from Oliver's plate and an uneaten potato from Agnes's. The younger children were delighted with him. Edie became excessively polite.

'Do you find the meat to your taste, Mr Considine?'

'I was brought up on prayers and spuds, mum, so a good piece of beef is a treat to me. I'll have a slice more if you don't mind. I don't like to see good food going to waste. Here youngster, don't you want them beans? I'll eat them for you. Push your plate over here.'

Edie saw a roast she had meant to last two meals vanish in one. Bluey sat at the table sucking skewers and string. 'You're a good cook, mum. You don't mind me sayin'? But the Reverend here, he eats like an old maid with lockjaw. Too much going on up top, eh? Got to fuel the engine, Reverend. Don't want to get top heavy. Now mum, you make him eat. You ask me here again, I'll show him how to eat. And if you don't mind me sayin', a bit of hot mustard with that gravy would improve it.'

'You are not married, Mr Considine?'

'I nearly got married once. That was in Australia. Half my life I'd been wandering, and I said to myself, It's time you settled down. So I found me a girl—a little slip of an Irish colleen she was, and a refined wee thing. Why you'll never believe it, she wore scent. It's the truth now, and I don't know how she could put up with me.' He gave a grin: he was not blind to himself. 'But,' he said, 'her mother died, and me being broke she gave me some money to buy a wreath. Well you know, I put it on a horse, and I'll give you a guess where that horse ran. Dead last, Reverend. Dead last, mum. It's a way all my horses have, of running last.'

Edie was shocked.

I said, 'It must have been in Australia you got your name.'

'Bluey. Because of my hair.' (It was redder than mine.) 'I was glad to get rid of the other. Francis is what I was christened. Now there's a good Catholic name, and it's no wonder. The town was crawling with priests where I grew up. Like beetles in a log, they were—and always telling me I'd burn. I got out of there Reverend, I got out on my feet, as soon as I knew which was the way to Dublin. I only had my uppers left when I got there.'

I took him to my study. We talked about books and religion and the labour movement. I respected him. He was his own rough-and-ready creation; dishonest only in things that did not matter. (Edie told me he had slipped a baked potato in his pocket.) From Dublin he had gone to Liverpool, from Liverpool to London; from there to the world, as stoker on a series of broken-down freighters. In San Francisco he had jumped his ship. He bummed his way (his term) back and forth across the continent. At one camp somewhere in the Mid-west he had shared his frying pan with Jack London. Later he had been a 'mate' of Pat Hickey; witnessed the birth of the I.W.W. He had seen the strike-breaking tactics of the American company police—had his head broken in one encounter by a brawny Mick from his home town of Clonakilty. Lately he had come across Hickey again; been with him in Blackball in the miners' strike, where the workers had won a great victory, half an hour for lunch instead of a quarter. 'And,' Bluey said, 'there's trouble brewing here.'

'Where?'

'On the wharves, Reverend. It's not long now and we'll be coming out.'

30 Two weeks later the Thorpe waterside workers went on strike. They had been encouraged by the miners' success. It wasn't more time for lunch they wanted but a fair day's pay. And though the strike petered out after several weeks for a while it seemed we were in for a long bitter fight. The union was fined for breach of its award; refused to pay; saw distress warrants issued against its members (Bluey one of them, but he had nothing), and property carted into the streets for auction. It organized the bidding and so spiked that gun. (Chairs were bought for a penny ha'penny that day.) Garnishee orders were served and the fine collected. But meanwhile more serious events took place. The employers got together a team of farmers to load the ships. Scuffles, blood, arrests, much bitterness; and the first signs of hardship in the strikers' homes. At that point a message came across from the employers that certain concessions might be made providing matters went through the proper channels. So the strikers went back to work, against the wishes of Bluey and his committee, and the grind of the Court began. The watersiders got little in the end, but by then the spirit had gone out of them.

A small strike; but the first of several events that turned my life upside down.

At first I felt helpless. I was a talking not a doing man. I felt uncomfortable with Bluey; and even more with the strikers and their wives in my congregation. I drew my fat stipend (relatively fat) and fed my children, while they had nothing and saw theirs begin to go hungry. I made a number of speeches in the town, in halls here and there. This was my usual activity—gab. But at last I could not hide from myself a way in which talking might be changed into doing. I had turned my steps away from it too long.

Edward was in church that day, John Jepson too, and John Findlater. (Not Andrew. Nothing would bring *him* past the door.) I chose as my text James 5:4: *Behold, the hire of the labourers who have reaped down your fields, which is by you kept back by fraud, crieth: and the cries of them which have reaped are entered into the ears of the Lord of saboath.* It was the first piece of text-hunting I had enjoyed in years.

I began moderately, telling my congregation of the obligations of honesty that lay on men in their dealings with one another. I said the relationship between man and man reflected that between man and God. Very much one of my bread-and-butter sermons. But then I was launched. There was, I said, an event taking place in our town that touched every one of us. We were fortunate, I said, that we in Thorpe had been given the opportunity of taking part in a skirmish, a frontier skirmish, in a war that was being waged throughout the world, and right to the gates of Heaven. The Lord of saboath, who was the Lord of hosts, of armies, had heard the cries of them which have reaped and had gathered His armies about Him, the armies of the workers of the world, and was marching on the citadels of privilege. He was battering at the gates and the walls would tumble down and the labourers enter in to claim their hire. I kept on in this vein for a good long time, and saw Edward restrain himself with effort from crying, 'Hear, hear.'

Then I paused, climbed down from my soapbox; and asked

very reasonably, had not Moses led a strike, and at the Lord's command? Were not the twelve Apostles, the chosen of our Lord, working men, labourers with their hands? Fishermen, not ship-owners. And, I asked, was not Jesus himself a working man, a carpenter, with callouses on his palms? For almost twenty years he had earned his daily bread with hammer and saw. He had strained his muscles in the shaping of timber, in the lifting of beams. He knew the agony of labour, the aching bones, the sweat, the pittance for pay. Never forget, I said, those years of his life before he became a teacher. Never forget that in the figure of the saving Christ there lives another, the man with calloused palms, Nazarene Jesus, the Carpenter. He never forgot it. The labourer, He said, is worthy of his hire; a belief that informs His teaching. And more. For what, I asked, was his moral creed when it was boiled down? What was it? (And I made them wait.) Why, I said, it was simple. We must not be frightened of it. It was the creed behind whose banner the working men of the world had assembled themselves, the waterside workers of Thorpe amongst them. It was the creed of the future. It was the future. What was it, the teaching of Jesus? Why, I said (for I had wound them tight enough), it was socialism. Simply that.

Edward said, 'Bravo!'

Here and there I saw a face that glowed. The rest were closed up tight.

We prayed. We prayed for the sick and suffering; for the hungry and exploited; for a softening of the hard-hearted. Afterwards we prayed the usual prayers, sang the usual hymns.

A strange and threatening stillness marked the going out of my flock. Their clothes seemed to rustle less and their shoes strike the floor more softly.

Our little band crossed the road to the Manse: Edie and I, the children, Edward and the two Johns. We sat in the sunshine on the wooden seats by Edie's conservatory. Andrew came round from the back garden where he had waited beyond the sound of hymns. I told him what I had said. He was elated. He was always one for large brave happenings; and he flapped his arms like a rooster and almost crowed. Kings, capitalists and priests were on the slippery slope. The age of the common man had dawned. All at a sermon from the Reverend Mr Plumb.

'Oh Andrew,' Edie said, 'they looked so angry.'

'Angry? So they should be. We'll have a battle, never fear. We'll have a fine old battle on our hands. They'll fight to the last ditch, while there's still a penny they can get their greedy paws on.'

'There'll be Session trouble, George?' John Jepson asked.

'It won't stop there, I think.'

'Presbytery?'

Bluey Considine came through the gate, with a bag of sweets for the children (he was penniless and must have stolen them). They ran to him and soon he had them lolly-scrambling on the lawn—to Edie's anger and my disapproval. I had not told Bluey what I meant to do. He might have tried to pack the church and I wanted to speak only to my usual congregation. He came to us and Andrew told him the story.

'Aye Bluey, you should have been there. I had a wee look George, I admit it. It did my heart good to see all yon donsie faces comin' out o' the temple.' (He called it temple, implying dark and bloody rituals.)

'Well Reverend, I wish I had been. But it'll do no good,' Bluey said. His eyes had a beaten expression I had until that moment put down to hunger.

'Why Bluey, what's the matter?'

'We've lost, comrades. Our friends have lost their nerve. Their wives want them back to work. So we've agreed to arbitration. You'll read about it tomorrow in your newspapers.'

'But,' I cried, 'it's the Arbitration Court we're trying to get rid of. We'll never get anywhere through arbitration.'

'It's the tool of the profiteer,' Andrew said.

'Of the master class.' We used this language. We were not the hungry ones.

'And so we lose. Well, there'll be other battles,' John Jepson said. The rest of us could not manage this larger view. We sat

85

there a downcast band. The children, seeing their chance, ran and screeched about us in a way that had Kate frowning out from her kitchen.

'Don't think of your sermon as wasted, George,' John said. 'Whatever the outcome of this strike the struggle for minds goes on. You've struck a blow in that.'

'Aye, the scoundrels have been set back on their heels. They'll be quaking tonight over their port and cigars,' Andrew cried.

John laughed. 'Andrew, you should have been a pamphleteer.'

These two and John Findlater strolled down to the orchard to look at the blossoms.

'Is it really over, Bluey?' I asked.

'Over,' he said. 'The wives have won the day.' He was more cheerful. He was looking ahead to his dinner.

'I wish you had let us know, Mr Considine,' Edie said. 'Then George might not have had to preach his sermon.'

'No Edie, that's not fair. I should have told Bluey what I meant to do. And anyway,' I said, 'the time had come. It would have been cowardly to behave in any other way. Edward, a church is not a lecture hall. You don't cry out Bravo.'

Edward turned pale. 'I was carried away, George.'

I laughed. 'So you were. And I was pleased to hear you. That was an awful silence.'

'Mrs Porter cut me dead when we came out. Willis, come down from that tree,' Edie said.

'Porter is one of your elders?'

'Oh yes. There'll be consequences. Willis, you heard your mother. Wait for me in my study.'

'Ah now, don't beat the lad. That would be cruel,' Bluey said.

'Willis is being disobedient, Mr Considine,' Edie said.

'Why mum, he's probably hungry. Boys suffer in that way. I hope you've got a good piece of beef in the oven.'

The others came back, with fallen petals decking their Sunday clothes. Andrew was in mid-poem:

'See yon birkie ca'ed a lord,
Who struts and stares and a' that;
Though hundreds worship at his word,
He's but a coof for a' that.'

I was heartened. I had friends. I had friends down through the ages. Men of sense and goodwill had always been on my side.

John Jepson, Andrew, John Findlater, went off to their homes. Edie and I, Edward and Bluey, went inside. Edie played the piano. The children made off to corners of the garden. I watched through the parlour window. Oliver read. Felicity brought the little girls their dolls. Willis, believing his punishment forgotten, made Emerson bend over and mimed a beating. Then he patted the smaller boy on his head in just my forgiving manner. I burst out laughing. I let him get away with it.

31 That was Sunday. On Monday Session called me to a meeting. I was dealing with civilized men—or so they seemed after Cheeseman and Hay. They acted with firmness rather than savagery. And at first they were inclined to charity. My error could be mended by a show of penitence. They wanted to keep the matter within St Andrews.

I sat and reasoned with them. We went through my sermon's argument step by step. Some of them had memories like rat traps. But I would not give way. It was my duty, I said, to indicate the course of Christian behaviour in any matter involving my congregation. The strike involved it, as I had made plain. And there was nothing doctrinally wrong in presenting Christ as a tradesman. The scriptures were clear on that point.

They replied that my error lay not in doctrine but in my use of my pulpit to preach a political creed. Socialism belonged on the street corners: the Lord's House to the Lord's business. And there we rested. I reminded them as I left that they had no

87

right to exercise discipline on me. As a minister I was not subject to their court.

I cycled home. It was a fresh Spring day. A shower had left everything brightly coloured. Well, I thought, this little business is launched and it will end soon enough, one way or the other, but the seasons go on. It seemed, as such things do, an original discovery, and I wondered at the pettiness of men.

Edie met me at the front door. Her face was drawn, she looked in middle age. I smiled to give her courage and took her hand and we went inside, through the entrance hall she loved so much (an imposing place, with leaded windows and carved seats and a profusion of mirrors: in style quite unlike my Edie), and into the parlour.

I told her I thought this thing would soon blow over. 'They're men who prefer private dealing. And they like to control things themselves. If it gets into the hands of Presbytery they'll find their importance shrunk.'

'Oh yes, George,' she said, 'I see that. But this is only the beginning, isn't it?'

'Are you frightened, my dear?'

'A little.'

'Would you have me stop?'

'No. But . . .'

'But, my dear?'

'I love this house. And the children must be fed and clothed and educated. George I will stand behind you in everything you decide. But before you decide, look at these things too.'

'If we feed their minds we are doing our duty by them. And do you think I haven't considered these things?'

'I know you have, George. I didn't mean to doubt you. But we've been so happy here.'

'Edie, I've had a hard morning. Bring me a cup of tea. I'll be in my study.'

And when she brought it I said, 'Don't be afraid. I'll do nothing that harms you and the children. But I must follow my conscience. You would not have it any other way.'

'No, George. I would not. I'm sorry.'

'I'll do nothing without your knowing. You knew about my sermon. And my dear, I'll tell you this, I won't quarrel too deeply with my church over a matter of politics. If that were all our quarrel I'd have it out now. But there are things that go deeper. When we do face each other, Edie, it will be on other ground.' I looked about the study. The books frowned down on me: a stern, not unfriendly frown, calling me to duty and honesty. 'If they can show me anything I should apologize for then I'll apologize. I think that's all they want. I'm not guilty of heresy, Edie. It hasn't come to that.' I implied, and she took my meaning, that soon it might.

'We may have a little time yet, my dear. But don't love the house too much. Or our comfort too much. There are more important things.'

She came and kissed my brow. I took it to mean she would follow me where I led.

32   I was wrong in thinking Session would keep the matter to itself. Several of the members were men of substance. They were threatened in their purses.

I had a visit from the Revds Mr Downie and Mr Mitchell. They were, they explained, appointed by Presbytery to look into certain remarks I had made in my sermon; which, they were bound to say, had an unorthodox sound. But their inquiry was an informal one. They were anxious I should understand that.

I took them to my study, where I fed them tea and cake. Soon they began to feel very much at home. They were two courteous and gentle men, though each, I think, had some iron in him. The books soothed them (they were both short of sight and could not read the titles); my bible, open by chance on the desk, lent the room an air of piety. Mitchell approached it and marvelled at the wealth of annotation. 'May I?' And he turned the pages with decorous motion, reading aloud to Downie; first a text and then my comment on it.

' "I will be as the dew unto Israel: he shall grow as the lily, and cast forth his roots as Lebanon." And of the lily Mr Plumb notes, "No plant is more productive. One root often gets 50 bulbs. Pliny." You are a scholar, Mr Plumb. Now what have we here? Amos 9: 2 "Though they dig into hell, thence shall mine hand take them; though they climb up to heaven, thence will I bring them down." And the commentary is "Sinner leave yr sins & fly to yr Saviour's bosom; this is the only way to escape punishment." '

It startled me that I had written this. It must go back to my days in Kumara. Could not Mitchell see the ink was faded?

'Do you mind if I turn to the Gospels, Mr Plumb? My word, there's not a free quarter-inch in the margins. Look at this, Mr Downie. Remarkable.' He browsed for a good quarter-hour. I poured him more tea. 'Thank you. Thank you. Listen, Mr Downie. "For where two or three are gathered together in my name, there am I in the midst of them." And Mr Plumb says, "The advantages of social worship. I. It promotes spirituality of heart. II. It is a stimulus to secret worship. III. It affords a lesson to the household." Very true, Mr Plumb. It's a practice that unfortunately is not as widespread as it used to be. Why in my day . . .'

And Downie came to the desk. He found: ' "And some fell among thorns; and the thorns sprung up, and choked them." The annotation says, "Ground not thoroughly purged & cleansed! Strangled by secret sins!" '

This made them happy; and me depressed. Well, it was they who must be satisfied. And when we came to chat about 'this other little matter' they wanted from me no more than the smallest nod at Mitchell's suggestion that perhaps my judgement had been a little astray. I gave them their nod, willingly. I undertook to keep politics out of my pulpit. For I saw my quarrel with them was of another sort.

Mitchell laid his hand on my bible. 'The Scriptures are close to your heart, Mr Plumb.' He was a kindly old man.

So ended the first of my battles with Presbytery. My sons would have called it a fizzer.

33 Willis 'phoned me before we left for the station. The stupid fellow had trudged a mile to the box, quite forgetting I cannot converse on the 'phone. Esther had to act as my voice and ears.

'He says to give his love to Felicity. Oliver too. That's an after-thought.'

'I will.'

'He will, Willis. And he says how are you getting on?' I hadn't said that, but no matter.

Esther yelled, 'He's got rheumatism in his wooden leg.'

'Tell him to rub it with alcohol. It'll stop him drinking the stuff.'

'Dad says rub it with alcohol. It'll stop you boozing.' Silence. 'He says Mirth has drunk all the alcohol. It keeps her warm.'

'She'd keep warm if she wore clothes. They all would. Ask him if he's taken any more wives.'

'Have you taken any more wives?—Do you mean other people's, dad?—No, just beginners.—He's got his eye on a little filly up the ranges. He showed her his wooden leg last week.'

'Tell him it's time he grew up.'

'Dad says you're nearly fifty, it's time you grew up.—He's been up and it's more fun coming down.'

'Tell him goodnight. We'll be late for the train. And give him my love. He's an idiot.'

'Dad says you're an idiot.'

I left them talking and went into the bathroom. I love Willis. He's a natural. Not in the old sense of that word, or the more recent one. He follows his nature, which is a pleasant enough

91

thing, not an iota of mean-ness or cruelty in it; but it leaves him without reason or understanding.

Fred and Esther drove me to the station. There I found Meg had booked me a sleeper. I was angry. I do not like to waste money. Nor do I like being treated as a child. The old are expected to put up with this. I never will. I told Fred to go along to the booking-office and change my ticket to a second-class one.

'It's too late now, dad. The train's nearly going,' Esther said.

'We've got ten minutes. Go on, Fred. And don't forget my refund.'

'Dad, you need a good sleep. Especially with that hand.'

'Fred.'

'O.K. George. Keep your shirt on. Here, give me the ticket.'

He went off, but I caught his wink at Esther. And now there was a bustle on the platform; porters and guards rushing about, children crying, and young people kissing in that open-mouthed way they've learned from Hollywood. No shame and no sense of cleanliness. Intimacy lies in another direction. I said, 'Go and get him, Esther. I'll miss the train.'

'Oh dad, make up your mind.'

'You know as well as I do he's round the corner smoking a cigarette.'

She burst out laughing. 'There's no flies on you.' She fetched him back and they got me into my compartment.

'Goodbye. Don't wait.'

'You're not angry, dad?'

'Of course not. I like being treated like an imbecile.'

'Cheer up. Don't lose your trumpet.'

Off they went, grinning; a modern couple, not much love between them, but a lot of laughs to be had. I sat down and pulled myself together. I'm not really bad-tempered. I've got my temper well under control; always have had. Never for a moment in my mature life, and I date that from my Presbyterian days, have I been without a sense of the divine. How can one admit temper, lust, etc, these flurries of the ego, when one has had my experience, entered into the Light, that is into Manhood. When Fred and Esther had gone, when the beating of my heart had subsided a little, I sat in that musty narrow box and experienced a moment of deepest peace. 'God comes to see us without bell.' I heard Him calling my name, and felt a lifting, a lightening, under my heart and in my skull. I wondered if my earthly life were ending, whether I would die on this worn red seat with the bustle of departure all about me. I was ready.

A young man came in. Ah well, the man from Porlock. I gave up dying and said Good evening to him. He looked a little taken aback to be sharing his compartment with an old codger like me, bald as a cricket ball, shining-eyed with the remnants of his vision, and armed with a weapon like a gramophone speaker. He was well brought up however, and he offered me the choice of berths and the seat by the window. I smiled at him; touched my ears. I did not want to talk. He settled down to read his evening paper.

Later, as the train was rushing through the fields of south Auckland, I noticed something had excited him. His wandering eye had picked out my suitcase label.

'Plumb,' he shouted. 'Unusual name.'

I agreed.

'—relation of Emerson Plumb?'

'He's my son,' I said. 'Do you know him?'

'—saw him land—Takapuna beach—nineteen-thirty.' Something like that. I grinned, inclined my head. I have lost the art of comporting myself in the light of my aviator son.

'What's he doing now?' the young man shouted.

'He's piloting flying boats across the Tasman.'

'Fair go? What a bloke, eh? The Sundowner of the Skies.'

The Australians called him that and it crossed the sea. It was many years since I had heard the name. It brought tears to my eyes. To hide my emotion I set about preparing for bed. The young man was helpful. He called the attendant and soon the seat was transformed into bunks and I was able to change. My companion found a reason to leave the cubicle. An octogenarian naked brings strong reminders of mortality—or perhaps

93

he found my shanks a comic sight. Anyway, I was alone; and grateful. I climbed between the sheets, switched off my light, and turned my face to the wall. And although I had gone there to examine what it was that had moved me so, I soon passed into sleep. I slept for a good long time.

34 The small hours. A moon-rayed closet full of dead air and burnt coal. A swaying circular motion that set my stomach floating as though on oil. As I put my feet on the floor they knocked over a cup of cold tea. It was another kind thought of the man sleeping above my head. He must have bought it at Frankton or Taumarunui and left it by my bed in case I should wake. I thanked him; and paddled to the window to see where I was. No difficulty. Close at hand Mount Ruapehu was shining in the moonlight.

I have always looked at scenery in an eighteenth-century way —a Johnsonian way that is, not Wordsworthian. It is the grandeur of man that moves me, not mountains. Mystical experience for me is not set in motion as for that good gray man of the Lakes. And so when he says:

> I have felt
> A presence that disturbs me with the joy
> Of elevated thoughts, a sense sublime
> Of something far more deeply interfused,
> Whose dwelling is the light of setting suns,
> And the round ocean and the living air,
> And the blue sky, and in the mind of man—

I say, Yes, and give my intellectual assent to his catalogue, but am moved to joy only by its last item.

The flanks of the mountain were certainly beautiful. They were smooth and pale, like cold butter. I enjoyed their slow turn about the train. No stirring in my soul, to be sure, but a calm enjoyment of beauty. I have been accused of lack of enthusiasm. A cold intellectual fish. But it's not so. I've seen a good deal of 'pure' response in my time, and seen what it leads to—fanaticism, self-indulgence, locked iron doors in the mind. I prefer the scalpel and microscope; and so have been accused of choosing them. It may have been true at one time, but not any longer. Dissect, experiment, by all means. But sooner or later one comes to the dark or Light. And entry cannot be made until the laboratory smock has been put off.

But my children have accused me of coldness, of pedantry. Even Oliver. Astonishing. A mountain to him is something to mine; a tree to mill for timber; a stream to dam. He's the cleverest of my sons, and the most limited. Full of sharp little thoughts that scurry about, pricking here, pricking there; but none escape from the box of his prejudices. His mind, it seems to me, is like an ant nest under glass. The little creatures are so busy, so full of purpose and hive-importance; they're never aware of the eye looking in. Well, Oliver; he is what he is; and he has, as they say, climbed to the top of the heap. Many people have told me I should be proud of him.

The train turned away from the mountain. I struggled into my blankets. My hand was painful again and I nursed it across my chest and thought of my sons. It had been kind of Willis to stump a mile on his wooden leg to say goodbye to me. He was full of natural goodness. And underneath, I was sure, was a good brain. But Willis was a vagabond, like Bluey. Adventure not knowledge was the object of his quest. I remembered him haled back home after his first escape; from Bluff, where he had joined an oyster boat. He took his beating like a man; and the next week was off again—to the Coast, the gold dredges. I had to let him go in the end. He signed on a freighter as cabin boy. And ten years later limped into Peacehaven on his wooden leg, grinning like a gargoyle. No letter for over a year; but in his seaman's bag a Finnish doll for Edie and a brass buddha for me. What could we do but cry over him and shake him by the hand?

Yes, my sons. Oliver the success, and Willis the failure. And Emerson, the Sundowner of the Skies. Plodding, courageous Robert. And Alfred. What was Alfred? On that night in the train I thought of him as Chatterton, dead at seventeen. Marvellous boy. But dead. And then became aware of my self-deception. I have noticed many times that I turn to some example or case from literature when I want to evade a clear sight of my behaviour. It will not do. And for the first time in twenty years I saw that Alfred's life had carried on. I felt the pain of his loss. Somewhere in the world Alfred was living; journeying as I was journeying. He would be forty-two: middle-aged. I could no longer feel that he was evil. I felt tears on my cheeks for the brilliant boy.

So in the witching hours I dozed and dreamed. The train murmured on. From time to time my hand dragged me to the surface and I felt the motion of rushing ahead. Dawn came. The young man climbed down from his bunk and fetched me tea and sandwiches. He took himself off again while I dressed. And soon we were in a long tunnel; then bursting on to the harbourside.

'—pleasure meeting you, Mr Plumb.'

We went through shunting yards, side-stepping over points; and rolled slowly at the side of a crowded platform. Smiling faces, hair blown by the wind.

And there was Felicity. My daughters are more reliable than my sons.

35 'Daddy,' she said, 'have you really stopped believing in God?'

'No, my dear, I have not. And never will. Who told you that?'

'Helen Brockie,' naming the daughter of one of my elders. 'She said she heard her father telling her mother. They said it was a disgrace and you'd have to be stopped.' At fourteen she is easily hurt by the bad opinion of her schoolfellows. 'I've been reading about Shelley. Was he really an atheist?'

96

'Yes.'

'But you're not?'

'No. Did Helen say I was?'

'She asked me what it meant, that's all.'

'Did you tell her?'

'I told her to go and look in the dictionary.'

'Good girl.'

'Dad?'

'Yes, Felicity?'

'If *you* believe in something it must be right.'

I was alarmed. I hid it. Now was not the time to disturb her faith. I took her hand and asked her to recite me the *Ode to the West Wind*. I told her the man who wrote that need not fear the judgement of the Brockies.

This took place in the garden behind the Manse. It was autumn 1910.

36 My children were growing up. Oliver, the oldest, was sixteen. Only three, Alfred, Margaret, Robert (new-born, red-headed, the last of our children) were not at school. They were handsome and lively, the Plumbs. We were complimented on their good looks and cleverness; but never on their piety. It was a scandal in my parish that my children were not regular at church and Sunday school.

I do not think I influenced Edie against her judgement. She followed where I led but tested every step of the way herself. She was an open-souled creature, yet robust, hungry in her religious nature as a new-born babe for milk. And she was no longer nourished by a penitential religion. That, I think, is why she loved our house so extravagantly. It was a cloak she drew about her so she might know warmth in her bodily life at a time when spiritually she wandered in the dark. We had not been so close in our Thorpe days as in Kumara and Emslie. I had thrown myself too much into my search for a political way and religious truth. But in the cold winter of 1909 we came together. I discovered that while I had been questing she had been taking her first wary steps, brave steps. *Audax et cautus*. I would like to say those words described my way. But I was less honest. I still kept Sunday in its box and entered it with the better part of my being held in check. I marvel that it went on for so long.

Edie was more in my study at the end. We spent long evenings together, talking and reading. One thing we never questioned: our vision of life was religious. What we sought was a form of worship that would not cripple us as rational beings. And more and more it grew plain that what we must do was put aside Christ, sweep Him into the past, those dark and superstitious times in which He had his genesis, and turn to the real person, Jesus the man. And go on through him, as an example of goodness, to God, to the One, of whom we were a part.

This brings into small compass ten years of searching, two years of it in the company of my wife. I will say nothing of our reading, or of that stretching of mind and spirit that set the air in my study trembling as at a charge of some force like electricity. Rather, I remember our companionship.

Her hand takes mine, signalling support of some new intention. I feel its roughness and have in that instant a knowledge of part of her life that has escaped me: the scrubbing, the sewing, the labour of her days as I drink tea and scribble in the margins of my books. We read again. We talk. She laughs with excitement. Later she cries. The cure is hard, often we are in pain—she more than I. I have been ten years on this way, my coming to health no longer requires cuts and dislocations.

We sit by the fire. Midnight chimes on the hall clock. Kate is asleep, the children asleep. The embers are taking on a coat of grey.

'And so it's decided,' she says.

'If you will stand beside me.' (I mean this metaphorically—there is no place for wives on the platform I have agreed to mount.)

'I will, George. You know that. I can even lose this house now.'

'We'll find another house.'

'Yes.' She is quiet. 'Oliver's going to be upset.'

'Oliver must learn courage. He cares too much about what people think.'

'He's very good at school, George.'

'He's clever.'

She sighs. 'The others won't mind so much. We'll be able to feed and clothe them.'

'Educate them. Feed their minds. They won't suffer. Not in any way that matters.'

'We'll have to let Kate go. She'd stay without wages but we can't ask that.'

'Can you manage?'

'I can manage, George. Felicity's a help now.'

We are quiet for a moment. Windows rattle in a gust of wind.

'George?'

'Yes, my dear?'

'Will you be able to buy the books you need?'

'I may have to cut down. John will let me use his library.'

'You must buy what you need, George. The rest of us will get by.'

Again we are quiet. She smiles.

'What is it, my dear?'

'I was thinking of Rebecca. She was at a birthday party yesterday and they asked her to say grace. The minister's daughter.'

'Had she forgotten?'

'Listen. "God in heaven, thank you for the party, which looks very nice, especially the jelly." '

We laugh delightedly. 'Were they scandalized?'

'I don't know. At least, Rebecca doesn't. She was too busy eyeing the jelly.'

We laugh again. We are very pleased with our children.

37 All except Oliver. I am not pleased with him. Worship for our eldest son was an act of conformity. He had a saintly style, or should I say monkish? and a jesuitical manner of argument. Legalism was his vice, even at that early age. There was no spirit, no emotion, in his religious behaviour; but a narrow-eyed concern for proper observance. For some time he had been unhappy with us.

'Oliver,' I said, 'your mother and I have been doing a lot of thinking.'

'What about?'

'About our faith. Our souls. And about our future. I mean,' I said, for he provoked me to exactness, 'our condition in eternity.'

'I thought all that was taken care of.'

'How?'

'We're Presbyterians aren't we?'

'Yes, we are. And I hope to remain one. If I can change one or two parts of the doctrine.' Hearing my voice say it, I became breathless, I felt myself shrink. There was no hope. I knew it. 'Oliver,' I said, 'I'd like you to share what your mother and I are finding. You and Felicity. And Edith, perhaps. The others are not ready yet. But you three could come to my study after tea——'

'No.'

'Why not?'

'I don't want to hear what you're saying. I know what I believe.'

'At sixteen?'

'I believe what I was taught. I'm not leaving the church. Not for you or anyone. People would . . .'

'People, Oliver?'

'You want to throw everything away.'

'No son. All I want to do is follow my reason and conscience. Your mother too.'

100

'Reason? Why? You've got your bible. You're a minister.'

'Has your reading taught you nothing, Oliver?'

'You made me do it. I never wanted to read half the stuff you gave me.'

'Stuff?'

'Emerson. Theodore Parker. All that bilge.'

'Listen, Oliver.' I clutched him as though he were drowning. 'You come with me next week. There's a lecture I want you to hear. There's so much for you to learn——'

'If it's McCabe I'm not going.'

'Why, Oliver?'

'Because he's Anti-Christ, that's why. And you should be getting up and preaching against him.'

'Is that what people are saying?'

'It's what I'm saying. And now can I go? I've got to get to school.'

'Oliver——'

'I'm a Presbyterian now and I'll be a Presbyterian when I die. And I'll go to heaven. And you and mother will go to hell and burn.'

All of this he said quite calmly; and kept a clear straight eye. He says it to this day.

38 Let them be original, I used to pray. A late prayer. Earlier I had planted in my son the doctrines of a narrow creed. There was no weeding them out. The certain torment of his parents in hell caused Oliver less pain than his own condition as child of heretics. This may be seen as original.

Felicity came to hear Joseph McCabe. So did Edie. Oliver went to his Christian Endeavour meeting. And I?

Well, some months earlier John Jepson had come to me with the news that McCabe was visiting New Zealand, and Thorpe, on a lecture tour for the R.P.A. of London. Spreading the word, John called it; a missionary visit. He was giving two lectures at the Choral Hall: 'The Evolution of Man' and 'The Present Conflict between Science and Theology'. John was chairman of the lecture committee.

I was excited. I knew all about McCabe: his Catholic upbringing, his twelve years in a Franciscan monastery—Father Antony —his struggle to shake superstition off: and then the books, the pamphlets, the lectures, the life lived with a purpose; the crusade, if you like, against the forces of religious obscurantism. I had read every word he had written. He was one of the shapers of my mind. And this man was coming to Thorpe. Yes, I was excited. When John offered me the chair at the second lecture I accepted without a moment's hesitation. I even brought forward a long-planned visit to Auckland so that I might be in Thorpe on the date.

McCabe arrived on the Christchurch express one Monday evening. A large party met him at the station. John introduced him to Mr Bridewell, the Deputy Mayor; and many of us saw the humour of the situation as this High Anglican gentleman cautiously explained that it was the custom in our town to extend an official welcome to well-known persons from the Old Country. However, we rescued McCabe, John took him off to his home; and later in the evening Edward and Andrew and I called there to take a cup of tea with him. What a glorious evening! The book-lined walls, the glowing fire, the company of like-minded men, the talk that threw a beam of whitest light down the road of the future. From time to time a wordless Mrs Jepson brought in pots of tea and plates of rich plum cake, which I must say was delicious.

'Mr Plumb,' McCabe said, 'I've had many fine chairmen on my tour but I can't remember that any of them have been men of the cloth. Now tell me, what are the consequences to be? Does the breadth of mind of your fellow ministers extend to having you stand on a public platform with an heretic like me?'

'No,' I said, 'it does not. Though one or two will support me privately.'

102

'I know them. Closet free-thinkers. Ah, what a place to be free in. You're expecting trouble, then?'

'I am.'

'The Presbyterian *Statement of Faith* is a tightly written document.'

'Very much so.'

'And the disciplinary powers?'

'All laid down in the *Book of Order*. Neat and tidy.'

'So, Mr Plumb, I've come at a high point in your life, I see. I'm pleased my talk will be your vehicle.'

'I'll not say much,' I said.

'But enough,' Andrew cried, who would have seen me hauled to the gallows and my children starve for a principle.

'Oh yes, enough.'

'Our careers are not dissimilar,' McCabe said. 'Will you write and let me know what happens?'

But our talk was mostly of a general future. I look upon the evening as among the happiest in my life.

McCabe's mind was an instrument of strength and delicacy. He had the reasoning powers of a John Stuart Mill and the wit of an Oscar Wilde, if one can imagine a marriage between those minds. His breadth of reference amazed us poor colonials; and his history caused us to look on him with awe, as on one who has spent a season in hell. He was a being of power. This though was not all. This, so to speak, was the then and now of the man. It was as seer, as prophet, that he impressed us most. The future was brought into John Jepson's library on that cold winter night.

'Our work is to lift the Christian dogmas from the human mind. What is good and true in men and women does not need this foundation to rest upon. Only when it is gone will we know that we act in a selfless way and not out of self-interest. The after-life is a mirage, an *ignis fatuus*—a glorious term I came across recently, the celestial honeypot. (Laughter.) Only when we fix our whole attention on this life, this life here, among men and women, our brothers and sisters not in Christ but in

103

humanity, only then will we discover this life's possibilities and enter our golden age.'

'Hear, hear. The future is with us,' Andrew cried.

Mrs Jepson came in, very still of face. She put tea and cake on the table.

'Thank you, ma'am. This is a very fine cake.' And when she had gone, 'A fine lady, Mr Jepson.'

None of us answered that. Edward and I smiled sadly at each other. We had a better knowledge of the lady. And Edward, skilled with his pencil, slipped me a little sketch of her (I have it among my papers) mouse-still in the half-light by the door, with one of her ears extended like a hearing-trumpet. Underneath he had written *The Ear of the Past*.

39 The lecture 'The Present Conflict between Science and Theology' was the second of the two. The hall had been packed for 'The Evolution of Man'; but there were not to be lantern slides in the second. And the weather was bad. Only a hundred people came along.

Joseph McCabe and I were alone on the stage. We chatted while the audience settled itself. The Choral Hall was built like a barn and we shivered as we spoke.

'Not nerves, I hope, Mr Plumb.'

'No. It's the cold that troubles me. I've had plenty of practice in speaking. Remember George Jacob Holyoake?' (McCabe had written his life.) 'No man who has studied Holyoake's method can be nervous at facing an audience.'

'Now there's a man who suffered for his convictions. They tried George for blasphemy, you know. And threw him in a dungeon. Poor stammering George.'

The example gave me courage. I had a quick look at my notes. McCabe touched my arm to wish me luck. I rose, had quiet (that quiet that always seems both slow and sudden and turns one's stomach once, like a falling lift) and began to talk.

McCabe had agreed I should state my position. So I said, 'Many of you will be surprised to see me on this platform. And for those amongst you who can see only my collar but don't know my face, I'm George Plumb, Presbyterian minister of St Andrews. You will want to know what I'm doing here. Well, the answer is simple. I'm introducing Mr Joseph McCabe, a great scientist, writer, and Haeckelian philosopher, whose words to you tonight will, I believe, send you out of this hall far better and wiser people than ever you are likely to be on coming out of a church—my church or any other. That's the truth of my presence here. And yet it's an evasion. So I'll speak plainly. I stand here as chairman of this meeting in protest against the absurdities of the orthodox teaching of the present day.'

'Hear, hear!' Edward cried; and Andrew echoed him.

I held up my hand. 'You are not in church, Mr Cryer.' A joke that won some laughter, though it puzzled a good many, including McCabe. Edie smiled faintly. She was sitting towards the back so her nervousness would not distress me. Beside her was Felicity, her face white and brave. I spoke to another quarter, hoping to turn inquisitive glances from them.

'As a Protestant I can understand the position of the Catholic authorities.' ('No!' Andrew shouted: a hot-head.) 'It is logical and consistent.' ('No!') 'But I remember that Protestantism began as a rationalizing movement and I cannot understand any Protestant person or body objecting to the teachings of science —of evolution, for instance. I look forward with hope to the complete rationalizing and liberalizing of religion as the work of Protestantism in its best sense. I hope that Mr McCabe's visit will have as one result the setting up in Thorpe of some sort of society for the study of the views which Mr McCabe will present to you tonight.' ('Hear, hear!') 'He will leave behind him the seed of his thought in all our minds, and our duty as thinking men and women will be to bring that seed to its full growth. There is a task for us that will test our strength and courage. We must show in intellectual things that same "nerveless pro-

105

ficiency" that a London paper gives us credit for in athletic pursuits.' I went on a little longer. I have made better speeches, but none in which I have felt so plainly my strength and nakedness. Then I introduced McCabe, and sat down.

I was astonished at my calmness, my enjoyment of my dislocated life. Here I had thrown away the easy future and laid on my back and on my family's back a burden that might break us all. And I felt like laughing. For the first time in many years I was my own man.

McCabe, in his plain polished way, said friendly things: he was happy in having such a chairman, my church in having such a minister. He said he had found much breadth of thought in our town—such as could not have been gained by the listening to sectarian pulpits. (One would have thought he wished me hanged for a sheep.) Then he spoke for an hour and a half on science and theology.

I heard very little of it. I was in a daze of happiness and optimism. From time to time I heard bursts of applause and Scottish shouts. But I watched a star of light winking on the rim of the water jug; and lengthening my sight, saw the pale blur of two faces dear to me; and I required no arguments to convince me of the rightness of my way or of my strength to travel it. McCabe wound up. Theology was demolished; but true religion left intact. For, he said, he knew many scientists who were deeply religious. As honest men they believed the evidence of their senses, of their researches, yet they must believe too in a great controlling Power. 'I respect such men,' said McCabe. 'They prove that science has not lost spiritual vision. Yet how different spiritual vision is from the creeds of the Christian churches. Indeed those creeds are dying. As the torch of science moves onwards through the world the lanterns of theology are fading out before it. We have evidence tonight of how far the cause of science is advanced. We have it in our chairman, Mr Plumb, who has moved from a position of orthodoxy, from the religion of the churches, to a new and noble ground from which he can utter his brave challenge to superstition. He is the man of the future, Scientific man. And yet I would ask you to remember that he remains deeply religious. That is not my way; but I respect it. To those of you in intellectual or in spiritual doubt I recommend it as a stepping stone.'

There was much applause; some of it for me. McCabe sat back with a happy look on his face. Even in such little halls as ours these moments were the high points of his life. I rose and invited questions. For a moment the hall was quiet. Then a man stood up in the shadows at the back. I saw the immaculate band of a collar like mine, and only then a face I recognized. Mr Mitchell, who believed in my love for the scriptures, had died, and the call of his congregation at Trinity had gone to Morrison Macauley, the type of coldly burning young fanatic who would have gladdened the heart of John Knox. He it was who said now, 'I have listened. I have come here against every inclination of my being, impelled by my Christian duty to face the Enemy of Life. I have heard filth and smelled the stink of the Pit. But even here I bring a message: That to sinners of the blackest dye the way remains open——'

There were cries of 'Shame,' and 'Quiet,' and 'Put him out.' And I called loudly that I had asked for questions not for speeches. Macauley was not to be stopped. 'The Christians of Thorpe are outraged by the presence among them of the Anti-Christ. We have met together today and formed the Thorpe Christian Evidence League. It will meet at my house on Thursday evenings, and for your salvation I implore you to seek us out and listen to the truth that we have for you. For the worst of sins is to deny the Lord——'

A pack of young men like a rugby scrum heaved Macauley down the aisle and into the street. As he went he chanted the 97th Psalm. And such was the power of the words that I felt my spirit shrink.

His lightnings enlightened the world: the earth saw and trembled.

The hills melted like wax at the presence of the Lord, at the presence of the Lord of the whole earth.

'These fanatics are interesting cases,' McCabe said.

We walked home in a group. For a time I felt threatened, wary of doorways and shadows. But the good company restored me to cheerfulness, and I made them laugh with tales of Macauley's zeal. A young man who had helped put him from the hall said, 'He's out for your blood, Mr Plumb. He said you'll be called to account for your words tonight.'

'I know I will. But Macauley has already been judged by a better band of men.' They applauded that.

We dropped them off one by one (McCabe with a quick handshake, for I would be at the station in the morning). At last only Edward was left. He lived on the other side of town but asked if he might walk as far as our gate. Macauley's psalm had taken him on a raw part of his mind—he had not rid himself of superstition any more easily than I. Edie saw his need for company. She took his arm. I walked with Felicity.

'Well my dear, did you enjoy Mr McCabe?'

'I liked you better.'

'Now Felicity, that's not being sensible.'

'Mr McCabe had said all his things before. Yours were for the first time.'

'That's true.'

We walked in silence. She came close to my side, under my umbrella.

'Dad?'

'Yes?'

'I'm going into full communion next month.'

'Well, my dear?'

'I don't want to any more.'

'Are you sure of that?'

'I couldn't belong to the same church as Mr Macauley. He looked like a murderer. With his eyes.'

'He's the sort of man who used to burn people at the stake.'

108

'Yes, horrible.'

'Don't let him trouble you. He's a man of the past. But tell me Felicity, what will you believe?'

'What you believe.'

'No, child. You must work out your path for yourself.'

'But dad——'

'My days of telling people what to think are over. What are you smiling about?'

'Nothing, dad.'

At the gate Edward shook my hand.

'Well, Edward?'

'You've crossed your Rubicon, George.'

'And a better man for it.'

'You've friends who'll stand by you.'

He strode away down the wet street, his shoes making a lonely sound—back to his room above his florist shop. Edie and I and Felicity went inside.

40 The weeks that followed were a trial to our patience. For nothing happened. The town simmered like a pot but did not boil over. Our lives appeared to keep their even flow. We read reports of McCabe's Dunedin lectures. Edie, I believe, began to hope we would be able to stay on in the Manse. I found her walking in the frozen garden, and from her eye knew she could see the seedlings of the Spring. But I knew my fellow ministers too well. Somewhere they had come together. This time there would be no fraternal visit.

. I stayed away from the next Presbytery meeting. In the afternoon the clerk brought me a letter, explaining that the members had not wanted me to discover its contents from the morning paper. I thanked him; offered him tea, which he refused; saw him on his way; and retired to my study. There I read that at the meeting the Revd Mr Macauley had moved that 'in view of Mr Plumb's having appeared and presided at a lecture delivered by Mr McCabe, the Rationalist, and in view of the statements made by Mr Plumb at the meeting, and of other disquieting utterances, the Presbytery ask him to meet them in conference at Trinity Hall, Thorpe, on August 16 at 11.15 a.m.' The Revd Mr Oddie seconded the motion, which was put and carried without dissent. Mr Plumb was therefore asked to present himself at the appointed time and place.

As the young man had said, they were out for my blood. I called in Edie and showed her the letter. And saw a light die from her eyes; and another take its place. She said, 'You had better work on your defence, George.'

'It will not be a defence, my dear. It will be an attack.'

Yet we were both in pain. In spite of everything I had kept a hope that I might be able to stay on in the church. I was attacked from several quarters in the weeks that followed—once in a newspaper editorial—for not resigning when it became clear to me that my beliefs were no longer those of the church. But I was not a destroyer, I was a reformer—honourable profession (Luther, Calvin, John Knox—a trio I no longer care to stand with!). And I refused to admit that a statement of faith is set for all time. *Tempori parendum*, was my cry. (I had not, I see now, an institutional nature. But a religious nature, yes.) I suffered at being struck in the face by men at whose side I had worked for fifteen years. I had grown and wanted to make them grow along with me.

Edie's concern was more for the children. She was sure of her way. But for Oliver she had a mother's pain at seeing him go off down his blind narrow street. She blamed herself. And she saw how the others must suffer at their schools, at the hands of other children. I believe she exaggerated their trials. Felicity, and her sisters in her train, Edith, Florence, Agnes, little Esther, became my ardent supporters. There were enough of them to keep out the cold. Willis saw the whole thing as a sporting event. I was David taking on Goliath. He would have liked nothing better than to keep me supplied with stones. Emerson

110

was so busy building a trolley he did not know anything unusual was going on. The rest were too young to know.

It was Kate, our broad kind Kate, who dealt them their hardest blow. She came to us in the study and said she was giving notice. She wished to leave at once.

'But why, Kate? What's happened?' We thought some piece of naughtiness had been too much for her.

'I can't watch the children brought up without religion.'

'Oh Kate, oh Kate,' Edie cried. And I said, 'But they won't be, Kate. They'll be brought up without superstition, that's all.'

'I won't listen,' she said. 'I won't listen to that.'

'But Kate,' Edie said, 'we'll be giving them a new religion. A better one. They'll still believe in God.'

'I won't,' Kate said. 'I won't. Oh those dear little things'— and she began to cry—'denied their eternal comfort.'

Where had she learned such phrases? But I knew. And I shook my head in a rage at my blindness—at the damage I had done. I had thought faith and worship were simple for Kate, like the taking of food; and in a sense I was right. A bitter gruel was her nourishment and she could not live without it. This was the food I had brought her and told her to like. And brought to how many others? Poisoned how many others in this way?

'I'll say goodbye to them in the morning,' Kate said. 'Will you say I'm going home to nurse my mother?'

'Oh, Kate.'

'It's true. She's very old. She can't walk any more.'

'Stay with us, Kate. At least for a little while.'

'I can't, Mrs Plumb. I can't.' Tears dripped into her bosom. She raised her hands to ward us off. Edie followed her to her little room, but Kate would not allow her past the door. She came back to me.

'Oh George, she thinks I'm bad.' And she wept. We loved Kate. She had been with us fifteen years.

She left the next day. All the children cried. Oliver cried.

41 But now there were other things for me to think of. Two more Sundays I presided in my church—a packed church now. I preached careful sermons that raised not a single eyebrow. At home I worked on my defence/attack—let me call it statement. I wrote to the Presbytery clerk saying I would be present at the meeting, but that it must be open to the press. I would not, I said, suffer the fate of Mr Bridges of Templemore, who some years earlier had been rebuked by his Presbytery for unspecified misconduct, and not been allowed to defend himself in public. I would have full publication of both charges and defence or I would leave the meeting.

The morning came. We sat around the table, chatting politely, until the Moderator, Dr Green, called us to devotions. These done, he told us the meeting would be private, in accordance with the *Book of Order*. He asked the reporters to leave.

I protested. But Green would not hear me until the two young men, one from the *Herald*, one from the *Post*, had left. Then he said, 'Mr Plumb, this is a fraternal conference and the *Book of Order* provides that conferences of this sort be private. If you like I'll read you the section.'

'I know it,' I said. 'It's a rule made to be broken. I won't be bound by meaningless rules.' I looked at these men gathered at the table—nine ministers and five elders—at kindly, bumbling, ordinary Green, trying for authority like a bad actor, and granite-souled Oddie, and troubled, sad McGregor, and puzzled Downie, who remembered my bible and Mitchell's approval of it, and angry Gates, and angry Matheson, and smooth smiling Graham, who wanted a quiet recantation, and the rest; especially Macauley, who had me speared like an infidel on his eye; and I said, 'I ask you to behave as Christian charity dictateth. At the moment you're hiding behind a book. You're carrying on as if you have something to hide. I have nothing to hide. Let's have the press in. Let's have some light in the dark places.'

112

'You can move to have the press in, Mr Plumb. You have that right,' Dr Green said.

'Very well. I move that the press be invited back.'

'A seconder?' Green asked.

There was none.

'So, Mr Plumb. We remain a private meeting.'

'I can't agree to it. I wrote to Mr McGregor telling him I wouldn't discuss the matter unless in open meeting. And I won't go back on that.'

'But Mr Plumb'—Green was puzzled—'I think you misunderstand what we're about. We've made no charges against you. We're asking you to explain your behaviour, that's all. Fraternally. Who knows, we may be satisfied?'

I laughed. 'You may be, Dr Green. But not Mr Macauley. He won't be satisfied until he carries out my head on a platter.'

'I protest at this language,' Macauley cried.

'And I,' Oddie said. 'I think we should put an end to this bickering and get on with our business. Mr Plumb has been called here to explain certain things—called not invited. So let him get on with it. Or let him leave. We can do quite well without him.'

I looked at Green. 'We're a private meeting?'

'We are. That is my ruling.'

'Then good day, gentlemen. And good day Mr Oddie and Mr Macauley.' I walked out.

In the street the reporters came at me with their pencils drawn. I told them why I had left.

'What happens now, Mr Plumb?' the *Herald* man asked.

'You'll have to ask Dr Green. But you may say that I won't discuss anything unless in open meeting. I have my defence, my statement. And if they refuse to hear it publicly then I'll give it to you gentlemen. And you can publish it. They can shelter behind the *Book of Order* if they wish. I'll come out in the open.'

'Will they suspend you, Mr Plumb?'

'I don't know. They'll no doubt frame some sort of Libel against me. That's the procedure. But you'll have to ask them.'

113

'What will you do if you are expelled?'

'Continue telling the truth. They have the power to take away my living but they can't take away my principles.' I remember saying too that the most pathetic being in the world is a minister cut adrift, but I meant that in no self-pitying way, as some accused me of.

While I was talking out there and, being no politician, saying too much, the Presbytery was deliberating inside. They produced the following resolution (a copy to me, a copy to the press):

'Whereas the Revd George Oliver Henry Plumb, of St Andrews, presided at a meeting held in the Choral Hall, Thorpe, on 13 July, 1910, when the well-known Rationalist, Joseph McCabe, spoke on "The Present Conflict between Science and Theology", and

'Whereas Mr Plumb stated that he took the chair in protest against the absurdities of the orthodox teaching of the present day and hoped that a result of the meeting would be the setting up in Thorpe of a society to study Rationalist views, and

'Whereas it appears that the Revd Mr Plumb is a member of the Rationalist Press Association, of London, recognized as one of the leading infidel organizations in Britain, and

'Whereas Mr Plumb has publicly recommended some of the Rationalist publications of this Association, and

'Whereas Mr Plumb, while a Presbyterian minister professing the Christian faith as held by this Church, preached on 3 July, 1910, in the Unitarian Church at Auckland, which church was about to become vacant, and

'Whereas such conduct is totally at variance with the principles of this church and inconsistent with the solemn vows which every minister makes at his ordination, and contrary to the principles of conduct expected from a minister of a Christian church, and

'Whereas Mr Plumb has refused to meet the Presbytery in private to have a brotherly and frank disclosure of his opinions,

'The Presbytery hereby requires Mr Plumb to furnish the

114

Presbytery with a written explanation of his conduct, and the Presbytery resolves to adjourn for a fortnight to receive this explanation and further deal with the case.'

42 'Five charges now.' And Edward, more innocent than I, scratched his head.

'It seems your errors are breeding, George,' John Jepson said.

'Aye, and if we didn't live in a civilized age yon priests would be at you with the thumbscrew and the rack,' Andrew said.

'You'll not go to a private meeting, George?'

'No. I'll write to them.' I was tired. As soon as I laid down my pen, which was not often, I became oppressed with a sense of having mismanaged the affair. This country walk, promoted by Edie, was meant to cheer me up. But I was not easily cheered. John Findlater read us his latest poem and I offended him by saying, 'There are no poets in this country. Apart from one thing of Bracken's there hasn't been a single true poem yet.'

Bluey was gobbling licorice straps. He offered me one. 'Reverend,' he said, 'I'm sorry I missed that McCabe. Now there's a good Mick name. And a rebel priest, you say? I'm sorry I missed him. But those Dunedin pubs are hard to get out of.' He had gone south to a Saturday race meeting and stayed for a week. Jobless, he came to the Manse for two or three meals a week. He was a disappointment to me, yet I could not dislike him—as the others did, thoroughly, by now. I had him placed as vagabond, a class not without its uses. His place as workman in our group was filled by Dan Peabody, a young railway stoker I had found in the town library one night asking for Marx's *Kapital*. I had taken him home and loaned him my copy and he had declared political ambitions so extravagant that at first I thought he was making fun of me. He meant to be New Zealand's first Socialist Prime Minister. He was impatient of our religious concerns; and thought poetry and rambling on the hills a waste of time. He thought Bluey a waste of time.

115

'Ah Reverend,' Bluey said, 'I wish I'd been there to help throw out that priest. I'd have had my little shillelah in my coat.' By coming after me on one of my side-jaunts he managed to get me alone. 'Is it true you're having to leave the Manse?'

'If they expel me, Bluey. And I think they will.'

'Now you couldn't reach some agreement with them, could you?'

'Let them buy me, Bluey?'

'Ah now, I don't mean that. But it's such a cosy place. I'll miss coming there.' This though was not his real concern.

'Now, Reverend?'

'What is it, Bluey?'

'You tell me about this rationalist business. Does it mean you don't believe in an after-life?'

'I'm not an atheist, Bluey, if that's what you mean.'

'So you think there's a God?'

'A power of some sort. Call it what you will. A Supreme Being.'

'But if there's that you need priests.'

'No, Bluey. No. That doesn't follow at all. There's just man and his Maker. Man facing God. Nobody in between. No priests. No Christ.'

He found the idea un-nerving. 'No hell, Reverend? No torments?'

'None, Bluey.'

'No?'

'None. That's superstition.'

'Aye, Reverend. That's what I think too.' He did not. Even at that age, far he believed from his death, he was a man in terror. They had had him from birth to young manhood and though he had escaped they crept back to haunt him in the night.

'Come Bluey,' I said, 'let your mind work. You're a man now. You don't believe in fairies any more. Or Father Christmas. So let this other stuff go. Just turn your mind on it and it withers up.'

'Aye Reverend, that's so. That's all I have to do.' And he

116

grinned and ate some licorice. But fear was not quite gone from the back of his eye. 'I'm ashamed of meself. I really am. I don't believe that stuff. Not in a beautiful world like this. Look at those clouds, Reverend. Lovely, aren't they? How can you believe in eternal punishment in a world like this?'

'True, Bluey.'

'But Reverend, if you could have heard those boyos spouting. Real artists, they were. Sparks crackin' from their lips and us poor little b------ curling up. Aye, telling how the red-hot worms would wriggle up our a---holes.'

'Now, Bluey.' (I can no more write down ugly words than say them.)

'Well, Reverend, it wasn't quite like that. But it was near.'

The others were stamping up and down to keep warm. We went back to them and the seven of us walked down to the town—a quieter group than usual.

'This whispering campaign, George. Who do you think's behind it?'

'Just my good God-fearing co-religionists.'

'Macauley?'

'Macauley doesn't whisper, Macauley shouts.'

'They'll have you taking black mass in the cemetery next.'

'Aye,' said Andrew. 'What haven't they accused you of? Atheism, Pantheism, Monism, Arianism.'

'They could make Arianism stick,' John Jepson said.

'Dictionary words,' Dan Peabody grumbled.

'They all have meanings, Dan. Arianism was Milton's heresy.'

'But still, I don't like isms,' I said. 'I'm a free-thinker, no more.'

'It's a grand title,' Edward said.

'And did you know,' said John, 'Nietzsche wanted a monastery for free-thinkers? Would you go there, George?'

'To an institution? No. They'd all end up believers soon enough.'

'But in what?'

'That's not the point. Belief closes the mind. Thought knows

117

no final decision. It looks forward always to new evidence. And speaking of Nietzsche, remember his terrible phrase "the castration of the intellect". That's the end of belief. I'll keep a free mind.'

Edie's stratagem worked. I was happier when I came down.

43 I sat in my study and wrote Presbytery a letter telling them I had their resolution and would come to a meeting with them and read my statement but leave if the press were kept out. Then I wrote a letter to the *Herald* and the *Post*:

'Sir, In your issue of Wednesday last I note the resolution of the Presbytery in regard to myself and remarks made when presiding at Mr J. McCabe's meeting. Does it not cause food for thought that two of the finest words in the English language, *freethought* and *rationalism* should have a kind of stigma attached to them by orthodox clergymen! That which is rational is sane and falls in line with common sense. My protest was a protest against the orthodox teachings of the day relating to the creation of man, and suggested by the teaching of evolution, which is now an accepted scientific truth. Outside of this I attacked no doctrine, and will answer no questions on any doctrine whatever, outside or inside the Presbytery. My worthy Scotch friends (and they dearly love a heresy case) who think that they are coming together for a good two hours enjoyment at my expense must be disillusioned. Trippings, trappings and pitfalls after the old inquisitional style will be useless. Samson with his eyes gouged out does not intend to make sport for the Philistines. Here is my reply to their charges:

'Yes I am a member of the R.P.A.—proud of the fact. It is not an infidel organization, but exists for the purpose of educating the ordinary people out of their superstitions by putting into their hands in a cheap form the results and verified conclusions of modern science. It is resulting in a loud clamour the world over for a liberal religious view. Ultimately it will save people from the materialistic and atheistic drift. Man must and will worship, but he must do so in a rational and sane way. I have faith in the religious instincts of man, and know he will return to a sensible shrine when the message is modernized and brought into line with reason and fact. No sir, the publishing of the R.P.A. literature does not mean the destruction of the Christian religion, but only of the obsolete and useless parts of it, and the building up of a newer and brighter faith. The list of subscribers to the R.P.A. is fairly well sprinkled with the names of clergymen, so I do not stand alone, excepting that I am the only minister in New Zealand. But this Dominion is conservative in religious matters, and about fifty years behind the rest of the world. Even so, I know of Presbyterians who believe as I do, and ministers amongst them. Let the Revs Oddie and Macauley go round the Presbyteries of New Zealand with the hot pincers, they will find more than one who will give a good healthy squeak.

'Yes again, I procured a student to conduct my services, and went for a holiday to Hamilton and Auckland. At Hamilton my kind host asked me to preach in the Wesleyan Church, which I did. At Auckland I stayed with Unitarian friends, and again was asked to preach. I did not go as a candidate to a charge becoming vacant. But yes, I stood in that pulpit, unashamed. My query to the minister, Mr Jellie, as to what line I was to go on, brought forth a reply that clings to me yet with a peculiar fascination. "Mr Plumb, when you stand in my pulpit, bring your religious message into line with the latest scientific knowledge and the latest and most scholarly results of the historical criticism of the Bible. In fact, take off the muzzle and be free."

'Blessed thought—it refreshes the mind like the scent of the spring violets coming through my window. Much of the orthodox teaching affects my mind like the smell of mildew and fungus. See, I would gladly give my right hand to hear the Presbytery say to me what the Revd Mr Jellie said. I preached in the Unitarian Church to one of the finest congregations of young people

119

I ever saw, and on the Monday was asked to become a candidate. Yes, there is no denying it. I feel a strong, strong pull that way. Still I must await events. The Presbyterian Church will reach that point in time. It is a weary waiting. This reminds me of a southern minister, an M.A., holding a Presbyterian charge, telling me some time ago that he moulded all his sermons from Unitarian literature, and especially the *Hibbert Journal*. Now this journal is the leading philosophical journal in the world, and is edited by Mr Jacks, a Unitarian, and filled with articles written by Unitarian ministers, and those in orthodox churches holding Unitarian views. So the poor old world wags on.

'While I say all this, let me add that although I have dropped many old views overboard I still hold to the great moral verities of the Christian belief, and would not have introduced the subject of Unitarianism only for the Presbytery mentioning it. A word more, and I finish. All kinds of rumours are abroad, and some members of Presbytery seem to have a greedy ear for gossip, which they even whisper to the papers. The *Book of Order* I do not know well. If given the choice whether to read a page of that book or take a dose of castor oil, I would take the oil gladly. There is one sentence in the *Book of Order* that clings to my memory. It is this: "Hearsay evidence is not admissible."

'I am etc.

'George O. H. Plumb.'

44 Felicity brought in my tea.
'Where's your mother?'

'Sewing a dress for Rebecca.'

'Oh yes.' I was seeing less of her now Kate was gone. 'Ask her to come in a minute. You come too.'

When they were standing before me I read my letter. It moved us all. I looked up from time to time and saw Edie's careful attention; and the face of my daughter. Her eyes grew bright at the smell of violets, moistened and shone at the loss of my right hand, sparkled with humour (an emphatic, dogmatic humour) at my mention of castor oil and the *Book of Order*.

'It's wonderful, dad.'

'Yes George, you've said it beautifully.'

These two, these women, were a pair of Aeolian harps through which the winds of my history whispered and roared. I heard their harmonies, which I took into my being like a food.

45 On the morning of my 'trial' I had a visit from Mc-Ilwraith, one of the St Andrews managers. We talked of the painting of the belfry, but when this was done he came to his real business.

'Many of us support you, Mr Plumb. Mr Kydd and I will be at the meeting to say so.'

I shook him by the hand and told him I regretted not paying more attention to the good people of my congregation: in my pride I had thought myself alone. I apologized. And I said I was sure I had spoken no heresy from my pulpit.

'We know that, Mr Plumb. I won't say we're happy about what you've done—or said for that matter. But we think you're impetuous, not that you're unChristian. And if there's any disagreement it's for us as a congregation to iron out. We won't be told what to do by Mr Macauley. I've come to tell you that. And I'll tell Presbytery this morning.'

'If they'll let you speak.'

'They'll let me speak.' I heard the swish of the claymore.

So I went along heartened and ready, knowing I was not to stand alone. Edie, holding Robert in her arms, saw me off at the gate. I rode my bicycle.

46 The faces were the same: Green, Oddie, Macauley, Graham, etc. In addition there were a dozen members of the public: McIlwraith, Kydd, Brockie, from St Andrews; Scroggie, who had followed me at Kumara; Geddes, observing for the Christchurch Presbytery, and looking as lemonish as ever; Buttle, a visiting Wesleyan; and three or four I did not know. No women. No Edward or John Jepson. I had told them to stay away. There were six reporters.

The meeting opened with devotions; and how weary I found that. I uttered a silent prayer for strength and patience. This, as it came at the end, was noticed. Macauley took it for hypocrisy. I looked around the faces of my peers, who were judging me, and noted those that were closed, those that were open, those that hungered for the fight, and those that wanted no trouble. They were practical men, and men of intelligence—albeit intelligence strictly set within bounds. By their lights they would be fair with me. By their lights. How dim those were. The bare room, the hard seats, seemed chosen with a strict propriety. And I had a premonition of defeat. So that as sad McGregor read the minutes I spent the time steeling myself. I was here to fight, and if I must go down would go down with my sword weaving a band of light about me. They would find my body by the wall. It helped to dramatize things so. I was smiling by the time McGregor finished.

Green cleared his throat. The man was a soft and woolly bear; and like a bear must not be enraged. I had always treated with him formally. He fixed me with a reddish eye and I saw that he had missed his breakfast honey.

'I wish to underline a point made in the minutes, and that is that the Presbytery has offered to meet Mr Plumb and talk this matter over with him in a friendly way. Mr Plumb has declined that, although it would have been in his own interests and the interests of his congregation and indeed of the whole Presbyterian community of Thorpe. We did not wish for a public enquiry, but a public enquiry has been forced upon us. It is Mr Plumb's doing, and if news of today's proceedings is blown abroad and takes other shapes as it travels, and I know it will do that, knowing the world, then Mr Plumb must bear the responsibility. That, Mr Plumb, is something I felt I must say.'

We inclined our heads at each other, like a pair of ancient clubmen over brandy. Green then moved that the meeting be held in public. Macauley seconded, saying the Presbytery had nothing to fear. It was carried without dissent.

Then Macauley's voice—a sharp voice, a cutting instrument —came again, and I saw it was to be very much his day. He waved some newspapers about. 'I have here some copies of the Thorpe *Herald* and the Thorpe *Post*, and two Christchurch papers. They contain statements made by Mr Plumb, and I move that they be held *in retentis* as documents in this case.'

So the field of possible charges against me widened. I could have challenged the correctness of this, but I did not. I was here to attack, not quibble, to strike with a sword not prick with an inky nib. The motion was carried and McGregor shuffled the papers nervously.

'Now,' Green said, 'I must raise another question about the nature of this meeting. And that is simply, whether we now begin a formal enquiry? If we do this then Mr Plumb has the right to decide whether he wishes to be tried by libel. And I would remind you—remind you too, Mr Plumb—that in that case he's suspended *ipso facto*. And that of course takes us into deep waters. My feeling is that a formal enquiry should not begin until we've heard Mr Plumb's explanations.' As he warmed up on that cold morning, as his position and the flavour of formal language comforted him, he began to mellow. Benevolence was his habit of mind. So alas was the desire to please. Now and then he became aware of it. His kindly smiles were interspersed with anger and hard judgements.

Oddie said, 'I must disagree. We could go on having meetings endlessly while Mr Plumb examines his beliefs. The charges are

123

laid. Let's hear them answered. Now. And an end to the talk. I move that this meeting be the first step in a formal enquiry.'

Macauley seconded it; and it was carried.

'I disagree,' Green said. 'But as chairman I'll carry it out. Perhaps you won't object if I give Mr Plumb the option of saying whether he wishes to be tried by libel.'

I was impatient by now, and growing angry. I was a little drunk with my cause, and these words, these procedures, were brambles and bushes, preventing me from coming at it again. 'I don't mind. Try me how you will. Just let's get it done with. I have an explanation and I'd like to read it.'

So trial by libel it became—I saw Macauley's eye glisten at that—and Green gave me leave to read my statement. I stood up. From behind me came a clapping of hands.

At once Macauley cried, 'I protest. I protest at this behaviour.'

Oddie said, 'Mr Plumb's supporters are turning this into a circus.'

'Throw them out,' Macauley said.

'Gentlemen,' Green interrupted, 'I remind you I'm in charge of this meeting.' He turned to the clappers (Kydd and McIlwraith) and said, 'This is not the occasion for applause. Public or not, it's a meeting of the Thorpe Presbytery, and I'll have it conducted in a seemly manner. Any more clapping and I'll have to ask you to leave. You'll not though be thrown out.'

It did me good to see Macauley go pink. I'd forgotten he was human. I had made up my mind not to leave him unscarred, and now I said, 'Before beginning, I wish to have my protest recorded against the attitude of one member of this Presbytery, the Revd Mr Macauley. Mr Macauley has prejudged my case. He'll deny it, of course. Yes, I hear you Mr Macauley, but please allow me to finish. I ask him to examine his conscience, and if that won't do examine his memory, and he'll find there evidence that he's prejudged me. He's said on the streets of this town, and I can prove it sir, I can call unimpeachable witnesses if you wish, he has said that I'm as guilty as the devil and that he'll

124

not name the place I should go to preach in. No, it's true sir'—for Macauley was shouting by now—'it's true, the words were spoken, and similar words at other times, and I'm placing them before this meeting and I ask to have them written into the records of this meeting.'

The clamour that rose was like that of a children's party, for I had placed on the table a most exciting toy, and they played with it for a while with enjoyment. Green had trouble getting order; and he turned an unfriendly eye on me when he had managed. All the same, it went down in McGregor's nervous hand that Mr Plumb had accused Mr Macauley of prejudging him, and Mr Macauley denied it. A victory, I suppose, and a shabby one I take no pride in now. But then it was important. It gave me a foothold in their camp, and I stood firmly there to read my message. I'll not record it here (in 1927 I printed it as an appendix to my book *The Growing Point of Truth*), but say how they received it.

The argument is a simple one: that a false theology, and in particular the false dogmas of creation and fall, stand in the way of scientific truth: that the Christian churches lose ground because they hold to a foolish theology and so close their doors to rational men and women; that our Christian duty is to open our minds and admit the truth and so stop the drift to atheism and materialism. To this end, I said, I had stood with McCabe, and made my famous 'utterances'. To this end I read and recommended the publications of the R.P.A. of London. To this end spoke freely from whatever pulpit was handy. We must rescue, I said, the great word 'faith' from degradations, separate it from outgrown and outworn dogmas. Our cowardice, our hypocrisy, prolong the discord and confusion of religious thought, the anguish of religious doubt. Let us be true and brave, I said, and in time we shall 'know the truth and the truth shall make us free'. To know, to love, to serve—these are the ends of life; these are alone what makes life worth living, and better far to sacrifice life itself than profane it to the conscious and deliberate slavery of error.

It took me half an hour to read. It fell on deaf ears. I am not surprised today. But on that day I believed, believed increasingly as I went along, that I might find a path into their minds. Their silence when I finished, their cold closed faces, struck me like an iron fist. I was stunned by the sight of them. Presbyterian clergymen. I am not being cruel. I am not being unfair. Or if so, to myself. Naïvety, enthusiasm, are not to be sneered at. I honestly believed I could reach them, these men in their iron cage. And my head, when I saw them there, rang with the weight of their blow, and I almost lost my senses.

Green said, 'Thank you, Mr Plumb.' The rest said nothing. Until at last Macauley moved that my statement be held *in retentis* by the clerk. And Oddie moved that the Presbytery meet in private to consider it. I was too stunned to object.

The public began to move out. I stood up to follow them.

'No Mr Plumb, no. You're still a member of the Presbytery.' So I sat down again.

47 And then came an interruption. McIlwraith and Kydd approached the table. McIlwraith asked permission to speak.

'Who are you?' Green asked, though he knew.

'My name is McIlwraith. And this is Mr Kydd. We're two of the managers of St Andrews Church. We'd like to put some evidence before you.'

'We've called for no evidence. We need no evidence, do we?' Green asked round.

'It's a simple matter of fact I want to state. It can be done very quickly.'

'Simple or no sir, that is not the point. We're a private meeting. You have no status here. I must ask you to leave.'

'I move that we hear Mr McIlwraith's evidence,' I said.

'If you hear his you'll hear mine,' a voice cried from the door. Brockie came forward. But now everyone had something to say,

126

and the most persistent voice was that of Macauley, saying that we had met for a certain purpose and no other business could be introduced. If parishioners of Mr Plumb wished to make statements they could do so after the meeting.

'Exactly,' Green said. 'Now I must ask you to leave. At once. Without a further word.'

'The matter concerns us. Mr Plumb is our minister.'

'At once,' Green cried, going the colour of port.

'We're used to him. He's unorthodox but he's honest. We want to keep him.'

'We do not,' Brockie cried. 'The man's an atheist. A tool of Satan.'

'Mr Kydd and I have canvassed the entire congregation——'

'Out, sir, out!' Green bellowed.

'Every name in the communion book. Fifty-eight want Mr Plumb to go and a hundred and fifty-six want to keep him.'

'Not me. Never,' Brockie cried.

'That is our evidence. And I ask this committee to receive it.'

'No, sir, we will not. We will not receive it.'

'Then I think you'll have to obtain two new managers for St Andrews as well as a new minister.' And with that McIlwraith left, Kydd along with him; and Brockie in the rear, looking as if he meant to strike at their backs.

Two courageous men. How had I overlooked them? Their support gave me no help, damaged my case in fact, but I was grateful for it.

'Mr McGregor, have you noted that? A hundred and fifty-six for, fifty-eight against.' But that only brought another bellow from Green, and McGregor dropped his pen and had to crawl under the table to retrieve it. 'A circus,' Oddie said. 'You are responsible for this, Mr Plumb. You seem to have a congregation entirely without discipline.'

'A congregation of free men, Mr Oddie. They think for themselves.'

'Not so,' Macauley cried. 'A divided house. For. Against. What sort of language is this? We're a church sir, not a debating society. Your congregation is in tatters. In rags. This is the greatest shame that has fallen on our church since it was founded.'

'Mr Macauley, Mr Macauley,' Green was calling out. But Macauley was not to be stopped. 'I move that we abandon formalities. We have a soul here to be saved. We must pray, we must mend our house. The fire of Heaven rains down. The sinner is taken. But there is time. That is the joy of it. There is always time. A second will suffice. The barest word. Ours is the duty to bring his salvation before him. We must—' etc, etc. He went on for quite a long time. His was the old apocalyptic style: fire in the eye, froth on the lips, and rivers of blood everywhere. As McCabe had said, these fanatics are interesting cases. But at last he was quiet; and looking spent, drank a glass of water. And Green, in some embarrassment, got the meeting under way again.

48 'Mr Plumb's statement,' Oddie said, 'makes it clear that he is no longer a Presbyterian. He is not in fact a Christian. Surely this is clear to you, Mr Plumb. I am at a loss to understand your desire to continue in your charge. Is it simply that you need the money? We know you have twelve children. No, I am not being offensive. I am simply trying to reach the truth of the matter.' In his way, he was. The truth for him was like something hooked out with his little finger from a narrow hole.

'The Presbyterian Church is my spiritual home,' I said. 'Not a comfortable home, I admit. But I've no desire to leave it simply because I'm no longer happy there. That would be cowardly. I wish to improve it, sir. To alter it. Not run away somewhere else.'

'This is sheer arrogance,' Oddie said.

'Perhaps. But Luther was arrogant. And Calvin. And John

Knox. Every reformer has some arrogance in him. If it wasn't for this you gentlemen wouldn't have wives. You'd be sunk in Mariolatry. You'd be turning your faces to Rome instead of burying them in the *Book of Order*.' An unworthy jibe; and so good Downie made me feel by saying, 'We turn our faces to our Saviour, Mr Plumb, and in no other direction.' And he went on, 'I honour your desire to improve the Church. It can do with improvement. We all see that.' (Oddie did not, his expression made it plain.) 'But improving a church and altering the basic tenets of its faith are two different things. Our doctrines are unchangeable and eternal. They come from the scriptures, and with the scriptures there can not be any quarrel. There can not be any quarrel within the Church. Outside, well sir, that's for you to say. But inside, no. Now, Mr Plumb, already you've denied two of our doctrines. The doctrines of the Fall and of the Creation. And what I want to know is, does it stop there? Are there any other doctrines you deny? I think we've a right to know. Could I ask you simply perhaps, do you still hold to the doctrines of Incarnation and Atonement? Are you a Christian, in fact?'

A good question. I could not answer it. I had simply to say I did not know; my beliefs were something I examined daily. They were living things, they changed their shape. I told Downie the doctrines of the Incarnation and the Atonement were open to more than one interpretation. But, I reminded them all, they lay outside the charges brought against me. I would not discuss them, I said.

Downie sighed and shook his head. 'Mr Plumb, I think you're an honest man. And I don't think that honestly you can stay inside the Church.'

129

49 And Macauley came to life. The fellow was like a battery. He shot out electrical charges, and ran down, and slumbered while his strength built up again. He was ready now. He asked for the papers he had given McGregor and spread them on the table. 'These are part of our business. And with the chairman's permission I'll read from them. Now, we've heard Mr Plumb's statement—and I must have my opinion recorded that it's a thoroughly impertinent document. Arrogant and outrageous. But for Mr Plumb it's expressed in moderate terms. Let me give you the true man. Let me show you what he really thinks of his church. I have a letter of Mr Plumb's written to the Lyttelton *Times*. And in it he declares that the Christian Church at the present time is one of the most immoral institutions in the world. And as if that's not enough, he goes on to characterize the Presbyterian Church, and I quote, as "that great lying Church". Yes, gentlemen. Most of you have read these letters. But they're new to some of you, I see. And I ask you to forgive me. There's more. From the Christchurch *Post*. Listen. "If the Presbyterian book were before me now with my signature beneath the vows I would with my broad-nosed J pen put a mighty stroke through it that could not be mistaken. I would not on any consideration put my name to anything of the kind again. It would not be true and sincere." Now gentlemen, these are Mr Plumb's opinions. He may wish to deny them now——'

'No,' I said.

'—but they stand here, in public newspapers, over his name, and he cannot. And I submit that they constitute a resignation from the Church. "I would put a mighty stroke through it that could not be mistaken." Very well Mr Plumb, we make no mistake. The action is clear. But as for mighty, dear me no, never mighty. Childish rather, I think. The action of a naughty little boy, wishing to shock the adults. You may come to manhood

130

one day, Mr Plumb, but at the moment you're simply pulling wings off flies.'

'I protest,' Downie said. 'We're not here to bandy insults about.'

'I think it's improper language too,' Oddie said. 'Mr Plumb is not playing with flies. He's putting his immortal soul in peril. And worse, the souls of the people in his charge.'

'I agree, and withdraw my words,' Macauley said. 'But I wish to move now that we take this letter as Mr Plumb's effective resignation from the church.'

They turned that over for a while. I kept silent. I was trembling with anger and would not trust myself to speak. That terrible phrase came back to me, 'the castration of the intellect'; and I looked at these men, leafing through their rules, knew them for what they were, a tribe of eunuchs. I grew sorry for them. I came to pity them. And that I did not want. I was tempted to offer them comfort, but knew my real task was to lead them into the cold light of their reason. I had not strength for it. But resolved to try again.

In spite of Macauley's insistence, they decided my letter was no resignation. At that point I said, 'Gentlemen, can we go back now to my statement? It hasn't been properly considered yet. It's not my business to run this meeting but it seems to me charges have been made and charges answered, and we should be keeping to those.' Green agreed. He was tired and needed his lunch. He had learned his procedures thoroughly and saw the way to the end was to stick to them. So we looked at my statement. But no good came of it. It might as well have been written in Sanskrit. My hope that I might persuade even one of these men to my view I saw to be a piece of wild optimism. They had not the language. But no—that they had. And they had my frame of reference all right. It was as if two universes existed side by side, and in mine the inhabitants had an extra sense; could see the monsters in the thickets, the supernatural beings, God and the devil, for what they really were. They shone a torch where the

131

others hid their eyes. This I tried to explain. But they saw my cloven hoof and made signs against me.

'Have none of you,' I cried, 'done any reading? Look at Darwin. Look at Huxley and Haeckel and Romanes. Gentlemen, I beg of you, open up your minds. These dogmas that you live by are dangerous. They poison the souls of men. I don't exaggerate. They kill.' (I was thinking of Oliver, who on the last two Sundays had cycled over the hill to Macauley's church.) 'Why, I'd rather face a doctor, a drunken doctor with a rusty lancet, than a Presbyterian parson armed with dogmas.' I sank my boat (but could not have saved it). And several of them, seeing it, became quite gentle with me.

Green was first. 'It's foolish in you, Mr Plumb, to suppose we haven't read these books you mention. It's simply that we read them from a different point of view. We see them on the one hand, and on the other Christ. He made certain claims. He promised certain things. And we believe Him. Our ways are very different, Mr Plumb. Do you really wish to stay with us?'

And Matheson said, 'Romanes died a Christian, Mr Plumb. He died in full communion. It's a history full of instruction. And I think I speak for all of us when I say that our hope for you will never be lost.'

He did not speak for Macauley. Macauley had not finished with me yet. He had sat there trying the words 'drunken doctor' on his lips. Now he cried, 'Enough argument. Haven't we had enough? There are some of us here who wish to get out in the air. I'll not try to describe the smell in here. And I wish to move that Plumb, the apostate Plumb, be deposed from his charge of St Andrews, and have his name struck from the books of this church.'

'Mr Macauley,' Green said, 'the *Book of Order* makes no provision for this. Deposition, yes. But it says nothing about striking names from books. No, sir. I will not accept that motion. Not until you phrase it in a moderate way. And you will refer to Mr Plumb—a member of this Presbytery still—as Mr Plumb. Apostate indeed!'

132

'We are not an inquisition,' Downie said.

'We're a court,' Macauley cried. 'An ecclesiastical court. And this man is the accused. He's charged with heresy.'

'I don't see it here. Five charges. But no mention of heresy,' Downie said.

'Heresy, Mr Macauley, translates in your Greek lexicon as choice,' Green said. 'And before we hear any talk about deposition I suggest we offer Mr Plumb a choice. I think we've considered everything now, Mr Plumb. And we want to act towards you in as brotherly a spirit as possible. (One moment, Mr Macauley.) I'm sure you see this church is no longer the place for you. Therefore, I advise you as strongly as I can to withdraw from it. Withdraw from your charge, withdraw from the ministry. And I think it's fair if we adjourn now for a further fortnight to give you time to think it over. (A moment Mr Macauley, if you please.) Now I'll ask the clerk to phrase that as a motion and if we can find a seconder we'll put it to a vote. Now Mr Macauley, you had something to say?'

'Evidence, Dr Green. I have further evidence. We must not let him have more time. We must not let him sneak out of here today. Or else he's made a joke of us. Listen.' He snatched a piece of paper from his pocket. 'Mr Plumb, did you say this? Do you deny you said this? "My brethren of the church are men who mince and prance, equivocate, cough, sneeze, amble, sophisticate, and lie like troopers to save themselves and their livings." You said that. Do you deny it?'

'No,' I said, looking about me. Forewarned of a dreadful anger in myself, I was, in this moment, sad: sad at the ending Macauley had brought on us. I was ringed by a group of hurt and decent men—and the one or two charlatans I had meant my words for, and one or two bigots. Their eyes were fixed glowingly upon me, their silence had the threat of a back-drawn fist. 'No, I don't deny it. But she must have a very good memory. Or perhaps she just writes fast.'

'What do you mean, sir?'

'You had that scrap of paper from a lady who was listening

at a keyhole.' For I had spoken the words to Joseph McCabe, a little drunk with talk and company. And outside the door pious Mrs Jepson had written them down.

Poor Downie looked as if he had been struck. Green was the colour of port again, and Oddie the colour of tin. I had not had them in mind. Not had Macauley in mind. But Graham, smiling Graham. I hardly knew the man—yet he existed in my mind as arch-equivocator (ambler, prancer, sneezer, liar yes); Graham, closet free-thinker, coward. There were a good many of him in the church. I do not misjudge him. He came to me in the street the day before my trial and told me insistence such as mine was ungentlemanly, that no one would think the worse of me if I quietly crossed my fingers and said I was sorry. Looking at him— he gazed at his finger nails—I had no regret for my words. I regretted hurting Downie though, and Green and McGregor— and said so. But said that as Macauley had tabled the words I would let them stand. They had been spoken privately. Men say such things and laugh and enjoy themselves. It is a part of good-fellowship. The crime, I said, was in the posting of spies, in the creeping about of people with long ears. I would remove myself from that, I said.

McGregor had some paper in front of him. I shot out my hand and took a sheet. (The poor man jumped a foot into the air.) Angry talk went on all about me. I dated the paper (with my broad-nosed J pen), addressed it to Green, and wrote: 'I herewith tender my resignation of the St Andrews charge and withdraw from the Ministry of the Presbyterian Church of New Zealand.'

I signed it; pushed it in front of Green; and left.

I went out of the Church into the air. Into fresh air.

50 The wind blew down the bare street and through the naked trees, bringing an icy drizzle. The little group of people standing under black umbrellas appeared like arctic birds on a shelf of ice. Half a dozen peeled away: reporters, rushing at me, shouting questions. I told them my statement said all I wanted to say, and asked them to print as much of it as they could. I had resigned, I said, but they must have the rest of the story from Dr Green. I went to McIlwraith and Kydd and thanked them. I told them I hoped they would stay on at St Andrews to help the new minister. Then I turned to Geddes. He surprised me by coming forward to shake hands. 'Aye laddie, it's Robert Elsmere over again.'

'You tried to warn me,' I said.

'You get a nose for these things. What are you going to do now?'

'I don't know. I've a message. And if God wills I'll deliver it.'

'Aye, I see that. Good luck, then.' Life had changed him. 'We're all toilers in the same field.' He went away to sit in the church.

Scroggie approached me next. He had a charge in Hokitika but visited Kumara still. The people there sent their good wishes. Our talk was inconsequential. He wanted to show kindness, that was all. We did not know it then, but he was to be my successor at St Andrews.

I fetched my bicycle and rode home. And there were Edward and John Jepson, keeping Edie company. Edward had closed his shop. They took my news well; managed to see a victory in it. Edie remained calm. She spoke of our future with some lightness, even gaiety. Over lunch we began to see our way clear. John and Edward had a plan. I listened; and soon agreed.

In the late afternoon I walked over the road to my church —mine no longer. So, I thought, the easy living is gone, the Manse and glebe. And this is gone too. I had pain, but no regret.

For a greater agony was gone from me—a soul agony. No more tossing up of theological balls, no more of the spiritual three-card trick. Now I had the task of knowing God. But I would make one last sentimental journey into the building that had seen so much of my life. When I wrote to McCabe I described the moment to him. I can do no better now than quote from my letter:

'It was evening, the sun had found a gap in the clouds, and its rays were striking through the coloured-glass windows as I opened the door of the church. I walked up the aisle slowly and stepped into the pulpit. I looked at the old bible, the bars of red and blue and yellow light falling on the empty seats. I saw the patch on the carpet where the nap was worn off by my standing on the spot for so many years. There I had dispensed Communion to the people who had trusted me and believed in me. To this spot and the messages from this spot, I had consecrated my life. This was the end of it and the last visit. I had never really knelt there before but I did so now. And I re-consecrated my life to God and Social Service and Truth at all costs. With these vows I rose to my feet, and since then I have not been on my knees! There is something better than that—it is never getting out of touch with the unseen forces—continuing instant in prayer. God is real to me now in a wonderful sense. To find God I had to leave the Church!'

Felicity was waiting in the porch. I took her hand and we crossed the road to the Manse.

I threw away my collars and called myself 'Reverend' no more.

51 Others kept it up. Bluey for one. And many years later Felicity's husband Max Waring adopted the term. He even came to say Rev, as one says Ken for Kenneth or Tom for Thomas. 'How are you this morning, Rev?' He is a man of ironic temperament. It amuses him that he, an atheist, should be married to the Catholic daughter of an 'unfrocked' Presbyterian

parson. He has too that fascination with religious behaviour one finds so often in unbelievers; and being a man who never in his life will rock the boat, he judges me a rogue. If I had not been unfrocked (his term) he would not have abbreviated my title.

Max is my favourite son-in-law. He's a gentle creature; caught somewhere on the middle of the public service ladder, unable to move up, or to fall off. He suffers from paralysis of the ambition, perhaps of the will; but it has not led him into spite or cynicism or self-pity. Nose like the beak of a flesh-eating bird; cruel mouth; small red eye. But how kindly in his nature. I have found the physiognomical method of judging character misleading nine times out of ten—and think of Edward Cryer, who was called by the sharp-tongued girls of our town Dr Crippen, but who in his nature was saintly. Max reminds me of Edward. Both men loved Felicity. The strange thing is that Edward who knew her as a child came to love her as a woman; and Max, who married her, who married this strong and emotional and opinionated creature, loved her for the child he saw in her, and never knew what to do with the grown-up person.

They met in 1922 when Felicity came to Wellington to teach, and married in 1928. Max was her faithful attendant all through those years. I have no way of knowing how many men entered and left her life (apart from the one who dominated it); but Max waited, concealing his unhappiness, and won her in the end by a combination of persistence and hard circumstance. The latter they have never confessed—not to me. But I have some detective ability. Their son Peter was born four months after their (registry office) wedding—an only child. I look at him and see who his real father is. He's a good-looking boy.

E*

52

'What are you writing, dad?'

'Oh, nothing. Just putting my thoughts in order.'

But her sharp eyes had covered a couple of lines. As I closed the notebook she thrust her hand inside. 'What is it? A family history?'

'No, no. Reminiscences that's all.'

' "They measure things by the marriages they made." Who, Esther and Meg? They won't like that.'

'They won't see it.' I managed to get the book closed again.

'What have you said about me?'

'Nothing yet.'

'Probably that I fell into superstition.'

'No my dear, your spiritual life is your own affair.'

'I don't like the way you say that. Like something illicit. Out in the lupins at the end of the beach.'

'Don't talk like that, Felicity.' I put down my trumpet so I would hear no more. It pains me that life has coarsened my daughters. Life should refine, should burn away the dross. Felicity feels it too. But her delicacy, her refinements, are selective. She keeps her life in compartments. The spiritual one is closed to me; a mystery. There, for better or worse (worse, I believe), the white flame burns, behind doors locked to me, and Max, and indeed all other humans (except for one or two celibates clad in black). There her soul meets its maker—both in a form I do not recognize. And because her energies are employed so strenuously there, the social, the family mask she wears is a rough-and-ready thing. She sees it herself and becomes girlish in apology—and for me almost the old Felicity. But soon goes back and is lost. She is the sort of Catholic, ardent and secretive, who must cause embarrassment in her church. It is frequently so with converts, I am told.

'Sorry, dad. Didn't mean to shock you. Come on now. Come

138

into the lounge. We've got a fire going.' She took my hand. I was unwilling. For fifty years I have sat alone at night and read or written. But print and solitude, Felicity says, are drugs I am 'hooked on'. She is going to break me of the habit. People are more important than books. Besides, she said, pulling me to my feet, Max wanted to change my dressing.

In the lounge Max was stacking pine cones on the fire. He collects them in coal sacks from the Tinakori hills. His Sunday outing, while Felicity goes to mass and Peter sleeps off his Saturday night. They are not a sharing family. But they like each other and give each other licence.

'Now Rev, I'll just get my kit.' When he was back he made me get up from the plain chair I had chosen and sit in a great winged affair like a throne. He lifted my legs and slid an upholstered footrest under my feet.

'Now.' He would have made a good doctor. He had that rare combination of passionate interest and unsentimental concern.

I said, 'Did you ever think of being a doctor, Max?'

'Yes.' He was kneeling by the chair, unwinding the old bandage. He threw it on the fire and began smearing ointment on my raw palm.

'Sorry.'

'It's all right. What stopped you?'

'Money. My father was a railwayman. Railwaymen don't put their sons through medical school.' His predator's beak and ferine mouth were poised above my flesh; but he said mildly, 'Of course if I'd had any gumption I would have put myself through. Plenty did.'

'Everyone should have an equal chance.' I spoke without force. My hand was throbbing painfully.

'I had my chance. I just couldn't face the hardship. Besides Rev, I wanted to be other things as well. A lawyer for one, and a poet, and a concert pianist, even though I can't play a note. And an All Black, believe it or not. I was going every which way, you see. Dreaming it all and not doing a thing. So I ended up a civil servant. In the great rubbish bin.'

139

I did not like that. It was a humorous statement, but I saw the pain that escaped its cover. He understood he had wasted his gifts.

'Why don't you resign? It's not too late to do something you want.'

'Ha ha!'

'How old are you? Fifty? You're a boy.'

Felicity said, 'That's my meal ticket you're trying to subvert.'

'He can do it. I did it. And nobody suffered.'

'That was because you had wealthy friends. We would have starved without them.'

'Nonsense. I could have gone back to the law. But I had a message and my friends thought it was important. And Edward wasn't wealthy. Edward was poor.'

'John Jepson had plenty.'

'John Jepson built the hall. But his interest stopped there. Rich men don't understand hunger. It was Edward who kept us in food. And John Findlater and Andrew Collie.'

But the strain of catching their wispy shouts had tired me. I had endured three days and nights of it. I put down my trumpet, saying I wanted to rest, and as Max finished bandaging my hand stared into the fire and remembered those hard joyous days. Memory with me is an active thing, not an undisciplined dreaming. It can be, and was now, an acceptable substitute for reading and writing. I get a hold on acts, words, gestures, worry them out of the corners they've got themselves lost in, and brush the dust away. And yet because they come from far away, from lost realms, and because their shapes are refined and mysterious, they have a visionary force. The processes of memory are religious. Each image I contemplate is an answered prayer.

I see a stage in a draughty hall and a small balding man passionately speaking of the True, the Good, the Beautiful. His clothes are well-worn grey, a minister's clothes; but his collar secular. The audience responds. This is the Litany of the Universal:

'It is the will of our Mother/Father God, that the people of Fellowship "stagger not back to the mummeries of the dark ages, but rather that they found a New Church of men to come, having heaven and earth for beams and rafters, science for symbol and illustration" . . .'

'Our Mother/Father God, help us to do Thy will on the earth.'

'Immanent Spirit of Universal Oneness, may we loyally co-operate with Thee to create Thy Kingdom on the earth for "We doubt not through the ages One increasing purpose runs, and the thoughts of men are widened with the process of the suns." Amen!'

The years pass. The hall is the same, the man a little balder. Now the emphasis falls less on theology:

'It is the will of God that the eyes of the people be opened to the anti-social spirit of modern Capitalism, Militarism, and Imperialism—a trinity of evil—resulting in the folly of fraternal slaughter; so that the reign of reason and love may appear, and the dominance of hate and bitterness be ended; that swords be turned into ploughshares and spears into pruning hooks, and that nations learn war no more.'

Oliver's troopship has sailed out of Lyttelton harbour. Men are dying at Gallipoli.

'It is the will of God that his children of the Spirit, extend their horizons and cultivate the true Patriotism—Loyalty to Humanity—and the Communal Consciousness of the New Age . . .'

Now there is a small house in the country, children four to a bedroom, two to a bed. Out the back a fruit garden grows, and at the side cauliflowers, cabbages, corn. Fowls scratch among the trees. A boy milks the house-cow and dreams of flying-machines. Another has gone to sea and will not come home. The girls go barefoot, breaking ice on the puddles with their red toes. Heavy plaits hang down to their waists. Their father wheels home a bolt of striped cloth. It lies on his bicycle like a roll of lead. One of his friends has had it cheap at a fire sale. Their mother sews, treadling into the night. And they wear

141

identical dresses, like butchers' aprons. Children hiss at them. The word is, 'Passifisst.'

A chain appears on the iron gate of the Unitarian Hall. A policeman with a key unlocks it for Sunday services, but Thursday lectures are not allowed—not when they are called 'Militarism—the assassin of Demos'. The speaker brings a stool with him—a nursery stool, painted pink. He mounts it in the street. And stones fly. He tastes his own blood on his lips. The Unitarians do not care for this. Half a dozen stones, two or three shouts of 'Judas', 'Traitor', two or three threats of death: the movement in Thorpe lies down and will not get up.

At home the speaker broods, thinks of new lands. He must preach or die—so it seems to him. Over the seas is America, the great Democracy. He does not see it as the New Jerusalem. But Woodrow Wilson sits in the President's chair, and Wilson has said there is such a thing as a nation being too proud to fight. The man does not fully believe him. He has been watching politicians for half of his life. But Wilson has the sort of face he trusts.

So they talk into the night. His daughter says, 'You'll be able to say what you want there, without being put in prison.' And his wife thinks of her budding trees and the blossoms she will not see. She weeps a little, then dries her eyes and smiles. 'Another shake of the kaleidoscope.'

53 I spoke of these things with Felicity. She leaned forward and touched me on the mouth. 'You've still got the scar.'

'It broke one of my teeth.' And our going—I did not say it—broke Edward Cryer's heart. He had told me of his love for Felicity; deluded in so far as it had its beginnings in his love for me. But it was a pure passion when one considers the impurity of most, that begin in self. I told him he might speak to her, and could not tell him what the end must be. It took place on a country walk. I saw from his dead look when it was over, and Felicity's pallor and a kind of shame in her eyes, how it had gone.

Our train pulled out. Edward and John Jepson ran along the platform crying, 'Good luck,' 'God bless you,' 'Come back when it's over'. And behind them a man cursing us and waving a Union Jack. John Findlater tripped him up. Andrew Collie tore his flag in two. Tears ran down Edward's cheeks. 'God bless you, God bless you all.'

He died while we were at sea, suffocated by smoke when his shop burned down. His will left all he owned to Felicity. It was less than a hundred pounds.

54 In California I preached again. I was looked on neither as evil, nor as an oddity. That place is the land of a thousand creeds, a thousand contending voices. Weird beliefs, distorted truths, the verities in costume prancing madly; and plain lies of course. But my own simple message won some attention. I became a regular speaker in halls in San Francisco, Oakland, Monterey. My religious message was broadly Unitarian, acceptable to various congregations. In my anti-war activities I was sponsored by groups whose beliefs ranged from the altruistic to the crudely isolationist. Sometimes I spoke seven nights a week. So I was active, and believed myself useful. But I never felt at home. I missed the cold of Thorpe; the climate of Calvinism; missed the flag-waving, the jingoist hatreds; Empire Day, the Steinway piano axed in the street. Missed, that is, my known enemy. I missed the plains and the mountains, the trout rivers, the shingle beach and grey cold sea. I sorely missed my friends. We knew very soon that we would not stay in California. But for two years we pretended we were settled.

We rented a timbered house in a suburb of Berkeley called Thousand Oaks. The boys dug up a lawn and Edie planted vegetable seeds. We were in a well-to-do neighbourhood but were poor. In the hot summers the neighbours splashed in their swimming pools. Our children listened over the garden wall. But soon our pretty daughters found their way in. They were happy. At school they concealed their lunches of home-baked bread.

Edith and Florence left school and took jobs in a clothing store. That was a sad day for me. They were clever girls. I had thought they would be teachers at the least. But a fever flushed their cheeks in this rich noisy land. A kind of infection struck them. They laughed more loudly, made their eyes glitter and their hair take unnatural shapes. Their voices quickly had a nasal twang. They spoke words strange to me—a language of possessions, pleasure, clothes, romance, and dancing. Edie was troubled by it too. But we quarrelled, for she said it was simply that they were growing up. 'Yes,' I cried, 'and in the land of Baal.' She agreed with that.

So a year went by—two years. A dreadful loneliness came on us. Clouds of greed and hatred enveloped the land—and my voice was like a plaintive bell in a sea-mist, warning of danger. It seemed to reach no ears. I sank to making a noise like a sparrow-squeak. And the land of Baal rushed into the war—a great river of foulness swept us away. (In everyday terms—and unmixed: the police closed my lectures. I was an alien, they said, a charge against me would be more serious than a charge of sedition.)

Again we talked into the night. We sat like conspirators in my little study, we hunched at the desk with paper and pen, counting our cents, while in our creaking house the children slept. We plotted to betray them. California was theirs. They had grown into it. (All except Meg: she pined, she failed to grow.) They slept unsuspecting; while a gladness fell on Edie and me. We scraped our money together. Enough, and some dollars to spare. We could go home. In the instant I knew it an image of grey streets came to me, and cold crashing waves, and humourless faces. It made me happy. There—that was mine.

It was like one's knowledge of Effectual Calling. I said, 'If I'm going to prison let it be a New Zealand prison.' Edie only smiled. She saw Linwood and her father's fruit garden.

The next day she told me I must go to Philadelphia to see my mother. 'Yes,' I said. 'We won't be coming to this country again.'

I travelled by train. In a brownstone house in a quiet neighbourhood I faced a woman who let me kiss her cheek but then sat me down and kept me at a distance of many years. The lady of the peacock hats was gone. The widow Mrs Weedon and I found a great chasm between us. It was distressing to me, but did not appear to give her any distress. I saw my own face before me, my round features, softened by femininity and hardened by belief. We spoke of religion. I could not get a word in. And I wondered if I affected others the way she affected me. I grew resentful. With my fluency but without my weight, her voice ran on, persistent as a stream on pebbles. 'Sin is in the mind, George. Sickness is in the mind. All cause and effect is mental. Even death is mental. Death can be healed. All the great fevers that infect our minds—all can be healed by a proper understanding of the Scriptures. Jesus was a healer and a teacher. His divinity lies in his teaching. Now, let me tell you of my good friend Hannah Brown. She discovered a lump in her groin that grew and grew . . .' And so on. For the five days of my visit. Except that on the final afternoon she discovered my hardness of hearing. It warmed her to me. 'George, this is no deafness, this is Error. We can banish it, we can put it out. All that you must do is know the Truth . . .' For the whole of that afternoon she dragged me about Philadelphia, showing me to her friends and testing my hearing. They planned assaults on my unbelief. I did not mind. It made a change.

In the morning I said goodbye. Weedon had left her well off. 'George, I feel bound to warn you, you can expect nothing from me. Everything I have will go to the church. That is where my heart lies.' A frank disclosure. Perhaps my visit had not been without pain for her. 'But George, if you'll send me your address when you get to New Zealand I'll post you some books explain-
145

ing the Christian Science teaching. Your hearing can be cured. Remember that.' I took my cab to the station. And never saw her again.

She had not once asked about Edie and my children.

55 I said to Felicity, 'Do you remember Wolfie Rendt?'
'Oh yes,' she cried. 'How could I forget him? He was the love of my life.'

'No, not really?'

'I was wild about him. I nearly fainted when we said good-bye.'

Wolfie came often to our house in Thousand Oaks. He was not the only one. An underwear salesman, Phil Critch, came to see Edith. A high school boy whose name I forget came to see Florence. Even Agnes, Esther, and little Rebecca, had their 'boy-friends'. I flushed them out from corners of the garden and drove them away. But Phil Critch was 'serious'; and Wolfie Rendt was serious. He was not a boyfriend. He was Felicity's young man. They shared intellectual interests. They wrote poetry, they read Thoreau and Emerson aloud. I liked Wolfie. I liked his immigrant parents, who ran a small ironmongery shop and struggled to put their son through college. I would have been happy to see Felicity marry this German boy. But she did not. She chose to come back to New Zealand. And, it seems, nearly fainted on saying goodbye. Wolfie went to the war and was killed.

Edith was the one who married. Edith married Phil Critch. I wept as I gave her away to this bullet-headed, loud and stupid man. He slapped my back and called me Pops. He told his friends I was in the God-business. He spoke of wops and kikes and niggers. He spoke of doing his bit to preserve democracy. And Edith loved him madly. She stroked his wiry hair and squeezed the muscles in his arms with a rapt expression. Like Felicity, she nearly fainted. My arguments made no ground
146

with her. So I left this daughter in the land of Baal, married to one of the natives there. She writes and tells me how happy she has been.

The *S.S. Ventura* sailed out of San Francisco with ten Plumbs on board. It steamed through dangerous warm seas into the south. I felt cold spray on my cheeks and knew I was going home, and going to battle.

We rented a house in the suburb of Shirley, Christchurch. I began to lecture at once.

56 Peter came home early in the afternoon, bringing a young woman with him. She was wearing the new style of dress, the 'new-look', and with her pink cheeks and curly brown hair I thought her very attractive. Nick Carter was her name. 'Nicola, Nicola,' the girl shouted into my trumpet, laughing at Peter. They were, Peter said, going to 'swot' together, and they went to his bedroom. That was too bare-faced. Straining with my dead ears, I could hear nothing. But when I put my trumpet to the door there was a sound of laughter. The place for me, I thought, was out of the house.

I sat in the garden, enjoying the autumn warmth and the scent of roses. Gardens I find calming to the mind; and calmness of mind a necessary condition for the quickening of the spiritual faculties; the stirring in its slumber of the soul; the sense of mystical union with the One. I have read that this is brought on by a change in body chemistry. But we penetrate *terra incognita*, we plumb the human deeps, search for the self, the soul, the Light within the dark, by means other than the scientific. Mystical experience is the chief. Science is busy in the margins. Or, to put it another way, science works on the vehicle but knows not the rider or his destination. Curious that I set such store by it in the old days. I was a limited fellow.

Such thoughts as these are not conducive to calm. Nor was my old man's curiosity about the two young people in the house.

I went inside, wrote a note to Felicity, and set off for town and my meeting with Oliver. I walked down the neat surburban street and came to a little station called Simla Crescent. Soon a unit swayed up to the platform. I got inside and was carried down the gorge into the city.

I knew where to find Oliver's court. But as I went towards it I saw Parliament Buildings off to the right, on top of their low green hill. Up there were half a dozen men I knew. I grew curious to see them at their work—curious especially to see Dan Peabody.

I went through the shadow of Dick Seddon's statue (the sculptor had him spouting, just as I had seen him once outside the Queen's Hotel in Kumara); up the steps, through the Grecian columns; and found my way into the public gallery. And there they were, in their rimu-panelled, padded-leather pit. I looked at them with emotion. A sense of the years came down on me and a grey oppression of spirit. So much left undone, so much that will never be done. I knew these important men must feel the same when they were out of this chamber, when they stood alone, facing their young selves. Fraser was there, Nash was there. I had seen them last in the flesh at an unemployed meeting in an Auckland hall in 1933. Savage had been there too (dead Savage, the 'hero', the 'saint': I still met people who believed in him). And Lee, not yet 'traitor'. I had made my mark on that meeting. I had given those men trouble. There had been too much oil on their tongues.

I found a seat and stared at them. I heard no words. My trumpet was on my lap. Bill Parry was speaking. I had heard Parry before. And the bitter-faced man beside him, the man with the Calvinist eyes and bar-room vocabulary. Semple. I had missed him by less than a year in Lyttelton jail.

Dan Peabody was in the second row, leaning back with his arm on the rest, and a patient expression on his face. A meaty face, Dan had, and the face of a disappointed man. It seemed to me only half alive. It had not the lightness, the inner life, one sees in the faces, however gross, of men who still have am-

148

bitions to realize. Dan was going nowhere. He had never made it to the front bench; had entered cabinet all right; but his portfolio was minor. Even now, I had trouble remembering it. Mines? Broadcasting? It did not matter. He could not have been further from the post he had told me so confidently he would fill one day. Even his seat had become marginal. And he had an election to face in less than a year. It seemed his life in politics was over. It was the only life he had.

Felicity had loved Dan Peabody. She had borne him a son. And I thought with a painful amusement of my old faith in the 'science' of eugenics. Eugenic betterment, eugenic sense, the the eugenic ideal: I had bristled with weapons, carrying these phrases. 'The higher sense of marriage.' 'The Divine right of maternity.' 'What God cannot do the child can.' Well, I would have said that Felicity, my daughter, intelligent girl, and Dan Peabody, Socialist, man of courage, would have a child who must carry on God's work. And I thought of that child: ordinary-minded, pleasure-seeking Peter, blank in the eye at the great old causes, but lighting up at news of a football score.

Dan had stumped the country in the First War, talking against conscription. They had put him in jail for sedition. But in the Second he changed his tune and helped pass the law that gathered the conscripts in. There is no science that can measure behaviour. It is even less easy to understand than inheritance.

I looked at the other side. Holland. Now there was a name. Once it had belonged to honest Harry—a politician who rose above his trade. I was pleased this cramped man in the Leader's seat was not related: Sidney Holland. He had a cunning clever face. Ambition, the expectation of power, had set a gleam on his eye that was not on Dan's. In his ugly cheek was a bunching up that strained against the now. I watched him with fascination, with a prickling on the spine, as one watches a stoat. Beside him was the man I recognized as Holyoake. A pleasant enough looking fellow. But I felt a little sick, felt the blow. For I had been told this man (well-fed, well-dressed, on the Tory side) had a blood connection with George Jacob Holyoake, of the English

149

nineteenth-century radicals perhaps the greatest—certainly the man of greatest courage. How the line had twisted.

Bill Parry finished speaking and sat down. Dan leaned forward and spoke into his ear. Then, as he sat back, he saw me watching. For a moment his face was naked. I knew what he felt. Time rushed away from me too, the years made a hollow boom, and all was loss. Then Dan grinned at me, and winked elaborately.

I stood up. I made him a nod of farewell, and went out into the bright still afternoon.

57 My 1918 lecture tour took me to the Coast, to Westport, Hokitika, Greymouth. Back in Christchurch, I picked up Felicity, and we set off for Dunedin and Invercargill. On the way home I gave two talks in Thorpe. Mrs Jepson was dead. Felicity and I stayed with John.

Our meeting was sad, for we remembered Edward. But in the evening, back from the hall—my old Unitarian Hall, without a name—we gathered in the library, almost the old group: John and I, Andrew Collie, John Findlater, Dan Peabody; and the ghost of Edward became a companion presence, one that I turned to from time to time when I grew tired of words. I was close to tears that night, and cannot tell even now if they would have been of acceptance or of pain.

I was proud of Felicity. In the old days I had wanted a woman in the group. And here she was, my daughter. She held her own. She had passion, fire, and the prophetic mind; but an impatience of high-sounding talk, a practical good sense, an earthiness of expression (where had she got that? the single thing I was unhappy with) that pulled us up short many a time and made us think again.

At first we talked of the great exciting event of those days, the Russian revolution. The news had come late in the previous year. I had been sitting in my garden in the Spring sunshine. On
150

my knee was the paper, a great sore, with its four pages of New Zealand's dead and wounded. (One of those names, one day, would be Oliver's.) I sat in that sunny green place as though in a pit of ash and mud. Then my eye fell on the special headline: *Russia Has Turned Red, Troops In Revolt*. It was like a spiritual revelation—in quality, in intensity, like a first sighting of the One. I came alive in an instant, that which I had thought dead in me began to move. And I saw burning in the sky those words of Ezekiel, 'I will overturn, overturn, overturn it; and it shall be no more, until he come whose right it is; and I will give it him.' But soon I set my vengefulness aside; and I thought, Mankind is out of his trap, the blind turning is over, the hatred and greed. Glory, glory, glory. I breathed deeply of the fresh Spring air. And soon I hurried inside to my study, for I had work to do.

Four months later our enthusiasm was running even higher. The war went on, but so did the revolution. Imperialism, Militarism, Capitalism, were the past, and the war their last convulsion. The Red Flag (the red blood of humanity) was the future.

We spoke of it that night in John Jepson's library; many ringing (and alas unprophetic) words. But my second talk was 'The Glorious Bolsheviks of Russia' and I did not want to give too much away. So after a while we talked of other things: progressive religion, marriage and morality, poetry and love, law, justice, poverty and wealth, education, control of the mind— talked until the sky began to lighten, *de omnibus rebus et quibusdem aliis*. It reminded me of our evening with McCabe. Except that there was no plum cake, and no Mrs Jepson listening at the keyhole.

Dan Peabody was a month out of Lyttelton jail, where he had been put for sedition. Paddy Webb was out recently too and Webb's account of the horrors of the place was, Dan said, a good deal short of the truth. I liked Dan better on that night than I had before—or have liked him since. For a time he was without his political skin. His voice shook with emotion as he told us of the mad or haunted eyes of men released from solitary confinement, the 'dummy' as it was called. He told us he had worked alongside a rapist, a sodomite, a murderer. He was a damaged man, and I wonder now if he ever fully regained what Lyttelton jail crushed out of him. He discovered the terrible fact of human cruelty and was not coarse-fibred enough to let it pass through him and out; or, I must add, firm enough in mind, clear in mind and spirit, to hold himself steady, get a sight of the foe, and enter the battle. Felicity's eyes filled with tears as she listened to him.

'You must go into Parliament,' she said. 'You can do something about it.'

'Parliament,' cried Andrew. 'There is no hope left in Parliament. The ballot box is dead, lassie. It's gone the way of the horse and cart. And a good thing too. What has it got us? Men like Bill Massey. No, my friends, this is the age of the armed uprising. Revolution. And the ballot box goes into the dustbin of history.'

'You must work to get into Parliament.' She was alone with Dan Peabody. Andrew was only a bit of Scotch comedy on another part of the stage. The rest of us did not exist. I saw the girl give herself to this man. It could not be other. She was young, passionate, idealistic—and recently in love. And he, well, he was handsome, he thought as she did, he had suffered. He was too lost in himself to know what was happening, but the rest of us saw, even Andrew; and sanctioned her in her feeling. We were children in our view of love; romantics, idealists. Even I. Had not Edie and I understood in a flash? Besides, we were tested in our beliefs. These two were the 'fit'. And had not woman been bound for hundreds of years by scriptural texts? Now she was free. This was her century. I had declared it earlier in the night. She might select her man and have her babe and know that her act served the true morality. If God held the partners together in love what need of churching, what need of the sanctions of law? And speaking generally—for this was Felicity's moment—I said from Ecclesiasticus: 'If thou findest a good man, rise up early
152

in the morning and go with him, and let thy feet wear the steps of his door.' That was not, after all, fully scriptural.

Dan had a wife at home, but she was a silly woman. She was one of the 'unfit'.

58 John came to me privately in the morning. 'George, I don't want to worry you, but there were two men in the hall last night taking notes. I don't think they were from the newspapers.'

'Policemen, you think?'

'They had the look of it.'

'Ah well, I've been expecting them. We'll see if they're there tonight.'

They were, one on each side of the hall. They scribbled industriously in their little books. I remembered George Jacob Holyoake. When the police came into his lecture and ranged themselves round the walls in their shining hats he spoke an hour longer, not having foreseen, he said, such a chance of extending liberal views in official quarters. Well, I thought, I'll take him as example. And I let myself go. I spoke for an hour and three-quarters without drawing breath.

Felicity sat in the front row. Dan was beside her that night. Her face was calm and happy. I thought how like Edie she looked.

59 It took the police two weeks to prepare their charges. I had time for lectures in Nelson and Blenheim. But when I came back I was summonsed. There were two charges, both of seditious utterance. I appeared in the Christchurch Magistrates Court at the beginning of March.

On the morning of my trial I dressed in my warmest clothes and stoutest shoes. Edie put half a dozen handkerchiefs and a

153

pair of woollen gloves in my pockets and I chose a small volume of Emerson's essays. I said goodbye to the children and told them they must work hard at school. Then I set out. Felicity came with me. Edie was not well enough.

I had wished to defend myself, but when I showed my friends the statement I meant to read they were horrified. John Jepson and Andrew had hurried up from Thorpe. Even Andrew was horrified. They might have airy notions about love, but about the justice of courts they were realistic. What I needed was a smart lawyer. They made me retain John Willis. And John would not even let me on the stand.

That was a wrong decision. I see it now. My statement had been carefully thought out. I speak very well. In speaking I'm a professional. I would not have moved the magistrate—a little Oliver—but there was an audience in court that day and it went to waste. I might have planted a seed. And a seed can grow into a forest tree. I look at the statement today: Appendix 2 in *The Growing Point of Truth*. It begins with a short history of sedition, from Jesus to Mazzini and Kossuth. Today's sedition-monger, I said, is tomorrow's political hero. And I showed how the lawbreaker may be more important to society than the law-maker. Then I went on to the charges, and spoke of 'the patriotic poison' in our schools and the need to teach loyalty towards the whole human family. I explained why I wished for no victor in the war and why praying for victory is a blasphemy. I tabulated New Zealand's war profits and showed who is the real victor. I explained my attitude towards war loans. And I described the sort of revolution I wished to see in my country. Then I made a more personal statement (or would have made it). I explained my decision to come back to New Zealand. New Zealand had a destiny, this destiny drew me back, for it was bound inextricably to my own. I made my 'utterances' at the command of God and my conscience. My conscience would not let me hate seventy million Germans at the State command. Nor would it let me be silent. I spoke for myself but I did not stand alone. For 'God standeth in the shadow keeping watch above his own,'
154

(Lowell). And although my lectures had cost me this agony—public trial—I regretted nothing. I had simply obeyed a call to duty, duty to my country and to mankind. 'The truth,' I said, 'is my burden and not sedition'.

But all this sat in my pocket, unused. John Willis conducted my defence on technicalities.

The case was brought under the War Regulations, section 4, which defined what was seditious or had a seditious tendency. The first charge stated that on February 14, in a lecture entitled 'Julius Caesar or Jesus Christ', I said:

'You are under the heels of the War Lords. We have not enough population in our country, yet we are lusting after the annexation of Samoa. The patriotic poison is in our schools. The children are taught to salute the flag and sing the National Anthem. I tell my children when they come home not to sing the National Anthem. I am hoping with a fervent hope that in this war there will be no victor. To pray about a war is blasphemy. A woman goes down the valley of death to bring a child into the world; she nurses it, sends it to school, sees it through the sixth standard; then comes a call to arms, and it goes away to war. What for? To die for its country? No! To die for the profiteer.'

The second charge stated that on February 15, in a lecture entitled 'The Glorious Bolsheviks of Russia', I said:

'Russia wanted war, England wanted war, the upper class in New Zealand wanted war. Never has there been such a wonderful five days as the five days of the Russian Revolution. The old Russia has gone and the new Russia has come in. I hope before I die to see a similar movement in New Zealand. I hope the day will come in New Zealand when these war loans will be repudiated. I hope not a penny of the war loan will be repaid. You do not authorize them.'

These were my seditious utterances. I pleaded not guilty.

60 The prosecutor was a man called Malcolm. He was a matter-of-fact, a dry-as-dust sort of man, but I heard a detestation in his voice once or twice in the morning. We anti-war folk were looked on as worse than murderers.

The clerk read the first charge. Then Malcolm set the scene: hall, chairman, sponsoring body (the Labour Representation Council), the audience of one hundred and fifty persons. Dry stuff. But then he showed some passion. 'There can be no question that these words uttered by the accused are seditious. The only question can be, were they used? They were. That we shall prove. And we shall claim they were uttered not under momentary excitement, not in the heat of argument, but coolly and deliberately by an educated man brought to the town of Thorpe and speaking in a public lecture designed as part of an organized propaganda.'

He called a Senior-Sergeant of Police, Sampson by name: one of the men who had taken notes at the meeting. He was a burly man, slow-speaking, slow-moving, and even I could see an excellent witness. If in those rites of Justice we can look on the magistrate as the Godhead, then Sampson and Malcolm had the role of serving priests. And Sampson was the senior. Malcolm handed neutral objects to him and Sampson sanctified them. Thus:

'How long did the accused speak?'

'I timed the speech. He spoke for an hour and twenty-two minutes.'

'Was there any response from the audience?'

'There was frequent applause. There were shouts of "Bravo" and "Hear, hear".'

'Did you take notes of the words of the accused?'

'I did.'

'Now Sergeant, are you a shorthand writer?'

'No, sir. I take a fast longhand note.'

'Are the words charged in the information the only notes you took?'

'No, sir. Prior to those words I took the following.' (He opened his notebook.) ' "If Jesus Christ was now on earth he would be tried for sedition. The churches are the recruiting agent for the world's greatest tragedies. Some of the clergy are now known as the black militia. We are weeding out the best of of our manhood and leaving the weeds. Where is this going to land us?" '

I leaned across to John Willis and told him the Sergeant was not being strictly truthful. These words were not consecutive. They came from different parts of my talk, like the words in the charges. John nodded. He had seen it. And when he rose to question Sampson he began on that line. I saw very soon it made up the substance of our defence. I was unhappy at that. I persisted in thinking this trial was part of an argument and my job was to persuade. There was the box. I should be in it, delivering my message. John kept stolidly on, though he must have felt my disapproval pressing on his spine. In court he dropped his uncertainties, hid the dark side of his nature, and came out the honest legal tradesman. It was a good piece of acting. But I was too angry to admire him for it.

'Do you agree, Sergeant,' he asked, 'that Mr Plumb is a fairly rapid speaker?'

'Yes, sir. Fairly rapid.'

'And you are not a shorthand writer?'

'No, sir.'

'But you managed to take a lengthy note?'

'Yes, sir.'

'Did you copy down all his words or just some?'

'Some, sir. There was no time to take them all.'

'No time? Then there are gaps in your record?'

'The notes are not consecutive, sir.'

'How long are they spread over?'

'The whole lecture. An hour and twenty-two minutes.'

'You will admit then that there are many words left out from the body of your note that might moderate or qualify its meaning?'

'No sir, I will not admit that. There are words left out. But those words do not change the meaning. The note gives the general trend of the lecture. Each sentence is a complete consecutive rendering.'

'Sergeant, when Mr Plumb said that he taught his children not to sing the National Anthem, did he add nothing to that?'

'Not that I remember, sir.'

'Did he not go on to say that he taught them to sing "God save the people"?'

At once a shout of 'Bravo!' came from behind me (Scotch, of course) and a short burst of clapping, like a pattering of rain. The magistrate nodded sharply, and the orderly was on his feet, threatening to put the offenders out. John was cross. He looked sternly at Andrew. Then he put his question again. The Sergeant remembered my words, but the magistrate, still frowning down the court, seemed to make no note of them. John glared at Andrew. But it all struck me as a piece of comedy; and Andrew's cry as a good honest response. Sooner that than the legal splitting of hairs.

John went on for a while; he produced qualifying remarks; had Sampson remember some; and sat down at last well pleased with himself.

Malcolm called the second policeman, Wood. He was not a shorthand writer either. He had less control of himself than Sampson and spent his time on the stand glaring at me in a cold and weighty manner I found upsetting. He was, I should guess, a good hater. Wood gave nothing to John. He admitted taking down only the words he thought seditious, but declared roundly that my other words had not altered their meaning. He had no memory of 'God save the people'.

John made one good point. He asked Wood if he did not think it strange that he and Sampson had noted the same words.

'No sir, not strange at all.'

'But the words you took down and the words the Sergeant took down are identical. Down to the last full stop.'

'I didn't see what the Sergeant took down. We were on opposite sides of the hall.'

'You didn't copy from him later on?'

'No, I did not.'

'It's odd then that you should have what he has.'

'No sir, not odd at all. We took down the words we thought seditious.'

'From a talk that lasted an hour and twenty minutes—some eighteen thousand words—you both took down the same fifty. And you say it's not odd?'

'I do.'

'Coincidental, then?'

Wood made no reply, and John left it at that. Then, as Malcolm closed his case, he stood up again to defend me. He called no witnesses, but addressed the court. He did so in a stodgy manner. Eloquence would not have been acceptable to the robed individual on the bench; a man loose-lipped, dewlapped like a bulldog, and suffering a red collapse of his lower eyelids. His voice was like the creaking of a door. Appropriate, I thought, to the kind of justice that locked free speech away.

John began by admitting that the words in the information would be seditious if used consecutively. But, he said, they were not so used. The policemen had admitted it. And he submitted to the court that he had shown beyond any doubt—beyond the shadow of a doubt, he said—that they had taken their notes haphazardly and ignored the qualifying phrases I had used.

'This case,' he said, 'is very different from a case of indecent language. The words in a sedition case should not be taken out of their context. What the accused said should have been rendered in full. I could of course put him on the witness stand and ask him to render it in full. But that would take up too much of the court's time. I have shown already how all the remarks in the information were qualified. And I suggest to the court—and to my learned friend' (a lawyerly nod at Malcolm) 'that the

159

summons should have been drawn up to show where the intervals occurred between the sentences.'

The magistrate interrupted. 'There should have been a row of points between the sentences. That is the proper manner.'

John was encouraged by this. He droned on like a great black bee, but it was plain to me he was trapped in the bottle of his legalistic mind. How I longed to jump to my feet and tell him and Malcolm and the magistrate what this case was all about. Words, words. A point here, a point there. 'It is manifestly impossible for anyone to take down in longhand any sentence such as the one submitted by Mr Sampson. That contains fifty words and would have been uttered in less than twenty-five seconds.' The magistrate scratched with his pen. Sampson folded his hands. Somebody coughed in the body of the court. I looked round and Felicity smiled at me. Dan Peabody sat beside her. I had not known he was coming up.

At last John was finished. He sat down, pleased with himself again, and touched my sleeve, but I could not bring myself to speak to him.

The magistrate—Bradley was his name—kept his nose down. He scratched on with his noisy pen, sucking in his newborn baby's lip. Malcolm yawned and studied his thumb-nails. Wood kept his deadly eye on me as though I were his prey. John whispered encouragement—all of it nonsense. To cut him off I took out my Emerson and started to read. 'No, no,' John said, 'that'll make a bad impression on the court.'

Finally Bradley laid down his pen and folded his liver-marked hands. I had thought we would be in for some legal knitting but he surprised me my coming straight to the point. 'I have no doubt these words were used or that they are seditious. Naturally they are only part of what was said, but I accept the evidence of the police that there were no other remarks that modify to any serious extent what is reported here. The only modifying clause is the reference to "God save the people", and that, it seems to me, could very well be sung as well as the National Anthem. The two are not contradictory. However, we are not

160

concerned with that here. We are concerned with the reported utterance. And it is plainly seditious to say that children should not sing "God save the King". We shall confine ourselves to that, and to the whole tendency of the words in the information. That tendency is to excite disaffection against His Majesty's Government. I find the charge of seditious utterance proven and I direct the court to record a conviction against the defendant. However, I shall defer sentence until the hearing of the second charge.'

He nodded at the clerk. And so we went through the solemn farce again. John enlivened it a little by reading a sentence from the charge to Sampson and having him write it down. Sampson did it perfectly.

'Yes,' John said, 'well you probably know it by heart.' And he read two short paragraphs from a newspaper. Sampson got down only the opening words.

'Well, sir,' he explained, 'what Mr Plumb said impressed itself more forcibly on my mind.' I was pleased to hear it.

In his final speech John said it was beyond human probability that two witnesses should have noted the same few words in speeches lasting an hour and twenty minutes and an hour and three-quarters. This was the only point he had to make but he looked at it back, front, sideways, and from underneath. The magistrate played with his lip and wiped his damp fingertips on his robe. When it was his turn to speak he wasted no time. I saw he wanted to purge his court of me. He could not understand any suggestion that New Zealand should repudiate its war loans. He could hardly imagine that New Zealand should have a revolution such as was still going on in Russia. Anyone who wished such a thing must be mad. To see his infantile, his stupid eye fix itself on me, and hear his grating voice declare me mad, was more than I could bear. He spoke for greed, stupidity, cruelty, death. I tried to get my statement from my pocket, tried to climb to my feet, but John held me down by my arm and hissed at me. He was saying, I believe, that if I sat still I might get away with a fine. 'Nonsense,' I said, 'this man wants me locked up.'

161

F

'George, be still, be still.' And on my other side the court orderly restrained me too. So I let Bradley get on with it.

'I find the defendant guilty on both charges. And because in these troubled times a man holding beliefs such as his is too dangerous to be at large, I sentence the defendant to fourteen months' imprisonment on each charge. The sentences will run concurrently.'

61 Felicity cried, 'You cannot do this. Shame!' Her clear light voice was the first sound in the room as the door closed behind waddling Bradley. There was pain as well as anger in her cry. This was the point at which games stopped for her. Like Dan in Lyttelton jail, she looked into the dark. We had been until then, she and I, engaged in crusading. White chargers, gleaming swords, cannot have been far from her mind. Now she knew the truth. I leaned over the rail and held her hand. She kissed me and burst into tears. I asked Dan to take her home to Edie. He put his arm about her and led her away.

Because I was not a desperate criminal I was given time to say goodbye to my friends. They filed past and shook me by the hand. John Jepson. Andrew. Bluey Considine, who had come over from the Coast. Then men and women I did not know began to walk by. I felt the touch of many hands. Last came old Matthew Willis. 'You should have got yourself a good lawyer, boy.' He told me not to worry about Edie and the children. 'I'll see they come to no harm.'

Then I was taken out and put in a van, and delivered to Lyttelton jail.

62   I rested in the sun outside Oliver's court. People going by looked at me curiously. Perhaps they took me for a beggar and my trumpet for a novel collection bowl. It struck me after a while that the ones who grinned were not grinning at me but at something written on the wall above my head. I stood up and looked at it. *Goodlad rides again.* And above that an obscene drawing. I remembered that Oliver was hearing a divorce case that had roused much disapproval and delight. Goodlad was a racing journalist who had committed adultery with the wife of a well-known brewer. The papers were full of the case, printing detail I thought most improper. The whole thing stank to me of lucre and lust and hypocrisy. On the other hand, I was not sorry to see the bourgeois world held under a light.

The sun went behind a tall building and at once a wind sprang up. I remembered this was Wellington. The stillness of the day had been a rare thing. A coldness began to play about my head and down my back. It drove me inside—this and a curiosity about the Goodlad case and my son Oliver's distinguished part in it. (Its only other distinctions were of a low sort.) Because it was late in the day I managed to find a place at the back of the court. The room was full of people, all leaning forward breathlessly. A good nine-tenths were women. The hats there would have stocked a milliner's shop. I could not make out the parties in the case.

Oliver, set on a ledge, had the look of an eagle. His beaky nose, his wig and steel-rimmed glasses, added to it. He looked capable of spreading wings and swooping down on some squealing victim, some plump and hatted woman—a tasty bite. But, I reflected, the simile was too bold for him. He had a meaner nature. Everything about Oliver was clipped, controlled. His mind especially. In that garden with square beds and gravel paths, no proscribed plant, no interdicted insect, lived for long. Oliver had a well-stocked shelf of poisons.

163

I felt easier in his court after thinking this. It was necessary for me to get Oliver set, get him square, before facing him. My exaggerations were not malicious. They rose from disappointment. I had had high hopes for Oliver, my first son.

He made no sign of having seen me, but I knew he had. Oliver misses nothing. I lifted my trumpet to hear. At this the woman next to me shifted away, rolling her posterior like a ball. She probably took me for a tramp. (Meg can never get me to buy new clothes. If the cloth remains warm, I say, what does a frayed cuff matter? Waste is immoral.) I was pleased to have the space. I laid my book there—a Browning selection I had borrowed from Max. The woman looked at it suspiciously, and moved off another inch. I smiled with delight. Perhaps Browning and I could clear the whole bench. Then I began to hear words. 'Bedroom.' 'Bed.' 'Naked.' Was this what held these women spellbound? This squalid event? Two foolish people satisfying an urge—the hired room, the hired bed? How had Browning put it?—'the unlit lamp and the ungirt loin.' The words were too good.

The man in the box was an investigator, one who spied on guilty couples for money. He was saying, as far as I could make out, that he had shone his torch into the room. A strong torch. An orderly held it up as evidence. And then had the naked pair, blinded like possums, tried to hide from this light that murdered their joy? If joy it was. I began to be more troubled than I liked, and I put my trumpet down.

Oliver wrote; as Bradley had, so many years before. I wondered how he enjoyed doing this job. A scrubbed and Lysolled man, Oliver. He must feel dirtied by what he was forced to hear. He wrote; looked up severely; gave a ruling. He was at the top of his profession. Perhaps his sense of this served him like a doctor's rubber gloves. He could handle sores and take no infection. Down there on the floor, Goodlad and Mrs Mottram, taken in their carnal act: up here, Oliver Plumb, Supreme Court judge. I could see how the two need never meet.

Court rose until the next day. I turned sideways to let the women out. Several stayed in their places to watch the actors go by. And here they came. Goodlad, bold and smiling; a whisky face, broken veins high on his cheeks, blue jovial eyes; and was that pain, bewilderment in them, moving like shadowy fish, deep down? Now Mrs Mottram, heavily befurred; perhaps on this mild day so dressed to keep up her morale. Pale, dark-eyed, queenly. Lips set in a small manufactured smile. The women beside me gave a little, 'Ooh'. They would, I think, have curtseyed if they'd had room. And they came by me in a great hurry to follow the lady out, but drew in their skirts not to touch me, this shabby ancient.

I waited in my seat and presently an orderly in a black gown took me to Oliver's room.

'Dad.'

'Oliver.'

We shook hands.

'What have you done?' It was more complaint than enquiry. Sickness, injury, affront Oliver's sense of propriety. He believes in solitary confinement for the sick.

'It's a burn. Nothing to worry about.'

'That bandage doesn't look too clean.'

'It's all right. Max put it on.'

Oliver made a sour expression. 'And you've still got that?' He tapped my trumpet with the edge of his nails. It sent painful vibrations into my ear.

'Don't do that.'

'Isn't it time you got rid of it?'

'No.' But I took it down as it offended him, and that cut me off. I sat and waited for him to get ready. First he washed his hands. Then he took off his wig and put it in a cupboard. From the way he handled it I saw it was a sacred object. He put his gown on a hanger and hung it against the wall. Then he put some papers in a satchel. He snapped it shut. Every move was quick and bare. I remembered his skill in weeding carrots, his manner of eating his porridge. He had spooned his way round it clockwise; made an island of it with scalloped cliffs; then eaten round it again, and again, keeping it perfect all the way. He

165

kept milk and porridge in exact proportion so that the last of each came together in his final spoonful. A beautiful performance. Edie had become aware of it first, and made me watch. It worried her. And in fact if it was interrupted he screamed in an hysterical frenzy, and subsided at last into a trancelike state. A ritual disturbed, a certainty lost, the structure of his infant world came down like a cardhouse. Edie had to take him in her arms and warm him back to life. What warmed him now? He put on a tweed overcoat; drew on leather gloves; picked up a cane, his satchel, a homburg hat. I was impressed. He looked ready to issue from 10 Downing Street. But he looked too a plaster man, ready to be broken. And how then could he be fixed? To stay whole in his artificial shape, in this rude Dominion, he must walk on paths unknown to the rest of us. If I had to choose, I thought, I would choose to be with Goodlad and Mrs Mottram.

In Oliver's quiet car we drove to Wadestown.

63 Dante says, 'A lady appeared to me robed with the colour of living flame.' And in another place, 'I knew an angel visibly . . . Blessed are they who meet her on the earth.' Oliver's Beatrice rose from her seat and apppoached me. I felt her large cold hand in mine; saw her bitter mouth make sounds of welcome and her eyes simulate warmth. The joke is really too cruel. Beatrice Plumb is barren, or Oliver sterile. They adopted a girl but the child went to the bad: ran away from home, lived with a Maori; then came home one day blind in one eye from a punch and demanding money. Oliver had seen her last in 1944, drunk on the streets of the town, held on her feet by black American sailors. (I had this from Felicity.) He and Beatrice spoke of her no more. It's no use now asking who was to blame. But Beatrice is a woman three parts dead. Love is dead, pity is dead, the desiring part of her nature, that is dead. Alive in her is a sense of what is owed her. But this is not simple: it has a

positive and a negative side. The world she inhabits is, in a sense, religious.

We sat by a small electric heater in the living-room. Beatrice too frowned at my bandage and trumpet. I gave her news of Meg and the children. She was too well-bred to shout. She leaned close to my trumpet and closing her eyes as though she might see wax in it, spoke in the voice Esther calls la-di-da. The sounds that came to me were distant.

'—Emerson?'

Yes, Emerson was well. Still in love with flying machines.

'—Fergus?'

Fergus was all right. Starting to make money.

'—Esther?—husband, Fred?'

Oh Fred was well. Making money too. Barrels of it.

Oliver nodded approval. They did not ask after Willis. They did not approve of him.

In the dining-room we ate a frugal meal, blessed by the head of the house. We had boiled potatoes, boiled cabbage, boiled neck of mutton chops with parsley sauce. It suited me well. I prefer plain food. We drank tonic water sweetened with orange-ade. After the meal Oliver took me to his study. I wondered which of his brothers and sisters he meant to talk about. Willis and Alfred were blotted from his mind. Felicity, a Catholic, lived beyond the pale. We had covered Esther and Meg and Emerson. That left Robert. As I had seen him so often in his youth, Oliver sat down and folded his fingers—like a magistrate, I thought. And that of course was what he was. Better: a judge. This sudden rushing of past and present to fill one space confused me. The intervening years were thrown aside. All that time, all that human life, vanishing as though into a void, filled me with horror. Significance? Where was significance? It seemed to me I was gazing into emptiness: Oliver's life.

'Now. Robert.' His voice was sharp as scissors; excellent for my trumpet.

'No, I won't discuss him.'

'Why not?'

'Robert has made his choice.'

'Some choice.'

'It's his to make. He's nearly forty.'

'Robert's a child. We all know that. And he's fallen under an evil influence. This Parminter. The man's a lunatic.'

'As far as I can make out he's a fundamentalist Christian. Same as you.'

'I'm a Presbyterian. And we're talking about Robert. He's fallen in with a den of communists.'

'Wrong again, Oliver. There isn't any doctrine. They just hold things in common.'

'Including their women.'

'Is that so? I hadn't heard that. But it shouldn't upset you. Free love can be perfectly moral. And can you imagine Robert taking part in orgies?'

'I can. Under certain influences. Have you seen *Truth* this week?'

'No.'

'They sent a reporter out. And now it looks as if the police are going to investigate the place.'

'They won't find anything.'

'They'll find a man called Plumb. And where do you think that will leave me?'

'Ah, now I see.'

'It's all your doing. You have to take responsibility for this. Blasphemy, heresy, sedition. What chance did he have?'

'I don't think I was ever guilty of blasphemy.'

But Oliver was in a rage. His voice remained steady, his face still, but a trembling in his fingers gave him away. I wondered if he sentenced in this state. What an asset to a judge: to appear under control while in a moral frenzy. I was thinking on this, on the grotesque shapes the cramped mind takes, on my visionary knowledge, my consciousness of the One; and my love for poor pharisaical Oliver, whom I would have share my certainties, if a way of sharing could be found, if a path into his darkness could be found: thinking all this, in a state of sadness and confusion,

168

when I heard half a dozen words, a sharp little cracker-burst:
'—the miserable life you led mother.'

'What?'

'She had a miserable life. No money. Never any proper food. Did you know she used to eat our left-overs? You were in your study. You didn't have the slightest idea what went on. Meat and potatoes for you. The rest of us had porridge, even for tea. And all mother got was the scrapings out of the pot.'

'Nonsense.'

'It's true.'

'We had one or two hard years——'

'And clothes. Mother liked beautiful clothes. You dressed her in rags. And everybody stared at her. She couldn't stand that. She stopped going out. And the girls in bare feet.'

'Two years, Oliver. Three perhaps. It did nobody any harm.'

'And then you had to go to prison. To prison. My father. How do you think I felt in France, half of the calf of my leg shot off, and my father in prison for sedition?'

'Quiet, Oliver, quiet. You should be over it now.'

'I'll never be over it.'

That was true. I looked at him sadly, but from a great distance. Poor crippled boy. Edie came close to me. She stood by my side and put her hand in mine. Edie in her worn clothes, Edie with her troubled face. Yes, Oliver was right, her life had been hard—perhaps at times even miserable. But he did not understand: Edie knew love, she knew joy.

64 'Now Felicity, tell me, did your mother ever give you porridge for tea?'

'Who's been telling you that?'

'Oliver.'

'Trust him.'

'Did she?'

'It happened once or twice.'

'And what did I have?'

'Oh, meat. A chop perhaps. I can't remember.'

'Eggs?'

'You were doing brain work.'

'I see.'

'You're not going to worry about it now?'

The car was parked in a resting bay on the Rimutaka hill. The engine had become overheated and Felicity was letting it cool down. A stony gully dropped away from the roadside. Beyond it hills went rolling off to the north.

'And when I was in prison what did you eat?'

'Oh dad, fancy worrying now. It's thirty years ago. It's dead and gone.'

'I want to know how the rest of you got on. I had other things on my mind.'

'We did all right. Grandpa Willis looked after us.'

'Did you get enough to eat——?'

She moved impatiently. 'Why worry about food? I said we did all right. It was the talking that was hardest to bear. The way people treated us.'

'Yes?'

'Did you know they threw stones through our windows? And left white feathers in the letter-box?'

'Your mother didn't tell me.'

'She didn't want to worry you. And then there was the morning we found muck smeared all over the front door.'

'What? What was that?'

'Faeces. Excrement.'

'Good God.'

'They'd tried to print a word with it. "Judas." Oh, don't worry, mother didn't have to wash it off. Emerson did that.'

'Your mother——'

'She was all right. She was no wilting violet. It made her more determined, that was all. Florence and Agnes were the ones who got upset. Florence didn't get out of bed for three days after it
170

happened. And she went off to the States as soon as she could. To get away from the shame of it all.'

'Florence never forgave me.'

' "I was born to be a lady." I've got no patience with her.'

'A girl at that age feels things very deeply.'

'You don't have to tell me.'

'Were you unhappy too?'

'I was all right. I never let the flag-waggers worry me. My worries were something else.'

'What?'

'Nothing you'd be interested in.—The engine should be cool enough by now.'

'Religion?'

'I won't talk about religion with you, dad. You can stop right now.'

'But I want to talk. You believed the same way I did then.'

'I did not. I pretended to. I even fooled myself.'

'But——'

'Poor dad. You thought I was something special. Woman of the twentieth century. Mother of the new race. And all I really wanted was poor silly Dan. A house and babies.'

'I don't believe that.'

'I wanted him to divorce his wife and make an honest woman out of me. So much for the New Woman.'

'Dan's your own affair. I don't want to talk about Dan.'

'What then? God? The Oversoul? Don't you see dad, it was all too intellectual? Not an ounce of feeling in it. All that Unitarian stuff. Mother/Father God. It meant nothing to me. I didn't feel it. I needed something else. Anything. The old gentleman with the white beard. So long as it wasn't just a light shining in the sky.'

'It was more than that.'

'To you. But not to me. I needed something I could understand. Father and Son and Holy Ghost. I was getting all dried up. I was dying. And because of all your silly terminology, all your Nirvanas and Cosmic Souls, I couldn't find out what it was.

171

But now I know. I wanted something I could hold. Something I could get inside my body.'

'I'm not sure your priests would approve of that.'

'Bother my priests.'

'And Felicity, my religion is more than you think. I know God. I have seen him.'

'Bully for you.' She got out of the car and lifted the engine hood. In a moment a cloud of steam rose up. She went round to the boot and came back with a jar of water. I thought, I don't know her any more.

Her conversion was by self-surrender. She must—such a strong-willed girl—have wanted it to be volitional. (See William James on conversion.) But she came to Christ by an act of yielding. Then, as far as I can make out, she asserted herself on the next step, made it a willed one, made it intellectually, into the One True Church. But that step, in her latter days, has the appearance of a sitting down. The first was the vital one. Curious. Ironical. Her conversion took her that extra distance to Rome just because she was my strong-minded daughter. There, having proved to herself she was herself, she relaxed; and today she sits enjoying her patch of sun like a frog on a rock. I look at her and I think: What a waste of mind and passion, what a dreadful defeat.

She slammed the hood shut. The car bounced. And bounced a second time as she closed the boot. She got back inside.

'Did I ever tell you,' I said, 'that I once heard the last confession of a Catholic?' I told her about Joseph Sullivan, the Maungatapu murderer.

'Did you get the priest afterwards?'

'No. We buried him. Scroggie and I.'

'But a priest could have come. There was still time for extreme unction. As long as you got him there as soon as you could.'

'The man was dead, Felicity. Already he was face to face with God. What need of priests?'

She looked at me, and I at her. Near the house where I grew up a long culvert ran under the road. My playmates and I would stand at either end and shout at the tiny beings far away, against the foliage of another world. I saw Felicity as such a being; and in some such way she must have seen me.

'What will you do?'

'I'll have a mass said for him.'

'For the repose of his soul?'

'Exactly. Now put your silly funnel down. I've finished talking to you.'

65 In the week I arrived in Lyttelton jail a man called Eggers was hanged for murder. The morning I left on transfer to Paparua a rapist was flogged. I spent seven months of my sentence in that place, and everything that happened seems of a piece with that hanging and flogging. Locked in our cells we heard the trapdoor drop—heard the death of Eggers. But I did not hear the sound of the whip on the young man's back or hear him screaming. I went into Lyttelton jail hard of hearing. When I left I was stone deaf in one ear and could hear only faintly with the other. I told no one. The warders pushed me roughly or struck me between the shoulders to make me move.

They put me on light work: cleaning, painting, simple carpentry, much of it outside the prison walls. It was a great relief to come out of that building into the daylight. I might see women hanging out their washing or children playing hopscotch in the street. After the cold, the damp, the cells and iron doors and tasteless food, the shadow of the inhuman lying over everything, I had begun to doubt the world outside was real. Coming out, even under guard, was a visionary experience. I learned from Lyttelton jail that physical things, a sun-warmed stone, a flower, a human face, can be known spiritually; and Understanding be reached through the eyes and fingertips as well as through the mind.

But as winter came on most of my work was inside. We were put in our cells at half past four and kept there until morning.

173

I read very little. Bob Semple told me he studied in Lyttelton jail. A warder brought him all the books he needed. The man must have been gone by the time I got there. The governor allowed me one book at a time. My Emerson was returned to me, but taken away before I could claim something else. Edie brought out books on her visits, but only the safe ones reached me—safe in someone's uncertain judgement. Le Bon's *The Psychology of Socialism* was kept back. So was Laing's *Modern Science and Modern Thought*, published in 1885! They allowed me Dickens but not G. B. Shaw. I could follow their reasoning. But *Queen Mab* and not Amiel's *Journal*? Still, it was not important. I could not read in that place.

Nor could I think. Thinking cannot be done in darkness. And in Lyttelton jail I was afflicted by a dark oppression of mind. I could not hold myself steady. I heard in imagination the iron and wooden crash of the gallows trapdoor. I could not pray. I could not find God or Man. 'Out of the way of darkness cometh the path of light.' I held the words before me. But the path would not be found. I heard the trapdoor crash. I felt the noose choking me. And the bullets Eggers fired smashing into spine and heart. And bayonets cutting my flesh, gas burning my lungs. The hell and the despair of the world were in my cell. When I think of that winter I use the term 'a dark night of the soul'. And I think of Whitman's words, 'Agonies are one of my changes of garments,' and 'I am the man, I suffer'd, I was there.' Unlike Whitman I was not able to say, 'All this I swallow, it tastes good, I like it well.'

In the spring I was shifted to Paparua prison. Some of the weight lifted from me. Edie came to see me more often. I let her bring Felicity and Emerson, and once Rebecca and Esther. My friends came out. They gave me conversation for an hour or two a week, shouting their faint words into my ear. With my wife and children, they gave me love and warmth. So I came from my darkness into a kind of grey. It was neither dawn nor twilight, it did not promise day or threaten night. But in it I could think and I could live.

The war ended. Oliver limped home, but did not visit me. Felicity began her training as a teacher. Florence went off to America. (She came to see me before sailing—a sad little interview. She was caught between love and resentment and so could not do anything but cry.) Emerson left school. If I had been at home I would not have allowed it. He was too persistent for Edie. All he wanted was to drive motor cars or fly aeroplanes. He went down to Thorpe where John gave him work in his aerated-water factory.

Matthew Willis was true to his word. He paid my family's food and clothing bills and paid the rent. Edie's sister Florence helped if anyone was sick (there was much sickness in that bitter winter), and her mother had the girls go one by one to stay with her. She was a sharp old lady, very much against me, and she considered it her duty to talk good sense into my misled children. Late in the year she died. And at once old Matthew fell ill. It was plain he would not last long. He came to see me, very bent, very sunken in cheek and eye, and told me I need not worry about the future. He was leaving me more than enough to get by on.

Matthew lived through Christmas into the new year. But in the summer a new grief hastened his death. He rented a cottage at New Brighton beach so that Edie and the children might be away from the city during the worst of the influenza epidemic. They spent two happy months there. On the last Sunday our daughter Rebecca was drowned.

66 The Governor called me to his office. There was Edie with white face and bruised eyes. I knew it was death, and I asked, 'Who?' She could not shout, but I saw her lips say, 'Rebecca—drowned.' I put my arms about her and we wept. The Governor left us alone. For a long time we stood there, giving each other what comfort we could. It was not much. A

175

part of us was dead. I was taken by a dreadful sense of waste and of cruelty, and a love for the dead child that became more pain than love. I found no help in God.

67 The day had been colder than usual. The sea was rough with small sharp waves, blown to spume on their tops. Matthew and Edie and John Willis sat on the sand, watching the children swim. Rebecca did not swim well. She was a thin child and felt the cold. Usually she was first out of the water. But she was excitable and the broken waves exhilarated her. She squealed with pleasure as they slapped against her face. When the others ran in no one noticed she had stayed behind.

The cold must have caught her suddenly. She must have found herself too exhausted to swim. And she drowned silently, while her brothers and sisters, wrapped in their towels, were walking up to lunch.

Later everyone searched. John Willis found her, only a short way out. She was white and cold and dead. They tried for a long time but could not bring her back.

Rebecca. Thirteen. A quiet child. Her hair was the darkest in our family. Her eyes were brown. She was good at her school-work and wrote little stories about wizards and princesses. I did not know her well, but she came sometimes, saying no word, and put her cheek on my sleeve. That is the memory I keep of her.

68 The sea took one of our children. And the Spanish flu brought me near to my death. I lay in the prison in-firmary for many weeks, as near to a corpse as it's possible to be while remaining alive. My hearing was gone, my hair was gone, and most of my physical substance wasted away. I was bone, and an unhuman kind of silken skin. Manikin. Homun-

176

culus. Shrunken in my spiritual being too. I had strength for neither pain nor rebellion. Or even for complaint. I lay there week after week; passive, dry, physical, as good as dead.

In April the prison van delivered me home; put me on the steps like a parcel of groceries. My family carried me in. They set about the task of breathing life into me. Edie, Felicity, Esther, took turns beside my bed; and Meg, my youngest daughter, sat with me after school and drew pictures for me (Phoenix, unicorn) and modelled dragon-killing knights out of plasticine. My friends came often. Some of them, I saw from their eyes, thought me finished as a man. They could not look at me straight. But I came back to health; amazed, perhaps dismayed them. (Dan had seen uses for me as martyr.) Andrew began to talk of a lecture tour. It would be a triumph. The returned men would be for me one hundred per cent. I said no. That book of my life was closed forever.

'Edie,' I said, 'we must think what we're going to do.'

'Are you well enough, George?' (I had my trumpet now and she leaned forward and spoke into it clearly.)

'Matthew has left us well off. Well enough. I think we should leave this town.'

'We've moved about a lot, George.'

'This will be the last time. We'll find a house, a comfortable house, and never move again. I promise you that.'

'Do you really promise, George?' She was firmer with me these days, nurse with invalid.

'There's nothing to keep us here, Edie. Whatever we need we can carry away in our minds. Florence and John will look after her grave.'

'Yes.'

'So, my dear?'

'I want to go somewhere warm.'

In the spring we paid a visit to Auckland and hunted in the suburbs and the country round about. We found a little town out by the ranges; a house that seemed to have grown up like

177

a tree. It was of the style known as villa, but pieces had been added to it. One stepped up, stepped down, into green dark places or sunny places. It stood on a slope beside a slow-running creek, with fifteen acres of land up a tributary stream. There were gardens on the flat land, well-grown pines and wattle trees by the road, and an orchard running back to a neighbour farm. We bought it; and hurried to Christchurch for our children. We packed, we said goodbye, and we travelled north. (Oliver and Felicity stayed behind.)

'I'd like to call it Peacehaven,' Edie said. I agreed, though secretly I had wanted Journey's End. Instead I put that name on the door of the room I had chosen for my study. From time to time people say it's morbid or defeatist. Then I explain it comes from John Davidson's poem:

> At the journey's end I see a new world
> Where men are healthy, women beautiful,
> Humanity tender, good and dutiful.

For this green place, this warm, garden-surrounded, bird-echoing house, made me optimistic. Just a little. It was to be many years before I freed myself from weight and pain. But in moving into Peacehaven I made a beginning.

The children loved it. They grew. They bloomed. I think of it especially as Meg's place, Robert's place. They were the youngest. They made the creek, the orchard, the paddocks, their magic land. Robert ran there like a pagan, setting up over the years a blood-bond with those fifteen acres. I have seen him sniff the soil and would not have been surprised to see him taste it. It would not have startled or worried me to come upon him embracing a hillock or praying to a tree. Meg leaned more to house and yard. But she too formed a bond with growing things. We came upon her sitting among ripe apples ten feet off the ground, singing a little song of her own composing—a tuneless song, Edie told me, of love for branch and leaf and fruit. But she had sophistication enough to be ashamed. She cried out,
178

blushed, hid her face as though caught in some guilty act; and ran away among the trees and had to be hunted out at dusk and carried home in my arms.

Robert milked the cow and looked after the fowls. He would not let anyone share these tasks. There was though little danger of that. Emerson (he had left John Jepson's factory to come to Auckland with us) was an apprentice mechanic at a motor garage in the town. When home, which was seldom, he tinkered with his motorcycle, a filthy foul-smelling machine called Indian, decorated with a picture of a brave wearing a war feather. The sound of its engine as he tested it in the shed out the back penetrated even my deafness and gave Edie headaches. He came in to tea in greasy overalls; and ate dreaming. He did not see his brothers and sisters or hear what they said to him. He was blind and deaf. He dreamed his future: pistons and petrol, goggles and floating scarf. Already he was airborne.

And Alfred? Books were his passion. In a sense he was airborne too: in two senses. For he liked to sit in trees to read or write. From my study window I looked across the gardens and the stream and saw him high in a pine tree, up where the wind set it swaying. He wrapped his legs about its slender trunk and read with the needles pricking his throat and cheeks. Edie had a hard time washing gum from his clothes. She did not complain. Most of his poems were to her. But there were also odes to skylark, thrush, Ceres, Spirit of the Stream, and later hymns to Social Justice. At fourteen he looked like Shelley: small head round as a ball and cluster of auburn curls. I had great joy in him. He was the son who would carry on my work. And yet I never knew him well. I did not get close to him, as I got close to Robert, or even understand him, as I understood Emerson. He kept a part of himself hidden from me, and intuitively I did not try to uncover it. He admired me, came near to worshipping me, but I sensed he did not like me. I turned aside from this, and was pleased with his accomplishments. Yet I was afraid!

> Like one that on a lonesome road
> Doth walk in fear and dread,
> And having once turned round walks on,
> And turns no more his head;
> Because he knows, a frightful fiend
> Doth close behind him tread.

I had not had that glimpse and did not have that knowledge, but in the dark of the night, in my lonely times, I knew the dread.

But I was saying, Robert's preserves were in no danger from his brothers. With a startling lack of originality he christened the cow Daisy and the goat Nan. He knew which hens were laying well and which should be next for the pot. And it was Robert who got the tomahawk and chopped their heads off. He did it without regret or enjoyment. It was a job, and part of his life. He was patient with the Butters's boy Royce, who would come to watch, but turn his back, and peep over his shoulder, and squat to examine the entrails, and then run home and tell his mother how cruel Robert had been. But Robert was kind. He taught Royce to milk and to bait fish hooks, and during the Butters's Radiant Living phase fed him cold chops from our kitchen.

'Dad,' he said to me, 'I want to leave school.' He had a way of making decisions I must call elemental. There was no quarrelling with them. I looked at his plain honest face. It was time for him to finish with book-learning. He knew it. I knew it. His next season had come.

So Robert settled down to digging and composting, to planting and pruning. He ran a small flock of sheep on our fifteen acres: wormed and dagged and sheared them, put the ram in at the right time, and brought us his fattest lamb for Christmas dinner. He learned about bees and before long had half a dozen hives. In the summer and autumn he set up a stall at our gate and sold fruit and eggs and honey and vegetables. Edie and I rested on him. He was a piece of firm ground under our feet.

180

We loved him, and took him for granted; we trod on him unthinkingly. In the depression when I lost my money it was Robert who saved Peacehaven. For three years we bought practically nothing: fruit, vegetables, milk, meat, all came from his labour. He sold eggs and honey to the grocer, and kept us in tea and flour and clothes. He even gave me money to buy books. And as much as he sold he gave away. Sundays he set out with a sugar bag of corn or pumpkins slung on his shoulder and came home for lunch with the sack empty and no money in his pockets. And again he was taken for granted. One old man attacked him with his walking stick when he showed up late, and another complained of Codling moth in his apples. But Robert only grinned and shrugged. He made no judgements on people. People were in nature. He did not question the shapes they had grown into.

He brought home several girls. One, Barbara, we thought he might marry. But she, like the others, made the mistake of thinking his end was his beginning. He took her on a tour of his land—I thought of it soon as his—showed her his hives and his sheep and his fruit trees and squirted a jet of Daisy's warm milk in her mouth. They walked hand in hand, and lay on a blanket under an apple tree. They kissed—and maybe did more. I do not know. But sadly we watched the girl's happiness fade. She was an honest homely girl. She and Robert should have been right for each other. But the times had infected her with ambition, the world had made its brassy call to her, and she betrayed herself. She wanted possessions, glamour, the twentieth century. Poor damaged thing, she had gone past the point of finding happiness with a man who needed no more than a piece of land, seeds to plant, sheep to tend, potatoes and mutton for food, and a pine fire in the evening.

Edie heard their final argument. Robert said, 'I'll never change.' And the girl called him hick, hayseed, worm, imbecile. And stormed away, weeping. I believe she loved him.

Robert said, 'I don't think I'll ever get married, mum.'

69　His letter had said he did not want to see Felicity. She dropped me at the gate and drove away to visit a friend in Carterton. If she was hurt she kept it hidden well.

The letter-box said simply *Parminter*. But on the cream-stand someone had painted *F--- Farm*. Envy and hatred, I thought, even in this lovely place. For it was lovely. Over the fields mountains reared up like giants. Groves of native trees stood in the plain, sharp-edged as storybook islands. The red roofs of the barns and houses showed above orchard trees. Post-and-rail fences made geometrical patterns, bone-white, on the pastures. The cows were Jerseys, gleaming like bottle-glass. They chewed their cud placidly and watched me as I crunched up the shell-strewn drive to the settlement.

A child playing on a rope swing in a tree told me I would find Robert at the beehives. I went the way he pointed and found the hives on the far side of a row of guava trees. Robert was busy taking out frames of honey. Bees droned about him and crawled on his clothes. They seemed more bemused than angry. He banged a frame sharply on the edge of the hive and sent a small army of them tumbling back inside.

'Robert,' I called.

He waved at me not to come close. I watched as he filled his handcart with trays of honey. The white wax and brimming cells had a quality both rich and virginal. And Robert had the right to handle them. He too was in nature. It was fanciful in me to think the bees understood. They did not sting him. One of them stung me. Robert knew at once. And I supposed, fancifully again, that he had felt the pain of its death. He closed the hive he was working on and came to me.

'Is that the sting? Don't squeeze it.'

I could not for the fingers of my burned hand no longer worked. He took off a glove and scraped the sting out with his fingernail. Then he took a small tin of chalky powder from his

182

pocket, wet a little with spit, and rubbed it on the hurt place. That done, he turned to my bandaged hand. He took off his other glove and unwrapped the bandage. Half my palm and my fingertips were raw and red and damp. They had an unhealthy look that alarmed me. Robert straightened out my fingers a little. He slanted my palm at the sun. 'Let the sun get at it,' he yelled. Then he went back to his hives.

I had not seen him for four years. I stood and watched him work, with the sun making my hand tingle, and a pleasant fading itch in my bee-stung wrist. Four years in a prison camp had damaged Robert badly, but he was a man who had found useful work to do and was doing it well. Oliver should envy him.

He pushed his cart to a shed and stored the honey.

'Well dad, how are you?'

I gave him Margaret's love.

'Meg, how is she?'

'Well.'

'Meg's a good person.'

'She talks about you a lot.'

'We were together.'

'She'd like you to come and see her.'

'No, dad. Tell her I love her, that's all. What's Peacehaven like?'

'Much the same.'

'Do you still have sheep?'

We strolled through a field of tomatoes, where half a dozen people were busy picking, and a worked-out strawberry field, and a field of cauliflowers. The pickers looked up as we went by with a simple or glittering curiosity that gave me the feeling of being in an institution for the moon-struck and possessed. But Robert saw nothing unusual. He told me about his work, his troubles with insects and weeds and with a soil that was not all he would like it to be. His words came to me almost independently of sound. I knew what he would say before he said it.

'You never told me much about the camps, son.'

183

He had been in Strathmore, Whitenui, Hautu, and others whose names I forget; and in Mount Eden prison for a time. When I had gone to visit him he had smiled and said he was well. He had looked well. Nothing terrible had happened; nothing openly brutal or openly cruel. The camps were not as bad as Lyttelton jail. But a part of Robert died in them; died behind the wire, in the messes and dark icy huts; under contempt and restriction.

He said, 'I don't want to talk about those places.'

'I'd like to hear, Robert. I was in jail too.'

'No, dad. I won't talk about them. Come to see the new tank I'm putting in.'

Later we waited in the yard as people came up from the out-buildings and fields. They went into the dining-hall. An oldish man went by, bald like me, thick in his body and muscular in his face. He had cheerful and slightly mad eyes—the madness brought out by steel-rimmed glasses. Except for his working clothes he looked like a Californian evangelist. He nodded at me. Parminter, I guessed.

Presently a gumbooted woman came up. She approached Robert shyly. She had wispy hair and a bulging brow, almost hydrocephalic, and a body shaped like a bran-sack. I thought perhaps she was mentally retarded. Robert patted her on the shoulder.

'This is Betty, dad. My wife.'

The eugenicist in me was revolted. But I kept hold of the thought that Robert was happy. And I shook hands with the woman gravely and said I was pleased to meet her. We went into the hall. Robert gave me a chair beside his own. The table was a long planed board on trestles. There were fourteen adults and ten children. Parminter sat at the head with his sons (Robert's fellows in prison camp). This 'family' was, I saw, hierarchical. Parminter said, 'Our visitor is Bob's father. We welcome you to the Ark and to our meal.'

Everyone said, 'Welcome, Bob's father.'

Parminter blessed the food.

Yes, I thought, mad. But happy. Robert is happy. I thank God for that. I supposed I must thank Parminter too.

As we ate a young woman with red scrubbed cheeks and her hair in a bun—a look I associate with fundamentalist sects: less wholesome than they suppose—sat in a chair by the window and read aloud from the bible. I had put down my trumpet and so could not hear. Now and then Parminter stopped his chewing and said something, perhaps 'Hallelujah', and the table echoed him. Once he prayed, piercing the ceiling with his eyes. The others stopped their eating till he was done. Even I stopped. Then benignly he signalled us to carry on. The food was plain, home-grown, home-made: meal bread, butter, honey, sour cheese, apples, milk. Robert spread my bread to save my hand.

After lunch he said he had a job to finish in the carpentry shop. I watched him for a time; admired his skill with chisel and saw; but soon became restless and said I would wait in the gardens. I walked about until Parminter came out khaki-handed from the tomatoes and invited me to sit with him on a stile.

'How do you find Bob?'

'Very well. He seems to be happy here.'

'You sound surprised.'

'No. He's always been a simple person.'

Parminter took it as a compliment. 'One must be simple to come into the Ark. I'm sorry Mr Plumb, I can't ask you to stay.'

'Because I belong in the world?'

'The world is Satan's world. Gehenna. And yes, you belong in it. One must speak the truth. Baal, Mammon, Satan and his angels. You come from that, and I smell their smell on you.'

'It's good of you to let me visit.'

Parminter shrugged. 'Bob wanted it.'

'He's unregenerate then?'

'You may joke, but none will joke on the Day of Wrath.'

'Except those on the Ark.'

'There will be rejoicing on the Ark. And weeping and wailing and a rain of fire outside. You will see.'

185

'Will it be long?'

'Not long.'

I saw why a dirty word or two on his cream-stand did not up-set him. But looking at his mad good-humoured face, I felt pleased with him, almost fond of him. I would sooner spend an afternoon in his company than with Oliver, or for that matter with Sidney Holland or Peter Fraser. He saw behind the official face of things.

'I've heard you believe there'll be a Second Coming.'

'He is amongst us now.'

This was more than I had bargained for. I wondered if Parminter were about to reveal Himself. I admired him tremendously. To bring Ark and Second Coming together—what an achievement! But he still had surprises for me.

'He slumbers in one of our number. And on the Day a transformation will take place. The human skin will fall away and Christ will stand in His glory.'

This was theologically preposterous. This was out at the far reaches of delusion. But I was moved by it, and made aware that possibilities lay in me—that the rock of my sanity might under some chance encounter be cleft, and the waters of a crazy joy well out; and that I would call the event revelation, and believe. I pulled myself together.

'And who is the one?'

Parminter looked up—speared Heaven on his eye. Put a question, had an answer. 'I may tell you, Mr Plumb.'

'Not Robert?'

Parminter nodded wisely. He looked at me with pity, and with a respect that must have had something to do with my role as Joseph. 'Yes, Bob Plumb. Our Lord has entered the Ark by its lowliest gate and waits His time. And on the Day when the Vengeful Angels go forth Bob will be transformed. Bob will stand revealed as Christ and He will ride with His chosen ones over the fire.'

'But,' I said, 'but, none of this is in the bible. How do you know it?'

186

'The Lord called me into the mountains. He revealed it to me.'

'I see.'

'You do not, Mr Plumb. But never mind.'

'Does Robert know?'

'Only I know. And you. And I advise you to pray, Mr Plumb. There may still be salvation for you. You must have some special merit as father of the Vehicle.'

'But Robert?—you've let him marry.'

'That was his wish. Bob heals. He brings happiness. Betty has come out her sleep. She seeks her salvation. This is a miracle.'

'He works miracles?'

'He touches things and they heal. He is closing up the wound in Betty's mind.'

'Well, well,' I said. 'Well, well.'

'And I saw him touch your hand. That will heal too.'

'In the natural course of things. There's no miracle there.'

'Has it been getting better?'

'No, but——'

'You will see.'

'Who married them?'

'They came together at the Lord's command.'

'That's all very fine . . . What if they have children?'

'That would be a great joy.' He stood up, a solid and convincing man: he looked as if he belonged in a boardroom—except for those eyes, glittering with knowledge and craziness. 'But I think there will be no time for children. The Day is soon.' His eyes went red—the red of self-delight and righteousness and blood. I recorded through my sight the Voice booming in his skull. He turned and walked away from me, across his gardens, through the growing plants, towards the hills.

'Mr Parminter.'

'The Lord is calling me.'

'The police are going to raid you, Mr Parminter. I heard in Wellington.'

'We have no fear. He has chosen us.' He kept straight on. The others in the gardens knelt as he passed. And Parminter grew smaller, crossing paddocks, climbing fences. Cattle lumbered aside to give him passage. So might Moses have made his way up Mount Sinai.

Finding that thought in myself, I said, 'Oh no. This is just a case of religious dementia. I've seen them before.' And catching one of Parminter's followers grinning at another, I thought it unlikely they believed all he said. Wise of him to keep Robert's condition to himself. They might not be happy with it. Robert would be unhappy. But I watched Parminter out of sight with a feeling of regret. I liked the man.

Then I walked about the gardens and paddocks, seeing Robert's hand in everything: neatly carpentered kennels, firewood stacked in a special way, a compost bin built on the same design as the one at Peacehaven. Robert, I thought, might or might not be the lowliest gateway into the Ark, but he was plainly this farm's cornerstone. Parminter's saviour in the mundane sphere.

70 It was getting on for two-thirty when I went to the carpenter's shop. I came up on him quietly. He was sharpening chisels on an emery wheel. Cold sparks played on his hands. I touched him, 'Robert,' and pointed to my watch.

He switched off the wheel. 'Time to go?'

'I'm glad you're happy here, Robert.'

'It's a good place.'

'Come and sit in the sun for a moment.'

We found a seat at the head of the drive beside a grapefruit tree. Yellow fruit hung in the polished leaves. Over a trellis jasmine tumbled like water. But Robert himself denied the Arcadian setting. He smelled of sweat. Dry manure was caked on the soles of his boots. He wore a tartan shirt and an ancient grey silk waistcoat and a felt hat with its brim cut off. It sat on his head like a basin. He seemed to me neither a likely nor an unlikely vehicle for the time-marking Christ.

'How does your hand feel?'

'Better. Parminter says you heal people.'

He grinned evasively. 'I make them look after themselves.'

'But you look after Betty?'

'The others were getting at her. So I told her to keep with me.'

'And now you're married.'

He shrugged. 'It makes her happy.'

'How long are you going to stay here, Robert?'

He did not answer.

'You can have the cottage at Peacehaven.'

'Thanks dad, but I like it here.'

'What do you think of this ark business?'

'I don't take much notice of that. That's just Tom Parminter.'

'You don't believe the world's coming to an end?'

'I don't think about it.'

'He's gone off into the hills. God called him.'

'It happens all the time.'

'But this time it's different. He's going to announce the end of the world.'

'He's done that three times already.'

'Well,' I said, 'what happens? When it doesn't end?'

Robert shrugged. 'Tom just says God's testing him. He goes on a fast. And freezes himself in the trough. Or else he gets his wives to burn his feet with matches.'

'Good God.'

'Tom's mad. But he's not doing any harm.'

'You know who he thinks you are?' I had a vision of Parminter crucifying Robert, but put it out of my mind. It was too crazy, even for this place.

'I've got a fair idea,' Robert said. He touched my hand. 'The sun's doing it good. Don't let Felicity put a bandage on it.'

'But Robert, you know the police are coming out. They've heard about the free love going on here.'

'I keep out of that. Betty's enough for me.'

'They could close this place.'

'Then I'll go somewhere else.'

'With Betty?'

'She's my wife.'

'But not to Peacehaven?'

He shook his head.

'Why, Robert?'

He would not answer. I think he saw Peacehaven as part of the world, and the world had hurt him. The world in a way was hell; and this place, the Ark, stood outside it. Parminter's craziness was necessary to Robert. If he left here it would be for some place lost, some place where no one would ever find him. I knew I was seeing Robert for the last time. I loved him most of my sons. I took his hand and said goodbye to him.

Felicity's car drew up at the gate.

'Will you come and say hello to her, Robert?'

He shook his head.

'Goodbye, son.'

'Goodbye, dad.' He understood what was happening. I took some pleasure from finding him less simple than Parminter supposed, less simple than I had supposed.

I walked down the drive and got in Felicity's car.

'Is that Robert standing there?'

'Yes, that's him.'

'He looks like the village idiot.'

71 I told her she was stupid and malicious. I told her Robert was the best of my children.

The car boiled again on the Rimutaka hill. She lost her temper with it and sat on a boulder beside the road, waiting for it to cool off. I was feeling a little sick with the motion and I opened the glovebox to see if there might be something inside to settle my stomach. But there was only a rosary and a mess

190

of Catholic pamphlets. I shut it angrily. In my nauseated state I saw Felicity as crazy like Parminter.

The rest did us good. We apologized to each other. And as we drove along I reflected that my claim to have freed myself from the base emotions was a false one—and a good thing too. I was happy to be no longer a prey to my appetites; but the emotions? It had seemed to me once, after I had come into the Light, that I was about to be translated into a state of superhumanity. I could not feel as men feel. But, thank God, it did not last. Yes, I thank God. One does not live in the Light, one remembers it. That is the way. And remembering, one is both man and Man. Not always a comfortable state. For man may fall into anger, or rise into it (the healthy anger of the rational mind); and Man knows anger not, but only love; and a most unpleasant condition results, a kind of pins-and-needles in the mind.

We stopped for a cup of tea.

'Won't Max be worried?'

'He'll be all right.'

I guessed he would set about cooking our meal. I could not get used to that. To take my mind off it I told Felicity about Parminter. She gave a snorting Catholic laugh. 'Does Robert swallow that stuff?'

I explained about Robert: as much as she needed to know. I did not tell her his touch had set my hand mending. For that was so, I accepted it without question. Something had passed from the boy to me and I thanked him for it. Part of his goodness? Why should that quality not be transmittable by touch? and meeting no unbelief, why should it not heal body as well as mind? It met no unbelief in me. No question. For I loved Robert.

Felicity did not need to know about this.

A week later she cancelled my rail booking and announced she would drive me to Auckland. By that time my palm had grown a new skin.

72 When everything was in order at Peacehaven I began to write. I had tried the platform, now I would try the pen. Today I look at my books. They sit on my shelves in their brown covers, a trio without distinction of style or content: sunk without a trace. (In 1934 I posted copies to G. B. Shaw when he visited Auckland, and had a note from him from Panama. He had donated my books to the ship's library!) only *The Growing Point of Truth* found a publisher. The others I had to publish myself. That was a costly business.

But writing kept me busy. Through writing and my family I slowly came back to health. I won back the territories I had held before Lyttelton jail. I worked in a disciplined way. On weekdays only Edie and I were home. Edie was happy. Of all our houses she loved Peacehaven best. I would sit in my study, find a new thought, express it well I believed. 'We shall yet learn the healing effect of love! The world was full of hate when the post-war influenza epidemic swept over it. Hate prepares the body and mind for disease. But love heals literally!' Then I would look up and see Edie in the garden, weeding or planting, and, I could tell, humming a merry tune. I would think, what more does one need than useful work and a loving contented wife? I would write again. And then go out for lunch and find her playing the piano. It was in these years we began our 'paper chats'. I learned to read her lips a little too. She was the only one I could follow in that way.

In the weekends the view from my window changed. The landscape was filled with people. I would look out and see Alfred climbing to the top of his tree, Agnes picking plums with Meg, Robert building the summer-house, mowing the lawn, Esther in the shrubbery, hand in hand with butcher boy Fred Meggett, and Emerson setting out on his motorbike, with a sack of greasy parts strapped on the pillion seat. They did not always start me on a happy train of thought. I remembered Felicity. She was

192

teaching in Wellington, for Dan Peabody had entered parliament. She would find no happiness with Dan. I saw it now. And thought of Oliver, scratching away at the law, and Edith married to Critch, and Willis somewhere at sea. Having children is a stern course in reality. But I did not let myself sink into a despondent state. I looked out my window again. It was like a Breughel landscape: activity everywhere. Edie was cutting withered heads from the roses. Robert hammered on the summer-house roof. Down by the creek the goat nibbled blackberry leaves. Emerson broadsided home (and crashed into the rose garden once. Edie was digging thorns out of him for weeks). Fred Meggett went off with lipstick on his cheek. And here came Meg with a ripe plum for me. I knew a lot about these active beings (even the goat). Knew my children's discontents and dreams—Agnes fretting to get to California, Alfred to publish a poem, Emerson to fly. But they were not unhappy. And could I reasonably ask for more than that? My discontents were company for theirs. I would not admit to being unhappy either.

There was in any case no time for that. For here came Merle and Graydon Butters with news of their latest steps on their current Way. And look who was on the drive (Edie put her head down at her roses): my good friend Bluey Considine, puffing blue smoke in front of him; a broken-down steamer coming into port.

73 I had received a note from the Post Office asking me to call for a parcel. When I went along the Postmaster took me into his office. He was unfriendly.

'That's it, Mr Plumb. I think it's a bit of a cheek expecting us to deliver that.' The parcel sat in an ooze of pinkish brine in a tin tray on his desk. A length of twine still circled it and scraps of paper clung wetly to its sides. On one of these the Post Office staff had deciphered the surname Plumb.

'It is for you, I suppose?'

'Corned beef?' Bluey had wrapped it in several thicknesses of newspaper and tied brown paper round that. The letter he had put inside was now a glob of *papier mâché* held in place by twine. 'It's from my friend Mr Considine. I think he's coming to dinner.'

The Postmaster would not see the funny side of it. 'There's regulations governing perishable goods.'

I borrowed more paper, wrapped the corned beef up, and took it home. On the way Bluey began to overwhelm me. Who but Bluey would do a thing like this? I found myself hoping he was in Auckland to stay.

Edie was scandalized. She refused to cook the meat. I gave it to Robert who fed it to his dog. But I made her buy the same sort—brisket: silverside was short on fat, Bluey said—for our Sunday dinner.

And here now on the drive was Bluey himself. I ran out and we pumped each other's hands.

'Reverend,' he boomed, and the Butterses, approaching, stopped dead at the sound. Edie got in their way and side-tracked them into her roses.

'Now what's this, what's this contraption?' He took my trumpet and pretended to use it as a spy-glass, pointing it at Merle and Graydon, waist deep in greenery.

'Give me that, Bluey, or I won't hear a word you say.'

'A cornucopia, Reverend. A horn of plenty. But isn't that your good wife in the roses? I must go and give her a kiss.'

'She's got friends with her, Bluey. Come with me and I'll show you over the farm.'

So we walked about for half an hour, until Bluey began to complain of hunger.

'That was a nice piece of meat you sent, Bluey.'

'You got it then? I was worried. A friend of mine bet me it wouldn't go through.'

'You win your bet. But the Post Office wasn't pleased. So don't do it again.'

194

'I won't, Reverend. A nice roll of brisket, that was. I think I can smell it cooking.'

'Tell me what you're doing, Bluey.'

'Why Reverend, I'm working a system now. It's very demanding and I'm thinking of giving it up. There's too much paper work.'

'I haven't heard of this. Is it on the wharves?'

'No, no, Reverend, the gee-gees, the horses. I go over the whole field and pick out the ones that came first to fourth at their last start. Then I take the newspaper tips and tie those in with the totalizator betting. It's working against time that I don't like. And the running around. Bad for my feet. The returns are disappointing too. Sometimes I have to cover half the field. It takes all the fun out of it. I'm thinking of selling out.'

'Selling the system?'

'You can always find a buyer, Reverend. But my word, that corned beef smells good. Is she cooking it with carrots?'

He had no interest in union activities, or politics, or reading. His concerns were his next meal and his soul's destination. Yet because he was kind I loved him. And because he was strapped beyond hope of escape into the cruellest of his religion's torture machines I gave him my time and my arguments, and endured my wife's disapproval.

As we approached the house again she came from amongst her roses and gave Bluey a hand in a gardening glove. 'Mr Considine, how nice to see you.'

'Now mum, call me Bluey.' He had meant to kiss her. But Edie, as lady, was unkissable. Bluey was a man of resources though. He robbed her of her secateurs and cut a fine late bud from the nearest rose bush. 'Here, mum. Beauty to beauty calls.' It was not pleasure reddened Edie's cheeks. In haste I brought Merle and Graydon forward, and Graydon's mother (wearing her muse-visited look that day, and so to be introduced as Ella Satterthwaite). Merle and Graydon had the finest of social noses. It took them only a minute to sniff Bluey out; and sniff out too the discord he unwittingly sowed between Edie and me.

We sat about a cloth Meg had spread on the lawn and drank tea and ate scones spread with gooseberry jam. The smell of corned beef boiling in onion-flavoured water drifted out from the kitchen and stimulated Bluey's appetite. He sent Meg up to the house for another plate of scones.

Ella Satterthwaite, an ethereal lady, clad in something gauzy, pre-Raphaelite, hid her pleasure in this by raising her eyes. Her hearty appetite compromised her in her role as finer spirit, and she disguised it by looking elsewhere whenever she reached for food. Many a time I had seen her fingers come down in sugar or jam. Looking skywards, securing a scone, she said, 'You knew Mr Plumb in Thorpe, Mr Considine?'

'That's it, mum. When he was giving those bible-bashers what for.'

'I understand John Findlater was one of your circle?'

'He was. Drove us barmy, John did, with his poetry. All about singing streams and talking hills. I never knew there was so much gab in nature.'

'Mrs Butters—Miss Satterthwaite—is a leading poetess,' Edie said.

'Is that so? You've got the look of it mum, if you don't mind me saying.'

'You were privileged knowing John Findlater,' Ella said. She bit a scone with delicate greed. 'He is the best of our poets. He has the finest perceptions. One can forget the world in reading him and hear the voice that speaks from a leaf or stone.'

This was very much in her poetic style. There is a magic in naming. Ella had the beginnings of an understanding of it. John Findlater had it too. But only the beginnings. Their gaze was not clear enough, their understanding fell short in strength and stern-ness. Gentility and sentimentality spoiled them as poets. Leaf, stone. They could never leave it at that. It was too crude, it made them avert their eyes. So they added an adjective (and one led to two), a softening 'thought', a humanizing fancy. They posed their troublesome children in pretty clothes.

Ella said, 'John's most recent book is dedicated to Mr Plumb.

It compares him with the kauri, the forest giant, standing above the common trees and speaking with winds and storms.'

I blushed. And Bluey grinned. 'Have another scone, mum. They'll fatten you up. Too much poetry is a thin diet.'

'Thank you, Mr Considine. Delicious. Yes . . . "trunk as hard as iron and stern as love". I find the image a little unpolished myself.'

I was pleased to be twitched in their direction by Graydon and Merle—then alarmed. A kind of greed was on them to share their grief. They had not slept, they said; for they lived in the dreadful knowledge of having committed a crime against their son. They had damaged Royce, stunted the growth of his responses; they had allowed him to count, to read, to have black paint in his paintbox. All this before seven, before he had shed his milk teeth. The consequences were dreadful. A child's first seven years were years of natural response to his surroundings. The intellect must not intrude into this sacred time. Or notions of right and wrong. Why, Steiner said . . .

I understood. They had become Anthroposophists. Soon they would launch their campaign to convert me.

'Surely,' I said, 'Steiner has nothing against black paint?'

'Oh yes, it's not in nature,' Merle cried.

Not more than thirty feet away a blackbird (*Merle!*) was scattering pine needles. I did not think it would help to point it out.

'You probably used black paint when you were a girl. And look, it hasn't affected you. You've come to Steiner.'

'But my understanding is so misty. Our understanding. Isn't it, Graydon?'

'Yes. We're damaged beings. The trouble we have in perceiving the spiritual world.'

'The dreadful trouble. So often we've wished to be children again.'

'To begin again.'

'Yes.'

'Little children. Before the change of teeth.'

'Before the time of moral-feeling judgement.'

'And now poor Royce, we've done the same to him.'

They suffered. I was sorry for them. 'What is this spiritual world you talk about?'

'Reality. The substance behind the shadow.'

'We must come back from our exile.'

'To reality.'

'A lifetime's work,' I said.

'But we shall get there.'

'Yes.'

'Yes.'

Nudging each other along, they began to be happy. If I had told them that inside a year they would be into Radiant Living, or Christian Science, or psycho-analysis, or automatic writing, or tapping on the lid of Joanna Southcott's box (well, no, not that), they would have recoiled from me as from the serpent in their Eden. It was true all the same. How happy they would have been in California.

I did what I could for them: advancing the proposition of child as tough guy, who would be himself in spite of his parents' intentions. It was as near as I could get to saying Royce was a dull boy. (His only liveliness was in avoiding the demands made on him by Merle and Graydon's shifting beliefs.)

At half past twelve the Butterses went home and I sent Robert to muster the family for lunch. Bluey lumbered round the table and put a chocolate fish on the children's side plates, even Agnes's. They were too old to be amused by him. I had to say, 'Thank Mr Considine, please.'

'Thank you Mr Considine.'

'Gobble 'em up,' Bluey said.

Robert's excepted, their faces were hard and still. An ugly expression. I was sorry for them, and angry with them too. I set myself the task of making sure my family caused Bluey no pain. I am still at it. But at that Sunday meal I did not begin. It turned into a party, a celebration. Bluey became simply part of the background. For as I began to carve the roll of brisket we heard a sound on the back veranda. The clump of a heavy step, then a wooden tap: clump tap, repeated. (Even I heard: a psychic hearing.) It advanced into the kitchen.

'Whatever's that?' Edie was pale.

Something heavy banged on the floor. She rose, pushing back her chair. 'George?' I put down the carving implements. But we waited, we needed a sign. In a moment it came: a mouth organ playing a sailor's hornpipe. (He played it again later into my trumpet so I could share the moment fully.)

'Willis, oh Willis,' Edie cried. She ran. And we ran after her, jamming in the doorway. Bluey was left at the table, open-mouthed, looking at the corned beef, which would not be served for another half-hour now.

74 It happened in Copenhagen. A hawser snapped and the mashed lower part of Willis's limb went skidding on the deck. Into his wooden leg he carves the names of women he has known. Lately, I believe, he has run out of space, even though it's his fourth replacement he's walking on. But when he came home in 1923 there were only half a dozen names.

'Lily. Now Lily really was a stunner. She worked in a bar in Havana. Don't look so shocked, mum. You would have liked her. One of nature's ladies. And very kind. Very kind to me. I should have married Lily.'

All his stories ended in that way. 'Brigid. Ah yes, I should have married Brigid.' And Rosy and Dolores and Ingrid and Sue. The sea was not in his blood so much as adventure; and he had found his best adventures in women. He did not need to get on a ship again. The lovely creatures were everywhere. At first I took his talk of marriage for a piece of hypocrisy; but saw after a while that he expressed loyalty in this way. He did not exploit his women. They were true companions, loving and loved. And if he had to leave them in the end, well, there were plenty of songs to prove sadness was the lot of man. He sang them in the sunshine, in a tear-filled voice.

'What will you do now, Willis?'

'You're not going back to sea?' Edie said quickly.

'That little cottage down by the road? Is anyone living in that?'

'No. But it's tumbling down.'

'I've seen worse. Tell you what—you buy the paint and timber and I'll do it up.'

So Willis became our first tenant in the cottage. He relined the walls, put new iron on the roof, took out weather-boards feather-light with dry rot and replaced them with new. He painted the place red and white, put lino on the floor, sewed curtains, planted a garden. And soon I saw other men's wives entering or leaving the place at unrespectable hours.

'They're just friends, dad. They come to chat. They like my wooden leg.'

'I'm not a fool, Willis.'

'Dad, do you think I'd do anything wrong?'

'I don't know what that word means to you but I know what it means to other people.'

He laughed. He looked at me in a way both mischievous and honest. 'I make my girlfriends happy, dad. That's all. I help them enjoy themselves. You can't call that wrong.'

'The road to hell . . .' I said.

'You don't believe in that place.'

'All right, the road to trouble. To the law courts.'

And trouble came soon enough. The mayor of our town, relaxing one afternoon in a Queen Street cinema, looked down from his seat in the circle and saw his wife cuddling in the stalls with a wooden-legged sailor. They were eating ice-cream and resting their foreheads together.

At midnight I found at my door that sad and comic figure, the wronged husband. He bounced with rage, he trembled with indignation; and, alas, tears of pain overflowed his eyes and ran down his cheeks. He dashed them away with a show of manly

200

disgust. It took me a little time to understand what he was saying. Then I sent Edie in from the doorstep, ordered my craning daughters back to bed.

'Follow me.' We marched down the drive and through Willis's garden. A light was burning through his bright red curtains. I was glad we would not get him out of bed. A man in pyjamas is at a disadvantage. I had no hope of his innocence, but wanted him to keep what dignity he could. I marched in without knocking. And of course the woman was with him—a pretty buxom thing with tumbling hair. She was bare-footed and, I'm sorry to say, in her petticoat. They were cosily drinking large mugs of Ovaltine. I had not time to appreciate the scene. The husband, Richards, darted past me, shouting 'Slut!' I think, and aimed a slap at his wife. Willis came round the table, surprisingly quick for a peg-leg, and knocked him down. The rest is a mime. (I had not brought my trumpet.) I see the woman, Mirth, help her husband up and sit him at the table. I see Willis bring water in a basin. Together they bathe Richards' face. He cries, and pleads perhaps; and the woman weeps, but holds Willis tightly by the hand. Willis is kind and gentle. He is, I understand, something of a monster—a being of extreme simplicity, infinitely kind, moved to tears by his pain and the pain of others, but entirely without a moral sense. I wonder if this forty-year-old woman, Mirth, whose suitcase I now see through the open door, spilling undies and blouses on the bed, this apple-cheeked *bourgeoise*, understands the nature of the man she is leaving husband, car and bungalow for. I think not. Such simple people are never understood. But I see too she has caught a sight of happiness and is after it with both hands.

'Dad, you'd better get home. You'll catch a cold.'

'I'm not happy about this, Willis.'

'In the morning, dad. I'll see you in the morning.'

We met in my study. He told me Mirth was coming to live with him. I gave him notice. I would not have a *liaison* of that sort close to the girls. It was not as if it were a true union, I said, not in the eyes of God. And that was what mattered. A

201

man and a woman must be drawn together by more than the lusts of the flesh. Love in a higher sense, duty, the wish for children, these were the moral and eugenic and divine bases on which a 'marriage' rests. Anything less was a piece of self-indulgence. I would not have it under my nose. I would not have Edie insulted and my girls led astray.

Willis laughed. 'O.K. dad, O.K. I'll move out. As a matter of fact I was going to talk to you. I've got my eye on a piece of land up the valley. It's just right for grapefruit and lemons. Now if you could see your way to letting me have a couple of hundred pounds . . .'

75 I helped him buy the place. I could not be angry with him for long. He settled in with Mirth and lives there still. I'm told he and his wife and children and his other lady friends practise naturalism, which means apparently running round in the summer with no clothes on. Emerson told Esther, who repeated it to me, not without relish, that on a recent visit to Willis's orchard he had come upon the naked peg-leg chasing an equally naked Mirth among the grapefruit trees. 'He caught her too.'

He has, as he told me once, a talent for making his women happy. Mirth made a good choice. Nymph at sixty. Few women can have known that.

76 Agnes and Emerson left Peacehaven in 1925. They took the same ship for California. Emerson was off to see the world. He would go on to England and the Continent. 'When I come home,' he joked, 'I'll be flying my own aeroplane.' Agnes though meant to stay with her sisters in San Francisco.

I did not believe I would see Agnes again. That land, that rich, noisy, blue and golden land, for me, for Edie, a dry and bitter place, was full of a sweetness my daughters learned the taste of. It drew them fatally and made of them people whose language I do not speak. Agnes too. I waved. I felt the streamers snap, and saw the smartly dressed pretty girl waving madly from her high rail as the ship turned heavily into the stream. No, she would not come back. No more than Rebecca. Hers was almost as surely the 'undiscovered country'.

We went home sadly to our house by the creek. Esther, Alfred, Robert, Meg. We had four children left.

More than I had before I passed my time with them. I wrote my books, I lectured in Trades' Halls and Mechanics' Institutes and in the Unitarian Hall. But I came home to Edie and my children with a sense of having come out of a monochrome world into a coloured. I gardened with Robert, or walked in the orchard with Meg. I listened to Alfred's poems. His clear thin voice came down my trumpet like water. Esther, a loud, happy girl, kissed me on top of my head and wiped the lipstick off with her handkerchief. Even in her vulgarity I took pleasure. I had the sense of living in my own and my family's history, but not in the world's. In that decade the feeling was widespread. The war had been more than we could grasp. Difficult now to apprehend Mankind. It took the depression to bring us back to that.

One day behind the summer-house I came on Fred Meggett kissing Esther in what I took to be an improper way.

'Young man,' I said, 'you get off my property. And Esther, I'll see you in my study. At once, if you please.'

She stood there five minutes later, grinning. 'I'm going to marry him, dad,' she yelled. 'So you'd better cool off.'

'What,' I said, 'marry a butcher?'

'Hey, where's your socialism? One man's as good as another, isn't he?'

'It's not his trade I object to——'

'Besides, Fred's not a butcher any more. He's a land agent now.'

'I won't have him kissing you in that way. Not where Margaret might see.'

'Meg knows what's what, dad. Don't you worry about that. Besides, I've got to give poor old Fred something. I've had him on the string for four years now. He'll go off the boil if I don't keep him stoked up a bit.'

'I'm disappointed in you, Esther.'

'I know. But I like you. I think you're a good old stick. Now dad, I want you to do something for me. You can still marry people can't you?'

'I can. But———'

'Here on the lawn. I don't want any churches.'

'No Esther, I won't do it. I can't approve———'

'Come on, dad. For me. Now say you will.' She stroked the top of my head. 'I'd love to be married by you. By my own father. And Fred's not too bad. He's really quite human, you know.'

So in the spring, beside the blossoming plum tree, I married Esther to Fred Meggett. Everybody came. Oliver brought Beatrice up from Wellington. Felicity came with Dan Peabody. (Oliver was stuffy about that.) Willis and Mirth were there. The Butterses walked over the bridge, bringing Graydon's mother, who turned herself into Ella Satterthwaite the moment she understood that the man exclaiming over the plum blossoms was John Findlater himself. Edie could not prevent me from asking Bluey. I promised to set Andrew Collie to keep him out of mischief. For Andrew was there too, happy as a spaniel off its leash, and full of the songs of Burns for this happy day. John Willis, whom I had not quite forgiven for his bungling defence of me, and whom I associated with Rebecca's death, turned up in time to give the bride away. I found myself glad to see him. He was just on his feet again after yellow jaundice and had only decided to come at the last moment. These and a number of bright young girls, chattering like birds, were the guests from Esther's side. (There was too, I almost forgot, our new tenant in the cottage—a schoolteacher, Wendy Philson.)

Fred's people I did not see much of. They seemed to talk mainly about race horses.

I married Esther and Fred—the Unitarian service. Then we

feasted. I kept away from that. I have never liked to see people gobbling food. I sat down on the lawn and talked with John Willis. And gradually my friends came about me. I felt like Socrates. There was though an elegiac note in our talk, not just for John Jepson, dead of a stroke, but for times that were gone. Our beliefs were not dead, far from it, but we found they no longer led us into actions. Still, we were happy. The bowl of the lawn was full to its brim with sunlight. Over by the plum tree Willis was playing merrily on his mouth organ. Pretty girls were everywhere, in white and blue and lavender frocks. We could smell their perfume and hear their happy talk. (My trumpet had a sharpened sense that day. I heard with a fine-ness that had not been mine for years.) Edie strolled about with Meg at her side. They drew my eye like the focal point in a painting. I saw their mother-and-daughter likeness—a liquid movement, a happy eye; and saw too their spiritual beauty. Self had its proper place in them. They were loving and charitable beings (always excepting their dislike of Bluey).

I saw them a second time, and a third. Then the currents of my life flowed together. I passed into the room of my own soul. I faced the Light, and knew the way to go, and entered it. 'Behold I show you a mystery.' Which was made plain. And though I had not strength to endure it long it did not matter. As I have said, one cannot live in that place. Memory is enough for one's daily living. I had my glimpse, my time. It was the vision splendid. A great light, a bliss, a splendour, a white radiance, streamed through me. The whole of my life had been a preparation for this moment. I rose from the tomb of my body and its inheritance and, as Carpenter says, identified with the immortal Self of the world. 'I, the imperfect, adore my own Perfect.' These are better expressions of it than I can find. For myself I say, I knew with all my being, in every fibre, that love is Life. I had known it already. But this was more than intellectual knowing. All doctrines, all other beliefs, were blown away like dead leaves in a storm. 'When I burn with pure love, what can Calvin or Swedenborg say?' I had seen God.

'Are you all right, George?'

'Fine. Never better.'

John put his hand on my shoulder. (The others had wandered off.) 'It's good to see you looking so well. After Christchurch.'

'That was a bad time. It seems far away.'

'George, I've sometimes thought, you must hold me partly responsible for . . . certain things.'

'No.'

'Rebecca . . . I should have been watching.'

I comforted him. The jaundice weakens a man and makes him emotional. 'Enough now, John. We've come to terms with that time.'

'Yes, but——'

'No buts, John. Do you know, I think I could prescribe for you. Do you know what I'd prescribe?'

'No.'

'A good woman. A wife. You need looking after.'

He blushed. 'They're hard to find, George.'

'Nonsense. Look at my lawn. Full of them. Shall I find you one?'

'No, no.' He looked alarmed.

Andrew came back; and John Findlater (Ella not far behind). Felicity sat down and put her hand on mine. Dan lay next to her, resting his head on a fold of her dress. At this time their love was at its strongest. We spoke of the old days again: of the Thorpe strike, and my heresy, and mad wild Morrison Macauley, and street-corner spouting, and draughty halls. We spoke of John Jepson and Edward Cryer. Bluey came up with a plate full of food. 'Ah Reverend, that John Jepson. Many's the fine meal I've eaten in his house. There's a lot to be said for ill-gotten gains.'

'Ill-gotten, Bluey? You can't use that word of John.'

'A capitalist though,' Andrew cried. 'A man can earn so much with his own two hands. After that it's ill-gotten. John had more than his share. Someone went short, that's plain to see.'

'Well Andrew, we won't go into that. Let's remember old

friends kindly. Now give us a poem for my daughter's wedding day. Give us "John Anderson". I haven't heard that in years.'

He obliged—that beautiful poem. And then gave us 'The Rigs o' Barley'. Ella, I could see, found them too rustic; and the latter improper. She asked John Findlater to recite us something of his. But John had too much sense. He knew real poetry when he heard it. Pressed though, he extemporized a couplet:

'George Plumb, your name speaks true:
It tells of deeps and of the straight line too.'

It pleased me, for it was kindly meant. I said, 'Well, well, I hope it's true. It needs a bit of polishing.'

Off to one side I saw Alfred smiling. I had not known he was close. I grinned at him. The boy was wild about T. S. Eliot, and if he could make anything of that stuff had earned his right to look down his nose a little at John Findlater. Seeing him there, and seeing into his mind, I had a sense of time, of generations. Beyond him, private, but not I thought unhappy, was the young woman, Wendy Philson: square of body and, I saw, with eyes that were beautiful. Now there was a girl for John Willis. Not too young, not frivolous. In fact, a woman, not a girl.

John said, 'Your father tells me you write poetry, Alfred.'

'Yes,' said the boy, going red.

'I'd like to hear some.'

'So would I,' John Findlater said.

'No, I'm sorry. I don't read in public. Besides . . .'

'Besides?'

'I don't think you'd understand it.'

'Ah, I see, it's in the modern manner.'

John Willis persisted. 'I'd like to read it though. Will you give me some?'

'All right,' Alfred said ungraciously. 'But it's a waste of time. You won't understand it.'

His arrogance pleased me. Everything pleased me on that afternoon.

77 Alfred was nineteen, and full of scorn at the jollity and back-slapping of Esther's wedding. Walking about among Fred's racing acquaintances, listening to Meggett senior's ribald talk, and observing Fred's mother weeping like a rainstorm, he gave to his mouth a Byronic twist. Esther's chattering friends—and there were some pretty girls amongst them—might as well have been a tribe of monkeys. He silenced them with a down-slanting look. Esther herself had always been close to him, and he had an affection for her that he tried to make appear tolerant. It was in fact as strong as any of the multifarious loves that kept our domestic air humming with the noise of a giant top. He was angry with her for marrying Fred, a 'peasant'.

The couple came down from the house to set off on their honeymoon. People threw rice and confetti (Robert frowned to see it on his lawn) and two young men tied an old boot to the car. A girl wrote *Just married* with lipstick on the window. Earlier I would have turned my shoulder on this. (Oliver turned his shoulder.) But I took Edie's arm and we moved through the crush to kiss Esther goodbye. She was looking coarse and happy. 'Goodbye, Esther,' I said. 'I wish you joy, my dear.'

'Don't worry, I'll have plenty of that.'

'I'll look after her, George,' Fred Meggett said. I had not invited him to call me George.

They got in the car. 'Dad,' Fred called, and his father came to the window. Fred handed him a scrap of paper. 'Will you get that on for me?' Meggett senior looked at the paper. 'Pot Luck? It hasn't got a bolter's, son.'

'You just get it on.'

'Goodbye, goodbye,' everyone called.

'Goodbye mum, goodbye dad. Alf, come and kiss me,' Esther cried.

Alfred kissed her cheek through the open window. Rice rattled on the car like hail; and Fred drove his unblushing bride away.

78 Edie would have liked to see the guests go home after that. But they stayed for another two hours, drinking beer Fred's father brought out from his car. 'Can't let me boy get married without having a snort or two, George,' he explained. Soon the young ones were dancing to the sound of Willis's mouth organ.

I looked for Alfred. A sense of superiority can be a painful thing. Meg told me he had gone into the orchard. I found John Findlater strolling there with Ella Satterthwaite. John recited his verses; and listened to Ella's with only the faintest appearance of bending down. I left them to it. Alfred, they told me, was down by the creek with John Willis and Miss Philson; holding forth on a poem of Eliot's—'The most unmitigated tosh,' John said. They had had to come away to avoid saying hurtful things.

The three by the creek were cooling their feet in the water. I came up on them and sat down to one side. John looked at me gravely. He gave a small nod I took to mean he found my son a remarkable boy. I angled my trumpet at Alfred long enough to hear him say, 'We are the hollow men, we are the stuffed men, leaning together, headpiece stuffed with straw,' and then put it down. Clever young people cannot help being taken in by the current nonsense, even when it has a death-smell about it. It would not help to condemn this stuff to him. I did not doubt, in my glowing state, that he would come through on his own. I was pleased to see him treating Wendy Philson as an equal, and pleased to see Wendy attending to him with an interest more than literary. Many a boy has been helped on to his path and given a push along it by a sensible older woman. Wendy was sensible, no doubt about that: sensible clothes, sensible manner, sensible opinions. But older? Not by more than a year or two. She wore graveness like a garment, covering her accidental youth. I was pleased she thought Alfred worth listen-to. And I hoped if she meant to befriend one of these men it would be Alfred. John, I saw now, was too old for her. And alongside her would become conscious of his lightness of weight. While Alfred might take weight. I thought too that friendship with Wendy Philson was something *I* might try for.

'I wouldn't look on Eliot as a god,' she said, 'or even as a prophet. If he's anything he's a doctor. And not a healing one either. A diagnostician.'

'He's a poet,' Alfred said sensibly; and that was a point to him.

Wendy smiled. 'Yes,' she said, 'and it seems to me a damaged one.'

'How?'

'Damaged by the times he lives in. Oh I know, all poets and all people are that, although you can put it a different way. Shaped, I mean. But it seems to me these new poets have nothing to celebrate. True poetry is celebration.'

'What is there left to celebrate? After the war?'

'Why, God. He still exists, doesn't He? Poetry is an attempt to find God.'

'No. Not for me.'

'What is it then?'

'An attempt to understand man.'

'Isn't that more or less the same thing?'

John Willis smiled at me. He felt left out. I plucked him by the sleeve. I wanted to stay and listen, but wanted more to leave Alfred and Wendy to themselves. John dried his feet with his handkerchief and when he had his shoes on we took ourselves off. We strolled down through the orchard. Angling my trumpet cunningly, I heard Ella say:

> 'The sparkling thrush, the sparkling thrush,
> Upon the orchard bough,
> He sings of past and future,
> But never of the now.'

'I would have thought the opposite,' I said.

'I like it better though,' John said, 'than headpieces stuffed with straw.'

79 John was ill again that night. He should not have travelled. We put him in Esther's bedroom; and kept him with us through the spring.

Edie enjoyed looking after him. For her he meant the old times: her mother, Florence, the house in Linwood. He made her face Rebecca's death again. It strengthened her and brought her peace. She never lost her belief in a personal survival for the soul.

It was a happy season. Alfred sat his university exams and said they were laughable (meaning easy). In his holidays he worked on farms about the district, making hay, cutting scrub. I did not worry about him. I no longer had the sense of secret places in his mind. He was open, glowing with happiness and expectations of fame. He did not read me his poetry, knowing I did not care for its new direction; but read it to Wendy Philson. Good. She had a better understanding than I of modern verse, would indicate to him more acceptably, though no less plainly I hoped, that it was muddy stuff, diseased—'rats' feet over broken glass'—and that Alfred must raise his eyes and study Man.

He and Wendy spent much of their time together. I saw no more than a friendly affection between them. That was exactly what I had wished for. I thought of Alfred as setting off on a long journey on which he would make himself. And Wendy I saw as a rock, herself already. He might come back to her when he was a man, but now it was enough that they should put their heads together and talk about poetry; and laugh more freely than they laughed with other people. John, I thought, was jealous of that. Wendy was formal with him.

My own explorations continued. My experience of the Light

211

lay in me like seed. It was the business of the rest of my life to make it grow. I do not mean I abandoned my work for social justice. But my larger work was to reach understanding of my revelation. I was swollen a little with pride, but sufficiently aware of it not to be damaged. And as I read through that Spring it burned away and dropped from me as a kind of ashes. Spiritual excitement burned it away. I read everything I could get my hands on about the great cases of illumination from God. I read the Gospels in a new light. And studied the lives and teachings of Mohammed, and Paul, and Gautama the Buddha, and Plotinus and Jacob Behmen. I looked into Dante again, Pascal, Blake, Spinoza, Edward Carpenter, my old friend Ralph Waldo Emerson. I had not read so intensely before, and have not again. And I came to believe I was candidate for a second illumination, a more glorious one. I had only stood in the margins. It was enough, more than enough, for the rest of my days. But I saw I might be one of the few called to the Heart of things. Earthly, domestic, mortal cares became a black and troublesome weight, but could not hold me back. Man's dual nature was shown me clearly; soon I would be free of the lower part. I kept before me Edward Carpenter's lines: *That day—the day of deliverance—shall come to you in what place you know not; it shall come but you know not the time.*

The time would be soon.

One Saturday morning I set off to walk into town. I kept up my habit of walking and often covered five or six miles at a time. Edie and Meg were visiting Esther, Alfred was working on a neighbour's farm, and Robert helping Willis in his orchard. John had said he would keep me company but cried off at the last moment to write letters. He was in his last week with us. I joked with him, saying perhaps he meant to slip down to Wendy's. He blushed again. He was a man for black-blushing and for pallors.

I walked along the road at a good brisk pace. The creek ran on my left, a chain of deep slow pools of a muddy green linked by yellow-white rapids. On my right a clay bank rose from the

212

side of the road, which swam a little in the bright Spring sun. I thought of Lyttelton jail and the darkness that had fallen on me there; and of my present quest. I had come to think of the goal as 'cosmic consciousness'—R. M. Bucke's term—a consciousness of the life and order of the universe, an intellectual enlightenment, a state of moral exaltation and quickening of the moral sense, and a knowledge of immortality. All this, Bucke said, comes to one in an instant, as a fire within the self, and it may never come again. But one remembers; and possesses a new sense or faculty. It has had many names. Jesus called it the Kingdom of Heaven; Paul called it Christ or the Spirit of God. For Buddhists it is Nirvana; while Mohammed called it Gabriel. Dante: Beatrice. Whitman: My Soul. I thought if it came fully to me I would call it Love. I remembered too, as I walked along, that Bucke who had had the faculty himself had never lost it, even in periods of black depression. I found that a comforting thought, both in its upward and downward looking directions. I did not think I would care to be entirely without troubles.

My thoughts were broken by the distant cry of 'Reverend', coming, it seemed, from the most unilluminated times of my past. When I had shaken myself back into the world I saw, and was glad to see, Bluey hoisting himself to his feet from his resting place in the shade of a tree. I shook hands with him and indicated my ears.

'It's lucky I heard you at all, Bluey. I haven't got my trumpet.'

He shouted something about finding himself barred from the Avondale race-course. (I never discovered why.) So he had got on the bus and come to see me. He also said something about lunch.

We walked back together. Bluey talked but I heard only a word or two. It was, I think, all about horses and hellfire. I told him there was no such thing as hellfire.

When we arrived at the house I sat him down in a cane chair on the veranda and went to fetch John. I felt I would like help

213

with Bluey that day. But John was nowhere in the house. I took Bluey a plate of biscuits and told him I would not be long.

'No hurry, Reverend,' he said, munching.

I went out into the orchard to look for John. I did not hurry. Bluey was happy and the morning beautiful. I crossed the brick bridge and turned into the apple trees, where the green fruit was taking a blush of pink. Far away in the Butters's garden Ella in something gauzy and blue was walking in the roses. The white of Wendy's cottage shone through the trees. I hoped I would not find Wendy in John's company. I was jealous for Alfred's sake. I told myself that was unworthy. Wendy was free to do as she chose. I reminded myself she seemed not to care for John. I went through the pear trees and the peach and climbed a little hill overlooking the corner where our quince tree grew. There I stood. To the couple in the grass I must have risen like some frightful beast from their most hideous dreams.

I saw what it was inevitable I see. It stunned me. I had a moment of utter blackness. I almost fell. When I came to my senses I found I had gripped the branch of a tree to hold myself on my feet. And my mind became full with a clamorous boiling rush, full of Old Testament bloodiness. I cried that they were unclean, that they were filth. And I called down death upon them, I called down brimstone, fire; I smote them so they died. It is true. I saw life go out of their eyes. I saw a death come on them. Their flushed men-faces grew white and bestial. They croaked like toads. And I fled from them, I fled back through the orchard, but it was an orchard no longer, I ran through the slimepits of Siddim, where the kings of Sodom and Gomorrah fled and fell. I ran on the plain and did not turn my eyes, for behind me the smoke of the evil cities went up as the smoke of a furnace.

So my early training kept a kind of doubtful sanity in me. It held me on a course. I remember thinking Edie would become a pillar of salt.

When I came to the house I ran to my study. But there was no refuge there. My books had turned to ashes. And in a moment I was scrabbling in my drawer, bringing out the little tin box in which I kept a store of golden sovereigns. I did not count them. I took a handful and ran out of the house.

Alfred and John were coming over the bridge. I met them, raised my palm to ward them off.

'Don't come into my house. You are dead. You are dead to me, Alfred. Never come here again.' And I flung the sovereigns on the bricks in front of him. 'Your name isn't Plumb. There's money to change your name.' And I fled again, for I saw the danger of his face becoming human.

I shut myself in our bedroom. I lay trembling on the bed in which Alfred had been conceived and borne. It was my right to kill him, kill the beast, as God had killed those creatures of filth long ago.

So in my mind I killed him; and killed him again.

Bluey found me there when he came searching. He covered me with a blanket. Somehow or other he made a cup of tea. And he sat with me until Edie came home.

80 It is not surprising I behaved as I did. I had believed my spiritual strength, my certainty of my self, gave me the power to gaze steadily on human depravity. Gaze; and forgive. It was not so. More than I knew, I was a man of my times. I might question religious doctrine, or struggle to alter a political system, even smile on a daughter's irregular union; but my location was fixed in the matter of sex between men. I had never made a study of it, had prevented it from even crossing my mind. It was there all the same, a black invisible planet in a sky of stars. Many years later I opened my bible at Genesis, chapter 19, and read of the sins of Sodom and Gomorrah, and of those cities' destruction. The margins are blank. Mitchell had said there was not an empty square inch. He had not looked there. But how had I understood what was spoken of, what that 'knowing' was the men of Sodom planned? Someone must have

whispered it to me. (The commentary I used kept a decent silence.) Did something in myself whisper it? In any case, I knew. For the language of that chapter boiled from my mouth when I discovered Alfred and John Willis under the quince tree.

I told Edie I had sent Alfred away. I had found him sinning. And when she pressed me, said his sin was the sin of Sodom. Her calmness was extraordinary. I guessed she had known, below full consciousness certainly; but known the truth of his nature, and forgiven him. Now it was out in the open she was calm. Her love was deeper than mine. It gave her the means to forgive him fully.

I said, 'You're not to see him, Edie. I forbid it.'

'You don't have that power, George.'

'You're my wife, and I forbid it.'

'George, you must listen to me. We have the rest of our lives to spend together. And so we must never talk of this again.'

And we never did. But Alfred lay between us for the rest of our days. I saw her on Saturday afternoons put on her hat and gloves and walk off to visit him. She smiled at me like a stranger. And I thought, Edie has become a pillar of salt. There was no understanding of what she was doing—not for me—and the biblical words gave me a painful comfort. They pointed to mysteries; and where mysteries were there was hope of miracle. But I could not come to her. We reached out our hands but only our fingers touched.

She met him, I think, at Esther's place. (I wonder how Fred liked that.) Esther never spoke of Alfred to me. Nor did Robert or Meg. Willis was the only one who dared. I had made up my mind to call him Theo, but he refused to answer to the name.

'You chose Willis dad and now you're stuck with it. Now tell me what this nonsense is all about.'

I told him to mind his business; and that I would call him what I pleased.

'Did you catch them in the act?'

'Willis,' I cried, 'be quiet.'

216

'Look dad, I've been on the ships. I've seen it all. You can talk about it with me.'

I put down my trumpet. But he simply bent close and raised his voice. 'What were they doing? Kissing? Holding hands?'

'Will you get out of my study.'

'A little bit of -----, eh?' (Even today I'm ignorant of whether the word is slang or clinical.) 'It happens quite a lot, dad. In the best of circles.' (And today I see he meant this as a joke.)

'Will you go away?'

'And you turned him out for it? You old parsons really take the cake.'

'I won't have you talk to me like that.'

'O.K., dad, O.K. I guess it's time he got out in the world. He'll manage without your blessing.'

'I won't have him mentioned, Willis. *Theo.* Not in my house.'

'Banished to outer darkness, eh? Well, if that's how you want it. But -----.' (The word again.) He laughed. 'Poor old dad. You've got a lot to learn.'

A few months later he told me John Willis had come to Auckland. He and Alfred were sharing a flat. And Alfred, though he had left my sovereigns lying, had changed his name.

I said I was not interested.

For more than twenty years no one spoke his name to me again.

81 Meg must have wished to many times. For a girl of her affectionate nature and sentimental habit of mind it must have been agony to have a brother banished. She thought love could heal all wounds and bridge all gulfs. The affair was a lesson in reality for her. She was wounded by it in her courage and faith. Hardened by it, I think, and checked in her growth. But through the joyless Christmas that came on us soon she gave Edie and me the loving company we could not give each other. She left school at the end of that year and enrolled at the

217

Teachers' College. I had wished her to go to university. She said she was not clever enough. That was true. Her mind was receptive of 'thoughts' not ideas. Her reading had already disappointed me. She was moved to tears by the novels of Mary Webb. She kept by her bed a shelf of favourite books: *Precious Bane*, *The Constant Nymph*, *The Forest Lovers*, *The Small Dark Man*. They were there for many years—are still there, I think.

Sentimentality was her vice, as gentility was Edie's. She was in touch with the springs of the religious life, in a sense one of the elect. Goodness was natural to her. Love was natural. But between response and understanding her feelings were spoiled; between conception and expression they passed through a falsifying element. It took her many years, our loss of Alfred, marriage, motherhood, to come to terms with the real. By that time she was a diminished being.

But Christmas, 1926. She gave us love. We were not critical. I took to eating alone again. Meg brought my evening meal to me in the study. Sometimes she stayed to talk. I tried to explain to her my belief in man's spiritual destiny. She could not grasp the logic of it, but found the idea beautiful. I talked in large optimistic terms—because I had lost my path. I was in darkness again and felt I might never come out of it, and so I made loud noises to persuade back my memories. For unlike Bucke I had not retained them in my deep depression.

Meg sat with me, listened; now and then made a response— that she thought something I said was true or beautiful. And when she really thought so tears came into her eyes. As I came to think of my own cares less I saw I had done a great wrong to her in letting her get that way. I did not see how I could go about undoing it.

82 Edie came to me in my study. 'Will you have tea with us tonight, George? Meg's young man is coming.'

'I didn't know she had a young man. Is it serious?'

'Everything Meg does is serious. He's a plumber's apprentice.'

'A plumber's apprentice? What's his name?'

'Fergus Sole.'

'Can't she do better than a plumber's apprentice? There must be young men at the Training College.'

'She likes his dirty hands, George. She thinks they're honest.' She tried to joke, but I saw she was troubled.

'Have you met him, Edie?'

'Once. In the street.'

'What's he like?'

'Very polite. He behaved very well.'

'Is that all?'

'He's good looking. At least Meg thinks so. And he dances well. She said to tell you he plays cricket too.'

'I don't like the sound of this.'

'He's a pleasant boy, George. Be nice to him. It mightn't go any further.'

Fergus Sole was late. And when he came he beamed at me in a way I thought idiotic. I could not see that he was good-looking. His face was flushed and his eyes, I thought, slightly crossed. He gave me a handshake that made my finger bones creak. Meg was the colour of a tomato. She looked as if she might be going to punch him.

We sat down to eat our meal. With the first thrust of his fork Fergus Sole scattered peas over the table cloth. He looked at them stupidly. Then he began to spear them one by one. He worked with a fearful concentration. It took several minutes. One elusive pea he trapped under his water glass. ' 'Scuse fingers.'

He popped it in his mouth. ' 'Licious peas, Mrs Plumb.' Then he scattered his second forkful.

'Oh Fergus,' Meg screamed. She jumped up and dragged him from the table and out of the room.

'What's wrong with that young man?' I said. 'Is he sick?'

Robert grinned.

'Well, what is it? Tell me.'

'He'll be all right, George,' Edie said. 'He needs a little sleep, that's all.'

'Why should he need a sleep?'

Edie made no reply. I pointed my trumpet at Robert.

'He's blotto, dad. Pickled up to the eyeballs.'

'Robert, I won't have that language,' Edie said.

'Well anyhow, he's drunk.'

I could not believe it. I had never had a drunk man at my table, or in my house. I could not believe Meg would introduce one.

In a moment she came back, very still in the face.

Edie said, 'Where have you put him dear?'

'On the sunporch.'

'Will he be warm enough?'

'I don't care if he freezes to death.' She began to cry. Edie took her away. That left Robert and me.

'Do you know anything about this fellow, Robert?'

'He was in the first cricket eleven at school.'

'And?'

'The girls all liked him.'

'Anything else?'

'I think he's a good bloke.'

'A good bloke. I must look up my dictionary.'

'A nice person, then.'

'Nice can't be used in that way.'

Robert shrugged. 'You'd better get used to him, dad. Meg's going to marry him.'

'But why for heaven's sake?'

'She's in love.'

220

'Love, love. She hasn't the faintest idea what the word means. And I'll say whether or not she gets married. Your mother and I.' Robert just grinned at that.

Later Meg came to me in the study. She crept in in her old way and sat on my footstool.

'He's not usually like that, dad.'

'I should hope not . . . I hope you're finished with him now, Meg.'

'Oh no. Oh no. I love him.'

'Nonsense, my dear. Love is for grown up people.'

'I'm eighteen.'

To me she seemed no more than eleven or twelve. She was open, eager, silly. She saw things that were not there. I shuddered when I thought of this creature thrust into an adult world. At thirty, I thought, she would become a woman. She would be fully grown. And worth knowing. And ready to love and be loved by some adult man. But the world would not leave her alone to grow. Fergus, or whoever replaced him, would not leave her alone. She was not to have time. I saw it plainly. I saw how life would break her.

'He's a drunkard, Meg. He'll make your life a misery, my dear.'

'No, dad. He doesn't drink. He hardly ever drinks. He was nervous about meeting you, that's all.'

'Am I an ogre?'

'No. But you do frighten people.'

'Me?'

'You're clever. And Fergus is not.'

'I wouldn't have expected him to be. A plumber's apprentice.'

She looked at me reproachfully.

'All right, my dear. I'm sorry. That was unworthy. But tell me, has he any interests? What do you talk about?'

'Oh, everything.'

'Does he read?'

'No, but . . .'

'Meg, it just won't work. You're a clever girl. Well, you've got some imagination. You want to write books, don't you?' Even, I added to myself, if they are just romantic twaddle. 'He won't understand that. He won't understand any more than a Hottentot. My dear, you're in different worlds. And if you get married he'll never be able to come into yours. You'll have to go into his. And you'll be unhappy there.'

'But we love each other.'

Always it came back to that. I became angry to hear her use the word. She had not earned the right. Children speak of God, and think of a kind old man with a long white beard. We allow it. And Meg spoke of love, and thought of what? . . . a cloud of pink cotton-wool on which she and Fergus would float away into the future. That I would not allow. So I forbade her to think of marriage, I forbade her to think even of an engagement. She was eighteen. I told her to come and see me again when she was twenty.

She said, 'All right, dad. He wants to finish his apprenticeship anyway. We can wait.'

'You'll get over him. You wait and see.'

She touched me on the cheek as though I were the child. 'I love him, dad. And I know you'll love him too.'

So Fergus became a fixture. He learned to sit at table with me without the aid of strong drink. He brought me gifts: a pineapple, a jar of Chinese ginger. And because he was a generous person, because he played draughts with me in the summer-house, and because Meg did not seem to be getting over him, I began to take trouble with him. I gave him books; which he thanked me for and carried away and did not read. I tested him. He looked embarrassed and mumbled something about being short of time. (It also embarrassed him to talk down my trumpet.) 'To tell you the truth Mr Plumb, I haven't read it. But I will. I've put it aside to read. It looks like a good one.' He did not even know what a bolshevik was. Come to think of it, he did not know the name of our own Prime Minister. But the ginger was tasty. I beat him at draughts. And he took me to cricket matches. So I told Meg he might come again, or that she could go with him to a ball or a movie in town; but she must not think of an engagement yet. I watched for signs that she was getting over him. I watched. But they strolled hand in hand and her face glowed, her eyes looked into that sparkling unreal future. Or he hit a six and she clapped as though he had made a speech to the nation. I saw I was going to lose. My pity for her increased. I began to be sorry for Fergus too. Some of the pain would be his.

What little there was to him I came to like.

83

I have never got used to riding in motor cars. It is a method of getting about that flies in the face of nature. As we hurtle along at forty miles an hour missing by no more than a foot or two cars that hurtle towards us at the same speed I expect to be punished. I grieve for man, who has travelled so far from himself. The twentieth is not my century. Nor, I fear, is it mankind's. He took a wrong turning, is on a wrong road. As technological man he has entered the time of his death. The signs are plain to see. Unless he turns aside and passes through the Door he will stay mere man, the thinking brute, until he dies—which is soon—and never be Man.

Meditations of this sort shorten my journeys in motor cars. I derive no pleasure from them—but take them like the pills that prevent car sickness.

We spent two days driving home from Wellington. Many times I wondered if I would see Peacehaven again. And when we reached it, at last, at last, thank God, I climbed out of the car with the speed of a boy and stood by the gate trembling. This was land under my feet. I was back in nature. Thank God.

I swung the gate open. Felicity drove through.

'You go on. I'll walk up.'

'Are you all right?' she mouthed.

'Perfectly.' I turned away from her and looked at the name

223

on the weather-warped board: Peacehaven. Edie's choice, and Edie's work with the brush. The white paint of the background was flaking away and the letters themselves were gone. I read them in bare grey wood. (Fergus wants to repaint the sign. No, I say, when I'm dead. I can beat him in argument any time with my death.) Peacehaven. I remembered her painting those plain shapes on a piece of wood yellow as butter.

Her presence reached out to me. Patience my dear, I thought, I'll be with you soon. Of course, I attributed impatience to her wrongly. There can be nothing of that on the Other Side. But the mortal Edie was my real listener. I walked up the drive and turned away from the house towards the creek. She became less a presence than a memory. And this made her less easy to face. For those last eight years were a dark sad time. The shadow of Alfred lay over them. We never spoke his name but he was there—in the smallest of our exchanges, in kitchen, garden, bedroom, he was there. Her love for us was perfect—painful to her. It struck her with a mortal wound, her life bled away. She saw both of us as outside nature. Alfred because of his practices—equally with me she believed them unnatural—and me because my love had proved insufficient. Hers was sufficient. It began to kill her. (The doctors said the trouble was her heart. They were right, though they did not know it.)

I tried. I tried with the whole strength of my mind and will. *Homo sum; humani nihil ad me alienum puto.* I tried to make it true. But I was preacher, teacher, moralist. I could not do it.

But now, I thought, resting in the summer-house, now I can do it. I can love Alfred. I can forgive myself. I am a man. Nothing human is alien to me.

I had Robert to thank for this. This had only been possible since his touch on my hand. I said, 'Edie, you would be pleased with him.'

'Dad, dad,' a voice cried at my ear. And there was Meg waiting to kiss and hug me. 'Talking to yourself?' she cried. I saw her eyes wet with emotion at having me back, and her cheeks pink with happiness, and felt her strong plump arms about my body, and I returned her kiss, thinking, 'This is a good girl too.'

We went inside. Felicity was buttering pikelets and wanting to shuffle me off to my bedroom so she could gossip with Meg. She had had me for three weeks: I did not blame her. But Meg made me sit down. She poured me tea and gave me pikelets and shouted all her news into my trumpet: Fergus and Fred had quarrelled over the plumbing in the new shops and Fred had been forced to back down; Rebecca had won the mixed doubles title at her tennis club; Emerson's flying-boat had turned back on its Sydney flight with engine trouble. The last affected me. I did not like my children to be in danger. And only half an hour ago I had been reflecting on the petrol engine. How much more presumptuous the aeroplane than the car. And a son of mine entered the great tin belly of the machine and pulled the knobs that made it fly, and mounted close to the sun. I feared he would be punished like Icarus.

'I'd like to see Emerson,' I said.

'He's coming on Saturday.'

'And Willis.'

'We can drive up there.'

'And Alfred.'

Meg dropped her cup. Then there was a great to-do: mopping out, sweeping up. I waited till it was over. 'Alfred Plumb, or whatever his name is now.'

Felicity was less agitated than Meg. Meg believed the journey had made me delirious. She wanted to put me to bed. But I said, 'Stop fussing Meg. Felicity's got something she wants to say.'

'I just want to ask if you're sure you know what you're doing.'

'I think so. Why shouldn't I?'

'For twenty-five years you pretend he doesn't exist. And now you think you can snap your fingers and have him come running to see you.'

'I don't think that. I'll be surprised if he comes.'

'So will I.'

'But I'll go to him if he won't come to me. And now Meg

225

dear, I think I'd like to lie down.' For I was very weak suddenly. I felt as if I might topple off my chair. But Felicity said, 'His name's Hamer, you know. Alfred Hamer. He didn't take your money but he took your advice.'

'Stop it, Felix,' Meg said. She helped me to my feet.

'And while we're on the subject,' Felicity cried, 'you might as well know John Willis is dead.'

'Is he?' I said. 'I'm sorry.'

'He and Alfred lived together. Like any old married couple. They made each other happy.'

'Felicity, stop it. Come on, dad. You don't have to listen to this.'

'When did he die?'

'Three years ago. Another attack of yellow jaundice. His liver wouldn't stand it. Alfred's a widow now.'

'Felix,' Meg shrieked.

'My dear, I've been cruel,' I said to Felicity, 'but is there any need for you to be?' I let Meg take me to my bedroom.

'Is it true his name is Hamer?'

'Yes.'

'That must have pleased your mother.'

'I don't know.'

'She didn't talk to you?'

'Not about that.'

We were quiet for a moment.

'I'm glad you want to see him,' she said, 'but . . .'

'You think he won't want to see me?'

'No. Not that. What I was going to say was, why now, after all these years?'

'It was Robert, I think.'

'Robert?'

'Not anything he said. Or did either . . . He healed my hand Meg, see. But it's more than that. I've been possessed. For twenty-five years. And after seeing Robert the madness has gone. Nothing human is strange to me any more. He showed me love.'

226

I could say no more than that, and understand no more. Meg placed her palm on my healing one. She kissed me.

'Go back to your sister, dear,' I said.

But she stayed with me. Presently I went to sleep.

84 Meg and Fergus were married in a Presbyterian church. The Presbyterian was Fergus's communion—though, he said, he hadn't been to a service for two or three years. He meant to please me.

I went along in a state of sorrow for Meg. I did not believe in this marriage. But for myself I was excited. I had not entered a Presbyterian church since my last visit to St Andrews eighteen years before. I sniffed the air of the place like a retired surgeon returning to the wards. The stained-glass windows, the bars of light striking through the gloom, the architecture of the place —even in this country box there was a lovely soaring—set me quivering with recognition and filled my throat with the pain of loss. I shook myself out of it. Used the old arguments. They were true after all. But the place set up echoes, a haunting moan, inside me. From some things there is no escape. Remembrance of this kind is another sense. I had not read Proust in 1928. But that day I stood for a time in one of his 'true paradises'.

The young man who married Meg and Fergus might have been Scroggie or my young self. He did well. He allowed the words to do their own speaking. Hearing them, I began to have hope for Meg. Love and a sense of duty might help her put unreality off.

There was no reception. Meg and Fergus drove away. We said goodbye to his parents. Fred and Esther drove us back to Peacehaven. And there we lived with Robert for six more years, and loved each other through the dark that had come down on our joy.

85　Six years. How much happened in that time. Felicity married, had her child. Esther, Meg, Mirth had children too. I published my third book, my last. I wrote for the radical papers, lectured sometimes three nights a week, supported Labour candidates for parliament. My friendship with Wendy began. Ella Satterthwaite died. My mother died and left her money to her church. Emerson came home—the Sundowner of the Skies—and went away again. In America Agnes married a car salesman. And we all lived through the depression.

But there is a deeper level in my experience. There only one thing happened. Edie died.

She was not afraid. Perfect love casteth out fear. But I was afraid. I was afraid to be without her. I was afraid to see her go before I had knowledge of the thing she knew. She had perfect love. And I did not. I believe she made herself live as long as she did in the hope I might find it. Her hope for me prolonged her life while her love for Alfred and me was killing her.

86　The new babies brought her much delight. And Emerson's triumph made her blush with pride while she laughed at the craziness of it.

Emerson learned to fly in England. He had a natural aptitude for it. It is almost as if he feels wings attached to his shoulders the way Willis feels his amputated leg. People liked to believe the first time he flew was solo. It caused the kind of sensation in flying circles a new immaculate conception would cause in religious.

Emerson saved and bought himself a Gypsy Moth, for which he gave his car in part exchange. For a year or two he flew it about Britain. It kept him poor. Then one day in 1930 he walked into the Croydon airfield carrying a few clothes tied in a bundle and a packet of sandwiches wrapped in a brown paper bag.

From a British newspaper:

Mystery Airman

A light aeroplane landed at Croydon yesterday and from it stepped a young man who announced his intention of starting at 4 a.m. today on a flight to Australia.

This morning he reappeared and after stating that his name was Emerson Plumb and that his home was in Auckland New Zealand, he climbed into his machine and flew away.

Aerodrome officials have no idea where he came from.

Legends are made in this way. A pity it could not go on. I like to think of him chugging over the Arabian desert, munching sandwiches, singing a tuneless song; or speeding south from Timor over the shark-infested sea, with his silk scarf flying behind him and his bundle of dirty clothes perched on his knee. He lands at Wyndham in Northern Territory, and is found there in the dusk tinkering with the engine of his plane. Eighteen days out from Croydon. The Australians name him the Sundowner of the Skies.

But soon we had too many details; the magic went out of Emerson. For me it was as if Theseus, arriving from the north, had recounted his adventures in Frazerian terms. Still, he was a hero. The right hero for his times. His plane came on a ship from Australia and he flew in triumph about the country, from Whangarei to Stewart Island. He was welcomed by mayors and mobbed by little boys. People began to say he should be knighted. And soon *Kia Ora* disappeared from the fuselage of his plane and the name of an oil company took its place. I thought it a great pity.

But when we had Emerson home we found him unchanged. He was gay and dreamy by turns, as he had been in his motor-cycling days. In the midst of a conversation he would go off somewhere; would take to the skies and fly into the sunset. He had an inviolable self. Fame could not alter him. He looked ahead to his freedom—Emerson Plumb soaring in his machine above wind and weather. The mayors, the little boys, were no more than a bit of fun.

And faced with him I began to recapture some of the magic of his flight. There was more than daring in it, there was spirit.

Croydon: *Only one or two people were out to see him as he taxied his tiny blue and silver machine across the aerodrome in the grey light of the morning, and with a wave of his hand started on the first lap of his eleven thousand mile journey.*

Lympne: *The weather conditions were only fair when the lone flyer took off on the six-hundred-mile hop to Munich. A southerly breeze was blowing banks of fog in from the sea; and the hills were shrouded in mist, although over the Channel the sun was breaking through.*

At Munich he swung the propeller while the throttle was open and the plane came alive like a bucking horse. He threw himself flat; then chased it, caught its wing, and climbed aboard.

At Aleppo he ran out of petrol and made a forced landing. And another at Baghdad after flying through a sandstorm. From Jask to Karachi he flew in company with the Hon. Mrs Victor Bruce, who had been lost in the desert. Then on to Jodhpur, and through a strong headwind to Jhansi, where in the dark he could not find the airfield. After circling for half an hour he came down in a ploughed field. The plane turned over and broke its propeller. And during the night the monsoon rains began. But with his little money Emerson hired some villagers to turn the plane on its wheels. He unstrapped his spare propeller from the fuselage and fitted it. Then he had the villagers haul the plane two miles to the only dry ground in the district and took off between trees that almost clipped his wings on either side. Calcutta. Rangoon. Singapore. Batavia. Bima—where he stayed overnight with a tribe of Malay headhunters. Koepang. And then the shark-infested seas; and Wyndham, where three hours after his arrival someone found him overhauling his machine.

I felt a ridiculous pride. It needed Emerson's presence to keep it alive. Edie's delight was girlish. She escaped into her aviator son. She had no fear for him. It seemed she thought of him as a being under some other dispensation. I thank him for the happiness he brought into her last years.

Soon he went back to England. And from there to South Africa, where he formed a flying circus. He sent us a photograph of himself wing-walking. Edie laughed with joy.

87 Joy. In those years it was in short supply. The dream of a Utopia in the southern seas, of God's Own Country, had never been more than that: a dream. Holes had been shot in it before the depression. But in the depression it rusted like an old tin can, it fell to pieces. All we had left was human kindness. Without it we would have become a nation of beasts.

On the level of simple survival the Plumbs survived. My few invested pounds fell down a great hole. But Robert saved Peacehaven with his hands. Willis struggled on, copying him. Felicity was all right: Max kept his job. And Esther's husband was a bookmaker. The parasite class keeps food in its belly. Meg suffered most. Fergus lost his job early and was on relief through most of that time. Their third child was born in 1932.

They lived in a three-roomed shack a mile down the creek from us. One Saturday morning I shouldered a sack of vegetables and walked round to see them. I found the two older children playing in the front yard, while the baby slept in a butter-box under a tree. Meg was boiling the copper to wash napkins. She lugged water from the rain-water tank to a lean-to that served as a wash-house, using an old kerosene tin as a bucket. Fergus had fitted a wire handle to it. It cut Meg's fingers cruelly, but she would not let me help. When she had the copper full she dropped the napkins in, trying to hide the

231

stains from me. Poor Meg. Genteel even in this extremity. She took me inside for a cup of tea. The children ran in and she gave them baked crusts of bread—Edie's *zwieback*. The baby cried. With her back to me she fed it from her breast. Now and then she turned her head and shouted something into my trumpet.

Fergus was out on his bicycle. He was off relief for a time, finding his own work. He had managed to put together a tool-kit that would do for plumbing and carpentry. Each morning he rode off to the local timber yard with his kit over the handlebars. Whenever a loaded truck came out he pedalled after it. Often he fell too far behind, and cycled back exhausted to wait for the next truck. But when he managed to follow all the way (one of the drivers helped him by slowing down) there was sometimes work for him stacking the timber; and now and then a day's plumbing or carpentry. He preferred this to relief. He was his own man.

But that morning he had gone out on other business. I was close to Meg's shoulder watching the baby's peaceful greedy sucking. (Edie had fed our children locked in the bedroom.) I saw its eyes jerk open with shock as a tear from Meg's eye splashed on its forehead. At once she was contrite. She cooed. She wiped the tear away. She helped the tiny pursed mouth find her nipple again.

'What's the matter, my dear?'

'Nothing.'

'Is it Fergus?'

She made a movement of her head. I took it for a nod.

'What's he done?'

'It's not his fault.'

'Of course not.'

'He's so proud.'

She told me the story. She spoke quietly and I held my trumpet almost to her mouth. The baby became still as a bird, watching this strange black object hovering over it.

Last night the nightman had come. (Meg blushed.) He was

232

a young man who had been at school with Fergus. And of course
he was in steady work. (Her colour deepened.) Fergus made a
joke of him, but liked him: a friendly young man and very kind.
Well, last night was his night. She had heard him rattling his
cans at two o'clock while she fed the baby. And heard something soft land on the step. After the baby was asleep again
she had gone out to look. And there it was, lying on the doorstep: a sack of old clothes and shoes. She pulled them out
gingerly, with great fastidiousness, but saw that after a boil the
shirts and dresses would be all right. The underclothes, no. One
had to draw the line. And the shoes—one could not boil shoes.
She would pass those on—although a pair of walking brogues
looked her size. She washed her hands and went back to bed.
Two dresses she could wear; and a shirt Bobby's size; and a
dress for Rebecca. It was like discovering buried treasure. But
she lay awake worrying: Fergus would not be pleased.

She got no further for Fergus himself came in. He was
flushed from riding his bicycle. Meg laid the baby down. She
poured him a cup of tea.

'Well,' he said, 'it's done.'

'I suppose you punched him on the jaw?' This was sharp
for Meg. I looked at her with sorrow and respect. She would
come through. I did not like to think of the cost.

'I told him to keep his cast-offs,' Fergus said.

'What did he say?'

'Nothing. He was in his pyjamas, the lazy b-----.'

'Fergus! Dad's here.'

'Sorry, Mr Plumb. But still, at ten o'clock in the morning.'

'He was working all night,' Meg said.

'You call that work?'

Fergus had stood in the front yard and called the nightman
out. And when he had appeared, pyjama-ed and rubbing his
eyes, Fergus had thrown the sack of clothes at his feet. The
man had said nothing; picked up his sack, gone inside and
closed the door. And Fergus, back home and drinking tea, was

233

ashamed of himself. He blustered. 'I don't need any man's charity. I can look after my family,' etc.

'One of the dresses was just right for Rebecca. We've got nothing for her. And winter's coming.'

'We'll be all right.'

'But Fergus——'

'We'll be all right, I said.'

'Yes, Fergus.' After a moment, she said, 'Dad brought us some vegetables.'

'Thanks, Mr Plumb. But I can grow my own.' As if to prove it he went out to his garden.

'He's so touchy,' Meg said. 'He hates taking things from other people.'

'Shall I take the vegetables back?'

'Oh no. He didn't mean it. As soon as you've gone he'll come in and say he's sorry.' And very soon she said, 'Listen, he's whistling. Just like a boy.'

'Your mother wants you to come round for dinner on Sunday. Robert's killing a sheep.'

'Oh, the poor thing. Why does he have to be so cruel?' This was my Meg. I smiled at her. But in a moment I saw she was crying again.

'What is it, my dear?'

'I don't know. I don't know. Something seems to have gone out of things.'

I tried to cheer her up by giving her the book I had brought: a little volume called *The Kingdom of Love*, by Ella Wheeler Wilcox. She had read it as a girl.

'Thanks, dad.' She laid it on the table. 'I don't get much time for reading. I'll put it away for the children.'

'Do you still write?'

'I told you,' she cried angrily, 'there's no time. Besides, Fergus wouldn't understand.' We both thought of the warning I had given her. She jumped to her feet. 'And anyway, I don't want to. That was a silly game. I'm married now. And Fergus is a wonderful man . . . Oh, my copper. The fire will be out.'

234

She ran to the wash-house. She sent Fergus rushing for wood.

I did not know who to be sorrier for. But I find today that when I think of the depression I think most often of Meg crying at her kitchen table; and of the nightman, dressed in his pyjamas, turning back into his darkened house with his sugar-bag of used clothing in his hand.

That was the depression. It was not a simple thing.

88 I played little part in the politics of it. My failure to find a course of action confused and disappointed me. I understand now I'm not a political man. My eye has always been fixed on ends, I've not had a clear view of means. Politic-ally I am a child. Always the action I have wished to take has been impossibly direct or wildly idiosyncratic. I was not a Com-munist, though I was often accused of it. I was a member of no party—had been free of them all since the U.L.P. swallowed the old Socialist Party. What I wanted was a workers' revolution. I wanted spontaneous uprisings all through the country. Though with the rational part of my mind I saw that Savage and Nash and Fraser were the men of the future, the political idealist in me would not accept them. They were too mundane, men not Men. As the swell mounted behind them I watched them set their feet on the rocks of tradition. They would not be carried away. Someone has said that political parties are a breed. When new they have some marks of individuality, but they revert to type. And for the radical that means they become conservative. It is true. Under a Labour Government there would be, I guessed, two or three years of reform of a half-baked kind, and then would come the old cry that economic realities must be faced. And the new order would change its shape to the old. What I wanted was not a new order but new realities.

I sat one evening with Bluey in an Auckland hall. It was full of hungry men. Savage and Fraser and Nash were on the stage. Lee with his empty sleeve. Semple. Dan Peabody. They were all there. I did not hear what they said. Deafness can be a blessing. Now and then Bluey scribbled something on a piece of paper and handed it to me. I saw the politicians were at their old game of buying votes with promises. But Bluey wrote too: *They don't like it.* And I heard a murmur about me and saw angry faces. These men were not to be fed with words. They had suffered enough. I rose to my feet. Nash was speaking: scattering his handfuls of tin tacks about the hall. My voice has a wider range. The pulpit trains more thoroughly than the soap-box. For a moment or two we fought in single combat. He scratched my surface like a rasp, I beat on him like a hammer. The men in the hall enjoyed it—egged me on. But when Nash sat down and the chairman threatened to have me turned out they began to bellow with rage—a frightening sound (made hollow and other-worldly by my deafness). For a moment I thought I had unleashed revolution. The weight of the noise beat the chairman back to his seat. I saw him put up his hand to ward it off; and I thought, This is honest anger, this is the voice of the people. And at once said so, and told the politicians they were right to be frightened, that unless they obeyed the people's will they would be swept into the gutters of history. But I kept it short. There was heat here and unless I used it quickly it would grow cold. So I said, 'Your way is wrong. It can only end in repression. This parliament you want to take over will take you over, it will swallow you up. Six months in that place and you'll be a new bunch of Coateses and Wards. These men down here know it. They can hear it in your voices. They've got hungry wives and children at home and that has given them an extra sense. They don't want you going to Wellington to take over old institutions. They want new institutions. Or no institutions. They want a movement, a revolution, a people's government. And if you are too cowardly to talk of it up there, why we'll talk of it down here. We'll talk of it. No, by heaven, we'll do more than that. We won't just talk of it, we'll do it.' And I cried, 'I put a motion to this meeting, this meeting of the unemployed workers of New Zealand. I put the

236

motion that we declare here and now that our country belongs to its working people and that henceforth its government is a people's government, a dictatorship of the proletariat. There's the motion for you. And I see your chairman won't put it to the vote, he's frightened, he's hiding under his chair, so I'll put it. All in favour say Aye.'

I saw the cry that went up as much as heard it. For a moment I felt the intoxication demagogues must feel: they drink their followers up and swell with power. But I was no demagogue, no leader. Just an angry man with a good voice and a sense of other people. I had made my speech. Another man, more ambitious or braver, might have led his followers out of the hall: there would have been broken windows and broken heads. But I was not ambitious, not a man of action. Having got my crowd roaring and ready to move, I did not know what to do with it. I was forced to hand it back to the politicians. I said, 'There you are, gentlemen. We've changed the shape of the country for you. It has a new government now. The people have voted. Now you know what you're at the helm of. Let's see whether you can steer a straight course.'

I walked out, with Bluey and one or two others at my heels. I do not know how Nash and Fraser and Savage (they are interchangeable) pointed the meeting back in their direction. They were clever. They managed it all right. I waited on the windy footpath, stamping my feet to drive out the cold. After another half-hour the men came out. They were still-faced, grey-faced, sour. The fire was out in them. They turned up their collars, put their hands deep in their pockets, and trudged on their broken shoes off home. Only one or two came up to speak with me. But the politicians came out hearty. Semple rushed up and shouted at me—gutter language. It was a performance. He was not angry. In fact I think he was pleased with me, and his attack a tribute from one clever performer to a person he took for another. The others left me alone. Except Dan Peabody. Dan sidled up.

'That was a foolish thing to do, George.'

'You wouldn't have thought so twenty years ago, Dan.' I looked at him with pity. I could not dislike him. He had abandoned my daughter to avoid upsetting the Grundyites of his party—the bible and purity boys. He was an object of pity not dislike. And as well as Felicity he had put his young self aside and with it all that was honest and simple in him. He was on his way now, after the job at the top. And I saw in his eyes the fear that he was not going to get it. The others were tougher than he was and had more brains. He was starting to understand. He said, 'We're going to be the government, George. At the next election. There's no way we can fail.'

'You've failed already.'

He smiled. 'Double talk again. It's always double talk with you. You're too clever, that's your trouble. And you see where it's got you. Way out on the end of a limb. All by yourself.'

'I stand with the Reverend,' Bluey said, 'and proud of it.'

Dan looked at him absently. It was a shocking moment. Dan was a politician now, to his core. And that meant people had no essential being. They were fuel to stoke a career with. He looked through Bluey; but spoke to me because I might have uses—political decoy-bird. I turned away from him, shied away almost, as though from a suddenly incarnate dark angel. I walked up the street. Bluey kept at my side. He too had understood. He retained his good practical sense and his nose for moral decay.

We were shaken. We went to Bluey's room and drank several cups of tea before we were better.

89 One night (the 20th August 1934) I read late in my study. The house shuddered in a winter storm. Draughts stirred the curtains in the windows and when I looked into the night I saw blown leaves plastered to the glass in the shape of eyes. I had a sense of foreboding. Pursuing the Light, I had been deep in my books.

238

> I go to prove my soul!
> I see my way as birds their trackless way.
> I shall arrive! What time, what circuit first
> I ask not: but unless God send the hail
> Or blinding fire-balls, sleet and stifling snow
> In some time, His good time, I shall arrive.
> He guides me and the bird.

But I had no sense of being guided, or of being about to arrive. On that night I felt I might be struck down. I shook myself; I put it down to tiredness, too much print.

Towards midnight I went to bed. I slipped in beside Edie. In the light of the night-lamp I looked at her sleeping face. It was drained and cavernous. Her beauties were gone. But I knew of other beauties. Behind the suffering mask of the sick Edith Plumb was girl, wife, mother, loving heart, courageous spirit. My tiredness, the pushing restless ideas in me, and perhaps the elemental night, perhaps my love for her, opened a door between us, and I had a vivid and terrifying glimpse of her immortal soul. It was Light. It was Love. But it was not for me to look upon. I backed away. This was a forbidden mystery. I had thrown away my right to look on it. I must concern myself with the mortal part of her. So I thought of her sufferings.

Mirabeau dying after many days of pain signalled for pen and paper and wrote down in two words the only desire he had left: *To sleep*. This was the desire Edie had for herself. I understood. I was even able to hope it would come soon.

I woke at 3 a.m. (the 21st) and felt her beside me fighting for breath. She had no wish to struggle. Her body was fighting of its own accord. I turned on the light and saw she was suffering her last attack. I called out to her, 'Edie, don't go. Don't go.' And I ran to Robert's room and sent him cycling for Wendy and the doctor. When I came back Edie managed to fix her eyes on me and know who I was. 'George.' She felt for my hand and took it with a strength that had in it all of our life together. 'George.' She wanted to say something, but had not

239

time. She died. I know she would have told me I must make peace with Alfred and love him as my son. I would have obeyed. Why, knowing her wish, have I failed to carry it out?

I closed her eyes. For a moment I shared her arrival, shared her joy. Where she was gone was deep and lasting peace. For both of us I heard in my skull, *Non omnis moriar*. Horace had been speaking of fame and poetry; but the words had a better meaning. I looked down at my dead wife. Grief descended and struck me its hammer blow. But still I kept my eyes on her face. And I thought in the words of the ancient philosopher, See the shell of the flown bird.

90 Wendy arrived and the doctor. In the grey dawn Meg and Esther came. I went to my study and locked myself in. But there was nothing in that room to tell me who my wife had been. I put my head on the desk and struggled to find her. Later in the morning I crept through the house to her sewing-room and took from the cabinet there the exercise books in which she wrote her thoughts and memories. I turned the pages over. But I could not get into the times and places she wrote of. I was like an insect on a window. A hard transparent substance lay between me and Edie. She wrote: 'That little woman had a *dirty apron* that she wore nearly all the fortnight she was with us. She used to bring in my meals with a *knife sticking* in a jar of jam. One day she said to me, 'Would you like a wee lick of chicken broth?' I said I would, but when the broth arrived I *changed my mind* as it looked so horrid. It looked like hot water with a lot of little bits of *oil and feathers* in it.' I knew who that was: Mrs Evershaw the nurse who tended her in her confinement with Rebecca. But I could not hear the woman's Scotch voice, or see the broth, her dirty apron; or hear Edie, even in that word so dear to her, *horrid*. And I read, 'He loved his garden and flowers. He used to say nothing compared with a *dark red rose*.' Her father. I had always felt I

knew him. I did not know him now. I read on, '. . . a trellis with purple grapes . . . a brick footpath . . . the dining-room window wreathed in climbing roses.' I had seen and smelt them for myself. The colour, the scent, were gone. I began to feel my life was leaking away. 'We had beautiful rata wood fires. The minister used to put on a *big log* and it lasted all evening.' Was I that minister? I could not remember. A glass wall stood between me and George Plumb. I put the books back in their drawer and went outside. The wind had dropped and the rain fell straight and heavy. I sat in the summer-house. And there I began to find myself and my wife. I sat on the wet seat. The rain came down in drops as large as bantam eggs and splashed on my head and cheeks. 'George, come out of that,' I heard her say, 'you'll catch your death of cold.' I thought, The light of my life has gone and I will miss her as long as I live. There is a pain in my heart which cannot be removed.

Meg found me. Then there was a great commotion. The girls undressed me and rubbed me with towels. They scolded and screeched like parrots and cooed like doves. I stood like a wooden man. They put me to bed with hot bottles about me and blankets six deep on my chest. Later, when Edie's body was taken away, they shifted me to the big bed. I was easier there. I lay shivering with cold and sweating in fever for many days. Someone else said the service for Edie. I did not mind. They buried the shell of her. I sought her shining soul in other realms.

91   I had been home two days without a visit from Bluey. I asked Meg if he was sick but she did not know. Sutton was always busy in the garden, so she supposed everything was all right.

'I'll go down and see him.'

'Here.' She gave me a sago pudding in a basin. 'Take him that.'

'Thank you, Meg. He'll be pleased.'

'He's the only person I know who can eat the stuff.' Meg had come a long way. In the hard modern manner she tried to detract from her kindness. I smiled at her and said again, 'He'll be pleased,' and went off down the drive with this mess Bluey would look on as a prize. It was Saturday. As I went through the gate Bobby rode past me on his motor-cycle. (Like Emerson's it was an Indian.) Rebecca sat on the pillion seat, dressed in her tennis whites and a blue cardigan. She waved her racquet at me. I waved my trumpet back. (It pleased me now that Meg had named her daughter for her drowned sister. At the time I had thought it unhealthy.)

I walked along the footpath and in at Bluey's gate, wondering at the little car parked outside. Bluey had no friends left that I knew of. Excepting Sutton, of course. The man was at the side window of the cottage, in a burglar's crouch. He saw me on the path and came at me in a lopsided run. With his finger on his lips, he drew me after him to the end of the garden. I do not care for mysteries. But I cannot be brusque with Sutton. He knows it. He exaggerates his vulture's hump with me. But now he had a violence about him. I liked it even less than his usual malice. I did not care for his clutching of my arm, or like the unnatural redness of his eyes. Until, with a start, I realized he had been crying.

'What's wrong, Mr Sutton? Is Bluey all right?'

'They've caught him, Mr Plumb. They've hooked him at last.'

'What do you mean?'

'He's got a priest in there.'

'Ah, that explains the car.'

Sutton hissed. The sound came so sharply down my trumpet it hurt. I drew away. Sutton had been crying with rage more than grief. He had owned Bluey as servant and friend for fifteen years. He must have felt safe. Nobody wanted the old man—even I did not want him. But now the Church claimed Bluey; and Sutton had enough sense to know a good part of his friend had escaped him forever. He was lacerated by his rage and pain.

I would not have been surprised to see him stamp himself into the ground like Rumpelstiltskin.

'Is this the first time he's come?'

'He's been once before. They took him to confession yesterday.'

'Bluey must have had a lot to confess. He'll be saying Hail Marys for the rest of his life.'

'You can do something,' Sutton cried.

'No, Mr Sutton. Less than you.'

'I thought you were his friend.'

'I am. I hope I am. I don't like his church, or any church for that matter. But I think he'll be happy for the first time in fifty years.'

'What will happen to me?'

'Why nothing, I should think. You'll have to share him, that's all.'

'I won't share him.'

'You'll have to, Mr Sutton. Now come on,' I said, 'you're his friend. You know how tormented he's been. They've got him back and that's a sad thing for us. But he'll be able to relax.'

Sutton would have none of this. He was in a sense Bluey's lover and Bluey's master—entirely possessive. He must have Bluey whole. I had seen Sutton first in 1934, walking along behind Bluey with a small happy grin on his face. It was Queen Street, Friday night. And Bluey sailed through the crowds like a barge, making a path for the cripple. He waved his heavy oak stick to clear the way. People watched them go by like a circus act. Bluey was unaware. But Sutton loved it. And now, after fifteen years, Bluey was getting away. I understood Sutton's pain, but could do nothing to help him. I offered him a bite of sago pudding.

'Aah,' Sutton cried, 'it's your fault. With your talk of souls. There's no such thing as souls. It's a dirty trick you church b-----s play on us.'

I left him in the garden and went to the cottage, where I sat

243

on the bench and waited for Bluey and the priest to come out. Poor Sutton. Bluey's care for him would increase, but I saw the cripple would take it as a loss.

I waited on the bench for a good half-hour. The sun warmed my bones. Off to one side Sutton crept along the garden path. He stationed himself at the cottage window again. I got up and peered round at him, but he bared his teeth so I left him crouching there. I did not think Bluey should be warned. He was probably expecting trouble from Sutton.

When he came out he grew red to find me there. We shook hands. He introduced me to the priest, a Father Pearce. I noticed I was Mister not Reverend, and took from this an unexpected pain. I had had my title from Bluey for forty years. But, I told myself, it was not important. What mattered was that Bluey had come to rest. In spite of this he was shifty. He wanted the priest out of there. Pearce seemed to understand. He was a large man, blue-jowled, bushy-browed; comfort-loving, I guessed. He looked at the sunny bench with longing; but allowed Bluey to ease him towards his car. I sat down again. Remembering Robert's advice, I turned my tender palm towards the sun.

Bluey came back and lowered himself on the bench. I gave him the sago pudding.

'What's this? Sago? Is this from Meg? Ah, that's a good girl . . .'

I wondered if his conversation was to be like this: full of clumsy gaps where in the past he would have said Reverend. 'Bluey,' I said, 'you'd better call me George.'

But he could not. Our friendship might founder on this rock. 'So you've come back to it, Bluey? I'm not surprised.'

'Eh? What's that? I can't hear you.'

'You've come back to the church?'

'It's me ears. They're getting worse.'

'The church. The church.'

But he simply grinned and tapped my trumpet. 'I'll have to get one of those.'

I gave up. 'Meg made the pudding specially, Bluey.'

244

'Ah, she's a good girl. I've always liked sago. I'll have it for lunch.'

I told him about my trip to Wellington, about Oliver and the Goodlad case (he told me Goodlad had shot himself: it was in the morning paper); about Robert, whom Bluey had always loved; about Felicity. Felicity would come and see him, I said. I reminded him she was a Catholic. (He had an attack of deafness at that point.) Last I told him Esther was arranging for me to see Alfred, my son Alfred Plumb. Bluey's pleasure in that shone on his face. He nearly called me Reverend again. With luck, I thought, we would keep our friendship going.

I said goodbye and left him at his door. Sutton crept round the corner and stood by his side. Bluey showed him the pudding. They went inside. I walked home. The whole business, I thought, was a defeat for good sense. It did not fail to make me angry. The priests who had crippled Bluey Considine in his youth would get no congratulations from me for providing him with a crutch in his old age. Still, he was happy, for the first time in fifty years.

I could not take the debate through to its end. It became too much for me.

92 In any case, I thought, it has no end. Or if it ends it will be with Man. And history closes its pages at that point. There will be a new book, a new reality.

Emerson roused me from that reverie. He came down to the summer-house where I had hidden and threw his arm round my shoulders.

'Lurking in the bushes, dad? Come and have a walk.'

I had not seen him for several months. In that time he had, as the newspapers say, brushed shoulders with death. Two hundred miles out over the Tasman Sea his aeroplane had started to sputter and smoke. He switched one engine off and flew back home on the others, whistling a tune, his co-pilot said, with thirty terrified people still as mice in the cabin behind him. His landing on the harbour had been a model of neatness.

I said, 'When are you going to give that flying up, son?'

He laughed. 'Soon, dad. I'm getting a bit long in the tooth. I think I'll grow grapefruit like Willis.'

'What tune was it you whistled?'

'I don't know. Something mum used to play.' He whistled it down my trumpet.

'I dreamt I dwelt in marble halls,' I said.

'Is that it? Anyway, it was all that kept the old pile of scrap in the air.'

I believed him. We strolled down the lawn and over the brick bridge into the orchard. The trees were dying. Nobody had pruned them since Robert had gone. I was not concerned. They and I kept pace. We would end together. Fergus would have the bulldozers in soon after my death. So it seemed a kindness to the trees to let them take the course natural to them. Age and weight split their trunks as cleanly as kindling.

Emerson shook some late apples off a branch. We ate as we went along. He took off his jacket and slung it over his shoulder. On his wrists I saw the tiny white scars made by an exploding bottle in John Jepson's aerated-water factory. I said, 'Do you see anything of Alfred?'

He took it calmly. The others must have warned him. 'We haven't got much in common.'

'When did you see him last?'

'Oh—' he shrugged. 'A couple of years back. At Esther's, I think.'

'How was he?'

'Seemed O.K. to me. He'd put on a bit of weight.'

'Did he talk about John Willis?'

'No.'

'John's dead.'

'So I hear.'

He was uncomfortable. He felt the same way I did about homosexuality. I changed the subject. But as we walked down

246

to the house he said, 'Mum used to meet him here, you know.'

'Alfred?'

'Esther told me. He used to come in through the farm at the back.'

The way, I thought, he had come to meet John Willis. I felt a tremor in my universe, and thought for a moment things would fall apart. But then felt a settling, and looked with a sharp eye at the new conformations. I did not like them. Edie had walked in the orchard, deceiving me; I had put her to this torment. So, in concealment, she had met the needs of her life. I did not like the part I played in this.

Emerson stopped on the bridge. He threw his apple core into the water. An eel rose from the deep, nosed it, and sank again. Emerson said, 'Alfred's started drinking.'

'Did Esther tell you that?'

'She wanted you to know. He's on it pretty heavily, she says.'

'Because John Willis is dead?'

Emerson frowned. 'Evidently.' He looked at the sky; wishing he was up there. 'Do you think it's a good idea to see him?'

'Yes. I do.'

'Esther told me to tell you he mightn't come.'

'We'll wait and see.'

Emerson flapped his jacket. He wanted to say something more but did not know how. I could not help him. He had extraordinary skills. He could loop the loop and do the falling leaf. He could fly under bridges. And given a single piston or shaft, like an archaeologist the bone of an extinct beast, he would probably manage to put the original machine together around it. But he could not say what he had to say to me. We walked up to the house. There, in the backyard, he managed.

'Dad, look, some of the others are still sore at you. For turning him out, I mean. But I want you to know I understand. I'm not saying you should have. I mean, he's my brother. But I see why you had to do it.'

'Thank you, Emerson.'

'But what I want to say is, why do you have to go and dig it up now? It's ancient history. Let it lie is what I say. You can't change anything now.'

'Don't worry, son. You won't be involved.'

'We're all involved.'

93 Meg called us in to lunch. I would have liked to have mine in my study but could not with Emerson visiting. So I sat between him and Meg and ate a piece of luncheon sausage and a lettuce leaf.

Emerson's words had set up a trembling in my mind. I was on the point of seeing my family whole. Of course they were all involved. The conversation was about motor-bikes, with Bobby and Emerson swapping anecdotes and Raymond and Fergus chipping in now and then. But the real conversation (Meg, Felicity, Emerson) ran like an underground stream beneath all this. I saw its progress in their unnatural ease, in their heartiness and sudden preoccupations, and in the glances they sometimes gave each other, or sent in my direction to see if I had changed my shape again. I remembered Edie's phrase, another shake of the kaleidoscope. I had shaken it, and now my children were jostling at my shoulder to see the new pattern. I had a more intimate sense of them than I'd had in years; since they had been neat-haired Sunday children assembled in the parlour at the Manse to sing to their mother's playing 'Saviour, breathe an evening blessing' or 'Flow gently, sweet Afton'. I even had dead Rebecca in my mind. And banished Alfred. I had Edie.

Felicity shouted, 'Wool-gathering, dad?'

I smiled at her but made no answer.

'A penny for them.'

'I was thinking of your mother.'

This made her frown, and made Meg's eyes grow misty. I

said, 'And Alfred. I'd better have a rest if I'm seeing him this afternoon.' I thanked Meg for the meal and went to my study. Fergus followed and opened the door for me. His tough man's-man face had an anxious look. But he was too proud to say what was on his mind—something, I guessed, about Alfred displacing the Soles at Peacehaven, or in my will.

'It's all right, Fergus. This doesn't change anything.'

'It's none of my business. I never knew him.'

'Look on it the way Bobby and Raymond do. A sporting event.'

He laughed; but was not amused.

94 I had not been in the study long before Meg let herself in. She carried a cup of tea and a plate of biscuits.

'Thank you my dear, but I don't want any.'

She put them on the desk and pulled up the stool. She had not come to talk but to sit with me. I would sooner have been alone. But this was the most vulnerable of my children and I could not turn her out.

'Felicity's doing the dishes.'

'Good. Good.'

I sat and dreamed a while and she sat beside me with her hand on my knee. My past was returning to me in colours unnaturally bright, in smells of cooking and burning and growth, and in sounds that I being deaf could never have heard. I remembered this child, Meg, bringing my tea to the study one night. It was 1917. She was nine. We were just back from America. She put her face against my shoulder and asked me why I was worried. I was worried about many things. I told her the least of them. A man from the insurance company had called to say his firm would not insure our furniture because somebody might burn down our house. Meg stamped her foot. She had that beautiful strong sense of justice that resides in children—a primary sense that too soon becomes muddied. She

249

stamped her foot. She cried out with anger. Was he, she wanted to know, the young man who had come to see me late in the afternoon, the young man with the thick glasses and leather bag? Yes, I said, that was him. 'Then I wish he'd fall off his bike,' she cried. 'I wish he'd fall off his bike and break his neck.' I was astonished at this from my gentle Meg. I explained that it was not the young man's fault, that above him were the company managers, and above them the profiteers and war-mongers, and they were the evil men, not the clerk with the pebble glasses, who had been ashamed of the job he had to do. Tears ran down Meg's cheeks. 'It's not fair,' she wept, 'it's not fair the way they're cruel to you.' We talked for a long time that evening. I told her what Keats had meant when he called the world a vale of soul-making. And I gave her to read that same little poem of Ella Wheeler Wilcox's I had given Felicity: 'Let there be many windows to your soul . . .' The next night she had it by heart.

That had been more than thirty years ago. With a pain like that of bereavement I realized this was not a nine-year-old child sitting with me but a grown woman, and an unhappy one. I said, 'Do you remember the insurance man, Meg? The one you wished would fall off his bicycle?'

'Vaguely. Did he have pebble glasses?'

'That's him.' And I went on to speak of that night, of our talk about the soul's pilgrimage, and of the poem she had learned. I should not have. She did not remember. I took her hand. She was suffering, I thought, from a stupor in those bright life-giving cells where the past resides. The blows of the present rained too heavily on her. Unless she could learn to take them, ride with them in Bobby's phrase, she would not recover the lost part of herself and become whole again. It seemed to me the most simple of diagnoses, and I explained it to her. She did not listen.

'Oh dad,' she cried, 'what am I going to do?' She spoke of her troubles. Fergus was growing away from her. He lived for his work. He had become a stranger. And the children were growing up. They would soon be gone. What would she do then?

'You must look inside yourself, Meg. You still have yourself.'

'Some self!'

'It's all you've got, my dear. It's all any of us have. But it's enough. Because the Light is an inner light. And that's where we find God.'

'Oh God,' she cried. 'That old stuff. I thought you gave that up.'

'No,' I said, shivering a little, for I saw she was bent on self-destruction. I could not see how to save her. I would even have turned her at that moment towards Felicity's church, Bluey's church. But I did not know the way. So I kept on talking— religious waffle Willis calls it. And soon she began to pat my knee absently.

I said, 'Why don't you talk to Felicity?'

'About the Catholic Church, you mean? Don't think I haven't thought of it.'

'Why don't you then?'

'Because you've ruined that for me. All churches.'

'Good,' I joked.

'That's all very well for you . . . I've even been to see the doctor.'

'What did he say?'

'He thinks I've got too much time on my hands. He told me it's not too late to have another baby.'

I laughed.

'It's not funny. I've thought of seeing a psychiatrist.'

'And what would you tell him, my dear? That you've got an ache in your pineal gland?'

She did not understand.

'That's where Descartes located the soul.'

'Who's Descartes?'

95

Felicity said from the door, 'What are you two talking about?'

'Who's Descartes?'

'Des Cartes,' Felicity said. 'He's a cousin of Les Miserables.' They laughed. I watched them with astonishment. It made them laugh even louder.

'Dad's trying to talk me into joining your church,' Meg said.

'You could do worse. There's a woman out here to see you, dad. She says her name's Wendy Philson. Do you want me to tell her to go away?'

'You remember Wendy.'

'Never seen her in my life.'

'You met her at Esther's wedding. And she was at your mother's funeral.' I knew she remembered—she did not suffer from Meg's disease. She was provoking me. Like Meg she disapproves of Wendy's role in my life.

'Tell her to come in, Felicity. And I hope you'll remember your manners.' She grinned and went out. Meg followed with the cup and plate. A moment later Wendy took her place.

'Hello, George. How did the trip go? How's your hand?' She took it and opened it out. 'It's healing.'

'Yes,' I said. I told her about Robert. She had never been close to him. She thought him dull. And, I could see, thought my account of his present life sentimental. She gave a faint smile when I said he had healed my palm.

'You don't have to believe it, Wendy. I'm not trying to set him up as a faith healer.'

'It would have got better by itself.'

'Perhaps.' It was not that she disbelieved in supernatural forces. But they worked, she believed, through superfine souls. Robert, lumpish Robert, was not equipped. I was not going to argue with her. I knew him.

I put down my trumpet and handed her a writing pad and

pencil. This is an intimate act. It makes her blush, especially in the privacy of my study. 'Now my dear, tell me what you've been up to. Last time you came you said you'd been doing some reading.'

She put her head down like a child and wrote. (I'm not sure she doesn't put her tongue out.) *I'm reading Jung. All about the interpretation of dreams.* And she wrote on at length about the dream as the key to the world of one's psyche, the dream as empirical data. She claimed that all the evidence pointed towards the truth of reincarnation. When she paused I said, 'Is this in Jung? I haven't read him.'

Jung stops short, she wrote. *He didn't dream his other lives. But I do.*

'Tell me one of them.'

She wrote (and I read over her shoulder): *I was a young girl. I was fourteen. I found myself descending stairs which were of stone, and narrow and low. As I descended they became so low I had to crawl. They were fearsome, and ended in a large underground cavern out of which I came to a labyrinth of narrow dark passages. These led to a small room with no doors or windows. I was simply in it and did not know how to get out. I tried the walls for an opening. After what seemed an eternity I was walking along a wide light passage. I noticed a door on the right-hand side, and put my hand on the handle. As I did so I heard myself exclaiming joyously, 'And this is the room of light.'*

'But Wendy,' I said, 'isn't this the initiation ceremony of the Eleusinian mysteries?'

'Exactly,' she cried. And wrote: *It's the ceremony that confers the long memory. It symbolizes a journey, an inner evolution. But don't you see, it's more than that? This was a dream of one of my past lives. I must have been an Eleusinian initiate. Otherwise how would I know all that? The dream is data. I had one about the Egyptian mysteries too.*

'Perhaps you'd better teach me, Wendy.'

No, you are the teacher. You've always been my master in

253

our past lives. I'm your pupil. You're ahead of me in the evolutionary scale.

I did not take this lightly. Wendy was in earnest. She was no intellectual butterfly, like Merle and Graydon (two wings of the same creature). She would have tested her new belief for faults. I said, 'If you'll lend me the books I'll try to read them.'

You don't need to. You knew it when you had to know it. You're close to the Light now. You don't need dreams any more. The Light blinds you. And she wrote: *George, I think this is your last reincarnation. You're a long way ahead of me. I'll have to go on alone.*

She smiled at me from a very great distance. There was nothing I could do but pat her hand.

96 She was born in the year of *Peter Pan*. She hated her name. But could not use her second. It was Ouida. Her parents came to New Zealand when she was four. She grew up in a country town, attended university, trained as a teacher; and rented the cottage from me when Willis moved out. She was Alfred's friend; my friendly acquaintance. She withdrew from me in horror when I sent him away. She was inward looking. She learned to look even deeper. She had believed me a good man. I showed her a gross imperfection that led her on to views of human nature that almost cost her her reason. Evil was a force that battered on the doors of her sanity. (The words are hers.) Once she tried to drown herself in the creek. But the black water took on the nature of a hellish fluid and the life in her, the good, refused it entry. Finally she tried to save herself by refusing the world. She hid in the cottage. Robert told me he thought she was 'off her rocker'. I went down. I knocked at the door. But she would not let me in. I saw the curtains breathing, that was all. So I got in touch with her parents. They took her away.

When Edie and I entered the little cottage to tidy it up we

saw the pathetic childishness of her retreat. Everything was pasted over with brown paper. All surfaces: walls, floors, table tops. All objects: chairs, sideboards, pots and pans. Brown paper covered everything. She had used flour and water paste. When that ran out she had made do with condensed milk. It took Edie weeks of work to scrape everything clean. We decided not to let the cottage again but keep it as an overflow house for visitors. Then after more than two years we had a letter from Wendy saying she was well again and asking if she might have the cottage back. We did not hesitate. She had made it hers with that brown paper.

When she came back she was slower, older, and gave the impression of being less fully alive. She had closed off a part of herself. Spiritually, I thought, she would never be whole. (I was wrong in that.) But socially she was whole. She and Edie became friends. As Edie's illness worsened, Wendy was with us more, as nurse and companion to her; as pupil to me. And teacher. I will never forget her kindness to my wife. Or the part she played in my recovery.

I was deep in the pit of my own evil nature. This was my dark night of the soul. I had been close to the Light; and blind to the flaws in my nature. I had believed I was Chosen. And at the point of victory I fell. 'The radiance of Paradise alternates with deep and dreadful night.' I was in that deep and dreadful night; and believed there was no way out. Paradise was no more than a pinprick of light at the end of a tunnel I would never pass through. How could I move in any direction but down while my black hatred of my son Alfred endured? This is no rhetorical question. It fixes me in my location at that time.

The economic depression came. I wrote. I lectured. I left my small mark on events. Then Edie died. And her death moved me a painful step on my journey. I began to pass along the tunnel, for I knew that in the light beyond its end she had her new being. I worked towards it.

Wendy was my companion on the way. One evening she read me Whitman's *Song of Myself*. It was well known to me. But it

255

had been growing on both of us that Whitman was a key figure, and the *Song* a key text. It was a winter night. A fire was burning in the study grate. In another part of the house Robert was sleeping, worn out by his day's labour. Wendy had put on her coat to go home, and come to my side to say goodnight to me. I was depressed. Our talk that night had led nowhere. And yet I had in my mind the Persian text: *Whatever road I take joins the highway that leads to Thee.* She picked up *Leaves of Grass.* She began to read. From habit more than interest I turned my trumpet towards her.

'. . . What I assume you shall assume, For every atom belonging to me as good belongs to you.'

I accepted that, and I began to listen. And for the first time began to see a pattern. Wendy read the *Song* from beginning to end. It took an hour. And then, as if she understood her part ended there, went home. I sat and worked on it. I understood for the first time that in the mystical state all was not joy, that dark and light were complementary parts.

My *Commentary on 'The Song of Myself'* was the last of my publications. It came out as a pamphlet in 1939. I paid its way. And to my knowledge, not a soul noticed it. There are two copies in the General Assembly Library and two in the Turnbull Library. And three hundred more in a cardboard box under the house. It is not important. I wrote the piece for Wendy and myself. Its twenty pages are the fruit of three years' thought and conversation. Briefly, the *Song* is the record of Whitman's entry into, journey through, and emergence from the mystical state. I broke the poem into five parts: Awakening to self; Purification of self; Illumination; Dark night of the soul; Union. And these into smaller parts. Union for example is twofold, made up of faith/love on the one hand and perception on the other. I will not go into it. As I have said, the pamphlets are in the libraries and can be consulted there. And I have three hundred copies under the house. They are only sixpence each. What I must say is that the lessons of those dreadful sections 33–37 were the hardest to learn. Many a time beaten I cried with the poet, 'Enough! enough! enough!' But I learned. In the end I was able to say along with him, 'Do you see O my brothers and sisters? It is not chaos or death—it is form, union, plan—it is eternal life—it is Happiness.'

As I sent my *Commentary* off to the printer I knew that I would not re-enter the Light. I was too old, my imperfections lay heavily upon me. But I had gained three things: a knowledge and acceptance of my nature; a knowledge of the Cosmic order; and a fixed memory of my glimpse of God. Like Bucke's memory of the full experience, it would stay with me even in times of depression. It was, to use Wendy's later phrase, empirical data. And grasping it, and grasping my self, I had made the next-to-last of my journeys. Death remained.

Wendy was forty years younger. Wendy went on.

97 When the Second War started I wrote to Dan Peabody, and to Semple and Webb, reminding them of their stand against conscription in the first. I hoped they would make that stand again now they were in power. But it was just because of their power my hope was not real. Power had moved them beyond idealism. Sadly I watched the old men bury the young.

And the Hitler–Stalin pact? It did not surprise me. The Bolsheviks were men. Because I knew the way to super-humanity was spiritual I could not believe they had changed their essential natures. Many believed it. The last letter I had from Andrew Collie was full of bitterness at my defection. I had said to him that the stories coming out of Russia—of labour camps and blood purges and secret police—had the ring of truth about them. A human sound. Andrew damned me for a traitor. He had religion. It was complete not only with doctrine and prophecy but with revelation. 'I have seen the future and it works.' Faith carried him over inconsistencies. I wrote to him again, several times. I told him I still believed in communism, that it was the only just system, but that men being men it would be corrupted where it appeared; that man's salvation lay in another direction. I did not deny that we must keep on trying to improve our social organization—we must try for justice and equality. Unless we had a passion for justice we were less than men. But until we were more—until we achieved a higher consciousness —we would never inhabit Jerusalem. I should have known better than to use that language to Andrew. He never replied.

I was losing Wendy too. She wanted to marry me. I had overlooked a whole side of her nature. She wanted to bear my child. When she had taken us to the point of speaking of it, and I had told her why it could not be, there was nothing for her to do but pass out of my life.

She owned a little car and into it she packed her few belongings—her clothes, her books. She was going back to the town she had grown up in. When she had locked the cottage she brought me the key.

I was in the summer-house. Meg's children played on the lawn—a game full of shooting and falling down dead. (The kaleidoscope had been given another shake. Fergus had shocked us all by enlisting; and Meg and her children had come to live at Peacehaven.) Lifting my trumpet, I heard their agonized cries. Wendy walked by them with a middle-aged tread. She put the key on the ti-tree table in front of me.

'There you are, George. I've given the place a scrub. There's no brown paper this time.'

'Thank you, my dear.'

'Do you know yet who's going in?'

'Bluey and his friend.'

'That'll be a change. Is he still scared of hell?'

'You're not interested in Bluey. Talk about yourself.'

'I've finished with myself. That self, anyway. I'll make another.' She grimaced. 'Spinster living with her widowed mother. Not an original role.'

'It's one you'll play well, my dear.'

She narrowed her eyes angrily. But these days she was not able to keep her feelings going. 'You'll write to me?'

'Of course.'

'And if you want me to come back I'll come back.'

'I'd like you to visit me, Wendy.'

'No. Not for a long while anyway.'

'My dear——'

'I'll come back as your wife, George, no other way. Or as your mistress.' The word made her blush. She took my note-book and wrote: *We have been part of each other in many lives.* She looked at it. It seemed to surprise her. She wrote: *I love you. Our place is together.*

'My dear, I love you too. You are my child.'

She looked at me as if she meant to strike me.

'The time has gone by when anything more would be proper.'

'Proper!'

It did seem a mean little word. But I had meant it in a larger sense. Marriage would return me to a world I had left, would re-open rooms that were closed. Besides, I did not love her in that way. I loved only Edie. Wendy I loved as my child.

I tried to explain. (I had explained before.) She did not listen. She sank again into that half-alive state that enabled her to keep going. Now and then she looked at what she had written. It still seemed to surprise her.

After we had been silent for a time I gave her the present I had chosen for her: my copy of *Leaves of Grass*. She thanked me. She kissed me on the forehead and went away. Through the trees I saw her little car flickering off down the road.

I did not see her again for many years. She was a sexless being when she came back. Her body had thickened, a dropsical complaint had swollen her legs. And her beliefs had changed. She was reading books, following gurus, I had never heard of. It all seemed proper (again in a special sense). For the world had changed: mine and everyone's. Millions of people had died: been burned and blown up and bayoneted and gassed in specially constructed chambers. More than one sort of bomb had fallen, more than one sort of mushroom cloud hung over man.

I no longer knew all my children. Oliver was a judge, had sentenced men to life imprisonment. Felicity was Catholic. Esther, in her own words, had grown 'hard as nails' (while Fred swelled with money like a toad). And Robert had gone to live on Parminter's farm.

98 Meg was the only one I knew. Fergus, puzzled by his motives, had gone off to camp; to Crete, Egypt, Italy. He was guilty as he left and so he blustered, 'Somebody's got to stop him,' etc. I believe he saw his chance to step out of a role—husband, father, workman—that had him turning like a zoo animal in a cage. The war finished that, remade him. He came back tough, diminished, free—a freed carnivore.

Meg and her children lived out the years of his absence with me. For Meg coming back to Peacehaven was coming home. The pain of Fergus's desertion never left her. But the old house, her old room, the creek, the orchard, acted as a balm. And caring for Robert pleased her. She added him to her children; almost, I think, loved him equally. When he was sent to an objectors' camp she behaved as though he had died. I tried to tell her he was well off—told her how in the First War objectors had been sent to the front and tied to posts in no-man's land. Tortured, in fact. But she continued to mourn him. She knew better than I the effect imprisonment would have on him. At the end of it he went to Parminter's farm, he left the world; and Meg was not surprised. Nor did she grieve again. She had got over that.

We lived at Peacehaven as though on an island. Few people came to see us. Willis and Mirth and their children came. Esther came (Fred was busy). Sometimes she brought Emerson with her, sometimes an American marine or soldier. Bluey puffed up almost every day, tormented by his fear of hell. (Sutton peered through the trees.) And the Butterses walked over in the weekends. But they were remote. Their son had joined the Air

Force and died in a training crash. They were practising spiritualism and had succeeded in speaking with him. Their visits were charitable.

I spent much of my time with Meg's son Raymond. He was the quietest, the most thoughtful of the three. Rebecca was a tomboy, a noisy affectionate child, who would not let herself be loved. Robert, or Bobby as he came to be called, was a ruffian, an intelligent oaf; he was gang-leader, girl-chaser, jaw-puncher, eel-catcher—a manly fellow who knew the high value placed on his qualities, but knew he could not fool me. He kept out of my way. And he tortured his brother with the Chinese burn for, as he put it, 'sliming round the old geezer all the time'. But Raymond was not after anything Bobby would value. He was after my talk. For him being entertained meant having his understanding increased and his emotions stirred. So I told him about his grandmother and of our days on the Coast, of the Gardners and Joseph Sullivan and Johnny Potter. I told him about my friends Edward Cryer and John Jepson; about my trial for heresy, my street corner preaching, the Plumb family in California, my days in Lyttelton jail. In this way my history became part of his; and history slid into myth. He will carry it with him forever, an extra chamber in his mind. I did a good job there. It was though more than a job. I loved the boy. And though he has put himself at a distance now—girl-chaser himself—and chooses to play draughts with me more often than talk, I love him still. I am pleased to have given him something that increases him.

But I began with Meg. The child I loved best. Poor Meg. As her children grew she decreased. She put herself into them and got little back, and though she claimed to see this as natural she began to look on herself as nearing the end of her effective life. She tried to discover resources in herself, invent selfish roles. She tried to write, tried to paint; but found that cooking and sewing were all she was good for. She did not pity herself. But she came to pity her children, and love them desperately. She took her unhappiness as general evidence.

261

I disappointed her. She looked on my concerns as an elaborate game. She could not see their connection with her life, and I could not show her. Hers is the artist's type of mind, not the philosopher's or mystic's. She sees particular things, the simplest and hardest seeing to accomplish. (I have never managed it.) And I think takes the next step, transforms them imaginatively. But this is not the whole creative act. There is a final connection she never makes. She fails to find language. Poet *manqué*. She was close to being great—the closest of my children. As it is her life is a series of poems that never get written.

She survives. She cries on my shoulder from time to time, but accepts her condition; the fact that she and Fergus are strangers to each other, that her children are 'beings from Mars'. And that she and I fail to meet. These things wound her, make her cry inwardly. But this she accepts as part of the natural order; believes it the same for everyone.

I have not given up hope for her. She comes very close, close to expressing it. One day the wall may go down.

99 Felicity put her head round the study door. 'Time we were off, dad.' Wendy said goodbye. I wished her pleasant dreams. But she's a serious girl. She does not understand jokes. I kissed her cheek. She has the look of a person setting off on a long journey.

When she had gone I picked up my walking stick and trumpet. The stick is a present from Bluey. Its handle is made in the form of a swan's head with two black beads for eyes. I don't know why I took it. I'm steady on my feet. When I got out to the yard I found I was to travel in Emerson's car. Meg was going with Felicity. I made the Sundowner of the Skies promise to drive slowly. No aerobatics, I said. But the drive was a nightmare. We left the girls far behind. The winding road up the valley was a challenge to Emerson: he was incapable of not responding. Dust sprang up like a smoke-screen behind us. We whistled over bridges, slid round corners sideways, clipped bracken fronds that hung down from the banks. If I'd known which of the knobs to push to stop the car I'd have pushed it. Instead I closed my eyes, even though it made me feel sick. I have claimed to understand Emerson. On that ride I lost my understanding. He pulled up at Willis's gate. 'There you are, dad. A nice steady drive.' At least that's what I think he said. I was too busy getting out of the car to take much notice.

'I'll walk up,' I said.

'It's a quarter of a mile.'

'I'll walk up.' I was grateful for my stick. (If he'd tried to make me get back in I'd have attacked him with it.)

He grinned. 'O.K., dad.' He opened the gate and sped away up the drive.

To avoid his dust I retreated into the trees. How grateful I was for their stillness. Orchards are part of the world I understand. I struck in deeper. The leaves lost their coating of dust and became glossy green. Weeds lapped about my knees. The internal combustion engine seemed centuries away. I sat down beneath a tree whose fruit had been left to ripen. The golden orbs hung like suns above my head. I put my stick and trumpet in the grass and lay back on a natural springy pillow. Shortly we would be driving to Esther's house, and there I would meet Alfred. In the meantime how pleasant just to loaf in the grass —'loafe and invite my Soul'. Well, that was Whitman, and I a lesser being. And Alfred's path curved towards mine with a geometrical, a terrifying beauty. But I took this moment like a gift. A moment lying outside time and care. I closed my eyes. I folded my hands on my chest. The old are great improvisers. I went to sleep.

When I woke Willis was sitting beside me. He was smoking his pipe and smiling to himself. On his naked arm I saw the tattoo of a heart transfixed by an arrow. Underneath was printed *Rosy*.

He saw me looking at it and said a name I think was Liverpool. He knocked his pipe out (on his wooden leg) and stuck it in his belt like a cowboy's six-shooter.

'Come on, dad. The girls are getting stroppy.'

He helped me up. We walked through the trees to the house, which is no more than a collection of railway huts joined to an old tramcar. It grew as Willis's family grew. Mirth has painted sunflowers on the doors. Mirth herself was sitting on the lawn with Emerson, Felicity and Meg. My girls were ladies beside her. I make no judgement. But Mirth was an extraordinary figure: straw-hatted, straw-haired, roly-poly and brown as boot polish, clad in the briefest of shorts (a man's shorts with their top button burst open) and a ragged blouse fixed with a pin in the middle. The pin was a concession to my coming. Indeed the blouse might have been. I could count myself lucky not to have found her naked. Meg and Felicity cried out together, 'There you are, dad. Where have you been?' They claim to like Mirth but I thought their behaviour strained.

I sat down. Mirth took my hand. 'I'll get some tea in a minute, George. Unless you'd like something stronger?'

'Tea will be fine.' I had wanted as wives for my sons women who were beautiful, intelligent, fine-souled, spirited—rather like the young Felicity. But only Oliver and Willis had married (I could not count Robert as married), and I had as daughters-in-law Beatrice and Mirth. Mirth I would not swap for one of those imaginary creatures. She had the gift of making people happy. I had left that quality out of the ideal wives.

She made tea and brought it out on a tray. We talked for half an hour. Willis told us yarns—Rosy, Ingrid, Sue—while Mirth smiled resignedly. Felicity kept glancing at her watch, but Meg began to relax. Perhaps it was the sun, perhaps the air of contentment Mirth and Willis gave off. She lay down and closed her eyes; opened them again only when Willis said, 'Well, dad, so you're going to see our brother?'

'I am,' I said. 'Everybody seems to disapprove.'

'I think it's a good idea.'

'I don't disapprove,' Felicity cried. 'What I don't like is the casual way you're doing it.'

They debated that. I took no part. I put my trumpet down and enjoyed the sun. Mirth took no part either. Whenever I caught her eye she smiled at me. Willis was lucky to find this woman, I thought. She had left behind two grown-up children, an important husband, money; and built a home with sunflowers on the door. Her second family (she had borne sons and daughters until she was fifty) ran in the trees like dryads, fauns. She did not worry how they would fit into the world. She was not clever. My daughters have pointed out to her the damage she may do. But Mirth has knowledge from another source. She has instinctive wisdom. Her children are happier than Meg's and Felicity's.

I drank my tea; and looked at my watch; and saw it was time to go. Mirth helped me to my feet. The others had reached no agreement. Emerson was looking embarrassed and Meg distressed. Felicity had a steely gleam in her eye. Only Willis could muster up a smile. He put me into Felicity's car, lifting in my feet as though they were a separate item.

'There you are, dad. Comfortable?'

'Thank you Willis. Is there any message I can give Alfred for you?'

'No. No need. I see him all the time. He comes up here.'

'He does?'

'Sure, dad. He's my brother. Pansy or not.'

I have seen myself as the centre of the universe, around which everything revolves. My children surprise me with their independent lives. I held Willis's hand for a moment. I remembered I had told him nothing of Robert.

Emerson came to say goodbye. He was staying for tea. 'Emerson,' I said, 'tell Felicity to drive slowly, will you?'

'Sure, dad,' he grinned.

We drove away. I looked at Willis and Mirth out the back window: the peg-legged sailor and his fat old wife. One at least of my children has built his Jerusalem.

100 'He hasn't come yet,' Esther said. 'In fact I'm not sure he will.'

She took us into a sitting-room. 'Who'd like something to drink? Dally plonk.'

'Me,' Felicity said; and Meg nodded too.

'How about you, dad? You can't be a wowser all your life.'

'No thank you, Esther. I'll just sit here and rest.' And to make sure I would not be talked at I put my trumpet on the floor. The girls walked about. They could not be still. I watched them with sadness and love and amusement. Each had a glass of purple drink in her fist. They traversed the room as if in a dance. Esther turned. So did Felicity. And Meg. Felicity took out a cigarette. Esther lit up too. And Meg. One swallowed. They all swallowed. And puffed. They blew out clouds of blue smoke. Life had taught them no tranquillity.

I was calm. I did not congratulate myself. I was old and tired. I had learned not to waste emotion.

When they rushed to the window I guessed they had heard Alfred's car.

101 'Hello, Alfred,' I said.

He made no reply. He did not even look towards my chair. With a smile he closed on Felicity and kissed her cheek. 'You're looking well. How's Max?' More coolly he kissed Meg. He did not ask after Fergus. Fergus, I knew, had always refused to meet him.

Then he sat down on the sofa. Still he did not look at me. 'Well Sis, I'll have a glass of that purple death.'

I took this in through my trumpet. He had a clear reedy voice; a voice I remembered; but ragged now and with a damaged edge. I put it down to alcohol more than the years.

266

Alcohol was the fuel that kept him going—alcohol, memories, hatred. In spite of his friendliness to the girls that emotion radiated from him. I felt it in my chair across the room. I watched his ruined Shelleyan head turn slowly in my direction. His red-brown curls were gone: he was bald. He had a wet lower lip the colour of raspberries, and baggy cheeks, and red eyelids. His eyes were the yellow of a healing bruise, and whitish-blue, and blind with water not made up of tears. They stopped short of me, went back to Esther, who brought him a glass of wine and said something I did not hear. Alfred did not hear either. He cupped a hand behind his ear. At this I felt a shock of pain at our common blood, and terror at the blind progressions of life. I had given Alfred my deafness.

I said, 'I'd like to talk to Alfred alone.'

The girls began to move. But he stopped them with a lifting of his hand; then looked at me for the first time. 'Who are you? I don't know you. Have we got anything to say? Esther—' he turned to her—'who is this man? Introduce us please.'

'Go on, Esther,' I said.

'Oh, Alfred . . .'

'Well, he looks familiar.'

'Go on,' I said. 'He's got the right to this.'

But Esther could not play the game. She splashed more wine in her glass.

Alfred smiled. 'It seems we'll have to introduce ourselves. I'm Alfred Hamer. I lost my parents when I was quite young.' I saw he would not be able to keep it up. He was trembling. Twenty years of pain and hatred found no expression in elaborate games.

'Alfred,' I said, 'I don't know why I wanted to see you. If it's a mistake forgive me please. But I saw your brother Robert a few weeks ago. And when I'd seen him I knew I had to see you. He healed my hand.' I held it up. The connections were clear to me. I did not expect him to see them. Like Wendy he had looked on Robert as an inferior being. And now he cried, 'Robert. My half-wit brother. How is he? Still shovelling dung?'

'He could help you, Alfred. You should go and see him.'

He turned to his sisters. 'Who is this man? Who is he? Telling me what to do?'

'Dad, you can see it's no good going on with this,' Felicity said.

'Do you still write poetry, Alfred?'

'Poetry! My God! My God! Do you hear him?'

'Alfred——'

'He thinks he can turn this into a social chat.'

'It's more than that. I'm trying to find out who you are.'

'Why? Why should you care?'

'I don't know. I behaved very badly to you. If there's any way I can help you now——'

'My God! The stupidity. The blind arrogance. Help me! The only way you can help me is by jumping off a cliff.'

'Alfred,' Meg cried loudly.

'Help me! You heard him. After treating me as though I was some sort of maggot or slug. And pretending I was dead for twenty years. And John Willis too. John used to be his friend. And he treated him like filth.'

'Alfred, I'm sorry,' I said. 'I can't do anything about that now——'

'John was a good man.'

'I know——'

'You don't know anything. You have the nerve to offer help to me. After what you've done. Well I don't need your help. I've got plenty of money. More money that you've ever seen. And more friends too. No shortage of friends, thank you.'

He told me then that Edie had hated me. That was a lie. I watched him invent it. When he saw it fail he told me in gutter language what he and John Willis had done together, under my roof, and in the orchard at Peacehaven. I had seen some of it. The rest seemed to follow. But it upset me only to hear his rage, his rage to crush me. I would not hold myself responsible for it, but neither could I say I was not responsible.

When it was over he sat trembling. Meg had gone out with

her hand over her face. Felicity stood white-faced in a corner. Esther poured him another glass of wine. She opened his hand and put it in. She said, 'Don't talk like that in my house again.'

'I'm sorry. I'm sorry.'

'And dad, you go home.'

'All right.' I stood up.

'No,' Alfred cried, 'he's not getting away as easy as that.'

'Alfred,' I said, 'I'm sorry I've brought on this. I didn't want to go back into the past. That's done with. I just wanted to tell you about Robert. He touched my hand and now it's healed up. Why don't you go and see Robert?'

'To stop me being a homosexual?'

'I didn't say that.'

'What then?' And suddenly he cried out in a frenzy, 'Stop pointing that thing at me,' and he came at me three steps and smacked his open hand against my trumpet. It flew out of my grasp and sailed across the room. He ran after it, grabbed it like a club and battered it on the wall. Chips of black horn flew about the room. Esther tried to hold his arm. Deaf now, I could not hear their cries. But Meg rushed in again and ran to me. Felicity helped Esther. They wrestled Alfred's arm down to his side. They made him drop the ruined trumpet. Then they got him out of the room into Esther's bedroom. Esther stayed with him. Felicity came back. She bullied Meg and me out to the car, knocking us along with thrusts of her arms. On the drive home she raged at me. Her eyes were rarely on the road. I heard nothing. Being without my trumpet was an advantage. I knew I would not buy another one.

Halfway home Meg had her sister stop the car. She came into the back and held my hand.

102 Edward Cryer said to me, 'When morality triumphs nasty things happen.' He was quoting from somewhere. I thought of Alfred, the clever boy, the happy youth. Morality triumphed. But also something more. I can only call it evil. It was not all mine. John Willis was our guest, he corrupted our son. But then I slew my son. Yes, evil worked in me. I had thought of him as mine, as my achievement. His glory belonged to me. So when he showed his nature I destroyed him. This brings the event too much into the open. It took place in deep shadow. But I saw it clearly as I rode in Felicity's car. And did not judge myself. The time for judgements had gone.

Meg's hand lay in mine. I thanked her for its warmth. And closing my eyes found myself saying Edwin Markham's line: *Sorrows come To stretch out spaces in the heart for joy.* I had taken comfort from it many times. But no, not now—now it would not do. Alfred's ruined life, his ruined unhappy face: that was more than a sorrow.

Felicity brought the car to a halt in the yard—a skidding halt. I got out and walked away from the house. I told the girls I was going into the orchard. Meg made a move to follow me, but I waved her away with my swan-stick. I walked over the bridge and into the trees. Beyond the fence, shining in the sun, was the Butters's mansion. Merle and Graydon were standing in the garden hand in hand. They did not see me go by. Perhaps they were in a state of Wordsworthian—Plumbian they would call it—bliss. They caused me no amusement, no envy. I thanked them for their thirty years of kindness.

When I had climbed the little hill and looked down into the hollow I knew I was near my death. It would not keep me long. The rotting trunk poked up through the bracken. On that evening twenty years ago I had sent Robert out with an axe to chop the quince tree down. He had been unwilling, then defiant; but had gone when I raised my hand. He did not speak to me for several days. Robert, I thought, Robert. I prayed that Alfred would go to him. Robert would cure Alfred of his rage. But I knew they would never meet. Alfred would go down to a bitter death. His hatred of me was so great I did not believe he would survive me long.

I walked back through the trees and on to the bridge. I found a few crumbs of bread in my pocket and scattered them on the water. After a little while an eel floated up. I saw why people found them sinister. Dead mouth, snake's body. And they rose from dark holes in the slime. But I did not pursue it. They were God's creatures. And looking for symbols a game.

I went round the lawn, keeping by the creek, and peered through the trees at Bluey's cottage. Like the Butters's house it glowed in the sun. Bluey was sitting in his cane chair asleep. Something shining dangled from his hand. A rosary? He jerked awake; yawned and scratched himself; and went on with his interrupted penance. The sun shone on his sweating easy face. Sutton, black Sutton, watched from behind a bean row. He saw me, snarled. I moved away.

I could not understand life. I had, I thought, a better understanding of death. *On the earth the broken arcs; in the heaven a perfect round.* Browning: a useful poet. I went into the summer-house. 'Edie,' I said, 'I haven't got my trumpet any more. I can't tell whether your thrush is singing or not.'

Presently Raymond came down with the draughts. He set them out on the table. We played a game. I played hard. I saw no reason to let him beat me.

When I looked up Meg was in the door, smiling anxiously and making eating movements with her hands. I jumped Raymond's last piece. I thought, I'm ready to die, or live, or understand, or love, or whatever it is. I'm glad of the good I've done, and sorry about the bad.

Meg took my hand and led me in to tea.

Author's note

Lyndahl Gee, Bernice Kydd, and Muriel Parker helped me gather material for this novel. I had Lyndahl Gee's permission to include passages from the writings of her parents (my grandparents), James and Florence Chapple. Much of George and Edith Plumb's early history is Chapple history. Not all. For example, James Chapple did not meet Joseph Sullivan. He was though a Presbyterian minister, he did take the chair at Joseph McCabe's meeting, and he was sent to prison for sedition. His religious career, his opinions, his wanderings, were very like George Plumb's. However, George and Edith's domestic life is largely imaginary, and after 1918 wholly so. The twelve Plumb children are not the fourteen Chapple children. My uncles and aunts are not to accuse me of putting them in a novel. Felicity, Oliver, Robert, Alfred—the twelve—are fictional beings. Emerson is fictional, although his adventures are those of my father-in-law Oscar Garden. In one way Oscar Garden's flight was more remarkable than Emerson's: he made it after only two week's flying experience. Incidentally, he denies having a bundle of dirty clothes perched on his knee.

I have shown Parliament sitting in April 1949. In fact the session did not begin until June.

My thanks to the New Zealand Literary Fund for financial help.